Praise for the Novels
of Jo Beverley

Forbidden Magic

"Stunning . . . sizzling." —*Publishers Weekly*

"Delightfully odd characters and a thrilling plot, along with a generous touch of magic, make this an enchanting read." —*Booklist*

"A charming, outspoken heroine, a magnetic, unconventional hero, and a diverse cast of well-drawn secondary characters come together in a fast-paced, intriguing plot with a holiday setting that features a touch of evil, a dash of bawdy humor, and enough of Beverley's trademark page-singeing sensuality to satisfy the most demanding reader." —*Library Journal*

"A fabulous dream spinner." —*Romantic Times*

Emily and the Dark Angel

RITA Award, Best Regency
Romantic Times Award, Best Regency Rake
Named as one of *Romantic Times*'s Best Romances of the Past 20 Years

"This marvelous love story has all the makings of a long-standing classic." —*Romantic Times*

A Lady's Secret

"With wit and humor, Jo Beverley provides a wonderful eighteenth-century romance starring two amiable lead characters whose first encounter is one of the best in recent memory. The tale is filled with nonstop action." —The Best Reviews

Lady Beware

"Jo Beverley carries off a remarkable achievement in *Lady Beware*, the latest and possibly last in her Company of Rogues novels. . . . It is the unusual combination of familial comfort and risqué pleasure that makes this book a winner. . . . No doubt about it, *Lady Beware* is yet another jewel in Beverley's heavily decorated crown." —*The Romance Reader*

continued . . .

"[E]nchanting . . . a delightful blend of wit (with banter between Thea and Darien), intrigue (as evil lurks throughout) and emotional victories (as love prevails in the end). . . . Watching Thea and Darien spar is entertaining, and watching them succumb to the simmering love and passion is satisfying."

—*The Columbia State* (SC)

To Rescue a Rogue

"Beverley brings the Regency period to life in this highly romantic story [with] vividly portrayed characters. [Readers] will be engrossed by this emotionally packed story of great love, tremendous courage, and the return of those attractive and dangerous men known as the Rogues. Her Company of Rogues series is well crafted, delicious, and wickedly captivating."

—Joan Hammond

"With her usual beautifully nuanced characters and lyrical writing, RITA Award winner Beverley brings her popular Company of Rogues Regency historical series to a triumphant conclusion . . . [a] quietly powerful romance."

—*Booklist*

"Lighthearted and serious, sexy and sweet, this exquisitely rendered story is a perfect finale to this classic series."　　　　　　　—*Library Journal*

The Rogue's Return

"Beverley beautifully blends complex characters, an exquisitely sensual love story, and a refreshingly different Regency setting into one sublime romance."

—*Booklist*

"Jo Beverley has written an excellent character study. One of the best books I've read this season."　　　　　　　　　　　—*Affaire de Coeur*

A Most Unsuitable Man

"Picking up exactly where *Winter Fire* leaves off, Beverley turns a rejected 'other woman' into a fiery, outspoken, sympathetic heroine; pairs her with a dashing but penniless, scandal-ridden hero; and lets the fun—and the danger—begin. Once again readers are treated to a delightful, intricately plotted, and sexy romp set in the slightly bawdy Georgian world of Beverley's beloved Malloren Chronicles."　　　　　　　—*Library Journal*

Also by Jo Beverley
Available from New American Library

REGENCY
THE ROGUE'S WORLD
Lady Beware
To Rescue a Rogue
The Rogue's Return
Skylark
St. Raven
Hazard
"The Demon's Mistress" in *In Praise of Younger Men*
The Devil's Heiress
Three Heroes (Omnibus Edition)

OTHER
Forbidden Magic
Lovers and Ladies (Omnibus Edition)

THE MALLOREN WORLD
An Unlikely Countess
The Secret Wedding
A Lady's Secret
A Most Unsuitable Man
Winter Fire
Devilish
Secrets of the Night
Something Wicked
My Lady Notorious

MEDIEVAL ROMANCES
Lord of Midnight
Dark Champion
Lord of My Heart

ANTHOLOGIES
"The Dragon and the Virgin Princess" in
Dragon Lovers
"The Trouble with Heroes" in
Irresistible Forces

Jo Beverley

THE DRAGON'S BRIDE

A SIGNET ECLIPSE BOOK

SIGNET ECLIPSE
Published by New American Library, a division of
Penguin Group (USA) Inc., 375 Hudson Street,
New York, New York 10014, USA
Penguin Group (Canada), 90 Eglinton Avenue East, Suite 700, Toronto,
Ontario M4P 2Y3, Canada (a division of Pearson Penguin Canada Inc.)
Penguin Books Ltd., 80 Strand, London WC2R 0RL, England
Penguin Ireland, 25 St. Stephen's Green, Dublin 2,
Ireland (a division of Penguin Books Ltd.)
Penguin Group (Australia), 250 Camberwell Road, Camberwell, Victoria 3124,
Australia (a division of Pearson Australia Group Pty. Ltd.)
Penguin Books India Pvt. Ltd., 11 Community Centre, Panchsheel Park,
New Delhi - 110 017, India
Penguin Group (NZ), 67 Apollo Drive, Rosedale, Auckland 0632,
New Zealand (a division of Pearson New Zealand Ltd.)
Penguin Books (South Africa) (Pty.) Ltd., 24 Sturdee Avenue,
Rosebank, Johannesburg 2196, South Africa

Penguin Books Ltd., Registered Offices:
80 Strand, London WC2R ORL, England

Published by Signet Eclipse, an imprint of New American Library, a division of Penguin Group
(USA) Inc. Previously published in a Signet edition.

First Signet Eclipse Printing, August 2011
10 9 8 7 6 5 4 3 2 1

Copyright © Jo Beverley, 2001
Cover art by Phillip Heffernan
All rights reserved

SIGNET ECLIPSE and logo are trademarks of Penguin Group (USA) Inc.

Signet Eclipse Trade Paperback ISBN: 978-0-451-23340-0

Set in ITC New Baskerville
Designed by Alissa Amell

Printed in the United States of America

The Dragon's Bride is dedicated to
Romantic Times reviewer Melinda Helfer,
who sadly died in 2000. Melinda was a
steadfast friend of the romance genre, but she
was especially supportive of new writers. On
my first novel in 1988, she wrote in her review,
"The sky's the limit for this extraordinary talent."
I was stunned and moved to tears, and also
inspired to try to reach those heights.
For you, Melinda.

THE DRAGON'S
BRIDE

❧ 1 ❧

May 1816

The south coast of England

THE MOON flickered briefly between windblown clouds, but such a thread-fine moon did no harm. It barely lit the men creeping down the steep headland toward the beach, or the smuggling master controlling everything from above.

It lightened not at all the looming house that ruled the cliffs of this part of Devon—Crag Wyvern, the fortresslike seat of the blessedly absent Earl of Wyvern.

Absent like the riding officer charged with preventing smuggling in this area. Animal sounds—an owl, a gull, a barking fox—carried across the scrubby landscape, constantly reporting that all was clear.

At sea, a brief flash of light announced the arrival of the smuggling ship. On the rocky headland, the smuggling master—Captain Drake, as he was called—unshielded a lantern in a flashing pattern that meant "all clear."

All clear to land brandy, gin, tea, and lace. Delicacies for Englishmen who didn't care to pay extortionate taxes. Profit for smugglers, with tea sixpence a pound abroad and selling for twenty times that in England if all the taxes were paid.

In the nearby fishing village of Dragon's Cove, men pushed boats into the waves and began the urgent race to unload the vessel.

"Captain Drake" pulled out a spyglass to scan the English Channel for other lights, other vessels. Now that the war against Napoleon was over, navy ships were patrolling the coast, better equipped and manned than the customs boats had ever been. A navy cutter had intercepted the last major run, seizing the whole cargo and twenty local men, including the previous Captain Drake.

A figure slipped to sit close to him, one dressed as he was all in dark colors, a hood covering both hair and the upper face, soot muting the pallor of the rest.

Captain Drake glanced to the side. "What are you doing here?"

"You're shorthanded." The reply was as sotto voce as the question.

"We've enough. Get back up to Crag Wyvern and see to the cellars."

"No."

"Susan—"

"No, David. Maisie can handle matters from inside the house, and Diddy has the watch. I need to be out here."

Susan Kerslake meant it. This run had to succeed or heaven knew what would become of them all, so she needed to be out here with her younger brother, even if there was nothing much she could do.

For generations this area had flourished, with smuggling the main enterprise under a series of strong, capable Captain Drakes, all from the Clyst family. With Mel Clyst captured, tried, and transported to Botany Bay, however, chaos threatened. Other, rougher gangs were trying to move in.

The only person in a position to be the unquestioned new Captain Drake was her brother. Though he and she went by their mother's name of Kerslake, they were Mel Clyst's children and everyone knew it. It was for David to seize control of the Dragon's Horde gang and make a profit, or this area would become a battleground.

He'd had to take on the role, and Susan had urged him to it, but she shivered with fear for him. He was her younger brother, after all, and even though he was a man of twenty-four, she couldn't help trying to protect him.

The black-sailed ship on the black ocean was barely visible, but a light flashed again, brief as a falling star, to say that the anchor had dropped. No sign of other ships out there, but the dark that protected the Freetraders could protect a navy ship as well.

She knew Captain de Root of the *Anna Kasterlee* was an experienced smuggler. He'd worked with the Horde for over a decade and had never made a slip yet. But smuggling was a chancy business. Mel Clyst's capture had shown that, so she kept every sense alert.

At last her straining eyes glimpsed the boats surging out to be loaded with packages and half-ankers of spirits. She could just detect movement on the sloping headland, which rolled like the waves of the sea as local men flowed down to the beach to unload those small boats.

They'd haul the goods up the cliff to hiding places and packhorses. Men would carry the goods inland on their backs to secure places and to the middlemen who'd send the cargo on to Bath, London, and other cities. A week's wages for a night's work and a bit of 'baccy and tea to take home. Many would have scraped together a coin or two to invest in the profits.

To invest in Captain Drake.

Some of the goods, as always, would be hidden in the cellars of Crag Wyvern. No Preventive officer would try to search the home of the Earl of Wyvern, even if the mad earl was dead and his successor had not yet arrived to take charge.

His successor.

Susan was temporary housekeeper up at Crag Wyvern, but as soon as the new earl sent word of his arrival she'd be out of there. Away from here entirely. She had no intention of meeting Con Somerford again.

The sweetest man she'd ever known, the truest friend.

The person she'd hurt most cruelly.

Eleven years ago.

She'd been only fifteen, but it was no excuse. He'd been only fifteen, too, and without defenses. He'd been in the army for ten of the eleven years since, however, so she supposed he'd have defenses now.

And attacks.

She shivered in the cool night air and turned her anxieties on the scene before her. If this run was successful, she could leave.

"Come on, come on," she muttered under her breath, straining to see the first goods land on the beach. She could imagine the powerful thrust of the oarsmen, racing to bring the contraband in, could almost hear the muttering excitement of the waiting men, though it was probably just the wind and sea.

She and David had watched runs before. From a height like this everything seemed so slow. She wanted to leap up and help, as if the run were a huge cart that she could push to make it go faster. Instead she stayed still and silent beside her brother, like him watchful for any sign of problems.

Being in command was a lonely business.

How was she going to be able to leave David to his lonely task? He didn't need her—it was disconcerting how quickly he'd taken to smuggling and leadership—but could she bear to go away, to not be here beside him on a dark night, to not know immediately if anything went wrong?

And yet, once Con sent word he was coming, she must.

Despite treasured summer days eleven years ago, and sweet pleasures. And wicked ones . . .

She realized she was sliding again under the seductive pull of might-have-beens, and fought clear to focus on the business of the moment.

At last the first of the cargo was landing, the first goods were being carried up the rough slope. It was going well. David had done it.

With a blown-out breath, she relaxed on the rocky ground, arms around her knees, permitting herself to enjoy the rough music of waves on shingle, and the other rough music of hundreds of busy men. She breathed in the wind, fresh off the English Channel, and the tense activity all around.

Heady stuff, the Freetrade, but perilous.

"Do you know where the Preventive officer is?" she asked in a quiet voice that wouldn't carry.

"Gifford?" David sent one of the nearby men off with a quiet command, and she saw some trouble on the cliff. A man fallen, probably. "There's a dummy ship offshore five miles west, and with luck he and the boatmen are watching it, ready to fish up the goods it drops into the water."

Luck. She hated to depend on luck.

"Poor man," she said.

David turned his head toward her. "He'll get to confiscate a small cargo like Perch did under Mel. It'll look good to his superiors, and he'll get his cut of the value."

Lieutenant Perch had been riding officer here for years, with an agreeable working relationship with the Dragon's Horde gang. He'd recently died from falling down a cliff—or being pushed—and now they had young, keen Lieutenant Gifford to deal with.

"Let's hope that satisfies him," Susan said.

He gave a kind of grunt. "If Gifford were a more flexible man we could come to a permanent arrangement."

"He's honest."

"Damn nuisance. Can't you use your wiles on him? I think he's sweet on you."

"I don't have any wiles. I'm a starchy housekeeper."

"You'd have wiles in sackcloth." He reached out and took her hand, his so solid and warm in the chilly night. "Isn't it time you stopped working there, love? There'll be money aplenty after this, and we can find someone else who's friendly to the trade to be housekeeper."

She knew it bothered him for her to be a domestic servant. "Probably. But I want to find that gold."

"It'd be nice, but after this, we don't need it."

So careless, so confident. She wished she had David's comfort with whatever happened. She wished she weren't the sort to be always looking ahead, planning, worrying, trying to force fate. . . .

Oh yes, she desperately wished that.

She was as she was, however, and David didn't seem to accept that she had a strange unladylike need for employment. For independence.

And there was the gold. The Horde under Mel Clyst had paid the late Earl of Wyvern for protection. Since he hadn't provided it, they wanted their money back. She wanted that money back, but mainly to keep David safe. It would pay off the debts caused by the failed run and provide a buffer so he wouldn't have to take so many risks.

She frowned down at the dark sea. Things wouldn't have been so difficult if her mother hadn't set off to follow Mel to Australia, taking all the Horde's available money with her. Isabelle Kerslake. Lady Belle, as she liked to be known. A smuggler's mistress, without a scrap of shame as far as anyone could tell, and without a scrap of feeling for her two children.

Susan shook off that pointless pain and thought about the gold. She glanced behind at the solid mass of Crag Wyvern as if that would spark a new idea about where the mad earl had hidden his loot. The trouble with madmen, however, was that their doings made no sense.

Automatically she scanned the upper slit windows for lights. Crag Wyvern served as a useful messaging post visible for miles, and as a viewing post where miles of coast could be scanned for other warning lights. Apart from that, however, it had no redeeming features.

The house was only two hundred years old, but had been built to look like a medieval fortress with only arrow-slit windows on the outside. Thank heavens there was an inner courtyard garden, and the rooms had proper windows that looked into that, but from the outside the place was grim.

As she turned back to the sea, the thin moon floated out from behind clouds again, silvering the boats on the water, lifting and bobbing with the waves. Then the clouds swept across the moon like a curtain, and a wash of light drizzle blew by on the wind. She hunched, grimacing, but the rain was a blessing because it obscured the view even more. The sea and shore below her could have been deserted.

If Gifford had spotted the dummy run for what it was, and was seeking the real one, he'd need the devil's own luck to find them tonight. Let it stay that way. He was a pleasant enough young man, and she didn't want to see him smashed at the bottom of a cliff.

Lord, but she wished she had no part of this.

Smuggling was in her blood, and she was used to loving these smooth runs that flowed with hot excitement through the darkest nights. But it wasn't a distant adventure anymore.

It was need now, and danger to the person she loved most in the world—

Was that a noise behind her?

She and David swiveled together to look back toward Crag Wyvern. She knew he too held his breath, the better to hear a warning sound.

Nothing.

She began to relax, but then, in one high, narrow window, a candle flared into light.

"Trouble," he murmured.

She put a hand on his suddenly tense arm. "Only a stranger, that candle says. Not Gifford or the military. I'll deal with it. One squeal for danger. Two if it's clear."

That was the smuggler's call—the squeal of an animal caught in the fox's jaws or the owl's talons—and if the cry was cut off quickly, it still signaled danger.

With a squeeze to his arm for reassurance, she slid to the side, carefully, slowly, so that when she straightened she wouldn't be close to Captain Drake. Then she began to climb the rough slope, soft boots gripping the treacherous ground, heart thumping, but not in a bad way.

Perhaps she was more like her brother than she cared to admit. She enjoyed being skilled and strong. She enjoyed adventure. She liked having a pistol in her belt and knowing how to use it.

As well that she had no dreams of becoming a fine lady.

Or not anymore, at least.

Once, she'd been caught up in a mad, destructive desire to marry the future Earl of Wyvern—Con Somerford, she'd thought—and ended up naked with him on a beach. . . .

She physically shook the memory away. It was too painful to think about, especially now, when she needed a clear mind.

Heart beating faster and blood sizzling through her veins, she went up the tricky hill in a crouch, fingers to the ground to stay low. She stretched hearing and sight in search of the stranger.

Whoever the stranger was, she'd expect him to have entered the house. Maisie might have signaled for that too. But Susan had heard something up here on the headland, and so had David.

She slowed to give her senses greater chance to find the intruder, and then she saw him. Her straining eyes saw a cloaked figure a little darker than the dark night sky. He stood still as a statue. She could almost imagine someone had put a statue there, on the headland between the house and the cliff.

A statue with a distinct military air. Was it Lieutenant Gifford after all?

She shivered, suddenly feeling the cold, damp wind against her neck. Gifford would have soldiers with him, already spreading out along the headland. The men bringing in the cargo would be met with a round of fire, but the smugglers had their armed men too. It would turn into a bloody battle, and if David survived, the military would be down on the area like a plague looking for someone to hang for it.

Looking for Captain Drake.

Her heart was racing with panic and she stayed there, breathing as slowly as she could, forcing herself back to control. Panic served no one.

If Gifford was here with troops, wouldn't he have acted by now?

She stretched every quivering sense to detect soldiers concealed in the gorse, muskets trained toward the beach.

After long moments she found nothing.

Soldiers weren't that good at staying quiet in the night.

So who was it, and what was he planning to do?

Heartbeat still fast, but not with panic now, she eased forward, trying not to present a silhouette against the sea and sky behind her. The land flattened as she reached the top, however, making it hard to crouch, making her clumsy, so some earth skittered away from beneath her feet.

She sensed rather than saw the man turn toward her.

Time to show herself and pray.

She pulled off her hood and used it to wipe the soot around so it would appear to be general grubbiness. She tucked the cloth into a pocket, then stood. Eccentric to be wandering about at night in men's clothing, but a woman could be eccentric if she wanted to, especially a twenty-six-year-old spinster of shady antecedents.

She drew her pistol out of her belt and put it into the big pocket of her old-fashioned frock coat. She kept her hand on it as she walked up to the still and silent figure, and it was pointed forward, ready to fire.

She'd never shot anyone, but she hoped she could if it was necessary to save David.

"Who are you?" she said at normal volume. "What is your business here?"

She was within three feet of him, and in the deep dark she could not make out any detail except that he was a couple of inches taller than she was, which made him about six feet. He was hatless and his hair must be very short, since the brisk wind created no visible movement around his head.

She had to capture a strand of her own hair with her free hand to stop it blowing into her eyes.

She stared at him, wondering why he wasn't answering, wondering what to do next. But then he said, "I am the Earl of Wyvern, so everything here is my business." In the subsequent silence, he added, "Hello, Susan."

Her heart stopped, then raced so impossibly fast that stars danced around her vision.

Oh, Lord. Con. Here. Now.

In the middle of a run!

He'd thought smuggling exciting eleven years ago, but people changed. He'd spent most of those years as a soldier, part of the mighty fist of the king's law.

Dazed shock spiraled down to something numb, and then she could breathe again. "How did you know it was me?"

"What other lady would be walking the clifftop at the time of a smugglers' run?"

She thought of denying it, but saw no point. "What are you going to do?"

She made herself draw the pistol, though she didn't cock it. Heaven knew she wouldn't be able to fire it. Not at Con. "It would be awkward to have to shoot you," she said as firmly as she could.

Without warning, he threw himself at her. She landed hard, winded by the fall and his weight, pistol gone, his hand covering her mouth. "No squealing."

He remembered. Did he remember everything? Did he remember lying on top of her like this in pleasure? Was his body remembering . . . ?

He'd been so charming, so easygoing, so dear, but now he was dark and dangerous, showing not a shred of concern for the lady he was squashing into hard, unforgiving earth.

"Answer me," he said.

She nodded, and he eased his hand away, but stayed over her, pressing her down.

"There's a stone digging into my back."

For a moment he didn't respond, but then he moved back and off her, grasping her wrist and pulling her to her feet before she had time to object. His hand was harder than she remembered, his strength greater. How could she remember so much from a summer fortnight eleven years ago?

How could she not? He'd been her first lover, and she his, and she'd denied every scrap of feeling when she'd sent him away.

Life was full of ironies. She'd rejected Con Somerford because he hadn't been the man she'd thought he was—the heir to the earldom. And here he was, earl, a dark nemesis probably ready to destroy everything because of what she'd done eleven years ago.

What could she do to stop him?

She remembered David's comment about feminine wiles and had to fight down wild laughter. That was one weapon that would never work on the new Earl of Wyvern.

"I heard Captain Drake was caught and transported," he said, as if nothing of importance lay between them. "Who's master smuggler now?"

"Captain Drake."

"Mel Clyst escaped?"

"The smuggling master here is always called Captain Drake."

"Ah, I didn't know that."

"How could you?" she pointed out with deliberate harshness, in direct reaction to a weakness that threatened to crumple her down onto the dark earth. "You were here for only two weeks." As coldly as possible, she added, "As an outsider."

"I got inside you, Susan."

The deliberate crudeness stole her breath.

"Where are the Preventives?" he asked.

She swallowed and managed an answer. "Decoyed up the coast a bit."

He turned to look out at the water. The sickle moon shone clear for a moment, showing a clean, strong profile and, at sea, the armada of small boats heading out for another load.

"Looks like a smooth run, then. Come back to the house with me." He turned as if his word were law.

"I'd rather not." Overriding her weakness was fear, as sharp as winter ice. Irrational fear, she hoped, but frantic.

He looked back at her. "Come back to the house with me, Susan."

He made no threat. She had no idea what he might be threatening, but a breath escaped her that was close to a sigh, and she followed him across the scrubby heathland.

After eleven years, Con Somerford was back, lord and master of all that surrounded them.

❧ 2 ❧

SUSAN FELT dazed, almost drunk with shock. How could it feel as if eleven full years had disappeared like melting snow? And yet it did. Despite the physical changes in both of them, and a virtual lifetime of experiences, he was Con, who for that brief time had been the friend of the heart she had never found since.

Who for an even briefer time had been the lover she could never imagine finding again.

Con. Con, short for Connaught, his second name, because his first name was George and his two friends were called George, and they'd all agreed to choose other names. . . .

Her mind was dancing crazily, flinching off memories and feelings, then ricocheting back to them again.

He'd simply been Con when she'd known him.

She bit her lip on nervous laughter. In the biblical sense. The sweetest, steadiest young man she'd ever known in any sense. She'd teased him about being her Saint George, who'd save her from any dragon.

He'd promised to be her hero, always.

In almost the next breath she'd told him she never wanted to see him again.

The house loomed ahead with only the one candlelit window to break the blackness. Con was back, but he wasn't Saint George anymore. He was Wyvern. He was the dragon.

"There's a door on this side, isn't there?" he asked.

"Yes." She stepped past him, but even she had to feel for the door in the dark. When her unsteady hands found the iron latch, the door opened silently into light, for she'd left a lamp burning for her return. Once inside she quickly closed the door, then turned, afraid of what she might see.

She saw lines and angles that had not been there before, and two white slashes up near his hairline that hinted at danger narrowly missed. He'd been a soldier for ten years.

And yet, he was still Con.

His rebellious, overlong hair was now trimmed severely short. She'd run fingers through that long hair, sticky with sweat. . . .

His eyes were the same steady gray. She'd thought they were as changeable as the sea, but she'd never dreamed of seeing them so stormily cold.

He was earl. In theory at least, he ruled this part of England. In practice, the smugglers took the *free* in Freetraders very seriously. He looked like the sort of man who might try to stop the smuggling, and that could get him killed.

She was suddenly as afraid *for* him as *of* him. Lieutenant Perch had come to a bloody "accidental" end. That could happen to anyone who got in the way of the Freetrade. She didn't think David would kill to save himself and his men, but these days she wasn't sure.

David would kill to save her. She was sure of that.

"What are you going to do?" she asked, not even sure if she meant about the smuggling, herself, or everything.

Con was looking at her with an unnervingly steady gaze. He probably didn't approve of the jacket and breeches, but was there something more personal in his scrutiny? Was he contrasting her with the fifteen-year-old, as she was him?

"What am I going to do?" he echoed softly, silver eyes still resting on her. "Having ridden hard for far too long, I plan to eat, have a bath, then go to bed. The servants seem to be in short supply, however, and my housekeeper is also missing."

There was no choice but to admit it. "I am your housekeeper."

His eyes widened and it was wryly pleasant to shock him. "I was told my new housekeeper was a *Mrs. Kerslake*."

"Told? Told by who?"

"Don't pretend to be stupid, Susan. It won't wash. Swann has been sending me regular reports ever since I inherited."

Of course. Of course. She felt stupid. Not a spy, but Swann, the earldom's lawyer, who rode out from Honiton every fortnight to check his client's property.

"I am Mrs. Kerslake," she said.

He shook his head. "One day when I'm less tired and hungry, you must tell me how this all came about."

"People change." Belatedly she added, "My lord," desperate for distance and protection. "And a housekeeper doesn't actually scrub the grates and bake the cakes, you know. You will find everything in order."

She seized the lamp to lead the way out of the constricting room.

"But I didn't find everything in order."

She turned back sharply, alerted by his tone.

He was still angry. After all these years he was still angry. Fear surged through her in a sickening wave. This was a man to fear when he was angry.

He frowned. "Are you all right?"

She'd probably gone sheet white. "Like you, I am tired. If you expected a better reception, my lord, you should have sent warning. Come along and I will see to your needs."

She opened the door, wishing she hadn't used quite those words. What was she going to do if he wanted her in his bed? She didn't want to kill him. She didn't want anyone else to kill him. She didn't want to stir any more trouble around here than they already had.

She didn't want to bed him.

A slight but deep ache said that perhaps she lied. . . .

Aware of stillness behind, she turned.

He was giving that excellent impression of a stone statue. "If I choose to act on impulse, Mrs. Kerslake, it is for my household, my servants, to accommodate me."

"You inherited the earldom two months ago and haven't seen fit to visit here until today. Were we to stand in readiness, just in case?"

"Since I am paying you, yes."

She raised her chin. "Then you should have made it clear that you wanted to waste money. I would have had a banquet prepared every night!"

His eyes narrowed and danger prickled through the room. From fear as much as anything, she whirled and marched out into the corridor. "This way, my lord. We can produce simple food quickly, and a bath for you within the hour."

She kept on walking. If he chose not to follow, so be it. Better so. She needed time away from him to regroup.

Alas, she heard his footsteps behind.

"Are you alone, my lord, or have you brought servants with you?"

"Of course I've brought servants. My valet, my secretary, and two manservants."

She grimaced. She must be sounding like an idiot. But she kept thinking of him as Con, the ordinary young man she'd met on the headland and on the beach, exploring, teasing, and talking, talking, talking as if they'd make a world out of words and hide in it forever. They'd crawled into caves and waded tidal pools without stockings. Then one day they'd gone swimming in scanty clothing, and that had been their undoing.

He's the earl now, she told herself. *Remember it. Earl of Wyvern, with all the strange things that implies.*

"You have two footmen?" she asked to fill the silence as she began to climb the stairs. "That will be useful. The old earl didn't like male household servants, and I haven't engaged any since."

"They're not footmen, no. Consider them grooms."

Consider them? Then what were they? Soldiers? Spies? She wished she could slip away to warn David, but it would be pointless.

There was nothing to be done tonight. Was there anything to be done at all? They couldn't attack an earl without bringing the wrath of the nation down on them.

But someone could push him off a cliff. . . .

She realized that she'd thoughtlessly chosen one of the simple servants' staircases that riddled the house. So be it. If it was beneath his dignity, then he could go the longer way to find steps more suited to his noble feet. Her soft boots made no sound on the plain wood, but his riding boots rapped hard with each step.

Having him behind her began to unnerve her. She didn't really think he'd attack her, but her neck prickled. He'd thrown her down and unarmed her so easily.

She was a tall, strong woman, and she'd fooled herself that she was a match for most men. Perhaps she was, but more likely no man had ever seriously attacked her before.

Born Captain Drake's daughter. Now Captain Drake's sister. She was close to untouchable on this stretch of coast, but she understood the message of that attack. Anyone who threatened the new earl would be instantly and effectively contested, no matter who they were.

She opened the door into the south corridor, her lamp glowing on walls painted to look like rough stone.

He spoke behind her. "The dear old place hasn't changed, I see."

She turned and some trick of the lamplight made his eyes seem paler and more intense. "Oh, it has. You probably didn't notice the gargoyles outside in the dark. We have a torture chamber now too."

She answered his unspoken, startled question. "No, he didn't use it, except to scare the occasional guest. But he commissioned waxworks of victims from Madame Tussaud."

"Good God." She expected some comment, perhaps an instruction to rip the place apart, but he merely said, "Food and a bath, Mrs. Kerslake?"

She turned, stung by his indifference. What had she expected? So much time had passed, and he must have known many women. She'd given her body to two other men, but they hadn't erased a moment of the memory of Con, clumsy and imperfect as it had been.

She'd wanted them to, but they hadn't.

As they walked along the gloomy corridor she said, "You won't want to use the earl's chambers, my lord. The Chinese rooms are the next grandest. Everything is tolerably well maintained, though I cannot guarantee that the mattress will not be damp. Not having been given notice to prepare."

"I've endured worse than a damp mattress. Why don't I want to use the earl's chambers?"

"Trust me, Con, you don't."

She froze. She'd called him Con, and he was probably laughing at the idea of trusting her. She couldn't help it. She turned.

He looked more weary than amused, but like a man who could fight and even kill when weary.

She was suddenly aware of the sweeping curve of his dark brows above his dark-lashed pale eyes. She'd always thought his eyes the most beautiful she'd ever seen.

"Who is your husband?" he asked.

She blinked, puzzled for a moment. "I'm not married."

"*Mrs.* Kerslake?"

Absurdly, she felt her cheeks heat, as if she were caught in a lie. "It's convention for a housekeeper to be addressed that way."

"Ah, so it is. But I find your domestic incarnation surprising. How did it come about?"

"I thought you were hungry, my lord."

"I've known hunger before. Well? How?"

Buffeted by his will, she explained. "When the old earl died, Mrs. Lane wanted to retire. No one else suitable wanted the job, so I offered to take care of things for a while. Despite tonight, my lord, I am well trained in domestic economy."

"And your brother, David? Is he my butler?"

Susan suppressed a twitch, as if the truth would flare out. "Don't you know he's your estate manager?"

"Swann must have neglected to mention it. How very cozy, to be sure." He gestured. "Lead on to the Chinese rooms, Mrs. Kerslake. I remember them as being all barbaric splendor, but I suppose I will become accustomed."

The Chinese rooms were on the far side of the house, and since Crag Wyvern was built like a monastery around a large central courtyard, the walk there was long. A continuous narrow corridor ran along the outside walls, leaving the rooms facing inward, over-looking the courtyard garden. The only windows into the corridor were the narrow glazed arrow slits.

The effect was gloomy on a sunny day. At past midnight it was cavernous, especially with the trompe l'oeil stone walls and floor and the ornamental weaponry hanging on them. Susan was ac-customed to it. She was not accustomed to a dark presence at her back.

The weaponry was not, in fact, completely ornamental, and he could seize a sword or ax and decapitate her. She knew he wouldn't, but she walked between shining blades, nerves twitching.

"Old Yorrick's still here," he remarked as they turned the cor-ner that held a skeleton hanging in chains.

He touched the chains, setting the whole thing clattering and clanging. Susan did the same childish thing herself sometimes, but now the lingering rattle behind them raised the hairs on her neck.

Dear God, but she'd thought she was accustomed to this place, but tonight it seemed newly horrid—an outward sign of the tradi-tional madness of the earls of Wyvern. The last one had certainly been insane. Thank heavens Con came from a different branch of the family.

The walk seemed endless, and she flung open the door of the bedroom of the Chinese suite with relief. Golden dragons snarled in the lamplight, fangs bared against bright red walls framed in black-lacquered woodwork.

"Zeus," he said with a short laugh. "My memory had faded somewhat. I remember wishing I had this room. It's obviously wise to be careful what you wish for."

He swung his heavy riding cloak off and spread it over a chair. Beneath, he was neatly dressed in brown and buff. "Are there servants' rooms attached?"

"There's a dressing room, which includes a bed for a valet."

"The Norse rooms are next door, aren't they? I remember that my father had this room and Fred and I were in the Norse suite. To begin with."

A memory sparked like a falling star. She ignored it. "Yes."

"Put my secretary in there. His name is Racecombe de Vere and he's a rascal. My valet is Diego Sarmiento. His English is excellent and he will use it to complain about the climate and to try to seduce the maids. My other two servants, Pearce and White, are down in the stables in the village. The stables that are strangely lacking grooms and horses."

She didn't respond. He had to know that the Crag's horses were on loan to the smugglers tonight, along with most other horses in the area. What would he do when he discovered that Crag Wyvern had supported ten horses for years when the old earl never left the place? It would be an inconvenience to the Horde not to have those excellent, sturdy horses available.

Perhaps he sighed. "Light the candle and go about your housekeeping duties, Mrs. Kerslake. Any sustenance will do, but I want that bath within the hour, regardless of any other business taking place."

For some reason, Susan found herself reluctant to leave, and seeking words to bridge the gap that lay deep and wide between them. Did the words exist to make sense of their situation, past and present?

Probably not. She lit the solitary candle by his bed and left, closing the door on all the dragons within.

ꙮ 3 ꙮ

CON SUCKED in what felt like his first clear breath since that figure had walked up to him on the headland and he'd realized who it was.

Eleven years.

It shouldn't be hitting him so hard. There'd been other women.

They lay in his mind like ghosts, however, when Susan had always lived there in vibrant flesh.

Being rejected in the cruelest, harshest way was like a brand, it would seem. Something a man never got rid of.

Like a tattoo. He rubbed absentmindedly at his right chest. Another permanent mark.

He wandered the room, idly opening drawers that were, of course, empty. Everywhere he looked, the dragons writhed and snarled. He glared at one and snarled back.

Damn the mad Earl of Wyvern. Damn the whole line of them, and the last one for dying far too soon. If not for that, he would be in the peace of Somerford Court in Sussex.

The curtains and bed hangings were a glorious black silk with more dragons embroidered on them. The frame of the bed was black lacquer, as was all the furniture. The carpet covered nearly the whole floor with thick silk in paler, gentle shades, but still containing a picture of a coiled dragon. He hated to be walking on it in his boots, but he couldn't get them off without a jack or Diego.

His army boots had been more practical, but he'd thought he

should be fashionable now he was done with all that. Thus, he'd ended up with boots too snug to drag off himself.

He crossed the carpet to one of the long windows and looked down at the dark courtyard garden. Two lamps cast pale circles of light on paths and touched the edges of branches and leaves. He remembered it as a pleasant spot in the middle of the peculiar house.

Through a youth's eyes, Crag Wyvern had seemed a prime adventure, the crazy earl a figure of fun. Now he wasn't so sure. A torture chamber. He shook his head. The Devonish Somerfords had been mad since the first earl, who'd liked to be called Dragonkiller. He'd claimed to have killed a dragon here two hundred years ago.

Rumor said they dabbled in witchcraft. They'd certainly been blessed by good fortune enough to indulge their mad whims. Disappointing, then, to find the coffers almost empty now.

He wondered what was so peculiar about the earl's traditional chambers and felt a natural curiosity to go and look. He smiled. The boy never left the man entirely. He'd be happy to surrender to the boy again if he could, but life seemed to conspire against it.

His boyhood had ended when Susan Kerslake had ruthlessly destroyed it, and he'd taken the next step himself by joining the army. He didn't entirely regret it. As a second son he'd needed employment, and neither the navy nor the church had appealed. Men were needed to fight Napoleon, and he had decided that he might as well be one of them.

He'd served eight years and felt proud to have done his duty, but he'd also been damned glad when Napoleon had abdicated and it was over. He'd been needed at home anyway, with his father dead, and then his brother drowned in a silly boating accident. He'd become Lord Amleigh, and though he mourned his father and Fred, he had felt blessed to have lived through the war to become owner of his lovely Sussex home.

Those brief golden days had ended a year ago when Napoleon had left Elba to snatch back his power and his crown. Wellington's victorious, experienced army had been dispersed, so of course any seasoned officer had to return for the final battle.

Waterloo, it had ended up being called.

It had been a bloodbath, as he'd expected. Leaving England for Belgium, he'd known that neither general would be able to ride away to fight another day. It would be to the death, and somewhere in the months of peace and happiness in England he'd lost the calluses that made a soldier able to kill and kill, to wade through blood and mud, and climb over corpses, some of them of friends, to the only goal—victory.

No, he'd not lost the ability to do that. He'd lost the ability to celebrate afterward.

And somewhere in the mud and blood he'd lost himself.

His life before the army was a myth to him now, the memories of his life up till sixteen all invention. Perhaps he'd never been a happy child in Hawk in the Vale, a venturesome schoolboy at Harrow, an innocent youth on the rocks and beaches of Devon.

A precipitously impetuous lover . . .

He shook that away and looked around the extravagant room, catching sight of himself in a gilded mirror.

Dark, harsh, and somber—scoured down to the man that war and killing and constant, encircling death had made, a man who smiled only with conscious effort.

He still had purpose, at least—duty. And the earldom of Wyvern, including this house, was part of it. He'd avoided coming here for far too long. He must make sure that the place was being properly run, that his people here were being taken care of.

It would be nice to make some sense of the finances, too, so there was money to take care of Crag Wyvern without draining Somerford Court.

He'd come here knowing that he might meet Susan Kerslake. He'd never imagined meeting her so swiftly and directly.

And now? He was perfectly aware of all the irrational reactions sweeping through him, but he was not a boy anymore.

The important question was, What was she up to? Why was she

here, playing at being housekeeper? The smuggling didn't surprise him—it was in her blood—but the domestic work was as ridiculous as setting a thoroughbred to work a mine pump.

She was up to something.

He caught his breath. Could she be crazy enough to think she could try again to whore her way into the rank of countess?

A laugh escaped. She'd have to be as crazy as the crazy earl to think it possible.

And yet . . . and yet the panicked reactions swirling inside him said that it might be entirely too possible if he let his guard down. She was not the coltish girl he remembered, but she was more.

She was the same person grown devastatingly womanly.

Despite rough men's garments and a sooty face, she'd still had the clean-cut features he remembered, and the beautiful hazel eyes. She was tall and lithe and moved like a woman who could still climb cliffs like a mountain sheep and swim like a fish.

He took a deep breath and stood straight. He was an officer, and a damn good one. He'd faced many dangerous enemies and survived. He could face, and survive, Susan Kerslake.

Susan hurried down the corridor, fighting panic to try to think which servants could best be spared from the cellars to prepare food and heat bathwater for Con.

No, the earl. She had to think of him as the earl to remind herself that he wasn't the sweet-natured youth of the past, and that he held the livelihood of everyone here in his hands.

She'd left spine-twisted Maisie in charge of the main part of the house, never thinking she'd have to climb up to tell Diddy to light that candle signaling guests.

Who else could take care of Con? Middle-aged Jane and young Ellen.

Con, Con. What had he thought of her?

She knew what he thought of her! What else could he think after what she'd done all those years ago?

He was her employer now, that was all, and he wanted food and a bath.

She thoughtlessly started down the wide stairs that ran straight into the great hall, and hastily swung back out of sight—so hastily that her lamp tilted. *Get a grip on yourself, my girl, or you'll be up in flames!*

There were people down there waiting—two men—and here she was in men's clothing with dirt smeared over her face. Where were her wits? She might as well announce that she was part of the smuggling gang.

She knew where her wits were, and she didn't seem able to do anything about it.

She let herself lean against the wall for a moment, steadying herself as the white-gold flame steadied, taking the moment to come to terms with the situation.

So Con was here. Clearly he felt nothing for her now except old anger. If they kept in their proper stations, they need hardly meet. They were both adults now, and that insane youthful passion was a thing of the far past. He wasn't the same person, and neither was she.

Deep inside she didn't believe that, but she must. It was stark truth.

She took servants' stairs to the kitchens. Only Maisie was in there.

"Did I do right, ma'am? Took me a while to get up there."

"You did perfectly, Maisie. Don't worry. Everything's all right. It's just that the new earl arrived at last."

"He looked right frightening, though, ma'am."

"He's just tired. He wants food and a bath, so build the fire under the big kettle while I go get Ellen and Jane. And boil the small kettle for tea."

Tea! Wild laughter threatened. Would Con demand to know where the tea and brandy he drank came from? Most of England used smuggled goods if they could get them, but there were always those who stuck on principle.

Perhaps Con would follow the pattern of past generations and come to a gentleman's agreement with the Horde, but it didn't seem likely. He was a soldier, used to obeying orders and enforcing the law. He wouldn't find smuggling romantic anymore.

If he insisted, she'd buy everything, taxes paid, at ten times the price. She'd be the laughingstock of south Devon, though.

But most people couldn't afford those prices. Why wouldn't the government come to its senses and accept that there'd be more money in taxes if taxes were lower?

Of course if they did, that'd be the end of smuggling, and then where would the south coast be?

It was coming to a point where she didn't know what to pray for.

Maisie was moving burning coals under the big water kettle, and adding fresh so they crackled and flared.

"When you've finished there, Maisie, put together a soup of some sort."

Susan gathered herself, feeling slightly breathless, as if the world were whirling around her.

What now? What should she do now?

Go down to get Ellen and Jane, or change? She should go down first, but what if Con decided to pursue her here? She wanted to be safe in her severe housekeeper clothes when she had to face him again.

She hurried into her rooms, a bedchamber and small parlor that the previous housekeeper, bless her, had fitted out in a cozy modern style with pale green painted walls. Susan had added some of her framed insect drawings and a lot of books. Unexpectedly, she'd come to love these rooms, the only private space she'd ever owned.

She'd been raised at Kerslake Manor with love and kindness, but love and kindness couldn't produce enough rooms for everyone to have their own. That was why she'd spent so much time outdoors.

That was why she'd met Con. Why they'd—

A glance in the mirror showed her a pale face streaked with black, her hair simply tied back. Oh, Lord. This was not how she would have chosen to meet Con again.

The *earl*!

The Earl of Wyvern, who was no longer any personal business of hers.

She tore off her jacket, then shed the rest of her clothes. She washed off the soot, then slipped into a fresh shift, a light corset, and one of her plain gray dresses. She pinned a crisp white apron on top.

This wasn't how she wanted to look for Con either, but it was better. Much better. It was armor.

She twisted her brown hair up on top of her head and pinned it in place, then covered it with a cap, tying the strings under her chin. Not quite armored enough, she added a fichu of starched cotton around her shoulders.

Deep inside, like a tolling alarm bell, pounded the need to escape, to run before she had to see Con again. Counterpoint to it beat the desperate rhythm of need.

To see him, to hear him, the man the youth had become . . .

She swallowed, and as ready as she was likely to be, went out again into the kitchen. On the big hearth, steam was already rising from three pots, and Maisie was finely chopping vegetables. Susan praised her, picked up the lamp, and plunged down into the chilly depths of Crag Wyvern to summon the other maids.

It was only a temporary escape, however.

Above, the dragon still waited to be faced.

Con wondered if an earl in his noble home was supposed to stay in his grand chambers until service arrived. He wasn't in the earl's grand chambers, however—the Wyvern rooms, he remembered they were called—and the service was likely to be snail-slow.

The bed tempted him like a siren song. He'd been on horseback since early morning, pushing on as the light faded because of a need to get here, to get the first part over.

Or the need to escape.

Despite the call of duty, he probably wouldn't have left Somerford Court to come here if one of his oldest friends had not returned to his neighboring estate. Instead of riding across the valley to meet Van for the first time in a year, however, he'd lurked at home. When work had started on Steynings, indicating that Van might be returning for good, he'd discovered an urgent need to inspect this property in Devon and set off with no preparation at all.

He rubbed his hands over his weary face. Mad. Perhaps he was as mad as the Demented Devonish Somerfords.

Van had lost all his immediate family in recent years. And yet, knowing he probably needed a friend, Con had fled like a coward fleeing a battle.

Because Van might want to help him—

God! Con grabbed the candle and plunged back out into the corridor. *Dammit.* Which way did he go in this crazy place? It was full of staircases, he remembered. Circular ones at the corners. A straight one down into the hall. Servants' narrow stairs.

Right or left, he'd come to a circular one. Left, why not? He was left-handed.

He found the arch and headed down, remembering that his left-handedness gave him an advantage here.

In castles, these staircases always curled counter-clockwise so that defenders from above would have their right arm—their sword arm—free, while attackers from below would be cramped by the inner wall. The Crag Wyvern stairs curled clockwise because left-handedness ran in the blood of the Devonish Somerfords.

The old earl had been left-handed, and apparently so had most before him. Con was left-handed. Was that a bad omen? He could feel the pressure of madness in the very walls of this place.

He certainly wished he had a lamp or lantern rather than the candle he was holding in his right hand, instinctively leaving his left hand free, even though he carried no weapon. He wished he had a weapon, but the greatest danger he faced was that the wildly flaring candle might blow out, leaving him to feel his way down the stairs in the pitch dark.

He stepped out into a corner of the huge medieval-style hall with relief, pausing to let his hammering heart settle. The room was as peculiar as the rest of the place, the walls encrusted with weaponry, but it contained two relatively sane human beings.

"Ah, a human!" declared Racecombe de Vere, lounging on an

oaken settle with deceptive languor, golden curls framing a fine-boned face, smoky-blue eyes cynically amused at the world.

"If an Earl of Wyvern is ever human," Con replied.

"No? At least they seem to have been warlike." Race gestured at the walls.

"Not a bit of it. This stuff must have been bought by the yard."

"Alas. I was hoping some of the muskets and pistols might work. There's a distinct feeling here of imminent battle."

Race would know. He was an army man, but he'd missed Waterloo. He'd been part of the men rushed back from Canada who'd arrived too late. At which point he'd sold his commission in disgust.

Con put his candle with a stand of three others on the massive dark oak refectory table in the middle of the room. "The only likely battle would be against ghosts."

"Then why did you disappear for a solitary midnight stroll?"

Con met Race's mischievous eyes. "To stretch my legs. Servants are being roused."

"Roused from sleep on the heathy headland?"

Con merely gave him a look.

Race had been his subaltern for a while in Spain, and they'd met again in Melton Mowbray in February. Con had just heard of his mad relative's death. Race had decided he needed a secretary and appointed himself.

At the time it had seemed rather farcical, but Con hadn't cared enough to object. Race, however, had turned out to have a gift for administration. He still could be an imp from hell at times.

"You are tired, my lord." The soft, Spanish-inflected voice snapped his eyes open. He'd almost gone to sleep on his feet.

He shuddered and turned to Diego, a weather-beaten man nearly twice Con's age. He had dark Spanish eyes, but light brown hair touched with gray. Con knew Diego was here only to look after him. Once Diego was sure he was all right, he would return to his beloved, sunny Spain.

"We're all tired," Con said, rubbing scratchy eyes. "I can tell you where to bed down now if you want, but there should be food soon, and a bath."

There'd be hot water enough for only one bath at a time. It was a fact of being an earl that he would enjoy it first, a fact of life that Race and then Diego would use it after him if they wanted to. A tub of water could go through ten before it was cold and exhausted. Tenth in line for a tub had often been a dreamed-of luxury during the war. . . .

"I would be happy to oversee the servants and encourage them to greater speed, sir," said Diego.

The notion of Diego hounding Susan was vaguely alarming— vaguely because of invading sleep. "No." Con battled fatigue. "No need. The housekeeper has the matter in hand."

"The Mrs. Kerslake? What is she like, sir?"

"Young," he said, walking about to keep the blood flowing to limbs and brain. "And despite the Mrs., unmarried,"

"Pretty?" asked Race, sitting up.

"Depending on taste." Con suppressed an urge to growl a warning. "If you're interested, treat her as a lady, because she is one. She's niece to the local squire."

No need now to get into the more complicated matters of Susan's parentage.

To both of the men, he added, "If she asks any questions about me, don't tell her anything."

Diego's brows quirked, and Con saw mischievous curiosity flit across Race's face.

Damnation. But there was no point hiding all of it. "I knew her years ago and she might be nosy. The important fact is that everyone here is involved in smuggling, and for the moment we're going to pretend that it isn't happening."

"Which it is, of course," Race said, coming to full alert. "Hence the lack of servants in the house or horses in the stables. Fascinating."

"Remember, Race, we are for the moment blind, deaf, and very, very stupid."

Race subsided, giving Con a very ironic salute. "Sir!"

"My lord."

Con turned sharply to see Susan walking toward him. He couldn't help but stare. He'd not been surprised to see her in men's clothing, even though he'd never seen her dressed like that before. He was shocked to see her in dull housekeeper's garb.

Affronted even. He wanted to tear off the ugly cap and starched fichu. To command her not to wear dark gray that stole the color from her face. The outfit almost did the impossible and made her ugly.

He recovered and performed the introductions. He noted Race attempting to flirt and being frostily discouraged.

Good.

Zeus, could he sink so low as jealousy?

She turned back to him. "We have simple food ready for you all, my lord. Where do you want everyone to eat?"

Diego would normally eat with the servants, but Con didn't want him where he might see smuggling activity. Smugglers tended to keep their secrets with a knife. "In the breakfast room on this occasion, if you please."

She nodded. "If you remember the way, my lord, perhaps you could take your party there and I will have the food served within moments."

She disappeared again, and that was the last Con saw of her for the night. Two maids brought soup, bread, cheese, and a currant pie into the breakfast room. On request they returned with tankards of ale to go with it. One was past first youth and plain, the other young, thin, and bucktoothed. Con wondered whether Susan saw him and his men as a bunch of seducers and had chosen the plainest servants.

When they'd finished, he led Race and Diego upstairs, and found a steaming bath ready for him. By then he was almost too tired to care, but since coming home from Waterloo, he had tried never again to go filthy to sleep. He stripped, sat in the wooden tub, scrubbed briskly, and staggered off to fall into bed, asleep almost as soon as he was horizontal.

❧ 4 ❧

DAYLIGHT WOKE him. He'd neglected to draw the curtains.

Daybreak and birdsong—a very English awakening that he still savored every single day. He loved England with a passion built through all the days when loss of life and loss of England had rushed upon him. Perhaps if he could get enough of the true England he could heal.

The England he loved, however, was the England of the gentle Sussex downs, of tranquil Somerford Court and pastoral Hawk in the Vale. It wasn't this aberrant house on a heathy headland, haunted by madmen and criminals.

He climbed out of bed, snarled back at the dragons, and walked naked to the small-paned window to look into the garden. At Somerford his room looked out into the garden, but beyond that lay the valley and a view for miles. Here, the garden was enclosed by dark stone walls. At least the walls were covered with ivy and other growing plants, and the courtyard even contained two trees. They were stunted, however, and a sense of enclosure, of limits, pressed on him.

Such enclosure had doubtless been deliberate in a monastery or convent, but he had not renounced the world. Or perhaps he had. Perhaps riding away from Hawk in the Vale and his friend had been a renunciation of the deepest kind.

At least there were birds. He'd not imagined the birdsong, and he saw a sparrow fly across from tree to ivy, and swifts swooping up near the roof. He could pick out a thrush's trill and a robin's happy song. Maybe the birds were singing that there was a lot to be said for an artificial garden surrounded by high walls.

He began to see a pattern in the courtyard paths. Pentangles. An occult symbol. He shook his head. In the center stood a statue fountain that had not been here eleven years ago. There seemed to be a woman and a dragon. He assumed it was bizarre.

A torture chamber too.

Deeply, truly, he wanted no part of this place, safe or not.

A movement caught his eye, and he saw Susan come out of one side of the house and walk briskly across a diagonal of the courtyard. She was still in the dull gray and white that offended him, with that cap covering almost all her hair, but her walk was free and graceful.

Her clothes eleven years ago had been schoolroom wear, but more lively and becoming than this. Come to think of it, they'd been almost entirely pale colors, and she'd always been grimacing about mud, sand, and grass stains from their adventures.

What was his free spirit doing in gray playing housekeeper here?

Clearly not seeking to seduce him. She'd dress more becomingly for that.

She paused to study some tall, plumy flowers. He suspected that there was some interesting insect on them.

She had always loved insects.

What do you mean, always? You knew her for two weeks.

But it hadn't simply been a fortnight. It had been a lifetime in fourteen days. She'd loved to watch insects, often lying down on the ground or in the sand to study and wonder, to analyze their quirks of behavior. She'd carried a sketching pad and drawn them, showing real talent. That had been her key to freedom, the fact that she went out to study and draw insects, but it hadn't been pretense.

He watched her watch. Then she straightened, stretching her head back to take a deep, relished breath.

He inhaled with her, and carefully, quietly, opened the casement window to let in the same perfumed air that she was breathing.

Not quietly enough. With the window only half open, she started and looked up at him.

He conquered the urge to step back. The sill hit him at hip level, so he was essentially decent, though naked.

Their eyes held for what seemed to be far too long. He saw her lips part, as if she might speak, or perhaps just to catch air.

Then she broke the contact and turned to walk briskly, more briskly, across the courtyard and away.

He stayed there, arms braced on the sill, breathing as if breathing were difficult. For so long he'd told himself that their time here had been a minor thing, a passing moment, that her agonizing dismissal of him had wiped away any warm feelings and—paradoxically—hadn't hurt a bit.

He'd always known it was a lie.

Fifteen. He'd been fifteen, bedazzled, scared, eager. . . .

It had been a strange progression from sitting on the headland talking about everyday things, to lying side by side on their bellies talking about personal matters, to holding hands as they walked along the beach, to sitting in each other's arms sharing dreams and fears.

The moon had become full during that second week, and twice they'd sneaked out at night to sit on the beach surrounded by the magic music of the sea, to talk of anything and everything. He'd wanted to build a fire but she'd told him it was illegal. It could be a signal fire for smugglers, so it was illegal.

She'd known a lot about smugglers and shared it all, and he'd been romantically thrilled by stories of the Freetraders. Then she'd admitted her personal connection—that she wasn't a daughter of Sir Nathaniel and Lady Kerslake at the manor, but of Sir Nathaniel's sister Isabelle and the keeper of the George and Dragon tavern in the village of Dragon's Cove.

And then that her father, Melchisedeck Clyst, was Captain Drake, leader of the local smuggling gang.

She clearly didn't know whether to be proud or ashamed of her parentage. Though "Lady Belle" lived openly with Melchisedeck Clyst in Dragon's Cove, they'd never married.

Con was delightfully scandalized by this blatant sinfulness—things like that never happened in Hawk in the Vale. Overall, however, he thought it a grand connection, and it made Susan even more exceptional in his eyes.

He and his brother Fred spent time in Dragon's Cove, and he started to look out for Captain Drake. He didn't see him, and had no reason to go into the George and Dragon.

They had a grand time in the village anyway. The fishermen were mostly willing to talk as they cleaned their catch or mended nets. They picked up fishing lore and tall stories as they tried to spot which were smugglers and which weren't.

The truth was, of course, that they all were.

Sometimes the fishermen took them out in their boats and even let them have the huge treat of hauling in nets for them. Fred liked being on the boats more than Con, so he'd had time alone to wander the village straining to hear smuggling secrets.

Stupid boy.

He'd finally spotted Mel Clyst, a sinewy man of only moderate height, with a square jaw and Susan's hazel eyes. He wasn't exactly handsome—his bones were heavy and his nose had been broken a time or two—but it was easy to see him as a leader of men. He'd been dressed like the prosperous businessman he was in a cutaway coat and stylish beaver hat.

Another time he saw him with Lady Belle, who was dressed as a fine lady, though with a flamboyant touch that Lady Kerslake would never attempt. A wicked woman, and Susan's mother, although he gathered she had nothing at all to do with her children.

Lady Belle fascinated him, but Captain Drake fascinated him more. It became his dearest ambition to have a chat with his hero.

He got his wish, but it was not a chat he would have wanted.

He'd been sitting on the pebbly beach listening to old Sim Lowstock telling his version of the killing of the dragon by the first earl when they were interrupted. He was politely but firmly escorted into the George and Dragon. Not into the taproom at the front, but into a back room fitted out more like a gentleman's sitting room.

Mel Clyst was sitting on a sofa in gentleman's dress, Lady Belle beside him. It was the first time Con had seen her up close, and he noted plump, clear skin and large blue eyes, but above all he recognized her lush, carnal appeal. Her bodice was very low, and her wide hat held a sweeping, glorious plume dyed scarlet.

Captain Drake and Lady Belle sat on the sofa like a king and queen, and Mel Clyst had chatted about Con and Susan.

Now a man—and a man tested by fire—Con could still feel the sick nervousness and embarrassment of that interview. Or trial, even.

Clyst had not been cruel, but Con had felt all Captain Drake's power that day—the power of a natural leader, but also the power of a man who held the allegiance of most of the population of the coast. If he ordered one of the fishermen to take Con out and throw him into the deeps, it would be done.

In later years, developing his own authority, and using the power of the direct warning and the unspoken threat, Captain Drake had been one of Con's prime models.

All it had been, however, was a conversation, one in which Mel Clyst acknowledged that Susan Kerslake was his daughter, that she enjoyed great freedom to wander the area because surely no one would do her any harm. That a promising young man like Con Somerford had an interesting life ahead of him, one away from here, in the army perhaps, or the law.

It had been a silent but clear warning, man to man, not to do what he and Susan had done the very next day.

Had the warning put the idea into his head, sown some sort of seed? There was no way to know. His affection, his boyish adoration, had been essentially pure, but his body had been young, healthy, and lusty.

Mel Clyst had given one blunt order—no more nighttime meetings. Without a word of threat, Con had known that he, and probably Susan, would suffer sharply if they disobeyed.

So they had met in the afternoon the next day, in Irish Cove, a mile or more along the coast from both the fishing village and Crag Wyvern. It was not easily reached, since an old road there had been cut off by a landslip, and the way down to the beach was steep and treacherous. A smuggler's path, Susan told him, intended to be difficult. They'd scrambled down in search of privacy, aware now of being observed.

They hadn't been planning anything.

At least, he hadn't been.

They'd shared their grievance about interfering adults who didn't understand a friendship, and laughed at the suspicions.

Then they'd kissed to test it out, to prove that it wasn't . . .

Except that it was.

He had kissed a girl or two before. It had been mildly intriguing, but not something he particularly wanted to do again.

When he'd kissed Susan, it had been different. He closed his eyes now and could almost feel it again, taste it again, that soft, uncertain innocence that had left him hot and breathless.

He could still smell her—something subtle and flowery over the heat of her body in the sun. He could relive the hesitancy, the growing enthusiasm, the absorption. Then the breaking apart in shock, fear—and intense, burning speculation.

He'd had an erection. Astonishing, alarming, demanding. He'd had many erections before, but never one with such direct and present purpose.

She knew. She looked at his breeches and smiled, blushing. He was fiery-faced too.

"Cold water will cure that, they say," she said, and stood to strip off her dress. She hadn't even been wearing a corset on her firm, lightly curved body, only a shift, stockings, and shoes. She'd shed shoes and stockings, then said, "Come on!" and run down into the water.

Slim, lanky, but oh, so feminine in those subtle curves hinted at beneath her sturdy shift.

They were in view of anyone on the clifftop! But the road there went nowhere, so unless they were being closely watched, no one would pass by to see by accident.

If they were being watched he'd be married or dead come morning. Susan would likely receive the whipping of her life. Even so, he fought out of entangling clothes down to his breeches and ran to join her in the cool water.

Since she hadn't hesitated, he didn't, and plunged in to swim. She could swim too, better than he could, and they swirled back and forth in the salt water, her shift molded to her body now. It was a kind of dance, but as with other dances, awareness swam with them, heightened by brushing touch and glimpse of shape. Knowledge sat deep in eyes that rarely parted.

Then she stood, water lapping at her small, high breasts, hiding then revealing her nipples beneath opaque cloth. He couldn't stop looking at those flickering buds.

"You can touch them if you want," she said.

And he did, after one frantic glance at the deserted headland. He was dead—dead—if Captain Drake found out he'd touched his daughter's breasts.

Death seemed worth it.

Her breasts were cold from the water, and rough with the covering of cloth, but soft and firm, and sweetly unlike any part of his own body. They were womanly mystery in form, and he kissed them by instinct alone, wishing desperately that he were brave enough to uncover them, to feel silky warm skin instead of rough, cold cotton—

A squawk jerked him out of the past.

A red-faced maid stood in his doorway, a huge jug clutched to her chest. "I knocked, milord! Mrs. Kerslake said you were up—" She bit her lip, going puce at what she'd said.

He was stark naked and didn't need to look to know he had a full erection.

They both stood frozen for a moment. Then the maid scuttled over to his washstand, eyes averted, then out again. Except that she hesitated at the door, her color merely rosy. Her eyes slid to him, down, then back up to his face. "Unless there's anything else you need, milord."

He caught his breath as base temptation sank its teeth. She was willing, and though she was plain, with a heavy face and thick neck, it didn't seem to matter.

"No," he managed to say, "that's all."

The door closed, and so did his eyes as he struggled for control. It would be the last bloody straw to start using the servants as convenients.

He knew that wasn't the real reason he'd turned down the offer, though. The absolute barrier had been the thought of Susan's reaction when she found out.

Susan was in the kitchen supervising little Ellen in the making of toast when Diddy Howlock rushed in. "He were naked. Stark, staring naked! And ready to go, too!"

Laughter and exclamations ran round the five women in the room, young and old.

"And you just left him like that, Diddy," said Mrs. Gorland, the middle-aged cook who came in daily. "That's a turn up."

Diddy giggled. "I did offer. I'd not mind an earl's bastard. Likely set me up for life, and this one'd be able to, I reckon."

Susan bit back cold, angry words, knowing they'd be far too revealing. With a bit of prompting some of the local people might remember that she and Con had been . . . well, whatever they had been.

Friends. They'd been friends.

People would remember that meeting between Con and Captain Drake in the George and Dragon. No one knew what had been said, but enough guessed. Most thought it had been a youthful love affair, though no one seemed to think they'd gone as far as they had.

Who would think it? A young lady of the manor, even if a bastard, and a young gentleman of Crag Wyvern. Simple people persisted in thinking that the higher orders had less fleshy desires than they, even in the face of evidence to the contrary such as Lady Belle and Mel Clyst. And the old earl taking any youngish woman who was willing to his bed.

People would soon realize that the new earl was Con Somerford, that likable lad who'd hung around the village soaking up any story a body wanted to tell, and who'd spent dunamany hours on the cliffs with Miss Susan. He'd made a good impression, and thus haunted her for years after with the villagers' talk about "that young man of yours, Miss Susan."

It would start again. *Fancy the earl being that young man of yours, Miss Susan.*

How was she to bear it?

All around her, the women chattered and giggled about the naked earl, while she remembered the sight of him in the window earlier. She'd assumed he was wearing drawers, but now she knew he must have been stark naked. Despite logic it made that moment freshly embarrassing.

Or freshly stirring.

"Lovely body on him," Diddy was saying, relishing being the center of attention. "Good hard muscles, and no really bad scars . . ."

Yes, thought Susan. The sleek youthful body had grown and hardened to perfection. Wide shoulders, just enough muscle.

No really bad scars? There were scars?

Of course there were.

"Got a tattoo on his chest, though," Diddy said. "Can't say as I like that on a man."

So it hadn't been a freak shadow of the half-open window.

"A dragon it is. Not like the Chinese ones. I rather like those ones. . . . I know!" Diddy exclaimed. "It's like the one in the Saint George bedroom! Nasty old beast. Could be taken right off the walls there, it could. Coiled all around his . . ." Diddy circled her own large right breast.

Susan smelled burning and turned sharply. Ellen was watching Diddy, slack-mouthed.

"The toast's burning," Susan snapped, giving the girl a slap to the head, which she regretted immediately.

Ellen started to cry as she pulled the charred bread off the fork and grabbed a fresh slice. "I'm sorry, ma'am!"

Oh, Lord. She'd had little sleep last night, what with having to be sure the contraband was well settled down below, and then Con rattling in her mind like a spiked ball. But she shouldn't be taking it out on poor Ellen.

Susan rubbed the girl's cap for a moment. "I'm sorry. But watch the toast, not Diddy's boobies." She turned to the rest of the room. "Enough of this shameful talk. This is a decent house now. There'll be no goings-on, do you hear?"

Everyone hurried back to work, but Diddy said, "He be Earl of Wyvern, b'ain't he? And he thought about my offer. I saw him. So there."

Susan was sure he had. Diddy was plain, but she had a ripe body, a huge, generous curving of breasts and hips. She had plenty of suitors, and the only reason she wasn't married already was that she had an eye to bettering herself.

Diddy's ways weren't responsible for the churning inside Susan, however, or for her surge of bad temper. Nor was tiredness. "Heaven knows why the earl is awake so early," she said, "but we'll have a good breakfast ready for him. Get to work. Whatever he might desire."

Diddy chuckled.

Susan swallowed a retort and retreated to her rooms. There she sat, hugging herself.

It wasn't Diddy.

It wasn't even the thought of Con and Diddy.

It was the dragon.

If Con Somerford had a dragon tattooed on his chest, a dragon like the one in the big picture of George and the dragon in the Saint George rooms, it was all her fault.

✵ 5 ✵

THEY'D TALKED about his name, George, and why he didn't
use it. She'd heard about the other two Georges—Van and
Hawk—and how they'd chosen their names.

All three had been born within weeks of the time the French
were imprisoning their king, and so all three boys had patriotically
been christened George. They'd been born into neighboring families, too, and grown up as close friends, so the name became a
constant confusion.

Eventually they'd sat down to sort it out. They'd all wanted to
be George, not for the king but for the saint who slew the dragon.
To them the dragon represented all the evil in the world, and Saint
George was the perfect hero. They'd discussed drawing lots, but
in the end they'd decided that if they couldn't all be George, none
of them could. Instead they'd take names from their surnames.

George Vandeimen had become Van, George Hawkinville had
become Hawk, but George Somerford had balked at the sissy name
Somer. Instead he'd taken Con from his middle name, Connaught.

She remembered how she'd drunk in the stories of his close
friends. Growing up at Kerslake Manor, she'd had her cousins for
friends, but there were no other suitable young ladies nearby, and
her cousins, though very sweet, were not mates for her adventurous
soul. David was more in tune with her, but he was a brother, and
two years younger.

Con had been the first true friend she had known, the only

friend of instant, perfect connection. In her imagination, his friends were her friends.

The Georges, as Con had called them. Or, sometimes, the triumvirate. Con, Van, and Hawk.

He also had friends in the Company of Rogues, a group of friends at Harrow School. Twelve new boys gathered by a boy called Nicholas Delaney and formed into a band for protection from bullies—and for creative mayhem.

Fourteen good friends in all.

Riches beyond her imagination.

Yet all that happiness was now shadowed by that tattoo.

Con had loved the story of Saint George and the dragon, and all the dragon stories at Crag Wyvern. Though he had no high opinion of the Devonish Somerfords, he was thrilled to share the blood of a possible dragon slayer. He and his brother had been put in the Norse rooms together, but once he'd found the Saint George rooms he'd asked to move.

One day he'd sneaked her into Crag Wyvern and up to his room, to study the picture on the wall. Strangely, there had been no trace of awareness that they were together in his bedroom. That had been on the seventh day, before things changed.

"The George looks like me, don't you think?" he'd said, eager expectation in his eyes.

She looked at the saint, so covered in Roman armor, swirling red cloak, and huge crested helmet that it was hard to see him at all. She knew what friendship demanded, though. "Yes, he does. He has your square chin. And your cheekbones."

"I might be Con," he said, "but in my heart I'm George, defender of the weak and innocent. I'll defend you, Susan, if ever you are threatened."

"I'm not weak and innocent!" she'd protested, with a disgust that made the older Susan smile wryly.

He'd been so flustered, apologizing and protesting at the same time, that they'd fled outdoors again, where everything seemed so much simpler.

She remembered thinking that he might like her to call him George, but it hadn't seemed to fit him. He was Con, steady, fun-loving, beautiful Con. But in the aftermath of lovemaking, she'd said, "My George," and he'd kissed her and said, "Forever."

She could still remember that moment, perfect as a diamond set in gold. Lying in his arms in the warm shade of the cliff, sea-birds calling, waves chuckling around nearby rocks.

It wasn't what they had just done. It was that she'd found her person, the one she would be with all her life, the one from whom she would never want to part.

She'd known they'd have to separate for a while. They were young. People would make them wait. But they were joined for all eternity. And the perfect final detail was that her Saint George, her hero, her friend, would also one day be Earl of Wyvern.

She would be Lady Wyvern, queen of all she knew.

It had never crossed her mind that Con wasn't the older son. He had been as tall as his brother, and both stronger and more vigorous. Fred Somerford had even been painfully shy, and at ease only when talking about boats.

So, all through those magical days as she had fallen in love with Con, she'd fallen in love with a vision of the future.

She wouldn't be Lady Belle's bastard daughter, always being told how kind it was of Sir Nathaniel and Lady Kerslake to treat her and David as part of the family.

She wouldn't be a person who didn't really belong.

She would be Countess of Wyvern.

It would be perfect retribution for all those people who treated her and David as not quite members of local society, who discouraged their children from spending time with them, who watched constantly for misbehavior.

She would be Countess of Wyvern. She would belong without question, and everyone—everyone!—would have to curtsy and smile to her. And she'd take David into respectability too, so he could go anywhere, do anything. Marry an heiress. Become a grand lord himself if he wanted.

No one would be able to look down on them again.

So she had lain there in his arms, sure of complete perfection.

"I don't know when I'll be back," he said, stroking her, looking at her body as if it was a wondrous mystery to him.

She was looking at him the same way. What they'd done had hurt a bit, and she was sure there was more to it, but still, it had been the most magical thing she could ever imagine, and she wanted to do it again.

There was the danger of catching a baby from him, but if it happened it might not be so bad. They'd have to marry immediately then, wouldn't they?

"Don't be long," she said, tracing a pattern in the dusting of sand on his chest.

They'd had enough thought to spread their clothes beneath them, but some sand had still stuck on their skin.

"It might not be for a year. I don't see how I can bear it."

"A year?" She shifted so she could look at him. "You could ask to come back sooner than that."

"With what reason?"

She'd kissed him. "To see me?"

He smiled. "I don't think anyone would be impressed by that. They'll say we're too young."

"Say you want to learn more about your future estate then."

He blinked at her, lashes clumped, dark hair stuck to his temples by sweat. "It's not my future estate. It's Fred's."

She could remember, even now, the sick, aching coldness that had swept through her. "He's younger than you," she'd protested, already knowing it was stupid, that he wouldn't lie about such a thing.

"Perhaps he looks it, but he's thirteen months older. Sorry I'm not the heir?" He said it lightly, teasingly confident of a laughing denial.

But she'd been shivering as if they'd been tossed from August to November. It wasn't just that he wouldn't have Crag Wyvern, that he was a younger son who'd never be a lord. He didn't belong here.

He didn't belong back in Sussex at Somerford Court. He didn't belong *anywhere* any more than she did!

If she married him she'd have to go wherever he went, rootlessly with the army, or moving from parish to parish as a curate's wife, when all she'd ever wanted, above all other things, was to belong.

Here.

She'd given her maidenhead to Con to seal him to her. She'd seduced him. He hadn't been unwilling, but he'd never have done it if she hadn't taken the first steps. She'd done it to claim her place here at last, and instead she'd thrown her fate upon the waters, to be swept wherever the wind blew.

What if she was with child!

Looking back, she couldn't understand that girl. Why hadn't she seen that Con would have been her place, her security, her stability in the world? Perhaps she'd been misled by his gentle nature, his ability to simply enjoy life, and not thought him dependable.

If so, she'd badly misjudged what lay beneath.

She'd been only fifteen, though. What fifteen-year-old made subtle judgments about these things? Few sealed their lives with their folly, however.

No wonder parents protected their young from their very youth.

The light, the confidence, had faded from his face, and she had wanted to kiss him, to say that of course she didn't mind that he wasn't the heir. She could remember that. Remember feeling sliced into two parts, the part that loved Con Somerford, and the part that had gambled all to be Countess of Wyvern.

The lightness had gone entirely, and he said, "Susan?"

She'd wanted him so much, ached for him, the friend of her heart, that she'd only been able to leave harshly. She'd pushed away from him, grabbing her shift to cover her nakedness, to fight off the chill.

"Yes, I'm sorry you're not the older brother. I want to be countess. Nothing less will do."

Perhaps she'd hoped saying it like that would make it make sense. She had tried to add an apology, but eleven years later she still winced at its inadequacy: "I'm sorry."

He had simply sat there, naked, beautiful, the shock of betrayal stamped in every line of his face, so she'd tried once more. "You'll be glad when you think about it. You don't want to be tied to the bastard child of a smuggler and a whore."

It had been a mistake. She'd seen the spark of hope, the beginning of argument, so she'd clutched her clothes to her and fled, but not before shouting, "I don't want to see you again! Never speak to me again!"

And he'd obeyed.

If he'd come after her then, or sought her out in the remaining few days, if he'd argued with her, perhaps she would have seen sense. But being Con, he'd taken her at her word, and she'd not seen him or heard him speak again until last night.

Her heart had been shattered, but in a twisted way that had strengthened her will. Her mother had followed her heart and her desires into a shameful union, causing all Susan's problems. Lady Belle could have married well. She'd been courted by half the county, including the earl himself.

Instead she'd followed her stupid heart to a tavern in a fishing village, and even if Mel Clyst was Captain Drake, that didn't coat her shame with glory in the eyes of most of the world.

Susan would *not* be the prisoner of her desires like her mother. She would not run up to the Crag to sneak into the Saint George rooms to find her own George and beg him to forgive her. She would not send the letters she wrote to him after he left.

Looking back, she was awed by the steely will of that fifteen-year-old, able to crush every instinct in order to pursue a goal of being a grand lady instead of a charity case.

Hand over her mouth, she swallowed tears. She thought she'd forgotten better than this.

The fifteen-year-old had ruthlessly tried to scrub Con from her mind. With age had come wisdom, and then regret, but she had still worked at forgetting. It was done and couldn't be undone, and she'd felt at times that she might bleed to death if she let herself think of it.

She should have known it hadn't worked. For eleven years, every rock and plant and insect had reminded her. Irish Cove was intolerable. She'd never been there since.

But she'd thought she'd buried it all deeper than this.

She'd let two men seduce her solely to drive the memory of Con from her flesh. That hadn't worked either, not even Lord Rivenham, a skilled rake, who'd given her all the pleasure she'd expected, and still failed to dissolve the sweetness of that clumsy time with Con.

Fixed on her goal, she'd even tried to attract the attention of Con's older brother, Fred. After all, she'd given up heaven for Crag Wyvern, so she had to have it or her sacrifice would have been for nothing.

She could look back now and thank God that Fred Somerford had not been looking for a wife. Imagine meeting Con again after all these years as his sister-in-law.

She'd realized eventually that the prize was worthless tinsel, but it had been far too late. She'd dreamed sometimes of finding Con and trying to heal the wounds, but amiable Fred had visited a few times a year and brought news, so she'd known that Con had gone abroad with the army not long after leaving her, and was rarely home.

For some reason, his being out of England had made him even more lost to her. Even so, she'd written letters over the years to Ensign, then Lieutenant, then Captain George Connaught Somerford, letters she'd torn up and burned.

She'd known all about Con's career because Aunt Miriam had encouraged his brother, Fred, to visit the manor as often as he wished. It was partly true kindness, but also because she had two daughters and a niece, and why shouldn't they end up as Countess of Wyvern as well as any other young woman?

She remembered the time, at a family dinner, when Fred had produced a miniature that Con had sent him, done in his new captain's uniform. It had passed from hand to hand. Susan had watched it circling toward her with a mix of unbearable anticipation and terror.

Once in her hands it had stolen her breath. She'd had to pass it on before she'd had nearly enough time to absorb it.

She'd desperately longed to snatch it, hide it, steal it.

He'd been twenty-two when the picture had been done, the square chin stronger, leanness making the high cheekbones more pronounced. Following regulation, his hair had been powdered, seeming to emphasize his dark-lashed silvery eyes. He'd been smiling, however, and she'd genuinely rejoiced that he might be happy, might have forgotten her entirely.

But he had still been at war. Weakly, she'd checked the obituaries and casualty lists, praying never to see his name.

Through too many sleepless nights she'd relived the moment of decision, imagining what might have happened if she'd followed her weak heart instead of her strong will. They'd been only fifteen. No question of marriage unless she'd caught a child which, thank the Lord, she had not.

As a younger son Con would have needed a profession, but perhaps he would have chosen differently for her sake. Been safer. At the least she would have been with him, even following the drum.

It had been a pointless, painful circling that she'd tried to block, but which had often sucked her down, especially if she woke in the gray middle of the night. Over the years, however, it had become almost a fantasy, the people no longer quite real—people she knew rather than a person she had been. That had drawn its fangs.

Until now. Until here, with Con back marked in ways she would never have wanted him marked, but still Con. If she'd not been so willful, if she'd let herself love and be loved, might he still be the gentle, laughing person she'd once known?

He'd seen himself as Saint George, warrior against evil, but at some point he'd had a dragon tattooed on his chest.

She stood, and planning a route that would avoid any possibility of bumping into him, she hurried to the Saint George rooms.

⚹ 6 ⚹

T HE SAINT George rooms were decorated in a vaguely Roman style, with a mock mosaic floor and classical white linen draperies. The picture of George and the dragon was a fresco that took up most of one wall in the bedroom. This wasn't the first time that she'd come to look at it.

Saint George did look a little like Con, but now the saint looked softly unformed in comparison to the hardened warrior. He held his upright lance in an elegantly curved hand that seemed incapable of strength and violence. Con had touched her once last night, to pull her to her feet, and his hand had been hard and strong. The saint's cocked-hip stance seemed more feminine than masculine. There had always been a grace to Con's movements, but they were strong and direct, and now they were devastatingly, completely masculine.

The dragon was not dead. It reared up behind the saint, its head horned like a devil, the fainting virgin sacrifice chained to the rock behind it. Fangs and forked tongue were visible at the slightly open mouth. It was truly an evil dragon, and she wanted to shout to the stupid Saint George to look behind him—

The door opened, and she whirled to look behind.

Con stopped as if frozen, and perhaps a hint of color touched his brown cheeks. "I'm sorry. Are you using these rooms now?"

She knew she was red, and her mouth felt sealed by dryness. She made herself speak. "No. I have the housekeeper's rooms below. I . . . I was—"

"Don't lie." It was said flatly. "There was something special between us, wasn't there?" He came over to look at the picture, but carefully distanced from her. "I was an arrogant young ass to see a resemblance, though."

"No! No, you weren't." It was pointless to think she could soothe his pride after all these years, but she couldn't help it. "The first earl stood as a model for it, you know."

"I suppose that might account for it then." He turned to her, and there was even a hint of humor in him. "Though I'm not sure I want a resemblance to the Demented Devonish Somerfords."

A hint of humor only, like the promise of sun on a heavily overcast day.

She wanted to ask why he was here, but she knew. For the same reason she was—a pilgrimage to the past.

She wanted to ask why he'd had this evil dragon etched into his skin.

But she knew—because of what she'd done to him in the past.

Most of all, she wanted to ask if there was any way to undo the hurt at this late date.

But no. The wounds she had inflicted must have healed and scarred over long since. Scars, like tattoos, could not be rubbed away. There was no bridge back to sweet yesterdays.

And anyway, she realized, she was here to find the mad earl's stash of gold for David and the Horde. It was by rights the Horde's money, and desperately needed, but Con wouldn't see it that way. He'd see only a new, fresh betrayal.

Unless the run had gone smoothly.

It was a glimmer of brightness. If the run had gone as perfectly as she thought, then the Horde wouldn't truly need the money. She wouldn't have to betray Con again. . . .

There'd been too long a silence between them, and she was in danger of saying all the wrong things. To break the moment, she moved to open a nearby door in the wall. "There's been an innovation since you used these rooms."

Seeming calm, he strolled over and looked into the room. "A Roman bath?"

"Yes." She led the way across the short stretch of tiled floor and up the steps so they could look down into the huge mosaic bath. She hadn't thought about the picture, just about getting away from that other one.

Now she was blushing because the picture on the bottom showed a hugely endowed Saint George, identified by his helmet, which was all he wore, about to impale a woman who was presumably the rescued princess.

Rescued? She was still bound to the rock with iron chains and obviously struggling to escape her fate.

"Physically impossible," Con remarked, "or a bizarre form of murder. I'm not sure this bath is possible either. Are the taps functional?"

"Of course." She walked around the wide rim to put the width of it between them. "There's a cistern in the attics with a furnace below it. It takes time to heat the water, but the bath can be filled."

"Ah, I see the drain too. What an interesting anatomical position for it."

A laugh escaped her before she caught it, and their eyes met for a moment across a space both physical and temporal.

He looked away. "Where does it drain to?"

The tiled walls gave the room a slight resonance, and she felt that her pounding heart should be audible too. When he wasn't looking at her, she was drinking in the details of him, of his manly beauty so unlike—so like—the youth.

"Out of a gargoyle's mouth," she said, "and down on anyone who happens to be below." She pointed to a gilded chain. "It's polite to ring that bell first."

He looked around at the mosaic walls, where even the stylized trees were subtly phallic and gave tantalizing glimpses of other lewd activities. "Did my dear departed relative use this facility much?"

"Now and then, I gather."

"Alone?"

"I don't think so. It is rather large for one."

He looked at her, completely the earl. "I wish to move into these rooms, Mrs. Kerslake. I'm very fond of baths. See to it, if you please."

She almost protested. Having him in the Saint George rooms was too close to the past, and she hated to think that he'd changed so much that he liked this lewd display.

But she said, "Of course, my lord."

Whoever he was now, however, she didn't want him sharing this bath. With Diddy, for example. As they left the room she tried to establish some rules. "I run this house in a respectable manner, my lord. I hope you will not use that bath in any lewd way."

"Are you trying to dictate my conduct, Mrs. Kerslake?"

"I believe I have a right to concern myself with the welfare of the servants, my lord."

"Ah, I see. But if I were to bring in ladies—or others—from outside to share my bath, you would have no objection?"

She met his eyes. "You would be exposing the servants to impropriety."

"And they have not been so exposed before?"

"Times have changed."

"Have they?" He let it linger, then added, "And if I do not obey your dictates, Susan, you will do what?"

It was a neatly decisive blow.

The only possible retaliation was her resignation, but she couldn't leave Crag Wyvern just yet.

At her silence, one brow rose. There was a hint of humor, a lot of triumph, but also speculation. She didn't want him thinking about why she needed to stay.

She headed for the door. "I believe your breakfast will be waiting, my lord."

"I believe my breakfast will wait for me. There have to be some privileges of rank. Show me the late earl's rooms."

She wanted so desperately to escape, but she wouldn't simply be running from time spent with Con. She'd be fleeing the dream-memory friend of her heart. Her first clumsily wonderful lover. The youth she'd deliberately hurt. The man he had become.

More urgently, she'd be fleeing the dragon, coiled, patient, and the embodiment of silver-eyed peril. With a horrified glance back at the huge picture she saw that though the color of the saint's eyes was impossible to tell, the dragon's eyes were silver-gray.

"Mrs. Kerslake?" he prompted with a hint of authority.

She gathered her wits. "As you wish, my lord. They are next door so the earl had easy access to the bath."

She had to control her wretched reaction to him. If he felt anything at all for her it was anger. And yet . . . and yet he'd admitted he'd come here for the same reason as she, and that there had been sweetness between them once. . . .

She realized she'd almost walked past the first door to the Wyvern rooms, and stopped to unlock it. The key seemed to fight her about going into the lock, probably because Con was standing close beside her. She could swear she felt the heat of his body. She could certainly detect a faint but recognizable smell.

She'd not thought people had such a powerful individual smell, but even though he'd bathed, there was something, something in the air that carried her straight back to a naked tangle on a hot beach, and a youthful, muscular chest she had nuzzled and kissed again and again.

Stop it!

The key jerked home and she turned it, then thrust the door open, blessing the stale, pungent air that swamped sweeter memories. These smells—herbal, chemical, and the lingering hint of vomit—were all of the old earl. She walked briskly to fling open the window.

"He died here?" Con asked, as if he could smell death. Perhaps a soldier could.

She turned to face him, safer now that the large desk and wide worktable lay between them. "Yes. The room's been cleaned, of course, but otherwise left untouched. Some of these scrolls and books are valuable. Some of the ingredients too."

The walls were covered by mismatched shelves stuffed higgledy-piggledy with texts, jars, bottles, and pots.

"Only to another of his kind." Con strolled over to inspect a shelf of glass bottles. "Was he pursuing alchemy or chemistry?"

"Alchemy, with a touch of sorcery thrown in."

He turned to look at her. "Trying to turn lead into gold?"

"Trying to turn age into youth. He was seeking the secret of eternal life."

"And he died at fifty from drinking his own nostrum. How ironic. We are generally a long-lived family, barring accidents. My father succumbed to influenza, my brother to a careless moment on the water. My grandfather was thrown from his horse at seventy, and had the misfortune to land on his head."

For some reason she was clutching the windowsill behind her as if needing a tether to sanity. "He was afraid of death, and afraid of meeting his ancestor, the first earl."

"Why?"

"He had no heir. He was the one to let the Dragonkiller's line die out."

"He should have married."

She didn't explain the mad earl's ways. She couldn't talk about things like that with Con.

He settled his hips against the desk, long, lean, hard, and still dueling with her. "How do you know so much about him? You only came here after Mrs. Lane left, didn't you?"

She was reluctant to admit the truth, but it was common knowledge. "I was the earl's assistant for three years before that."

"Assistant?" he queried, and she could see he was thinking the worst.

"I copied old documents, did research, and found sources for his ingredients. I was a kind of secretary."

"My, my, you were keen to become countess, weren't you?"

She gripped the sill behind her more tightly. "I was his secretary, and I took the job because I wanted employment."

"The manor threw you out?"

"Of course not. I preferred not to live on charity anymore."

"And this was the only employment available?"

Why was she even trying to explain? But burdened by so many things she couldn't explain away, she would try to avoid guilt over this.

"It was the only employment locally for someone like me. A Miss Kerslake of Kerslake Manor could hardly be hired for menial work, and the offspring of a smuggler and a whore is not desirable for polite occupation. The earl offered me the position, and I took it."

"Did he offer your brother the position of estate manager, too?"

"Yes."

"Why?"

She hadn't considered the question. "I assume my father suggested it."

"And the earl did as Mel Clyst suggested?" A slight smile of disbelief touched his lips.

"They had an agreement." After a moment, she added, "Smuggling, Con."

"Ah." He pushed off from the desk. "You can tell Captain Drake—I assume you know the current Captain Drake—that there will be no agreement."

"Con—"

His sharp, angry look silenced her, but then the moment was broken by an outsider.

"Good Lord, what is this?"

Con's secretary sauntered in like a spring breeze into a stale cavern. Lissome, she thought, with his light, lithe body and soft blond hair. But no angel. Every inch of him denied angel.

Snatched from an entirely different existence, for a moment she couldn't remember his name. He smiled—a speculative, knowing smile. "Racecombe de Vere, ma'am, at your service. My friends call me Race."

Susan dropped a curtsy. "Mr. de Vere."

She realized then that she had never once curtsied to Con.

De Vere's lips twitched and charming humor glinted in his eyes. He was a lady-killer, but he was having no effect on her except a slight irritation—and huge relief that he had interrupted.

"What is this weighty atmosphere I sense?" de Vere asked.

"Equal parts witchcraft and exasperation," Con said. "This was the old earl's lair. He was completely barmy, and killed himself with some brew that was supposed to give him eternal life."

"Does he haunt the house?" de Vere asked, clearly thinking this a treat.

Con looked at Susan, so she said, "Not that anyone has noticed. Surprisingly, Crag Wyvern has no ghosts at all."

"That's because the torture chamber victims are made of wax."

"Torture chamber!" declared de Vere, eyes bright. "Con, you best of good fellows. Let us go there immediately."

"If you want to be stretched on the rack, we can do that later." Con seized the younger man's elbow and marched him to the door. "For the moment, I gather that breakfast is waiting."

At the door, however, he looked back. "After breakfast I want a complete tour, Mrs. Kerslake, and most of your time throughout the day. Also, make sure your brother is available with the estate records."

He didn't wait for a response, which was as well, as she didn't have one except a shiver that made her fold her arms and rub herself. Even when fighting, even when a third person had been present, they'd talked to each other in a ghostly reminiscence of past intimacy. As if they alone were real in an unreal world.

It was the other way around. The world was real and Susan Kerslake and Con Somerford were phantasms, ghosts of two young people from a summer so long ago, two people who no longer existed except in memory.

But ghosts could carry a potent aura. His friend had sensed it, and he was the sort to make trouble.

She had to get away.

How long would it take to hire a new housekeeper and make a dignified exit? Too long. Yet to flee was impossibly weak, and there still was the gold. She'd organized a complete cleaning of Crag

Wyvern over the past few months and found nothing. The old earl's hiding place must be obscure.

She left the room, locking it carefully, and went to her room to write a message to David. When he came up to see Con he could confirm that the run had been smooth. Then she would find a new housekeeper and make her escape, dignified or not.

Of course, where to go and what to do was another question entirely. Perhaps she should set off after her errant parents and head for the Antipodes!

As they went down a circular staircase, Race said, "I gather the lovely lady is out of bounds."

Con hoped he hadn't twitched. "Not particularly. As I said last night, you are free to woo her if it's honorable wooing you have in mind."

"Unlikely, but I might attempt an honorable flirtation if I'm not likely to feel your fist over it. She is the only good-looking woman in the place. The maid who brought my water was only one step more substantial than the skeleton in the corridor. This is a decidedly strange house."

"I hadn't noticed," Con said dryly, and crossed the courtyard to the breakfast room. He paused to look at the fountain statue. The dragon, as overendowed as Saint George, was about to have its way with the clearly unwilling, naked sacrifice. Around the rim of the basin was carved *The Dragon and His Bride*.

"I've never seen a dragon doing that with the traditional maiden before," Race remarked. "Throws a whole new light on the story, doesn't it?"

"I always thought Saint George's lance was pretty suggestive, myself."

"Especially the way pictures show him fondling it."

Con laughed as he led the way through the open glass-paneled doors into the breakfast room. The furniture was the usual dark oak, but white walls lightened it, and the open doors to the garden were pleasant.

And he was laughing. He was suddenly grateful to Race for attaching himself to him and bringing laughter here.

"Remind me to show you the bath in my new rooms," Con said as he sat down.

"The Chinese dragons too much for you?"

"The Saint George rooms have a very large, very interesting bath."

"Ah. You and your baths. So what's so special about this one?"

Con described it, and Race shook his head. "I've often wondered how those poor maidens felt about the price of rescue. I can think of a lot of heroes I'd not want to have to be grateful to. And what if the lady liked the dragon, and didn't want to be rescued by a boring saint?"

The thin maid bustled in with a coffeepot in one hand and a chocolate pot in the other. "The rest won't be long now, milord," she gasped, and rushed out.

"Why would the lady choose the dragon?" Con poured himself coffee. "A hoard of jewels wouldn't make up for being married to a monster."

"Some women lust after monsters."

"Then they deserve the monsters they get."

Race's eyes glinted with humor. "And those who choose saints deserve that fate, too?"

"Cynic."

"I ask you, would you like to be married to a saint?"

For some reason, the image of Lady Anne Peckworth rose in Con's mind. *Saint* was too strong a word, but she was gentle, kind, good, and devoted to practical charities to do with the education of children and the care of the old.

She was the woman he was probably going to marry. He'd certainly paid her enough attention in the past two months to give her reason to hope. . . .

Two maids came in this time, blessedly interrupting his thoughts.

They unloaded laden trays onto the table. Neither maid was the one who'd come upon him naked. One was the skeleton, poor thing; the other was the older one from last night.

"Anything else, my lord?" the older one asked.

Con looked at the enormous amount of food on the table. "No, thank you. I think we can make do with this."

The maids left and Con and Race shared a grin. "We could feed the regiment on this lot," Race remarked, helping himself to a number of eggs and half the plate of ham.

Con speared a slice of beef on his fork and put it on his plate. "Trying to make a good impression, I suppose."

"They're succeeding." Race spread butter lavishly on a roll. "So, who should a wise woman marry?"

"A good and boring man. Why are we stuck on the subject of women?"

"Something to do with the angelic Susan, I assume."

Con looked at him sharply. "Why?"

"My dear fellow, tell me to button it if you want, but don't pretend there's nothing."

Con evaded the question. "She's the least angelic woman imaginable. She was out with the smugglers last night."

"How splendid," Race said, mopping up egg yolk with his bread. "As for angel, have you not realized she has the look of one of those Renaissance angels? Too beautiful to be a man. Too strongly featured to be a beautiful woman. Perfect, however, for angels, which are neither male nor female, but pure spirit."

"I assure you, Susan Kerslake is entirely female and flesh."

Con regretted it immediately, and wondered if he was going to have to kill Race to stop him from talking.

But after a moment Race said, "So, what orders for the day?"

Con grasped the change of subject with relief. "I plan a physical inspection of the place. Your mission is the old earl's papers. The sooner I'm sure everything is in order here, the sooner I can leave, but it would be pleasant to pinpoint the leakage of funds as well."

"What about the smugglers?"

"I'm curious about the earldom's relationship with them, but otherwise we ignore them." He saw Race's mild surprise. "Race, smuggling is as much part of life here as the sea. If I put a stop to it people would starve. If I shipped every smuggler off to Australia, the coast would be empty. If there's murder, extortion, that sort of thing going on, I might have to act. Otherwise we might as well try to rid the world of ants."

"Right," Race said, but looked surprised. Of course he was from Derbyshire, far from any coast. Con had grown up in Sussex. Not on the coast, to be sure, but close enough to understand smuggling ways.

"Start in the office, which is next to the library. The estate manager should turn up soon to fill in the details. I want a complete report of matters here over the past year. Make sure the accounts are sound."

Race groaned, but Con said, "You can't wait. Admit it."

"You steal my little pleasures. I enjoy appearing to suffer."

"Then I'll make you spend your days squiring ladies around the shops, and your nights gaming."

Race laughed. "Tortures of the damned. Dashed peculiar, though. If I'd suspected I had such a taste for paperwork, I'd have taken a nice safe job in London instead of marching around in mud and dust for years."

"Heaven help London." Con watched Race absorb another plateful of food, wondering where he put it. "How long am I likely to benefit from your peculiar tastes?"

"Until you bore me."

"And I haven't done that yet? I'm a pretty boring man."

Race laughed, grabbing his serviette to cover his mouth. "Lord, don't say things like that. You'll kill me!"

Con leaned back in his chair. "I stick you in a quiet part of Sussex overhauling the antiquated administrative system of a minor estate, then drag you to this prisonlike place."

Race took a clear breath. "Torture chamber, remember. And all those lovely papers."

Con studied the curved handle of his coffee cup for a moment.

"You aren't by any chance playing the angel yourself, are you?" He looked up. "Guardian angel?"

Race looked back at him with perfect innocence. "Guarding you against what?"

Con almost answered, but then shook his head. "Clever, but no. I am not going to list possible answers."

Race dropped his serviette on the table, seeming to drop his playful manner with it. "You were an officer I admired, Con, and you are a man I admire. But you were a different officer and a different man in the Peninsula than you are now. If I can help you find that man, I will."

Con wasn't quite sure what to do with this. "And here I thought I was giving you needful employment."

"Employment is always nice."

"There you go again. . . ." But he might at least try to match honesty with honesty. "I'm not sure whether the Captain Somerford in the Peninsula was a better man, but whatever he was, he doesn't exist anymore. If you start chipping at this dry shell you may find only dust."

"Or a butterfly."

Con burst out laughing. "A *butterfly!*"

Race smiled. "There, see. I've made you laugh."

"I laugh."

"There's laughter and laughter. Remember the pigs?"

Con couldn't help but smile. "Piglets, Race. Piglets. What were there? Twelve? All tucked into the packs and jackets of men on the march. The company looked like a set of weavilly biscuits." He straightened his face and frowned at his secretary. "If your aim is to turn me into the sort of man who's always telling knee-slapping stories about army life, it's a forlorn hope."

"Talking of forlorn hopes," Race said. "Remember Santa Magdalena?"

Con stood, pushing his chair back roughly. "Enough. Sometimes war knocks the heart out of a man. But it seems possible to live without a heart."

Race stayed where he was. "Lord Darius is dead, Con."

Dear God, in what maudlin moment had he given Race even a sniff of Dare?

"Isn't that the problem?" Con said. "He's dead. I feel grief over it. Grief and laughter do not go well together."

"Sometimes they do. Is it grief, though? Or guilt?"

"I have nothing to feel guilty about. Dare played his part at Waterloo, and like so many others, he died."

"Quite."

"For God's sake. What the devil are you up to? Why are you acting as clumsy surgeon?"

Race frowned slightly. "I have no idea. I think it's this house. It worries me."

"It damn well worries me too. That's why I'm going to do my conscientious duty by it, then put it into good hands and ride back to the sanity of Sussex. Can I possibly persuade you to do your part?"

Race grimaced, but without a sign of repentance, and rose. "Persuasion is hardly necessary."

Wanting to argue with Race, or throttle him, or both, Con led him to the estate office, where most of the administrative papers should be housed.

Guilt.

Dare had been an old friend, one of the Company of Rogues, and a complete civilian. Con felt that he should have found a way to stop Dare from volunteering. When Dare's ducal connections had won him a role as a courier, he should have prepared him better. He should at least have kept an eye on him, though the devil alone knew how when Con was fixed in his regimental position and Dare was hurtling around all over.

He should definitely, however, have done the final duty of a friend and found Dare's body for decent burial.

In the cool part of his mind Con knew none of it was his fault, but most of his mind was not cool. Dare had come to represent all the death and suffering that had been Waterloo, and it hung over everything still.

He flung the door open. The estate office was a relatively normal room for Crag Wyvern, walled with orderly shelves and drawers, with only a solid oaken desk in the middle. The carvings on the desk didn't bear close inspection—though Race, of course, sank to his haunches to inspect them, and laughed—and the ceiling was painted with a vision of hell, complete with imaginative tortures of the damned.

Race looked up at it. "Clearly whoever ordered that did not enjoy paperwork. But it does remind me that you haven't shown me the torture chamber yet."

"I'm holding the treat back as a reward for work well done."

"Very well, what is my work?"

Con looked around the room, which would be a torture chamber to him. "Go through everything. Make sense of what's happened here. Find any shady goings-on or anomalies."

To him it sounded like ordering a troop to wade through a torrent, crawl through a swamp, and take a hill crowned with army guns, but Race smiled and said, "Right!"

By the time Con left, Race had already shed his jacket and begun to go through the desk drawers.

Con shook his head and returned to the breakfast room.

Damn Race. Perhaps he and Diego huddled in the evenings to share nursemaid reports!

So Waterloo had left him bleak. It hardly seemed an irrational reaction to monstrous slaughter including the deaths of many friends and colleagues.

And now he had scheduled an interview with Susan.

He felt as if he'd been ordered to wade through a torrent, crawl through a swamp, and take a hill crowned with army guns. . . .

He rang the bell.

When the skeleton maid responded—he found out that her name was Ada Splint, which seemed somewhat unfortunate—he asked her to tell Mrs. Kerslake that he was ready.

As he waited, he poured himself more of the excellent tea, sure that it had carried no tax, and planned the best line of attack.

First, he would treat her as housekeeper. That was the role she'd chosen for herself. She'd doubtless intended to be gone before he made his announced arrival, but now that she was caught she could damn well live with it.

Next, he must find out what she was up to.

Unfortunately she wasn't intending to seduce her way into the countess's bed. Being housekeeper was no route to that, especially with the clothes she was wearing. Or at least, she would think that way. In truth, he suspected that she could seduce him in rags. . . .

Ah, no. He forbade his mind to go in that direction.

Third, he would never, ever, call her Susan.

He drank some of the cooling tea and made himself consider why she was playing housekeeper.

Something to do with smuggling, he was sure. The Crag's horses were used by the Dragon's Horde, of course, and doubtless somewhere below were caves or chambers used for storage. Was that it? Was she simply guarding the Dragon's Horde's territory?

Susan came in from the corridor then, encased in her gray and white, blankly unreadable.

Hiding things.

Her chin went up slightly as she curtsied, and her eyes met his in a very unservile way.

✻ 7 ✻

Con saw immediately that Race was right. Her straight nose, square chin, and perfectly bowed lips did have that classical angelic look to them, especially with those clear eyes with smooth, arching brows. If Race had seen her at fifteen with her golden brown hair waving loose around her, he'd have thought he was seeing a heavenly vision. . . .

"My lord?"

Dammit. Keep this businesslike. He indicated the seat to his right. "Please sit down, Mrs. Kerslake. We have a great deal to discuss."

She obeyed stiffly, clearly wary.

"Now, Mrs. Kerslake, explain to me how things have been managed here since the late earl's death."

He saw the slight relaxation. She'd been braced for something else. What?

"The sixth earl died suddenly, my lord, as you know—"

"Was there any inquiry about it?"

She stared at him, and her surprise seemed genuine. "Do you think it suspicious? He was constantly trying new ingredients."

"Someone could have added a noxious herb if they had wished to."

"But who? He entertained few guests, and never took them to his sanctum, as he called it. And," she added with a direct look, "no one gained by his death but you, my lord."

"Gain? This place, and a property peopled entirely by smugglers?"

"And the title."

"I had a title. Many of us do not set such store on high rank."

It was a jab and he instantly regretted it. Not because she flinched, but because it showed he remembered. Perhaps cared.

If it stung, she hid it well. "Ah yes, Viscount Amleigh, was it not, my lord?"

"And I assure you I was content with it. As for other suspects, people sometimes have concealed desires and angers."

Her brows twitched, but it could be puzzlement as much as guilt. "His valet was with him when he prepared the potion, and when he drank it, and Fordham had been with him for thirty years. It is possible that some ingredient was not what it seemed, but the suppliers had no reason for mischief. They have lost an excellent and generous customer."

She sounded completely honest about this. He didn't even know why he'd taken that tack. He had enough problems without trying to create a murder out of nothing. "Very well. What happened after the death, Mrs. Kerslake? You had been acting as his assistant?"

She sat with a stillness that seemed all wrong for her—hands loosely linked in her dark lap, everything muted by white and gray until she seemed colorless. He had to concentrate to see that yes, her lips were slightly pink, her eyes hazel, her few visible curls that rich, complex brown. He'd always remembered her as vibrant, and despite the dark last night and dark clothes, she'd seemed so then.

Oh, yes. Susan was up to something.

"Yes, my lord."

Yes, what, dammit?

His mind was full of other things, but he pulled it back into order. Her employment here. That was what they'd been discussing.

"And you became housekeeper after the earl's death?"

"Yes, my lord."

"Why?"

She didn't flinch. "The earl left Mrs. Lane an annuity in his will, and she wished to retire. She was over seventy, my lord, and suffered in her joints, but she would not go until there was a re-placement to care for Crag Wyvern. So I took the position on a temporary basis. It is expected that you will hire a housekeeper to your taste now."

"Did your aunt and uncle not object to your taking such employment?"

Her brows rose slightly. "I am past my girlhood, my lord. Since I haven't married, I need occupation. I also need an income. My aunt and uncle are generous, but I cannot live forever on their charity."

"Ah, yes, I remember that you were always ambitious."

Another unworthy jab, and when she paled he almost apologized. But at the same time, the dark part of him wanted to see her flinch.

"Did your father not provide for you?"

She raised her eyes, but only as far as the silver teapot. He noted the delicate skin of her eyelids, the faint veins visible there, the dark line of her lashes. Her tense jaw. Did she want to let out honest, angry words?

He wished she would. He felt long overdue for a raging fight with Susan Kerslake.

"He purchased some property for me, my lord. It provides a small income."

"Yet you felt obliged to work here?"

"I need occupation, my lord."

"You should have married."

"I have not received an offer that tempted me, my lord."

"Held out for the Earl of Wyvern, did you?"

Look at me, Susan. I want to feed off every expression in your eyes.

As if he'd spoken, she did raise her eyes then, to fire a pointed, rather impatient look at him.

Ah, of course. Focusing on his own turmoil, he'd ignored the larger picture. Bringing an outsider here would be very inconvenient for the smugglers. Putting someone local in charge, someone in sympathy with the Dragon's Horde, had been the sensible action.

Why Susan, though? He couldn't believe that the area lacked women able to give basic care to a house, even a grand one like Crag Wyvern.

Perhaps, he thought, controlling every reaction, the question was, Who was the new Captain Drake? Susan had been out with the smugglers last night, but being the daughter of the old Captain Drake wouldn't entitle her to be there.

Being the lover of the new one might.

Hardly surprising if she'd followed in her mother's footsteps and taken up with the smuggling master. Hardly surprising if she was playing housekeeper for his sake.

It was the most reasonable explanation he'd come up with thus far, and without knowing the man he wanted him dead. Or at least captured and transported to join Melchisedeck Clyst in Botany Bay. He'd see to it.

No, dammit, he would not. He would not become the sort of man to harm weaker rivals over a woman.

He took a moment to clear his head, then asked, "Are you willing to stay on until I make decisions about Crag Wyvern, Mrs. Kerslake?"

He thought she would refuse, but then she said, "For a little while, my lord. I thought to begin the search for a replacement."

"Very well, but there is no need to seek a highly qualified woman. I do not intend to live here. I have a home elsewhere, and a family well suited there."

"A family?" The words were followed by a flush of color, and a quick, mortified lowering of her startled eyes.

He could have crowed with triumph. That had stung her.

By God, *did* she have hopes of entrancing him after all? He'd like to see her try.

Oh, yes, he'd very much like to see her try.

He'd also love to claim a wife and children and make her wounds bleed. If he'd a hope of maintaining the lie he might have done it, but it wouldn't stick.

"My mother and two sisters," he said. "They would not like to move here." But then he realized he had one blade that might cut deeply. "Also, I am to marry. Lady Anne would not be comfortable here."

You have a rival, Susan.

A serious rival.

What are you going to do about that?

He had met Lady Anne only a few times in London, then spent four days at her father's home, Lea Park. Nothing was settled, but he was thinking of making an offer of marriage. It wasn't an outright lie, and Lady Anne was too good a weapon to leave in the scabbard.

Susan was guarded now, however, and little showed, though her widened eyes gave him a bit of satisfaction.

"It is not good for a house to stand empty, my lord."

"I hardly think Crag Wyvern will appeal to many tenants."

"Some people have unusual tastes, my lord," she said with a slight, cool smile. "The earl had guests who liked Crag Wyvern very much indeed."

The smile was an act of pure bravery that made him want to salute her.

Damnation, Susan. Why?

"Then please supply Mr. de Vere with their names, ma'am. They may have first refusal. I know that leaving the chief house empty is always an economic hardship to an area."

Her brows rose, and her lips tightened, but it was a suppressed smile rather than annoyance, and it danced in her eyes.

"You're thinking of smuggling," he said. "Yes, at the moment the area is prospering from the Freetrade, but the end of the war is bringing hard times everywhere. On top of that, the army and navy have men to spare to patrol the coasts. That, I assume, is how your father was caught."

Her smile fled. "Yes, though if the earl had raised a finger to help him, he'd not have been transported."

"Remarkable that the mad earl for once did the right thing. The law is the law, and must be upheld."

There, that was a clear enough message for her.

"If there's any sanity in Parliament," he went on, "duties will be reduced and smuggling will cease to be profitable enough to justify the risks. The change won't come today or tomorrow, but it's on the horizon, Susan. People hereabouts need to remember that they once lived by farming, and by fishing for something other than barrels and bales."

"We know," she said softly.

"We?"

"The people hereabouts."

That was not what she'd meant. She'd meant herself and the new Captain Drake, damn his black soul.

And somewhere in that he'd called her by her name, which he'd resolved not to do.

Con stood abruptly. "The tour of the house, Mrs. Kerslake."

She rose with controlled grace and led the way back into the faux-stone corridor, heading toward the kitchen area first.

There weren't many surprises. He'd roamed this house as a youth and discovered most of its nooks and crannies. One startling new feature was a kind of drawing room off the great hall, plastered and painted in the modern style, furnished with spindle-legged chairs and tables.

"I persuaded the earl to have one room where conventional guests might feel more at ease," Susan said, standing composedly beside him, smelling faintly of lavender soap. Not the right perfume for her at all. She should smell of wildflowers—and sweat, and sand.

"Did he have any conventional guests?"

"Occasionally, my lord. People will drop by."

"How alarming. Perhaps that's why he constructed a torture chamber. I've known drop-by guests I'd like to hang in chains."

He intended it to be a joke but had forgotten whom he was with. When her eyes flickered to his, alight with startled laughter, he instinctively stepped away.

"Now I suppose we must tackle the upper floors," he said. "Including a more thorough check of the late earl's chambers."

Her face was carefully blank as she turned to lead the way. "They are not particularly alarming, my lord, but in some disorder. . . ." From the back he saw her slight shrug, which drew his attention to her square shoulders and then to her straight back.

Which he could remember naked . . .

Breathe, dammit, breathe. And listen. She'd said something about disorder.

"I remember he didn't like to leave Crag Wyvern," he said as she led the way up the wide central stairs. Her long back seemed to point down, down to the full curve of her bottom, which was bewitchingly at eye level. He sped up to climb the stairs alongside her, housekeeper or not.

He ached for her now as if she were a fire on a freezing night in the sierra. But fire burned. Fire destroyed. Even a safe fire, built within stones, could harm. He'd seen frozen men ruin their hands and feet by trying to warm them too close to a hot fire.

"He never left here," she was saying. "Certainly not as long as I've been aware of his movements."

"Why not?"

"He suffered from a fear of the outside."

"What did he fear out there?"

For Con, the danger was all within.

Could even fear enable him to resist the flaming power of Susan, especially if she was to stop, turn, approach, press, kiss, begin to shed her clothing . . . ?

She stopped, turned. . . .

"He had nothing real to fear as far as I could tell. He simply feared being outside these walls. He was insane, Con. It was mostly in subtle ways, but he was insane."

As insane as he was to imagine that Susan planned seduction! He gestured her to lead on and soon they reached the earl's rooms. She unlocked a different door this time and they entered the bedroom, though it did not seem a precise term for the room he saw.

The bed was there, huge, hung with faded red hangings that were actually moth-eaten to holes in places. It sat in a jumble of other furniture, however, as if the earl had tried to make this one room into a house.

The red window curtains were drawn against the courtyard light, but the holes let in some light. As his eyes adjusted, he saw a large dining table with just one chair, an armchair, a sofa, a break-front desk, and bookcases everywhere.

There were more bookcases than would fit around the walls, so many were the freestanding, rotating sort. All were full, with surplus books staggering on top. Con hesitated to try to move through the room, and for other reasons as well. The smell of musty books and vaguely noxious things hung heavily in the gloomy air.

Every surface was scattered with objects from riding crops to strange glass vials to stuffed animals. Con saw two human skulls, and not the neat, clean skulls found in anatomists' collections. There were other bones, too, which he hoped were from animals. Some were small enough to even be leftovers from the earl's dinners.

Presumably the crazy earl hadn't eaten the body of the croco-dile, however, leaving only the glassy-eyed head, or the rest of what-ever had owned the black and leathery claw hanging from the cobwebbed lamp near the desk. The upper rail of the bed boasted a fringe of other dark and shriveled things.

Curiosity made him work his way through the room to have a closer look.

"Dried phalluses," she said. "From as many species as he could obtain them. His most prized collection."

Con stopped, then pushed his way to the window to drag open the heavy curtains. The right one tore in his hand, spewing dust and other things over him so that he coughed, and had to brush off his face.

Through sunlight swarmed with motes he faced her. "Did you really think of joining him in that bed?"

She stared at him like a marble statue, and for a moment he thought she'd say a cold yes. But then she said, "No. I never came here before becoming housekeeper."

It was damnably ambiguous. "Then why spend so many of your years here?"

"I told you. I needed employment, and it wasn't easy to find. What's more, this was interesting employment. The earl was mad, but his madness was fascinating at times. After all," she added with a wry twist of her lips, "how many women in England have such an extensive knowledge of phalluses?"

It almost broke a laugh from him, and he looked away, at one of the two adjoining doors, the one that didn't lead into the sanctum. "What's through there?"

"His dressing room. Theoretically."

Susan worked her way carefully through the clutter to open that door, feeling as if she were constantly working her way through chaotic and often rotten obstacles to try to reach some sort of understanding with Con.

She could not recapture the past, but did they have to clash like enemies? Wasn't there at least neutral ground?

She stepped into the dressing room and stood aside for him. This room was blessedly clear of furniture other than two large armoires and the tin bathtub hung with draft-excluding curtains. The window curtains were open here, so the light was good.

She watched his reaction.

He stopped, staring at the figure hanging from the ceiling. But then he stepped forward and poked a finger into one of the flock-spilling gashes in the dummy.

A smile fought to show on her lips. Against logic she was deeply proud of the cool nerves formed in him by war. Against logic, a deep ache near her heart told her love still lingered in her. Love like a smoldering fire, threatening to burst into flame again.

Despite a growing longing to stay, she had to escape this place before she did something she would regret even more than she regretted the past.

He turned to a frame on the wall holding a number of swords and touched the blade of one with a careful finger. "Not ornaments," he remarked.

"He told me he'd been a skilled fencer in his youth, but along with his fear of the outdoors, he feared anyone near him with a weapon. So he fenced with that." She indicated the swaying figure that was suspended so that its feet almost touched the floor.

"Hanged by the neck?" Con asked.

She just shrugged.

"What a way to spend a life. There's that Roman bath, however. How does that fit in?"

"He developed an obsession about physical cleanliness, and would spend hours in the tub. Then he had the idea of the larger one. He decided physical cleanliness was the key to a long life and good health, and also to fertility."

"Zeus, that's enough to give a bachelor a distaste for bathing."

Their eyes met for a startled moment. She knew he too was thinking of the risk they'd so thoughtlessly taken eleven years ago.

8

I WAS YOUNG and foolish," he said, "and never gave the matter a thought. I hope . . ."

She wished she weren't blushing. "Of course not. There would have been hell to pay."

It was a delicate subject, but the wash of heat running through her skin was not only from that. Finally they were really talking about the past.

"That's what I supposed." He looked at her a moment longer and she held her breath, hoping for something that might weave a thread of connection, but then he looked around again. "Why haven't these rooms been put into better order, Mrs. Kerslake?"

She suppressed a sigh and regrouped. "Anything likely to turn to slime has been thrown away, my lord. And of course they were inventoried. But apart from that, the earl stated in his will that everything was to be left for your disposal."

"I hadn't realized quite what that meant. Very well, dispose of that figure for a start." He strode to the armoires and threw open the doors to reveal a collection of long robes. The drawers, she knew, contained a few suits of clothing, none younger than ten years.

"And get rid of this lot," he said. "Give them to the vicar for the poor if they're any use." He walked back into the bedroom. "Have the extra furniture moved out of here. Is there still empty space in the floor above?"

"Yes, my lord."

"Then put it up there." He looked at the bed. "Get rid of that. Burn that stuff hanging around it. And where the devil did he get those skulls from?"

"I don't know, my lord."

"I'll talk to the vicar about decent interment. And about whether any graves have been disturbed around here. All these books can go to the library, though de Vere had better check to see whether there's anything extraordinary about them." But then he frowned. "He has enough to do. Is there someone else in the area who could organize and evaluate those texts?"

"The curate is a scholar and would welcome the extra income," she said, enjoying seeing Con take command and issue crisp orders.

She might have enjoyed seeing him in battle except that it would have killed her, moment by moment, to watch him in danger. Bad enough to have known he was at war, to pick up each newspaper fearing to see his name.

She hadn't been able to help following Con's career through Fred Somerford. He'd entered the infantry. He'd made lieutenant, then captain, and once been mentioned in dispatches. He'd been at Talavera and wounded at the taking of San Sebastian—

Wounded!

—but not seriously.

He'd changed regiments three times to see more action.

Trying to pretend only polite interest, Susan had wanted to scream, "Why? Why not stay safe, you stupid creature?"

Her Con, her laughing gentle Con, had no place in fields of cannon fire and slaughter.

Yet it had made him the man she saw today. . . .

He was opening and closing drawers in the desk, glancing at the contents. "The curate had better go through everything," he said. "In fact, perhaps you shouldn't get rid of the bed. Just the hangings and mattress. There's a dearth of money in the coffers, so I can't afford the grand gesture of throwing away solid furniture."

Susan worked at keeping a bland expression but was jabbed

by guilt. She remembered Con saying years ago that his branch of the family was the poor one. It had sprung from the first earl's younger son, and what modest wealth the Sussex Somerfords had accumulated had been wiped out by royalist sympathies during the Civil War. Since then they'd lived comfortably enough, but more as titled gentlemen farmers than as members of the aristocracy.

Times were hard for farmers now, however, even gentlemen farmers, and the old earl had run the earldom's coffers almost dry with his crazy pursuits. And she must try to take what little coin might be left. . . .

One idea stirred. "What of the contents of his sanctum, my lord? The . . . specimens and ingredients. I believe some of them are valuable. Certainly the earl paid a great deal for them."

He looked at her. "So I shouldn't consign them to the fire? Hell. Is there an expert nearby who might be willing to organize the sale of them?"

"The late earl dealt with a Mr. Traynor in Exeter. A dealer in antiquarian curiosities."

"Is that what they call them? Well, waste not, want not. Give the details to de Vere and he'll summon Traynor. And the various peculiar objects in this room might as well be put in the sanctum for his assessment. Perhaps crocodile heads have mystic powers. We wouldn't want to deprive the world of such valuable artifacts, would we?"

A smile was fighting at her lips as she glanced at the withered objects hanging around the bed. "And those?"

"By all means."

But then he worked his way over to a sideboard and gingerly extracted something from under a pile of old magazines. It was a pistol. He carefully checked it, then tipped something out. The powder in the firing pan, she assumed.

He turned to her. "He feared invaders?"

"I don't know, but he liked to keep in practice."

"What did he practice shooting on if he never went out?"

"The birds in the courtyard. He was quite good."

He turned to look out at the courtyard. No birds were flying now, but the busy chirping and twittering was audible. "Not so safe after all," he murmured, and she wondered what he meant.

He put down the pistol and headed so quickly for the door that he bumped into a set of rotating shelves, sending it spinning and books tumbling.

"Hell!" He stopped to rub his thigh.

She hurried over to pick up the books, but he said, "Leave them," and continued out into the gloomy corridor.

She followed, wondering what was suddenly so wrong.

"How many keys are there?" he demanded.

"Just two. Mine and the earl's, which should have been sent to you."

"A large bunch of keys, yes. I thought they were symbolic." He pulled the door shut. "Lock it. We'll let this Traynor loose on all of it before touching anything."

As she turned the key in the lock, he spoke again, however. "Are there any more firearms in there, do you think?"

"I believe he had a pair."

She saw him brace to return to the room, and then give up the idea. "Before Traynor arrives, I'll have Pearce check the room for danger. No need to accompany him, Mrs. Kerslake. You can trust him with the key."

They were back to formality, when for a moment back there it had slipped. "Very well, my lord."

Then he said, "You'd have married him to become Lady Wyvern?"

"No."

"It never crossed your mind?"

Ah.

"I was a girl, Con." All she seemed to have to offer him was honesty, tarnished though it was. "Yes, I thought of it, but I'd never met him. I'd hardly seen him. He was as mythological to me as a dragon. I sought the position as his assistant with the idea in the back of my mind. But then I learned that he wouldn't marry anyone until he was sure they were carrying his child, and I could not do that. Which made me see that I could not be intimate with the mad earl before or after marriage. And that was before I saw that bed."

"He demanded a trial marriage? Did he think to get a local lady to marry him that way?"

"The local *un*-ladies were willing enough."

"He would have married *any* woman carrying his child?"

"Apparently."

"And no one fooled him?"

"He was mad, Con, not stupid. Any woman had to come here during her courses—and he checked to be sure it was real—and then stay here until she bled again. As you know, there are no male servants other than his valet, who was fanatically devoted."

"The old goat."

"They came willingly enough, and he gave them twenty guineas when they left. A handsome amount for simple folk. In fact," she added with a distinct flare of mischief, "some may come up here hoping you'll be interested too."

"Hell's hounds! I'll pay them twenty guineas to go away."

"Don't let word of that out in public."

She thought he might laugh, but then he shook his head. "We should progress to the dungeon, I suppose, and get this over with, but I promised de Vere the treat."

Con set off down the corridor, hoping it looked like a steady, well-ordered retreat, not the panicked flight it was. He believed her. She'd not seriously contemplated joining the mad earl in that bed, and yet the image haunted him.

She'd thought of marrying the old earl.

She was behind him. He sensed her even though she made no sound in her soft slippers—like a memory, or the ghost of a memory.

She'd only thought of it.

He'd thought of doing a good many things he was blessed not to have done. Suicide once, even. Only the thought of it.

He'd contemplated desertion once too. In the early days before he became hardened to men and animals in agony, to causing men and animals to be in agony. For a few days it had seemed the only sane choice, and he'd planned how to go about it.

But then they'd come suddenly under attack and he'd fought to survive and to help his comrades survive. Somewhere in the process he'd committed himself to the fight against Napoleon and been able to carry on.

He'd almost raped a woman once.

He'd been with a group of officers drinking in a taverna in a Spanish village. It had been not long after battle, though he was damned if he could remember which one or anything else about the place. Blood had been running hot still, and they all wanted a woman.

Some of the women were willing, but a few were not, and their protests and attempts to escape had seemed amusing. Exciting, even.

He could look back at it now as if from the outside and wonder how he could have behaved like that, but he also remembered feeling a godlike ecstasy. That the women were his warrior's due.

Pressing the struggling, sobbing woman down on a table with the cheers of the men and the wild Spanish music still playing . . .

His cock had been throbbing, jumping with eagerness and he'd had his flap half undone. Other hands had been helping hold her down.

But something in his mind had clicked. Some shard of sanity had shot icy reality through him.

He'd grabbed her up off the table and pushed out of the room saying something about doing this properly. Some had tried to stop him, but he'd fought free into the hot Spanish air and a touch of sanity, the woman still writhing and sobbing in his grasp.

He'd kept her in his tent all night and sent her off at dawn with some coins. Pausing before leaving, she'd asked, "Do you wish me to say that you can do it, Capitan?"

She'd thought the rescue was to cover up impotence. He'd

managed to hold back wild laughter, and simply said, "Say whatever is easiest for you, señora."

He heard days later that she'd spread tales of heroic virility. He supposed she'd meant well, but it had made life damned difficult at times. He'd never spent a whole night with a woman since in case she expected a heroic performance.

So he could understand that sometimes people did things in a kind of temporary madness, or thought of them. And that consequences, even of well-intentioned acts, were unpredictable.

And that people were often not what they seemed.

As they approached the office door he turned to her. "What do you think of Mr. de Vere as secretary?"

Her brows rose. "It is not for me to make such judgments, my lord."

"Drop the servant act, Susan. Do you think he'll be snoozing, or sitting with his feet up enjoying a book of questionable pictures?"

"I did, but now I assume not."

He opened the door to reveal Race, as expected, at the desk surrounded by stacks of paper and an aura of intense activity. He looked up impatiently and Con could almost see the words *Go away* coming out of his mouth, as in a satirical cartoon.

After a moment, however, he put his pen in the standish and stood.

"The records are in fairly good shape, my lord," he said, even giving Con the tribute of his title in front of Susan. "But you know, there's a great deal of money unaccounted for."

Ah-ha! Con turned to Susan. "Any idea where it might have gone, Mrs. Kerslake?"

"No," said Race. "I mean there's a lot of money that's appeared on the books out of nowhere."

Con turned back to him with a look. "Smuggling."

Race pushed hair off his forehead. "Oh, I suppose so. As I'm from Derbyshire, it doesn't come first to mind." He picked up a piece of paper to review it. "It must be a very profitable business."

"It is." Con glanced back at Susan. She had a rather fixed look on her face, as if she'd rather deny that such a thing as smuggling existed. "As the earl's secretary in the past," he prompted, "I'm sure you know something about his involvement."

The look she flashed at him was almost a glare. "The earl invested in cargoes, yes, my lord. Most people hereabouts do."

"And how much profit does a run make?"

With another irritated glance, she said, "About five times the investment, if all goes smoothly. There are always some runs that fail, of course, creating a total loss."

Con saw Race's eyes widen and said, "Remember this is illegal."

"So are a great many interesting things," Race replied. "Mrs. Kerslake, do you know the amount invested and raised on a good run? I ask only out of fascinated interest, of course."

Susan suddenly relaxed and smiled—at Race. A relaxed, friendly smile that made Con grit his teeth.

She moved toward the desk. "It's said that a cargo came in down the coast last year with a thousand gallons each of brandy, rum, and gin, and a quarter ton of tobacco. I hear that tobacco can be bought abroad for sixpence a pound and sold here for five times that. Spirits might be a shilling a gallon and six shillings here."

Race bent to make quick calculations on paper. "Almost a thousand pounds from an investment of about a hundred and sixty. Lord above."

She moved closer to look at his figures. "There are expenses, of course. The ship and captain, payment to the landers, tubmen, batmen, and for use of horses and carts. Everyone will expect a little of the goods to take home too. On the other hand," she added, "tea is even more profitable. Ten to one."

Race was looking decidedly dazzled. It was the profit, not the person, but Con's jaw was aching with the need to drag her away from his side.

"You know a surprising amount about it, Mrs. Kerslake," he said, and saw her remember discretion with a start.

"Everyone does in these parts." She moved away from Race, however, which was an improvement.

Race looked up from his papers. "No wonder the earldom seems to have taken in at least two thousand pounds on top of rents each year."

"Has it, by gad?" Con strode to the desk to look at the papers Race had spread in front of him. "Yet according to the records Swann's sent me, there's only a couple of thousand in the earldom's bank." He looked across the desk. "Any explanation of that, Mrs. Kerslake?"

"The sixth earl spent a great deal on what interested him, my lord. His antiquities." She was hiding behind her servant's manner, but he wasn't fooled. She was tense with knowledge.

" 'Eye of newt and tail of frog' being very expensive these days?" Con turned back to Race. "Any idea if there's any squirreled away?"

"It's 'Eye of newt and toe of frog,' actually," Susan interjected. He looked at her and was hard-pressed not to smile at the touch of mischief there—an adult mischief based on wit and wisdom rather than girlish high spirits.

"Tails may make more sense," she pointed out, "but toes must bring more profit, frogs having more than one."

"Tails would have rarity value, however, since they do not have one once they're fully grown."

Her eyes sparkled. "That would make them a symbol of eternal youth . . . !"

He picked up her thought. "And if the earl were still alive, I could make a fortune selling him frog's tails."

Con thought they both came to a shocked awareness of relaxation, of memory of past times, simultaneously. She certainly sobered and turned to Race at the same time Con did.

"Hidden profits?" Con prompted, aware of his secretary's intrigued interest, damn him.

"I've found none yet, my lord. Not all his incomes and expenditures are clearly itemized, however, and he clearly often dealt in cash. It is possible he spent it all."

Surely after being the earl's secretary for so many years, Susan would know. He challenged her directly. "I presume you don't know where the extra money is, Mrs. Kerslake?"

She looked him straight in the eye. "No, my lord."

That was the truth.

"Keep up the search," he ordered Race. "It will enliven your dull days. And note any records of the purchase price of his peculiarities. That might be the key to my fortune."

Susan's expression turned so perfectly blank he knew she was hiding something. He really must stop thinking her an honest woman. She was beautiful, fascinating, deadly.

But not honest.

She'd had years to play with the books here, diverting money at will. She was up against Race now, however, whose chief delight was finding the truths and secrets hidden in records and ledgers.

Raw from that moment of friendly banter, he had to escape. "I am going to inspect the estate."

Then he realized this would leave Susan free to get up to all sorts of mischief. "Mrs. Kerslake, I wish you to work with Mr. de Vere. You are familiar with the earldom's management."

"The torture chamber, my lord?" she reminded him.

"A thoroughly superfluous addition." He saw her puzzlement, but wasn't about to explain. Crag Wyvern was one huge torture chamber when Susan Kerslake was in it, and a trap too.

Race was showing absolutely no interest in rack and pincers, so Con left, shutting the door on them.

Then he turned to go back. Susan and Race, alone together? After a moment he made himself walk away from the door. Perhaps Race could save him from himself.

A few more days of this new Susan and he might be rolling in the sand with her again, and this time there was nothing to prevent him offering marriage and being caught for life.

Except, he suddenly thought, a prior commitment.

Last week he'd been drifting toward offering marriage to Anne Peckworth. Nothing had changed. She was well-bred, well-dowered, kind, and gentle. His mother and sisters liked her. She was the perfect wife for him.

She had another advantage—the reason, in fact, that he'd sought her out. Earlier in the year, a fellow Rogue, Lord Middlethorpe, had been about to offer for Lady Anne when he'd met and married his beautiful wife, Serena. Lady Anne had been led to expect that offer, and been hurt, but she'd behaved beautifully.

He'd decided that since he seemed to lack the ability to fall in love, he might as well take Francis's place with Anne, who had a crippled foot and thus didn't find it easy to attend social events.

It was rational, reasonable, and yet here, with Susan, he was in danger of losing his grip on that sane decision.

He went to his room and opened his traveling desk to take out a sheet of paper. After fighting an instinct to hesitate, he wrote a swift letter to Anne Peckworth.

A gentleman writing to an unmarried lady was tantamount to commitment anyway, but to make all safe he stated clearly that he intended to speak to her father as soon as he returned to Sussex, which he hoped would be in a week or so.

He did not sand the ink but watched it dry, knowing he was burning his bridges. He was burning bridges between himself and the enemy, however, which was an excellent military tactic.

Attraction, even love, was not always good. He'd seen men bewitched and entangled by unworthy women, often to their destruction. He would not be one.

The ink was dry.

He folded the letter, sealed it, addressed it and scrawled *Wyvern* across the top to cover the postage. Then he gave it to Diego. "Take this down to Pearce. He's to get it into the mail immediately. If he has to ride to Honiton or Exeter, so be it. I want it on its way."

So that I can't weaken and snatch it back.

He saw Diego's brows rise, but the valet only said, "Yes, my lord."

He sat back and considered his defensive position. It was perfect. Now he could resist any weapons Susan brought to bear.

9

SUSAN TRIED to pay attention to de Vere and the paperwork, but her mind and heart were still with Con. That brief moment of fun had been like a drop of water on parched earth.

Tantalizing rather than refreshing.

She could not endure more such encounters. They made her feel like the most fragile shell on the seashore, being worn thinner and thinner with every wave of interaction. She'd be transparent soon, and shatterable with the slightest pressure. She'd end up as sand, swept away with the next tide. . . .

"Mrs. Kerslake?" De Vere's voice broke into her thoughts.

She turned to him and saw his expression—intrigued, but not unkind.

"Perhaps you could explain how the earl recorded his investment interests. It seems somewhat unclear."

She concentrated on simple matters. "He was secretive by nature, Mr. de Vere."

He had brought over a chair so she could sit by him, and now asked a series of focused, intelligent questions. She was impressed by how quickly he'd grasped the arcane aspects of the records and by how clearly he understood what was contained in them, including what was implied.

She was also impressed and worried by his systematic approach. She had been efficient, but not so meticulous. Though de Vere was working with remarkable speed, he was stripping every sheet of paper of its information and organizing it for future reference.

She was almost sure that there were no details here about smuggling matters, but things might be learned between the lines. Payments were made to the George and Dragon tavern for wine and spirits, for example, which were disguised investments in smuggling. Would de Vere, from Derbyshire, realize that?

Large sums of money were entered under loan repayments without any record of the loan.

Also the earl had been inclined to scribble notes to himself on all kinds of matters on the edge of papers, or on scraps that often ended up mixed in with other things.

What might de Vere learn that way?

Might he learn that David was the new Captain Drake? If he did, what might he do with that, as an outsider and a soldier?

She needed to speak to David, to warn him, even though she knew such a warning was useless. There was nothing he could change, nothing he could do, except perhaps lie low.

And where was he? She'd sent the message saying he was wanted here. She needed to know the run had gone smoothly, that she could put aside the matter of finding the hidden money.

She gazed sightlessly at a row of figures. What if it hadn't gone well? What if David was wounded somewhere and that was why he wasn't here?

She made herself be sensible. She'd have received word. Someone would have told her.

What if no one knew? If her aunt and uncle thought he was staying with friends . . . ?

She realized that de Vere had asked her the same thing twice. He must think her an addlepated female.

Trying to speak calmly, she said, "You know, I think my brother would be able to help you more on these matters, Mr. de Vere. I wonder where he is."

"Until he comes, perhaps—"

She rose. "I will go and make sure the message was sent." Before he could object, she escaped.

She went to the kitchen and put Mrs. Gorland in charge. She

almost ran out as she was, but she disciplined herself and put on her plain, wide hat. She must be Mrs. Kerslake, respectable house-keeper, not Susan Kerslake, who'd tramped free on the hills.

Who'd gone adventuring with Con Somerford.

As soon as she was outside Crag Wyvern, her panic faded and she took a deep breath. She'd never liked the Crag, but until today she'd not felt its full constrictive power.

David was doubtless fine. Merely tired from last night and care-less about responding to commands. But she was outside now, and she'd make the most of it.

The most of her freedom.

She'd never felt quite like this before, but then, Con Somer-ford had not been inside Crag Wyvern before. Or not for eleven years.

She set off down the hill to the inland village of Church Wyvern. For a blessing, the sun was shining from an almost cloud-less sky. It had been a dreadful summer, apparently because of the eruption of a volcano last year half a world away. Sweet summer days were scarce, and after last night they could have expected overcast and even rainy weather, but heaven had sent sunshine when she needed it so badly.

She prayed that the run had been successful. Then she could quickly find a new housekeeper and be out of Con's orbit before she did something to destroy him, or herself. It would break her heart to separate herself from him again, but she knew she must.

Destroy, she thought, glancing back at the gloomy house. So strong a word, and yet she felt that kind of power swirling in the house between them.

He was so dark, so unlike the Con she remembered, even though her sweet, magical Con was there too. Trapped, perhaps? If he was trapped inside that dark shell, she didn't know how to free him. Even if it was all her fault, if she'd started the encrusta-tion all those years ago in Irish Cove, she didn't know how to break him free now.

But she could avoid making things worse.

Going down the hill, the pretty village was spread before her, with cottages clustered around the church spire. She saw Diddy's mother hanging out the wash in her back garden, little children running around her. Grandchildren, probably, though Diddy's youngest brother was still an infant. One little girl was solemnly handing Mrs. Howlock the pegs, and Susan thought wistfully of such simple pleasures. A home, children, daily tasks that didn't require much thought or anxiety.

She knew it was nonsense, that worry lived in the cottages as well as in the manor and at the Crag, but most people didn't deliberately entangle themselves with madness and hanging crimes.

Could she get David to forget about all of this? They could move far from the coast and live ordinary lives. . . .

She shook her head. The blood of a wanton and a smuggling master mingled in them both. David had been reluctant to become Captain Drake, but he'd taken to it like a cat to mousing, and she knew he wouldn't give it up now.

Anyway, it was his duty, and he knew that. The people here needed smuggling, and needed an orderly leadership. He couldn't walk away from his inherited responsibility any more than Con could.

She could go anywhere, however.

But where?

She was completely unsuited to be a governess or a companion, and her birth made her unattractive for that or as a bride to a gentleman. She wasn't sure she had the temperament to make a good wife anyway, and of course, she wasn't a virgin.

Where could she go?

What could she do?

She had enjoyed being the earl's secretary, but such a position normally belonged to a man. And she didn't want to leave here, the one place on earth where she belonged.

Jack Croker was working in his garden, ready to plant his beans by the looks of the long stakes he was setting, as he had for thirty years or more. A tumble of very young piglets was all over a sow in

Fumleigh's farmyard. Apple blossom carpeted the manor's orchard, promising autumn fruit.

There was no way to belong to a village like this without being born to it. Everyone else, no matter how pleasant, was an outsider. She belonged, but she was and would always be the daughter of Mel Clyst and Lady Belle, a couple who hadn't even bothered to put the gloss of marriage on the scandal of their union.

If she'd been willing, or able, to live like a young lady of the manor, she would have been accepted better. But no, she'd had to spend all the time she could outdoors, exploring, questioning, learning to swim and sail, so that soon people had begun to whisper that she was as wild as her mother and would come to the same end.

Which perhaps she had, though less happily.

She turned into the lane that circled around the village, noting the faint cart tracks in the soft earth. Last night's drizzle had softened the ground enough to leave the trace, but no more than a trace. The Dragon's Horde was skillful, and men always followed the cart with a roller, smoothing out the tracks a bit to make them look older, then superimposing footprints, even those of children. Everyone hereabouts was involved in the smuggling trade.

There were hoofprints too. The manor's horses would have been borrowed for the run, and returned around dawn. Farmers grumbled sometimes about tired beasts and men, but most accepted the payment in kegs and bales found among the straw.

She'd never been sure what Uncle Nathaniel and Aunt Miriam thought about smuggling. It was rarely mentioned at the manor, and only then as something that went on elsewhere. From being the earl's secretary and now helping David with the Horde's accounts, she knew they didn't invest.

Probably like most of the gentry along the coast, they were neutral, not noticing when their horses were borrowed, nor looking too closely at things hidden on their land, and not asking questions about kegs of spirits, packages of tea, or twists of lace that appeared—

"Mistress Kerslake!"

She turned with a start to see a horseman waving from a nearby rise. For a heart-jumping moment she thought it was Con. But of course not. Only one person used the old-fashioned term of address "mistress." Lieutenant Gifford, the riding officer.

He set his horse to a canter then jumped the low wall down the path a bit before trotting to join her.

She tried not to show her sudden burst of panic. He didn't suspect anything. He was new to the area and had not even realized yet that she and David were not Sir Nathaniel's children. But the ghostly cart tracks seemed suddenly deep and obvious beneath her feet.

He dismounted to stand beside her, such a pleasant young man with a slightly round face and soft brown curls, but also with a firmness to his mouth and chin that reminded her a bit of Con. Gifford, too, had fought at Waterloo. She liked him, and he was only trying to do his conscientious duty, and yet he was their enemy.

"A lovely day, is it not?" he said with an unshadowed smile.

She smiled back, and hoped it looked natural. "It is indeed, sir, and we deserve it after the dull ones we've had."

"That dashed volcano. And we're doing better here than on the continent and in America. You are walking to the manor house, Mistress Kerslake? May I walk beside you?"

"Of course." What else could she say?

The man was courting her, however, and it embarrassed her when it was so impossible. She cared nothing for him, and he would not wish to pursue it when he learned about her irregular birth. More than that, however, no riding officer could marry a smuggler's daughter without ruining his career.

She'd like to tell him, but could not point the way to David like that. Perhaps she could at least use this moment to find out about last night. "And how goes your business, Lieutenant Gifford?"

He pulled a face. "Now, Mistress Kerslake, don't play me for a fool. Everyone in the area knows when there's been a run, and there was one last night. Two, damn them. One I was allowed to stop, whilst another went on elsewhere along the coast."

Such a pity he was intelligent.

"I've been stuck up at Crag Wyvern all morning, Lieutenant, so I haven't heard any gossip. The new earl has arrived."

"Has he?" His eyes sharpened. "A military man, I understand."

She knew where his thoughts were turning. "I believe he was a captain in the infantry, yes."

"Then perhaps I'll have an ally in these parts."

She felt some sympathy for him, but had to say, "The earl doesn't intend to live here, Lieutenant. He has a family home in Sussex and prefers it."

He glanced up at the dark house. "Hardly surprising, but a shame. The Earl of Wyvern can make or break smuggling in this area. I heard talk that the old earl helped bring down Melchisedeck Clyst."

"What?" She collected herself, hoping her shock hadn't shown. "You must be mistaken. The earl was known to support the smugglers."

"A falling-out, perhaps. There's no honor among thieves, you know, ma'am."

Susan's head was spinning with the idea that the mad earl had not just failed to intervene, but had actively caused her father's arrest and the loss of a whole cargo.

Why on earth would he do that?

"I've heard rumors that last night's cargo came in near here," Gifford was saying, "but I can find no trace of it. I don't suppose you heard anything, Mistress Kerslake."

It sounded like a statement of fact rather than a question. He knew that no one around here would give him information.

"I'm afraid not, Lieutenant."

"There was a battle up near Pott's Hill with a couple of men left badly wounded. Doubtless a quarrel over the spoils, so the cargo must have been brought in near here."

Her heart skipped a beat. "A battle?" she said, thankful that shock would seem natural. "Whatever do you mean, sir?"

"One gang trying to steal from another. Happens all the time, my dear lady. These smugglers are not the noble adventurers some would have you think."

Lord above, did he really think anyone born and raised here had any illusions about smugglers? But what had happened? Had David truly been hurt? Had the cargo been stolen?

She tried her best to put on a look of innocence—or stupidity, maybe. "But then, can you not arrest the injured men?"

"Not without evidence, Mistress Kerslake," he said kindly. "They claim to have fought over a woman and will not be moved from that. Unfortunately, before we arrived, any contraband had disappeared."

She waited for a moment. If David was one of the injured he must surely mention it. When he didn't, she felt she could breathe again.

"Surely a fight over a woman is not so very unusual, Lieutenant."

"On the night of a run, Mistress Kerslake, even women are of lesser interest." But then he smiled. "That is, to lowborn wretches. To a gentleman, a lady is always first in his mind."

She could say something scathing about duty, but she managed not to. Thank heavens the gate into the manor orchard was only yards away.

"I see all too little of you, Mistress Kerslake. There was an assembly at Honiton last week that was blighted by your absence."

Susan managed not to roll her eyes. "I am employed, Lieutenant, and not free to attend such events."

"Come, come. Before the earl's arrival your duties cannot have been burdensome."

"On the contrary, sir. The late earl's eccentricities left the place in disorder. I have been attempting to set everything to rights."

"Indeed?" For some reason he seemed to disbelieve her. "But I'm sure you must be enjoying entertainment in some quarter or other. If you were to let me know, dear lady, I would make such places my special haunts."

This struck her as a very peculiar thing to say, as if he expected her to be spending her nights in taverns, but she had no time or patience for this now.

"I live a very quiet, boring life, Lieutenant," she said, opening the gate.

"You are funning! Very well, you pose a mystery for me to solve. For the moment, I am on my way to Dragon's Cove to solve another mystery, though I doubt there'll be anything to learn among that secretive lot."

He mounted his horse. "With that scoundrel Melchisedeck Clyst gone, they're doubtless in too much disorder to attempt a large run here, but I'll take a close look at the new tavernkeeper, and keep my eyes open for cart tracks."

Susan did not look down at the tracks beneath his horse's hooves, but she was hard-pressed not to laugh. The new tavern-keeper at the George and Dragon was Mel's cousin Rachel Clyst, a jolly middle-aged woman as wide as she was tall. She was certainly in league with the Horde, but a less likely Captain Drake was hard to imagine. She wheezed going up a few steps, never mind up a cliff.

Her humor faded as she watched Gifford ride away, however. He wouldn't find anything at Dragon's Cove, but he was clever enough and dutiful enough to find things eventually.

She went into the orchard worrying about that battle. When it came to smuggling, *battle* was an accurate word. Hundreds of men could be involved, some of them carrying guns. Deaths could occur.

What had happened?

Was David lying bleeding somewhere?

She cut through the kitchen garden past a sleepy-looking lad who was pretending to hoe between some cabbages. Nearly every-one along the coast would have gone short of sleep last night.

The lad called a cheery greeting, however, and her flurry of anxiety calmed. No one would be smiling if Captain Drake had been wounded or captured. And everyone would know.

She walked more calmly through a honeysuckle arch onto the lawn that ran up to the lovely house. It was as neatly rectangular as the Crag, but the dull stone was whitewashed. Set amid wholesome land and pleasant gardens and filled with warmhearted people, the manor was another world.

She paused to study it, thinking that she must be mad not to feel completely at home here. Her family here were good people and she loved them dearly, but she didn't think she'd ever truly felt she belonged, even as a young child. Once she'd learned the truth about her parents, she'd understood why. . . .

"Susan!"

She started, and saw her cousin Amelia running across the lawn waving. Amelia was twenty, plump, and excited, and typically her wide villager hat was sliding off her brown curls to hang down her back. "I hear the earl's turned up!" she gasped as soon as she was close.

"Yes, late last night."

"What's he like? Is he handsome?"

"He has been here before."

"Once, and I was nine years old! I do remember the father and two sons in the Wyvern pew at church, but it's a faint memory. This one was darker and steadier, wasn't he? I thought he was the older brother."

"Yes," Susan said, walking on toward the house, "so did I."

"I knew Fred Somerford, of course," Amelia chattered, falling into step. "Since Mother was always encouraging him to treat the manor as his home." She giggled. "Do you remember Father muttering about mad Somerfords, and Mother arguing that he was a perfectly sane young man? She had such hopes that one of us would snare him. I wonder what she'll do about the new one."

Susan could have groaned at the thought of Aunt Miriam matchmaking again.

"Shame he drowned," Amelia said. "Fred, I mean. But it's not really surprising. I always thought of him as Fred the Unready, like Ethelred the Unready."

Susan laughed, then stopped it with a hand. "Oh, dear. That isn't very kind."

"I suppose not. But is the new one more ready?"

Ready for what? Susan suddenly remembered Diddy describing him as "ready to go," and blushed at the vivid image that sprung to mind.

"I couldn't say," she said.

"I remember him as dark. Is he still dark? I like dark men."

"He could hardly be paler, unless he'd turned gray."

"Well, some people do, don't they? With stress, or fright. And Michael Paulet came back from the Peninsula with his light brown hair turned blond by the sun."

"I don't think dark brown hair does that." She wished Amelia would stop asking all these questions.

"There was that miniature Fred Somerford brought," Amelia said as they stepped onto the stone path that led to the back door. "I quite lost my heart to that dashing captain. Is he as handsome now?"

Susan fought not to react. Amelia and Con? She couldn't bear it.

"Are you going to toss your cap at him?" she asked as lightly as she could.

Amelia grinned, showing deep dimples. "It can't hurt to try."

"Even if he's not to your taste?"

"I won't know without trying, will I? And an earl to my taste would be very nice indeed."

"Even if you had to live at Crag Wyvern?"

Amelia glanced back at the house with a grimace. "A hit, I confess. But it could be changed. Windows on the outside, for a start. And white paint. Or stucco."

It astonished Susan that her cousin could be so lighthearted about all this, as if life presented only sunny options. This was the Kerslake way, though, and why she always felt like an outsider. An envious outsider.

"The earl has a very pretty secretary," she offered, knowing she was trying to deflect Amelia's interest. "A Mr. Racecombe de Vere, who has all the air of a fine gentleman despite his lowly status. In fact, I doubt his status is particularly low. You should look him up in one of Uncle Nathaniel's books."

Amelia's dimples deepened. "Two handsome strangers! It's about time something interesting happened here."

Susan glanced at her cousin. Surely Amelia knew.

"What's the matter?" her cousin asked. "Is it the new earl? Is he truly mad?"

"No. No, of course not. But he'll bring changes, and it's hard to tell what they might be."

"It has to be better than what's gone on before. He's young, he's eligible, he's handsome with a handsome friend. Will he be giving balls?"

Susan laughed. "At Crag Wyvern?"

"Why not? From what you say, it would be wonderful for a masquerade."

It was as if Amelia had turned everything to show a new aspect. "You're right, it would. And it might chase away some of the shadows. For the good of the area the place needs to become somewhere normal people might live and entertain their neighbors."

Not one of the crazy earl's crazy friends. Solid, normal tenants. She wondered how much it would cost to cover the walls with fashionable stucco. Perhaps those faux stone corridors could be painted cheerful colors too. And windows cut . . .

Astonishing possibilities.

✄ 10 ✄

THEY ENTERED the manor, finding Aunt Miriam working in the steamy kitchen alongside the cook and maid baking bread. Her round face tended to red anyway, and in the steam was puce, but her eyes lit. "Susan, love, how nice to see you. Give me a moment, and we'll have a cup of tea."

"I need to speak to David first, aunt."

The warmth of her aunt's smile was easing her, and stirring guilt. She knew Aunt Miriam thought of her as a daughter, and loved her like a daughter, and yet she could never be quite the daughter her aunt wanted her to be.

Conventional, happy, and married by now.

"He's probably still in the breakfast parlor," Aunt Miriam said, kneading away at a mound of dough. "I don't know what hour he returned home last night, or what he'd been up to. Young men will burn the candles, won't they?" she added with a wink.

Susan resisted an urge to state unwelcome truths, and went toward the front of the house hoping for a word in private with her brother. Aunt Miriam snared Amelia to help in the kitchen, which got rid of one problem, but when she entered the sun-filled breakfast room she found their cousin Henry keeping David company.

All the true Kerslakes tended to a comfortable roundness, and at twenty-eight Henry was developing a prosperous stomach. He had his hands clasped over it now as he watched David finish his breakfast and lectured him about the importance of the Corn Laws.

At the sight of Susan, however, he stood, beaming. "Now this is a treat!" He came around the table to take her hands and kiss her cheek. "We don't see enough of you, cousin."

Truly, everyone here was impossibly kind. She always felt like a thistle in a flower bed. David, despite being so like her, bloomed carelessly along with the rest.

She sat at the table, looking at the evidence of his hearty breakfast. "Anyone would think you actually worked for your living, love."

She saw evidence of tiredness, but none of fighting. He seemed his usual lighthearted self, thank the Lord. Everything was all right.

He flashed her a look from subtle blue-gray eyes. Apart from the eyes they'd been very alike when young, with their father's square chin and their mother's golden brown hair. By now, however, he'd grown heavier bones and six more inches of height, and a great deal of muscle.

She had the disconcerting concern of how it would go if he and Con got into a fight. David had inches and breadth on Con, but something warned her that Con might win.

"Aren't you supposed to be working, too?" he asked, forking the last piece of fried bread into his mouth.

"I am. I'm playing sheepdog. A message was sent commanding your presence up at the Crag."

"And you've come to nip me up there? Is the earl in such a hurry?"

"It's almost noon. And I don't know about hurry, but he's thorough. Or rather, his very efficient secretary is. He's going through everything like a miser hunting for a penny."

It was a warning. There shouldn't be anything in the Wyvern papers about smuggling operations, but it was possible.

"Right and proper thing to do," Henry said. "Take over the reins. See what's what. It's about time there was some order and decorum up there. He'll want your records and advice, Davy, and if you're ordered up there, up there you should be!"

David poured himself another cup of coffee and leaned back, mischief in his eyes. "If he wanted instant service, he should have sent warning of his arrival."

As he sipped from his cup, those smiling eyes slid to Susan carrying a question. *Trouble?*

She smiled a little to show that there wasn't. Which was true. Con wasn't throwing a fit over the smuggling run, which was all David would care about. She needed to talk to him, though, and Henry was stuck in his chair like a burr in a long-haired dog.

So she gossiped about the earl, and entered into aimless speculation with Henry on the effect on the neighborhood. Again, she passed on Con's message that he wasn't going to make this his principal residence.

"Shame, that," Henry said. "Perhaps he'll change his mind if we show him what a pleasant little community we have here."

David's brows and lips twitched in a humorous wince. There was nothing he wanted less than an earl in residence at the Crag. Even a friendly one had to be constantly thought of and pacified. "You'll have to see if Amelia can steal his heart, Henry. That would tie him here."

Henry reddened. "Marry her off to a mad Earl of Wyvern? I'll know the man a great deal better before I'll countenance that, and I'll go odds Father will feel the same way."

"Then if he's a handsome devil, perhaps we shouldn't encourage him to hang around."

Henry looked at Susan. "Is he a handsome devil?"

It wasn't hard to play her part. "I'm afraid so."

He pushed to his feet. "I need to talk to Father about this."

He paused however, to lecture David. "Obey orders and get up there, Davy. It's a nice little post you have, and if the earl isn't going to be in residence, an easy job with local influence. You don't want to lose it."

"How true." David was still lounging, however.

"You may think now that you do well enough as you are," Henry said with exasperation, "but one day you'll want to marry and set up your own establishment. That takes money. You need your employment."

"You're completely right, Henry," David said, eyes twinkling. "I'll just finish my coffee and be off."

Henry sighed and left to consult with Sir Nathaniel. Susan looked at her brother and suppressed laughter. She wouldn't hurt Henry by letting him hear them laughing at him, but David's prospects in life no longer depended on his post, and anyone aware of what was going on around them would know it.

The tendency to laughter faded. She'd rather David was simply an earl's estate manager.

"Everything went smoothly last night?" she asked quietly. As usual, there was no certain privacy here.

"Not exactly," he said, abruptly sober. "I'll tell you later."

Her stomach clenched. She chose her words carefully. "I met Lieutenant Gifford on the way here. He was on his way to Dragon's Cove looking for evidence of a run coming in there last night."

David drank the rest of his coffee. "I doubt he'll find anything."

So that wasn't the problem. She began to imagine different kinds of disasters.

"So what's the new earl really like?" he asked.

"Not mad." He needed a warning about the sort of man Con was now. "Strong," she said. "He was a captain in the army. He fought at Waterloo." Reluctantly, the word escaped. "Unforgiving."

Her brother became thoughtful. "You knew him when he was here, didn't you? In 1805."

She hastily picked up a piece of bread and nibbled it. What had David heard? The last thing she needed was antagonism between David and Con over her, but she equally didn't want to confess to David how badly she'd behaved.

"Yes, I knew him," she said. "We're the same age."

"Tom Bridgelow said something last night. About Mel thinking you two were getting too close, and warning him off."

"There was nothing to it," she said, trying to make it sound absurd. "We met here and there and were friends of a sort. He was here only two weeks."

"According to Tom once Mel had said his piece you and he weren't seen together again."

"Not surprising. No one would want Mel angry with them. A rare example of paternal concern."

"He kept an eye on us." Before Susan could ask what he meant, he added, "Shame there was nothing between you. It would be useful now if you were on close terms."

"It was eleven years ago, David, and we've not so much as exchanged a letter!"

He shrugged. "Just a thought." He pushed back from the table and stood, sober and thoughtful enough to please Henry, if he'd been here to see it. Susan suddenly saw a similarity between David and Con, an aura that came of being a leader, of carrying the lives and welfare of many on his shoulders.

It made her shiver. That way lay glory, but that way lay death too. Then she saw him wince and favor a leg as he moved from the table.

"What's the matter?" she whispered.

"Got into a fight," he said in a normal voice. "Lots of bruises, but no real damage, so don't fuss. I'll get my record books and we can be off up to prostrate ourselves before the demanding earl." He stopped to yawn, wincing again as he stretched. "I hope his questions aren't too deep or difficult, though. I've had only four hours' sleep."

Susan waited for him in the kitchen, smothering her anxiety with a hot bun running with butter, and chatting with her aunt about Con.

"A lovely lad," Aunt Miriam said. "Full of energy but kind with it. George," she added, pouring cups of tea all around. "But he preferred to be called something else. Ah yes, Con."

She passed Susan a cup and saucer, a twinkle in her eye. "I suspect he's grown into a handsome man."

Susan hadn't asked for the tea, but she took a fortifying gulp.

"Yes, he has." As a defense against that hopeful twinkle, she added, "He's betrothed to a nobleman's daughter."

Aunt Miriam pulled a face. "Ah, well. I remembered that you met him here and there when you were studying your insects. A shared interest is always nice."

"I doubt he's much interested in entomology anymore." Susan finished her tea, astonished by the complete lack of suspicion in her aunt's manner. Had she never thought it dubious that her almost-daughter was out with a young man, no chaperon in sight?

Sometimes it seemed to her that her manor family lived inside a soap bubble, disconnected from the reality of the Crag, Dragon's Cove, smuggling, or anything less than idyllic.

It must be lovely.

But she knew the notion of cozy complacency was an illusion. Four children had died in this house, three of Aunt Miriam's and one of Lady Belle's, and many members of previous generations. Aunt Miriam knew all about the less pleasant aspects of life.

Susan had been ten when her second brother had arrived at the manor. She'd been too young to question David's birth, but little Sammy had required explanation.

The truth had driven her to help take care of the frail baby, but had also stirred dreams and longings. She only vaguely knew Mel Clyst and Lady Belle, since none of the children of the manor were encouraged to go over to the village of Dragon's Cove.

But once she knew that Mel and Belle were her parents, her real parents, they fascinated her.

She'd fought to keep Sammy alive for his own sake, but perhaps as well she'd hoped to prove worthy of her parents' attention. She'd been heartbroken when the baby gave up the fight at six weeks, and guilt-struck as well.

She vividly remembered Lady Belle and Mel Clyst coming to the manor to look at the waxen body. Though she'd hovered nearby, Lady Belle—lush, queenly, and richly dressed—had paid her no attention. She'd looked at the baby as if he were an exhibit in a glass case.

Melchisedeck Clyst, who despite being a tavernkeeper had been dressed as well as Uncle Nathaniel, had seemed to feel something. He'd touched the swaddled child, and glanced at Susan in a way that might have been an acknowledgment. But no more than that.

They'd gone with the coffin to the church for the service, and then to the graveyard to see the small box settled in the Kerslake plot. To Susan, weeping, it had seemed that Lady Belle was profoundly bored.

From that day on she had put aside all hope that her true parents would clasp her to their bosoms. She didn't know why she had wanted it when she'd had the love of Aunt Miriam, Sir Nathaniel, her brother, and her cousins.

But from that day on she'd also longed to belong.

Sometimes she wondered if she'd simply needed to be in a position where Lady Belle would be forced to acknowledge her existence.

When David came into the kitchen and snitched a bun despite just having finished that huge breakfast, Susan rose and impulsively gave her aunt a hug. Her aunt hugged her back, but with a question in her eyes. Susan could see that she was touched, though, and was glad she'd done it. Had she ever shown her aunt and uncle how grateful she was for what they'd done for them?

"Is everything all right, Susan?" Aunt Miriam asked, holding on to her hand for a moment.

Susan felt a brief urge to burst into wild laughter and tears, but she said, "Yes, of course. Though the earl being at the Crag is going to bring changes. I don't think I want to stay there as housekeeper much longer."

"It always was a temporary thing, love, and it'll be grand to have you back here again."

Susan smiled, but she knew she couldn't do it. She'd taken a fork in the road, and she couldn't return to this coziness any more than she could explore the cliffs with Con again. She didn't say that, though, merely squeezed her aunt's hand and went on her way.

As soon as they were out of earshot of the house, David asked, "Is the earl going to make trouble?"

Trouble? What was trouble? Perhaps she should tell David the whole story so he would be warned. She was very afraid that if Con discovered that her brother was the new Captain Drake he'd turn against the Dragon's Horde for that reason.

"I don't think he'll fight the smuggling," she said, hoping it was true. "As things are at the moment. I suspect he won't invest, though, and he might not cooperate about the cellars and the horses."

"Inconvenient. Are you sure you can't persuade him to play a part? Smuggling has to continue, or I wouldn't be doing it."

"Truly?" She looked at him.

"Truly. I confess, I enjoy it in part, but I'm all too aware of the dangers. If you can, persuade the earl to be on our side."

Susan suppressed a shudder at the thought. "I think Gifford is more likely to persuade him into complete opposition. They're both army men."

"But isn't Gifford sweet on you?"

"I am not encouraging the poor man, not even for you."

"Ah, well," he said as they passed through the arch into the orchard, "Mel always said we had to play the hand we were dealt."

"Mel," Susan said, remembering. "David, Gifford suggested that the old earl helped bring about Mel's arrest."

He stopped to stare at her. "What? That's nonsense. They had an agreement."

"Might they have had a falling-out?"

"I'd have thought you'd know that better than I."

"I didn't see anything. . . ." They walked on. "But he might have hidden it from me. He wasn't stupid, and he'd know that I'd probably warn Mel of danger."

"Only probably?"

"We've no reason to feel kindly toward our parents."

He glanced at her. "I used to go down to the George and Dragon sometimes. I suppose it was easier, us being men. . . ."

For some reason it hurt. "Were you friends, then, you and Mel?"

"I don't know what you'd call it. Not father and son. Not friends either. I'm no happier than you about the way they ignored us, but I came to like him. He told me I'd have to take over if anything happened without giving him time to prepare. That's why he talked to me about the business."

She realized she was hurt by this connection, and by the fact that David had kept it secret.

But then, she had secrets, and now she didn't feel so responsible for pushing David into being Captain Drake.

"And Lady Belle?" she asked. "Were you friends with her too?" She heard the sour note in her voice but couldn't seem to help it.

His look said he heard it too. "She liked the company of handsome young men."

"Handsome, are you?"

"Stupid to say no. Susan, look, some women just aren't made to be mothers. I think Mel would have liked to be closer to us, but he wouldn't cross her for it. And he liked his children being raised at the manor as gentry. He didn't want us living in Dragon's Cove, part of his class. He kept an eye on us, and everyone around here knew better than to harm us."

Kept an eye. As Mel had by talking to Con. And she'd always felt safe roaming the coast. Perhaps her aunt and uncle had known she was under Captain Drake's protection, and that was why they'd given her so much freedom.

Her world had twisted again.

"How do you think he'll do in Australia?" she asked.

"Mel? If he's survived the voyage he'll probably thrive. I gather that after a while they can set up businesses."

"And Lady Belle?" But then she burst out, "I don't even *like* her, so why am I concerned?"

He laughed. "Blood will out? She'll be queen of Australia."

"On gold that doesn't belong to her."

"In a way, it did. Mel kept a handsome sum to back up the Horde in difficult times. He even paid people for sitting idle so they wouldn't get up to trouble. But it was his money. His profits."

Susan was bouncing from one shock to another. "The earl's gold is the Horde's though, isn't it? The earl didn't keep his part of the bargain."

"Assuredly."

So it was right to take it. She still didn't want to take it from Con. Or, to be more precise, she didn't want Con to know if she took it.

She shifted to something firmer. "What happened last night. How bad is it?"

"Half bad. We have half the cargo secure, though we won't be able to move it for a while with Gifford and his men poking around everywhere. The fight last night has them all over this part of the coast, dammit."

"What happened? How badly are you hurt?"

"Don't fuss. A line of tubmen was attacked. I think it was the Blackstock Gang, but I'm not sure. I arrived before they'd snatched all the tubs, but they got some and left a lot of men bruised and battered."

"Gifford said he knows of some of the injured. Were they ours?"

"Yes. I let him find them, since there was nothing to prove the cause of the fight—we had the cargo away by then. They'd get better doctoring that way. The others carried away their wounded."

She was afraid he might go after the Blackstocks to teach them a lesson, afraid he'd get more badly hurt, but she knew she had no say in such things. He wasn't her little brother anymore.

But there was an area where she could speak. "How much did we lose? What's our situation now?"

"About half the profit, but I've kept that quiet. I'll forgo my share, and if you do the same—"

"Of course." It would leave her with no money to finance an escape, however. Unless they found the money hidden at the Crag. "But the Horde will have no reserves."

They were out in the lane, and they stepped aside to let a man with a barrow pass, exchanging pleasant greetings. The man winked as he went past. "Grand night last night, weren't it, Cap'n?"

Susan took a deep breath. "Clearly he doesn't know of the loss. But I wish everyone didn't know about you."

"Don't be silly. How could it work if everyone didn't know? No one's going to say anything."

"It has to get out. Perch knew who Captain Drake was, but he accepted money not to know. Gifford won't do that." She said what she knew she shouldn't say. "David, I don't want him hurt."

He stopped to look at her. "Gifford? Perhaps you do fancy him."

She felt the color rush into her cheeks. "Of course not. But he's a good man simply trying to do his duty. It would be evil to kill him."

"You do think I've turned into a monster, don't you?"

"No. But when it comes to you or him. To your men or him . . ."

"I won't kill him or order him killed. It's not the Dragon's Horde way, Susan. You know that."

"But I don't want you hanged or transported, either!"

"Make up your mind, love." But then he linked his arm with hers and urged her onward. "Don't borrow trouble. But I have to say, it would be useful if you could get your hands on that gold soon. Once we move last night's cargo, we'll be able to pay the investors. But as you say, no reserves. We'll have to do another run. Soon."

"How soon?"

His glance said, *Too soon.* "Captain Vavasour has a tea cargo he couldn't get in farther up the coast."

"You can't bring it in here! And the moon's fuller every night."

"We're having such dull weather, the chances are it'll be overcast—"

"Chances!"

"Susan, smuggling's a chancy business."

"That's why I want no part of it."

"No, that's why you don't want me part of it. Stop it."

The firm command took her breath away. But he was right. Her panic was more likely to get him killed than help him.

"Of course we'd not bring it in here, but tea's a lighter cargo, so we can use somewhere tricky. Irish Cove, perhaps. That's not been used for years."

Her breath caught, even as she knew it shouldn't matter. It was just another bay along the coast. But in some twisted way it seemed another betrayal of Con to use that special place for a smuggling run when he was nearby.

"It's a hard climb up with the goods," she said.

"We could drop lines and hoist the tea up. It's equally hard for the Preventives to get at. Or get Vavasour to sink the bales with markers. Then pick them up by boat . . ."

He was lost in his plans, but Susan knew Gifford would be hawkeyed here. "David, if I find the gold, would you be able to wait?"

He looked at her. "It's a hard opportunity to pass up, a nice cargo just waiting. . . . But all right, if you find the money we can lie low for a month or even two. Isn't it going to be hard now the earl's in residence?"

"I don't think it makes much difference unless it's hidden under his bed, and it isn't. I've checked all such places already under cover of the inventory and spring cleaning. I confess, I expected finding it to be much easier. He had to be able to get at it, to add to it and take from it."

"Perhaps he spent it all on potions and dried diddlers," he said with a grin. She'd shown him the earl's bedchamber, and he'd nearly died laughing.

She swatted at him. "Remember, I was his secretary. I know what he spent. From what he received from the Horde, even just in recent years, there should be over two thousand in gold coin somewhere. That's not exactly easy to hide, even in small caches around the place, and if there were small caches, I should have found at least one."

"Perhaps a secret room, or secret chamber in the walls," David said.

"I know, but that could be anywhere. At least there's very little paneling."

"I need to let Vavasour know in two days."

"Two days! Very well, I'll buckle down to a ruthless search—for cunning hidey-holes in particular. Which reminds me. Con's brought a secretary with him."

"Con?" he said with interest.

She prayed not to blush. "I knew him as Con once. It slips out. Listen, his secretary—"

"Of course he has a secretary."

They were beginning the steeper climb up to the Crag, and perhaps that was why her heart beat harder. "Well, he's set him to going through all the records and papers. What if there's something there about smuggling?"

"Don't you know?"

"The earl was as crazy about his administration as about everything else. He scribbled notes to himself and pushed them in odd places. He did the same with letters he received."

"I very much doubt that Mel wrote him letters."

"I know, but I feel as if de Vere is bound to uncover something."

He smiled at her. "We'll play that hand when we're dealt it. It's not like you to be in such a fidget."

Again she longed to tell him the truth, but she'd hide her past—all her past, if she could.

"It is time for you to give up your job there, though," he said. "It's not suitable."

"If I can't tell you how to manage your affairs, you can't tell me." She stopped to catch her breath, something she couldn't remember having to do before. "You work for him," she added.

"I'm his estate manager," he said, not breathless at all. "That's suitable employment for a gentleman. Housekeeper is different. Are you all right?"

No, no, I'm not. I'm afraid, and confused, and both longing to see Con again and terrified of him.

"I'm just tired. I didn't get much sleep last night either."

He put his arm around her and hoisted her up the last bit of hill before the flatter land around Crag Wyvern. "I won't try to order you around, Susan, but I'd like you out of that place and not worrying about me."

She rolled her eyes. "I do intend to find a replacement, but I have to have a last try for that gold first. As for not worrying about you—how?"

"Perhaps you need to get away from here."

She stopped in the chilly shadow of the great house. "Away? You want me to go away?"

"I don't want you to, but I don't want you constantly worrying either. I can't promise to live safely for you. You know that."

"Yes, I know. I'm sorry. I'm just out of sorts today."

"Ah, that time of the month, is it?"

It wasn't, but she smiled and said, "You know too much about women."

He laughed and they carried on toward the gargoyle-crowned arch that led into the house of the demented earls of Wyvern.

❧ 11 ❧

CON HAD fled Crag Wyvern. His official excuse was to inspect his estate and tenants, but he'd taken young Jonny White and fled to the normal world, which was so easily forgotten inside the Crag's fortress walls.

After an hour or so he was soothed by the normality and good health of this part of Devon. He noted the strange quietness at first, and the absence of people other than the old and young. As the day advanced more people inhabited the scenery, all pleasant enough, and eager to talk to the new earl. All smugglers the night before.

He accepted the hospitality of one cottage to share a hearty midday meal, chatting about farming matters as if that were what put the food on the table.

He sensed all around him the unspoken question: What was his attitude to smuggling? He gave his answer as best he could without talking about it—he didn't intend to change anything.

It was true. Any attempt at sudden change would be disastrous. However, it was his duty to try to put a stop to the Freetrade eventually, and to prepare the people here for the change that would inevitably come.

He mentioned the naval cutters now patrolling the coast, and the number of army officers and men looking for peacetime employment. When an elderly woman blessed the fact that the war was over, he commented that they were also blessed that the government should need less money and could reduce the iniquitous duties on things like tea.

She agreed wholeheartedly, showing that none of the simple folk understood the implications—low taxes would reduce prices, and that would take away the profit in smuggling. No one was going to take on the risk and the work for a ten-percent return.

The burden of it pressed on him. This place needed a lifetime's care, and he didn't want to give it his life. He could leave the simpler part of it to his estate manager, but he needed to either give Kerslake more powers or hire a steward. That could wait until he had the measure of Susan's brother. He vaguely remembered a rapscallion with a toothy grin.

Zeus! He couldn't leave everything here in the hands of her and her brother!

The property seemed to be in good heart, at least, with crops growing and animals healthy. The sorry summer had not had too serious an effect in these parts. The cottages and farms were in good repair, and the people looked well fed. There was even a school in Church Wyvern run by the curate's wife with assistance from Miss Amelia Kerslake. He was invited to admire the large room furnished with benches, slates, a globe, and a good selection of books.

All paid for, he was sure, from smuggling, but there was much to be said for prosperity, no matter where the money came from.

He managed a word with the curate, who expressed himself delighted to help sort through the earl's private collection of books. The hearty young man confessed to great curiosity about them.

"Have an interest in the dark arts, do you, Mr. Rufflestowe?"

"Know thine enemy, my lord," said the curate, but a twinkle in his eye admitted to simple human curiosity.

Since he seemed an admirably down-to-earth man, Con asked, "What's the correct procedure for a skull, Rufflestowe?"

"Procedure, my lord?"

"There are two human skulls in the earl's rooms, and they look to me as if they were disinterred in the not-too-distant past. Have there been any disturbed graves?"

"Good heavens. Not as far as I know, my lord. But there are some ancient burial sites around here. Most interesting . . ." He caught himself up. "A little interest of mine, my lord. Perhaps it would be best to leave the matter of the skulls until I can inspect them. Tomorrow, perhaps?"

Another enthusiastic worker, thought Con. "By all means, sir."

He found Jonny sitting at a desk in the schoolroom, working his way carefully through the words on a hornbook. The lad had been a London orphan before taking the king's shilling just before Waterloo. He'd doubtless had little education. Con made a mental note to arrange reading lessons for him, but dragged him off on the rest of the circuit of the estate.

As the Church Wyvern clock struck four, he turned his horse back toward Crag Wyvern, as reluctant to return to the house as he had been to enter it the day before. The feeling reminded him of Waterloo. He hadn't wanted to go there either, but duty had left him no choice. Then, however, he'd known he was riding into hell. Now, he only felt like it.

He left the horses and Jonny at the stables in the village and walked up to the house. At the great arch into Crag Wyvern, he hesitated, tempted to linger outside.

He could walk across the headland. . . .

With a bitter laugh, he realized that he was dreaming of encountering a friend there, of exploring rock pools and caves, of lying in the sun talking, talking, talking. . . .

He squared his shoulders and walked through the gargoyle-crested arch into the shadows of Crag Wyvern.

He crossed the echoing great hall, heading toward the office, aware of being on the alert for Susan, both warily and eagerly. She didn't appear, but she might still be with Race.

When he opened the door to the office, however, he found someone else in the room with Race—a young man rising from an extra chair at the desk.

It could only be Susan's brother. The resemblance was remarkable, though no one would ever mistake one for the other. She might look like a Renaissance angel, but her brother, despite sensible country clothes, was all Renaissance warrior.

"Mr. Kerslake," Con said.

The man bowed. "My lord."

He was tall and strong, with an aura the officer in Con recognized. Things fell into place. This was Captain Drake. Of course he was. He was Mel Clyst's son. It was hard not to grin. Susan was certainly not the mistress of the new local leader. On the other hand, he thought, sobering, she was certainly neck-deep in smuggling.

"So," he asked Race, "how has the estate done in recent times?"

"Very well, my lord. Of course, it's suffering as everywhere with the end of the war and the fall in prices. . . ."

Con picked up a chair from by the wall and sat at the desk so the others could sit as they went through an efficient review.

Kerslake might be carrying two jobs, but he seemed to be doing this one well. If Race hadn't found any problems in the estate records, there weren't any to be found. Con asked a few questions and received sensible answers. When Kerslake had to look up some figures he seemed to know exactly where to find them.

After a while, Con held up his hand. "Enough. Everything seems to be in order, and de Vere will filter this all down to simplicity for me. Will you stay to dinner, Kerslake?"

There was a hesitation. "With pleasure, my lord. But you do know that my sister is your housekeeper?"

"Does that make a difference?"

"Some might think it would create awkwardness."

Con realized that the young man disapproved of Susan's being here, and was sending a subtle warning. It reminded him sharply of Mel Clyst's all those years ago.

That warning in the past had sparked trouble. What would this one ignite?

A touch of mischief.

"Then I invite her to dine with us, Kerslake," Con said. "She is hardly the common run of housekeeper, and she assures me that her duties don't include actually cooking." He was sure that Susan wouldn't like this move. And of course, it meant she couldn't hide from him, if that was what she planned. "Why don't you carry the message to her?"

Kerslake rose, but his eyes were steady. "Is this an invitation, my lord, or a command?"

"I'm an army man, Kerslake. If I give a command, you will be in no doubt about it."

When David Kerslake left, Con turned to Race and raised a brow.

"Honest, competent, thorough, and severely underemployed," Race said. "I'm not sure why he's still at the job."

Con sighed. "Smuggling, Race. Smuggling."

"It's that attractive to a man of such ability?"

"The best of games, and he's captain of the team. I'm sure of it. He is the old one's son, after all."

"What?"

Con realized that Race didn't know. "Both Susan Kerslake and her brother are the bastard children of Melchisedeck Clyst, tavern-keeper and the former Captain Drake—"

"Captain Drake?"

"The name taken by the smuggling master in these parts."

Race's brows rose. "But the manor?"

"Their mother is Miss Isabelle Kerslake of Kerslake Manor."

"The deuce you say. And they never even married?"

"It seemed unimportant to them. Their children were raised by the mother's relatives at the manor. Having the Kerslake name is useful, since everyone will look for Captain Drake to be a Clyst. I gather the Preventive officer is new. He might not even realize yet that David Kerslake is not a true son of the manor."

"What happened to the old Preventive officer?"

Con smiled. "You're beginning to get the feel of the place. Fell down a cliff one night. I gather the general belief is that he was pushed, and by one of the rival smuggling gangs hoping to make life difficult for the new Captain Drake."

"I'd think it would make life difficult for all of them, unless the old one was sharp and the new one blunt."

"Ah, but the key word there, Race, is *think*. Many smugglers don't often think. And no, Lieutenant Perch was middle-aged and obliging. Lieutenant Gifford is apparently young, clever, and ambitious."

"Idiots." He glanced at Con. "Kerslake doesn't like his sister being your housekeeper, does he? Strange that he permitted it."

"Do you think she is a woman who is allowed or not allowed?"

"I see you've found more amusement for me." Race tidied his papers and closed the ledgers. "First the anticipation. Will the lady attend the dinner or not? If she does, will she still hide in gray? Then the thrill of watching the byplay between you all . . . Does the formidable brother know about the past?"

"What past?" Con asked, but it was useless.

Race grinned. "Does the lady still desire? Does the lord? Will they speak their hearts? Will they be forbidden? It'll be as good as Drury Lane!"

Con swiped at him, and Race ducked, laughing like an imp from hell.

Susan was checking the preparations for the evening meal and preparing wines. As the Crag lacked a butler, the old earl's valet had done that job, and as she'd often dined with her employer she'd learned something about his cellars. She hoped the wines she'd chosen would be suitable. They were all French. All smuggled, of course, but she didn't think Con would raise the subject.

When arms snared her from behind, she almost dropped a bottle. For a startled, insane moment, she thought, *Con!* But then she turned to glare at her brother. "What do you think you're doing?"

"Scaring you."

She put down the bottle. "You do that all the time. Well, did you pass muster?"

"Of course. I'm a very good estate manager, and there isn't a great deal to do. For an earldom the property's quite small."

"So what are you doing now?"

"Playing messenger. You're commanded to dine with the lord and master."

Alarm shot through her. "Alone?"

His brows went up. "Of course not. Is he bothering you?"

"No." She tried to make it believable, which should be easy because he wasn't. Yet still she was bothered.

"I'm to eat with the earl and Mr. de Vere?" she asked, wondering what was behind the order.

"And me. Sorry if you don't like it, love. I probably caused it by saying it might be awkward to eat at the earl's table while my sister acted the servant. Come on. You used to dine with the old earl and me sometimes."

"I know, but I wore ordinary clothes when I was secretary. . . ." She gestured at her plain clothes.

"You must have something suitable up here."

Dress in a pretty gown for Con? A shiver of alarm collided with a stab of eagerness. The invitation was as good as a command. Or perhaps even a challenge.

So she would take it up boldly. Con had seen her only in schoolroom dresses, in men's clothing, and in housekeeper gray. Perhaps it was time to remind him that she was a lady.

"I do have a couple of finer dresses here," she said, adding with a smile, "mainly to stop Amelia from borrowing them."

"She's six inches shorter."

"But the same size around. She stitches up the hems but the gowns are never quite the same afterward."

"Can't you stop her?"

"Not when I'm up here and the gowns are down there. I brought my favorites to preserve them." She smiled. "She's welcome to borrow the rest."

She looked at the wine. "Would you help out by decanting the wine and spirits and taking them to the dining room?"

"Get him to hire a butler," he said rather haughtily, and she reflected again on how comfortable he was in his role as gentleman. Why couldn't she be the same?

He set to work, however, and Susan hurried off to her rooms, calling for Ada to help her.

She needed the maid's assistance with her fashionable corset. She could get into her working ones on her own, but the one she needed for her best dresses required back lacing. Once the corset was snug and supporting her breasts at a fashionable height, she had Ada help her on with her ivory muslin dress.

It had been through a number of changes over the years, but it was still her favorite. The upper layer, embroidered with white and just a touch of golden brown, veiled an underskirt which she had recently retrimmed with deep, pointed Vandyke lace—smuggled, of course. Since she'd cut eight inches off the underskirt to allow for the lace, it had created a delightful veiled effect around her ankles.

Was it too risqué? Too suggestive? Her only alternative other than her working clothes was a deep pink silk, which was much too grand, and a blue day dress with long sleeves and a high neck. Was there time to send down to the manor for her peach cambric? It was an altogether better choice for an informal dinner. . . .

But no, there wasn't time.

She plucked anxiously at the low front. It revealed a considerable amount of her breasts, which were thrust up by the corset. She'd worn the retrimmed dress a few months ago without a quiver of alarm—but then she hadn't been about to face Con.

As Ada worked on the pearl buttons Susan fought panic and pure excitement. The dress became her, she knew that.

It was suitable armor for a coming battle.

Had Con felt like this before battle—afraid, afire, eager?

Eager for what?

Her goal should be simple. Find the gold and leave. But another goal was stirring.

She couldn't recapture what they'd had all those years ago, and

Con had found happiness with another woman. She didn't want to leave Crag Wyvern, however, leave this area, without trying to get to know him a little, the man he had become.

And she ached to heal him. Whatever the causes of the darkness around him now, some were her fault. They had been friends once. Could she reach out now to help a friend?

She looked in the mirror and grimaced at herself. She might think noble thoughts, but in truth she was excited to be looking her best, to be able to show him that she was a woman able to attract men.

Attract men?

By the stars, she'd worn this dress six years ago when she'd let Lord Rivenham seduce her! It had been higher-necked then, sans lace, and with a trim of golden ribbons, but she'd been wearing this dress.

The next day, when he'd taken her for a drive to a conveniently private place, she'd been in pink jaconet, but the day before at the Bath assembly, it had been this dress.

Oh, what folly that had been.

Ada finished with the tiny buttons, and Susan sat so the maid could brush out her hair. She couldn't stop dwelling on past follies.

She'd been in Bath with her aunt and cousins. Her aunt had been advised to take the waters, and she'd taken her two oldest girls, as she always called them, along to enjoy society there. Cecilia, at twenty-one, had met her husband in Bath. Susan, at twenty, had seized an opportunity to try to drive Con Somerford from her mind and heart.

It hadn't been frightening or unpleasant. Lord Rivenham had been some years older, married, and a known rake. He was not an honorable man, but skilled. He'd even brought a sponge soaked in vinegar and shown her how to insert it.

It had all been very interesting, especially the contrast between Con's ignorant enthusiasm and Rivenham's expertise. It hadn't been an improvement, however, except in the simplest mechanical sense.

When they were leaving the rooms, strangely back to normal after that brief tumult, he'd asked, "Get what you wanted, pet?"

She could remember the moment as if someone had pinned it in a frame for eternity. Her face had burned, but she'd met his curious, cynical eyes and said, "Yes, thank you."

He'd laughed. "I don't suppose I'll ever know what brought you here today, but I hope you find the man you want for more than an afternoon."

She hadn't exactly lied to him. She'd wanted to wipe Con from her mind, from her skin, and she'd failed at that. But she had gained in knowledge, and not just about preventing babies.

This matter between men and women could simply be an act, but it wasn't always. What had happened between her and Con had been both less and more. It had been different because of the feelings involved. It hadn't caused the feelings; the feelings had caused the effect.

Therefore, she had set herself to fall in love. Cecilia and even young Amelia and most of the young women she knew seemed to find it easy to fall into love with handsome gentlemen and dashing soldiers. And just as easy to fall out again.

So she stirred herself into tremulous excitement about Captain Jermyn Lavalle in his dashing Hussar uniform. When she'd let him make fumbling, hasty, unsatisfying love to her in the gazebo of his colonel's country villa, however, she'd been used without care or even appreciation.

Too proud to protest, or scream, or weep, she'd known she was a mere physical convenience to him, and a trophy as well. She'd parted from him, chin high, terrified that he'd boast of it to his fellow officers, and knowing she was on a course to insane disaster.

At least Con wasn't a Hussar. She remembered thinking that, as if it were the crucial point.

The encounter with Lavalle had not made a scrap of difference to the secrets of her heart, but it had changed her behavior. She'd recognized at last that life would not be forced into the channels of her choosing, but must be lived with honor as it came.

Play the hand that was dealt her, as apparently Mel Clyst had put it. She wished she'd known her father better.

She'd spitefully wished Captain Lavalle dead in his first battle, but she'd overcome that too, and even managed to be glad when she saw notice later of his making major. She'd prayed, however, that their paths would never cross again, and that he would keep their assignation secret.

As Ada began to sweep her hair up, Susan adjusted the low bodice of her gown. At least she hadn't been wearing this dress with Lavalle. He'd thrown up the skirts of a pink dress trimmed with rosebuds. Immediately afterward she'd spilled blackberry cordial down it so it would have to be thrown out.

Ada screwed the hair up into a knot and jabbed in pins. Susan winced. Ada was no lady's maid, and Mrs. Gorland would be fuming that she wasn't out in the kitchen. In this gown, however, Susan couldn't reach up to arrange her hair for herself. In truth, fashion for women could be a kind of prison, but then, some men's tight jackets and high shirt points trapped them too.

Not Con, unless he dressed very differently for fashionable affairs.

Finished at last, Ada added a slender bandeau decorated with golden brown ribbon and tiny silk rosebuds. Susan thanked her and sent her back to her work, then put on her pearl earrings and necklace.

The pearls had been a gift from her father. She'd forgotten that. They'd been sent to her just before she was to make that trip to Bath. David had received a handsome set of pistols on his twenty-first birthday.

She touched the large pearl that hung in the center of a cluster in the front, thinking of David's words about Mel Clyst. Bitter because of her mother, she'd made no attempt to know her father. Maybe he had kept his distance because he'd seen his children bettering themselves through Lady Belle's family.

But why in heaven's name hadn't he married Lady Belle? The union would still have been a scandal, but not so much of one if it had been blessed. Had it simply been so that his children would be Kerslakes rather than Clysts?

She sighed and put the matter aside. If he'd meant well, it was far too late to acknowledge it now. It was probably too late for everything. The past happened. It set like concrete and must be lived with.

She stood and slipped on the silk slippers that went with the gown, raising her foot to the chair to tie the golden brown ribbons, thinking again of veiled ankles.

Would Con notice? Would he care?

She pulled on long gloves, draped a gauzy scarf over her arms, then reviewed herself again.

Elegant and ladylike. Not a bit like the housekeeper, or like the young girl scampering over the rocks and shore. Shorter tendrils of hair were already escaping around her face, however. She reached to repin them and found she couldn't. After a moment she decided the effect was becoming—in a wanton kind of way.

So be it. In fact, she'd go further.

She took a pot of rouge out of a drawer and subtly deepened the color of her lips, then added a touch on her cheeks. There. That completed the effect. With a laugh she thought of the warrior tribes of Africa and America who went into battle with their faces painted. Apparently it was supposed to frighten the enemy.

She hoped it made her dragon shake in his shoes.

❧ 12 ❧

Dᴀᴠɪᴅ ᴡᴀs waiting for her in the kitchen, chatting to the servants. "Lovely, but a little grand, isn't it?"

"I don't have anything in between," she said, linking her arm with his.

As they walked along the corridor he said, "You're not thinking of trying to marry him, are you?"

She wondered whether rouge hid or enhanced a blush. "Of course not. Why would you think that?"

"I can't imagine," he said dryly. "What are you up to? I always thought you might have fallen a little in love with him that time. You were strange for a while afterward."

"I didn't think you noticed."

"Of course I noticed. I don't want you hurt, love."

She tried to find a joke, to find any response that made sense, but then said, "I don't want to talk about it."

"As bad as that, is it?"

They'd taken the outer corridor toward the dining room. She stopped and faced him. "Perhaps there was a bit of love, but it was a long time ago and we were very young. We didn't part on good terms, though, and this invitation is a kind of challenge."

"What caused the falling-out?"

"None of your business."

"In other words, you were in the wrong. Would it be asking too much for you to say you're sorry?"

The idea appalled her. "After eleven years? What is all this to you anyway? Not still hoping I can turn him to your cause? Believe me, David, I can't apologize. It wouldn't help."

"As bad as that, is it?" He tucked her arm back through his. "Why do I feel you're ready for battle? Honey would serve the cause better than vinegar."

It was almost a command, and she narrowed her eyes. "Being Captain Drake is going to your head."

"Being Captain Drake is a real and demanding responsibility. I don't want things snarled by some petty disagreement between you and the earl."

"Petty!"

"You admit there's a disagreement."

"I admitted that we parted on bad terms. I will be civil as long as he is."

"I'm sure he will be," he said with confidence that made her want to throw something at him. "Come on, then. Let's advance together."

Con and de Vere were in the drawing room, and to Susan, walking into that conventional room seemed shockingly like walking into another world. The two men had both changed, but not into formal evening wear, probably because David would still be in day clothes. She was slightly overdressed, but she'd known she would be.

She noted Con's sharp attention before he looked away, however, and it was reward enough.

One glance at Susan was almost enough to knock Con off his feet. This was a Susan he'd never seen before—the beautiful, elegant lady. But at the same time it was the Susan he'd expected to see here. There was no clear connection to the coltish girl in rumpled schoolroom clothes, and yet the essence was the same, and it ignited the same urgent response.

He'd wondered if she planned to seduce him again, and now he saw that she did. He tried to be outraged, but something inside growled like a hungry tiger.

He managed a calm smile as he greeted her. "Mrs. Kerslake, I'm pleased you could join us." He gave thanks for the *Mrs.*, which reminded him of the Susan in gray and white, and set her slightly among the married.

However, Kerslake said, "I think my sister should be Miss Kerslake for this occasion, my lord."

Susan seemed as startled as he was. "David, that's not necessary."

"I think it is."

It was as if Kerslake had read his thoughts. Or perhaps he was an ally in the planned seduction. Con's sense and senses steadied. He would regard their hopeless efforts as an amusing show.

"Of course. Miss Kerslake, may I offer you sherry?"

There were no servants in attendance in the room, so he poured the wine himself. As he passed it over, their fingers brushed, and it took all his discipline not to start. It was like touching hot iron.

Even with control, he'd come close to knocking her wine down her lovely dress. Her lovely dress that revealed far too much of her round breasts, much fuller now than they'd been back then . . .

He snared his wits and stepped back. "If I am to be here for any length of time, it will be necessary to hire a footman. To serve wine, among other things."

He saw her eyes flicker to his with understanding, and her cheeks color. But then he suspected a touch of the rouge pot on those cheeks. She'd definitely come here all guns to the ready.

"And a butler, my lord," Kerslake said. "My sister had to recruit me to wine duty."

"My apologies," Con said dryly. "But in the chaos left by my predecessor, we all have to make do. It would seem excessive to engage a butler when I will rarely be here."

"I think the ladies of the area hope to persuade you to stay, my lord."

"Really?" Con shot Susan a look.

Her color deepened, but she was otherwise composed as she said, "Everyone hopes you will stay, my lord."

"Even the smugglers?" he asked.

He hoped Kerslake would have to answer, but Susan's brother looked admirably as if smuggling were a matter of scant interest. It was Susan who said, "That rather depends on your attitude to the Freetrade, my lord."

"And what is your attitude, Miss Kerslake?"

Her look told him that she thought that an unfair blow. "I cannot approve of any illegality, my lord, but in truth, the taxes levied by London are criminal themselves. And of course, I am the daughter of a man transported for smuggling."

A bold attack. A warmth that was almost tenderness spread through him. She was as brave and direct as she'd always been.

He turned to Kerslake. "And you are his son, Kerslake. Does the association cause you much trouble?"

"Very little, my lord. And of course he is no longer here."

There was a spark of mischievous humor in the young man's eyes that he'd do well to conquer. It cracked his otherwise excellent act.

"So there must be a new Captain Drake, I assume," Con said.

But Race joined the conversation then. "Captain Drake. Called after Sir Francis Drake?" Eyes bright and alert, he was, as he'd promised, acting like an audience at an enjoyable play.

No, he'd said *farce.*

Con let the silence ride, and it was Kerslake in the end who said, "Yes, but also from the associations with dragons here. A drake is another name for dragon, of course, as is wyvern."

"A two-legged winged dragon who eats children," Con contributed. "The earls of Wyvern do seem to have sealed their fate, don't they?"

"We can only hope it is not unfixably attached to the title, my lord," Kerslake said smoothly, then added to Race, "Have you visited Dragon's Cove yet? A guide to the area described it as a quaint fishing village. . . ."

Con watched with admiration as Susan's brother steered the conversation to local points of interest and other innocuous subjects. A young man of remarkable talents.

Susan smiled at David's comment, but her mind was buzzing with the effect of Con. That one, sizzling look had speeded her pulse, had alerted her to him in a way she'd not experienced before.

She watched him turn, and her breath shortened. It was such an elegantly powerful movement. He was by the fireplace, and his strong hand was framed for a moment, brown against white marble, stunningly beautiful despite the white slashes of minor scars.

When he'd smiled at David's comment, it had been a frank, open smile unlike any he'd given her here, though it recalled smiles of the past. If only he would smile like that for her again.

This was no good. She joined in the talk of local points of interest, and didn't let herself look at Con at all, but he still dominated her mind.

Her reaction was simply physical, but she'd felt nothing like it for eleven years. It had its own power, its own imperative. She was struggling to converse coherently.

Could she bear to part from Con without tasting this desire between two mature people with time and freedom to explore it . . . ?

A sip of wine almost went astray because of her unsteady hand. Was she thinking of trying to wipe away Lord Rivenham and Captain Lavalle in Con's bed?

Oh, no. There be dragons, indeed.

When Race and Kerslake fell into hunting talk, Con seized the opportunity to talk to Susan. "Your brother seems to be an excellent young man. De Vere is impressed with his administrative capabilities."

"He's very clever, yes." She was sipping her wine and looking at her brother, not at him.

"Is he moving with a limp now and then? A permanent affliction?"

She hesitated a second too long, but that was the only betrayal. "I gather he was involved in some sort of fight last night. Over a woman."

"Did he win?"

"I have no idea."

"I suppose it's not the sort of thing a brother tells his older sister. Do you mind him being protective of you?"

Her eyes met his then, a little startled. That he'd understand her impatience with it?

"It is the way of the world, my lord. But it's one reason I prefer to have employment."

"How very American." At her questioning look, he said, "The lure of independence. So, what will you do when you leave your position here, Miss Kerslake?"

"I have not yet decided, my lord." She met his eyes. "What is your opinion of the American states, my lord? Do you think they can continue to prosper?"

Thus she steered talk firmly toward different forms of government, leaving Con puzzled. He'd given her an opening and there'd been not a trace of flirtation in her.

Did she think her lovely and arousing appearance would do the work for her? Again?

Ah, no. He had to have learned better than that.

When Diddy came to announce that dinner was ready, Susan gave earnest thanks and took Con's arm to lead the way to the dining room. It had been rarely used in recent years, however, and despite polish and flowers had that strange aridity of an abandoned place.

The massive, dark oak furniture gave it a somber atmosphere even though she'd ordered the table reduced to its smallest size, and candles lit. Even the chairs were huge and carved, and upholstered on arms and seats with red velvet.

As they all sat, she felt as if they were a body of judges gathered to consider the case of the meal. As with all the other ground-floor rooms, glass-paned doors opened into the courtyard, but they were closed. It wasn't yet dark outside, but the two branches of candles created intimate ovals of light, intensifying the sense of a secret meeting.

She almost expected Con on her left to bang a gavel and launch an accusation against David for being Captain Drake.

Instead, Jane came in with the soups and placed them on the table. Susan was distracted for a moment by watching to see that the service was correct, and then by tasting her soup to see that it was good. Then she made herself put that aside. She was Miss Kerslake tonight, not the housekeeper, and she had other need of her wits.

David had adroitly engaged Con in talk about his home in Sussex, and Susan listened as best she could, remembering the fondness he'd shared for it in the past. She was pleased that affection lived on. He had a home he loved, and a woman he loved too. It gave her genuine pleasure.

Courtesy, however, demanded that she pay attention to de Vere on her right. "I hope you are enjoying your visit to Crag Wyvern, sir."

"Now, now, dear lady. You are Miss Kerslake, a guest here."

It was a mild rebuke, or perhaps just a reminder. More likely mischief, in fact.

She sipped some more soup. "Then I am two people in one, Mr. de Vere. I don't think anyone can put aside a part of themselves at their convenience."

"Can't we? Sometimes there are parts we'd like to put aside."

And that was true. "Then perhaps it can be done with strict effort." She looked at him. "You, Mr. de Vere, are also a Janus. One face is the idle, laughing man, but when it comes to paperwork you show a more serious aspect."

"Not a bit of it. Paperwork has me giggling with glee. There is something fascinating about it, don't you think? Especially confused accounts. Each item provides a piece of a mysterious picture."

"A picture of Crag Wyvern? Hardly worth your effort."

"A picture is a picture, and sometimes we piece one together for amusement. Have you seen such things? Pointless in a way to cut a picture up so that someone else can put it together, but engaging all the same. This picture is part of Wyvern's life, and that interests me. As do you, Miss Kerslake."

"I?" she asked, a sudden tension in her belly.

"You. You are a striking woman. I pointed out to Wyvern that you resemble a Renaissance angel."

She looked at him, tempted to laugh. "And what did he say to that?"

"He recognized the truth, of course. Too beautiful to be a man. Too strongly featured to be a beautiful woman . . ."

Jane came to remove her soup plate, which gave her time to think. "I could take that as an insult, Mr. de Vere."

"Now, would I be foolish enough to insult you with two ardent defenders to hand? Your looks are very attractive."

His words gave her an excuse to look away, at Con and David talking together as if they were just two gentlemen. "*Two* ardent defenders?"

"Definitely. So I suspect it would not be wise to set up a flirtation with you."

She looked back. "But why be wise, sir? I don't have much opportunity for flirtation these days." She leaned her elbow on the table and put her chin on her hand to gaze at him. "And you know, you have much of the look of an angel yourself."

A genuine smile fought to be free. It was so long since she'd played this game.

"Too beautiful to be a man?" he murmured, both wariness and amusement sparking in his blue eyes.

"But very attractive, even so."

His lips twitched. "And what, I wonder, do two fine angels do together in private moments? Shall we find out, Miss Kerslake?"

Slowly she lowered her arm and sat straight. She could not afford even the most playful entanglement. "It would doubtless not be worth the bother, sir. I assume angels pray."

"Or dance on the head of a pin. Easy to fall, wouldn't you say?"

She turned aside in an instinctive retreat, and found herself looking at Con, who had probably heard every word. The conversation switched so that she was talking to him.

"De Vere isn't the earl, you know," he said pleasantly, but with cool eyes.

"Goodness, I must have been confused for a moment."

His smile widened as his eyes chilled. "He is heir to a pleasant estate in Derbyshire, however, unless his disapproving father disinherits him. Worth your effort, perhaps, if you're not absolutely set on Wyvern."

Now she was smiling as falsely as he was, and praying that the other two men weren't listening. "Do I have a chance at Wyvern?"

He froze, looking at her, not smiling at all, and she wondered why she'd fallen into such a destructive exchange.

"Play your hand, Susan, and find out."

It was a challenge. A challenge to seduce him again in case he could be swayed? Surely he knew she would not do that.

No, perhaps he didn't . . .

She wanted desperately to speak to him directly, to talk about the past, to try to recapture the friendship and trust they'd once had. He was still angry and distrustful, however, and with reason, and she couldn't imagine how to change that.

Not with words, that was sure.

"And you, my lord," she said, directing most of her attention to her plate, "what ambitions do you have?"

"Ambitions," he repeated, in the same polite tone. "I am ambitious for peace, Miss Kerslake. International peace, and personal peace. For simple country days, and comfort for those I love."

She looked back at him, relieved that they'd found a safe subject. "Your mother and sisters."

"And Lady Anne."

Her throat tightened. She was trying to accept the idea of his chosen beloved, but it was hard. She prayed that the hesitation of her fork had not been visible, but the delicious lobster became like clay in her mouth, heavy and liable to choke her.

She chewed slowly to steal time, then made herself swallow. There was nothing between them anymore, so why did the reminder that he was engaged to marry create a painful lump in her chest?

She took a sip of wine. "Will your future wife like Crag Wyvern?" It sounded reasonably normal to her ears.

"No. We are remarkably in tune, Lady Anne and I."

"I see now why you do not plan to live here, my lord." She felt as if she'd reached solid ground again after wallowing in a swamp. It was not ground she'd have chosen, but it was solid.

"Remember, I do not want to live here either."

He was hammering the fact home, and she realized why. He was telling her that even if she somehow inveigled him into marriage she would still not catch the prize he thought she wanted.

Oh, Con, can we not do better than this?

She tried. "I do not like Crag Wyvern either, my lord," she said plainly. "Perhaps Lady Anne and I will find ourselves in tune, if she ever does visit here."

"Unlikely."

She raised a brow.

"You are the housekeeper, Mrs. Kerslake. You and my wife would be unlikely to discuss such matters."

It was so deliberately discourteous that Susan simply stared at him, and after a moment he looked away. That gave her a chance to squeeze her lips together to fight back tears.

Only pain would make Con into this hurtful man, and some of the pain—most of it?—was her fault.

She caught de Vere's all too perceptive eye on her, but that at least gave her an excuse to address a remark to him and switch the pattern of the conversation. She managed to force a bit more of her dinner down.

She had never expected this meal to be enjoyable, but she hadn't expected torture. Despite David and a stranger as safeguards, she felt as if she were being forced to walk on broken glass.

It was David who found a topic for four-sided conversation—a discussion of the role the newspapers should play in the setting of public policy. None of them had strong political leanings, so they could debate it warmly without friction. She could have kissed him. She didn't know whether he'd been aware of what was going on or not, but she was certainly coming to appreciate that he was a person well able to deal with the world, and not her troublesome little brother anymore.

Another end. A good one, but an end. Except possibly in the matter of the gold, David didn't need her anymore. It hurt a little, but it freed her. She could leave, and if Con was going to bring his bride here, even for the briefest visit, she would make sure to be elsewhere by then.

She'd never thought Con's marriage would hurt so much. She'd never realized how deeply she still cared.

Was there anything she could do to try to reclaim the treasure she had carelessly thrown away?

No. She must not think that way.

Though she was the only lady, she assumed she should behave in the conventional way and was glad of the chance to escape. At the earliest excusable moment she rose to leave the gentlemen.

All the men rose too, but Con said, "I don't think any of us wishes the freedom to get drunk and tell risqué stories, Miss Kerslake. I plan to move into the courtyard to enjoy port and brandy in the evening air. Please join us."

There was a distinct edge of command to it.

So she was not to escape so easily. Very well. She would advance with bravado. "With pleasure, my lord. I enjoy a good brandy."

"And I'm sure the brandy here is very good."

He flicked a glance at David, who responded with a bland smile, but she was suddenly sure that Con had guessed. He knew David was Mel Clyst's son, after all.

Would he move against David as a form of revenge? Though it seemed alien to the Con in her heart, she sensed that this man held darkness enough to do it.

Con turned toward the doors into the garden, putting a hand

on his chair back for a moment. Perhaps he had drunk a little more than he should have. How many bottles of wine had been served? She couldn't be sure, nor how much of it he had drunk, but she prayed he wasn't intoxicated. That tipped many a man—or woman—into doing and saying things they otherwise would not.

He flung open the doors into the courtyard. The enclosing walls cast shadows, but it was not yet dark. "Bring the decanters and glasses," he said to no one in particular, and strolled out along one of the stone paths toward the central fountain.

Susan noted that someone had turned on the water, probably trying to do their best for the new earl. Despite the unpleasant design of the fountain, the gentle splashing was soothing. She felt a desperate need for something soothing.

Susan looked back, but David said, "Go on. De Vere and I will play servant this time. Would you rather have tea?"

She made a lightning calculation. Tea would be so blessedly normal, but she knew she'd feel absurd attempting to preside over a tea table out beside the lewd fountain.

"I will drink brandy with the rest of you," she said, and followed, but slowly. She had no intention of having a tête-à-tête with Con by the fountain.

She also had no intention of showing how uneasy all this was making her. She'd drink her brandy, which she did enjoy, and then she'd politely say good night. And nothing short of a direct order would stop her from finding her rooms and staying in them.

Tomorrow, she resolved, pausing to inhale the perfume of some hyacinth, she would begin her retreat. There was nothing here for her or Con but pain. He was tied here for life, so it was for her to leave.

It wouldn't be hard to find someone to fill in as housekeeper, and in her remaining days she would conduct a thorough, clear-headed search for secret rooms, compartments, or other hidey-holes for the gold. If only she'd done that sooner, but she'd been so sure that the earl would have stashed the gold carelessly, and for safety's sake, she hadn't wanted even the servants to know when she took it. Now, with Con here, it was more dangerous, but she would do it. Even if she didn't find the money, she needed to know that she had done her best.

"Another insect?"

She started, and looked up to see that Con had walked back to her side.

❧ 13 ❧

"INSECT?" SUSAN asked.

"Wasn't that what you paused to study this morning?" Perhaps she, too, had drunk too much. It took her a moment to realize what he meant, and then she became freshly aware of him studying her from his bedroom window, of him being naked from the hips up—and invisibly, from the hips down.

Despite his clothes, her mind filled with the image of his splendid torso, and the dragon that apparently marred it.

She gathered her wits. "Oh, yes. But not now. Now I am simply enjoying the scent of the wallflowers."

She saw him inhale. "So English. Spain and Portugal are full of smells, and some of them are even pleasant. But not like the scents of an English garden."

It was so honest, so ordinary, so tender even, that she breathed it in as she had the perfume, holding on to the moment as if she could stop time. She didn't even dare to look back to see what had happened to David and de Vere.

Then she realized she had to say something. The only thing that occurred to her was prosaic. "The garden needs a gardener. It was Mrs. Lane's pride and joy. I've done my best, but I do not particularly have the gift for it."

"You're not a gardener?"

"No."

Did he feel it as meaningfully as she did, that he didn't know, and that he'd asked?

"Are you?" she asked.

"God, no. Though I appreciate a wholesome garden when I find one. Imagine Crag Wyvern without this."

He turned to look around, and she did too, seeing it with different eyes. It was quiet in the failing light, but during the day the garden buzzed with insects for which this was their entire world. Even the birds didn't seem to leave it. A world, a wholesome world, within the Crag. Without it, the place would truly be dead and rotten.

There was even the musical splash of the fountain to add to the magic.

He walked toward it and she followed, not so nervous now. A glance showed David and de Vere coming, decanters and glasses in hand, talking animatedly about something.

Almost a normal moment.

In Crag Wyvern.

Astonishing.

Then she almost bumped into Con because he'd stopped dead.

"I want this removed," he said.

She followed his gaze. "The fountain?"

"I want the figures out of here. Tomorrow." His eyes turned savagely to hers. "If you don't see why, Susan, you have been eaten whole by the dragon."

Shaking under that attack, she looked at the fountain, really looked at it. The maiden writhed beneath the dragon as always. The beast pinned her arms with its claws and spread her legs with its lower body.

She thought it horrid, but she'd learned to ignore it. The water was rarely turned on, however, because then the cistern in the roof had to be refilled. When it had been gushing water she hadn't looked at it clearly.

Now, however, she did.

The dragon's huge phallus spewed over the captive bride, some liquid filling her screaming mouth, more pouring off her outstretched, piteous hands.

After a horrified moment, she turned away. "Yes. Yes, of course."

She still heard the music of the water, but now the image made it foul.

He was right. The garden was the healing heart of Crag Wyvern, but by creating the dragon's bride fountain, the mad earl had introduced a blight.

"I don't know how it's constructed," she said, "but I'll find out what needs to be done to remove it. Tomorrow."

"I'm sorry," he said in very different voice.

She looked and saw a different man, less dark, less hard, closer surely to the Con she remembered.

"Sorry?" she asked, wondering if he was going to apologize for some of the darts he'd thrown at her tonight.

"You aren't my housekeeper at the moment, are you? I shouldn't be giving you orders."

She suppressed a sigh. "It doesn't matter, my lord. It should be done."

Her brother and de Vere were close, but Con moved away from the fountain. "There are benches beneath the lime tree, I think. We'll sit there."

David flashed her a look that suggested that he thought this earl was as mad as the rest of them, but Susan understood. Having been alerted to the abhorrence of that fountain, she didn't want to sit near it either.

There were two benches, and she ended up sitting beside David, while Con and de Vere sat on the other. She rather thought David had engaged in some clever maneuvering to achieve that, and she wondered what he was seeing here. As she warmed her cognac, the finest that the Freetrade had to offer, she wished this were a more wholesome evening.

The idea of sitting in a tranquil evening garden with Con and friends was something she had never dreamed of, and even in this flawed state it was sweet enough for tears.

"Miss Kerslake," de Vere said, "do you know what was here before this garden?"

She took a small sip of her brandy. "I'm not sure, sir. The original plans for Crag Wyvern show a garden here, but I've heard that before Mrs. Lane took care of it, it was in sorry shape. At one point it was all grassed to make a tennis court."

De Vere looked around. "And the windows survived?"

"I don't think so. Originally the lower windows were stained glass. There's a painting in one of the corridors."

De Vere shook his head. "Mad. And through the ages too."

"No one's denying it, Race," Con said.

"If I were you, I'd disown the lot of them."

Con took a mouthful of the brandy. "Ah, but that's the burden of the aristocracy. We can't disown our ancestors and keep the spoils." He turned to Susan. "Are there records of the first earl, Miss Kerslake? I would be interested to know more about the story of the dragon."

"I don't know, my lord. There's a room in the cellars full of boxes of ledgers and documents."

De Vere gave a faint moan, and surprisingly, Con laughed in seemingly true humor. "You are not getting a sniff of them until you've dealt with current matters. And in fact, I have engaged the curate to deal with the books. He might be willing to include archives."

"Unfair. Unfair."

"We'll probably not be here long enough to make any order of them anyway."

"I could stay," de Vere said, and flickered a smiling look at Susan.

That was unwise. She felt Con's cold disapproval like a lance. It seared through his words as he said, "You are my secretary, Race. Where I go, you go."

"Sounds more like a damn wife to me."

"For that, you lack certain essential qualifications."

De Vere didn't seem daunted by the sharp edge in his employer's voice. In fact he smiled in a deliberately winsome way. "Miss Kerslake said I was angelic."

Con looked across the gathering shadows at Susan. "Don't forget, Miss Kerslake, Lucifer is an angel too."

They were both speaking laconically, lounging at either end of the bench, but Susan wanted to scream at them to stop it, to stop sliding knife-edged comments through the conversation.

She drained her glass of brandy and stood. "I believe it is time I retired, my lord, gentlemen."

David stood too. "And I must return to the manor. Thank you, my lord, for an excellent dinner."

They went through the courtesies, but all the time Susan felt weighed down by Con's attention, quivering with the fear that he would command her to stay. There surely was nothing to fear, but here in the darkening garden at the heart of Crag Wyvern, she was afraid.

He didn't stop her, and she walked away with David, making herself not rush. They reentered the house through the dining room, and Susan was pleased to see that the servants had quietly cleared the table while they were outside. They had even restored the table to the usual seating for eight, which better suited the proportions of the room.

As they entered the corridor, David said, "De Vere is a damn strange secretary."

"I think he's more of a friend."

"A damn strange friend too. Are you all right up here with them?"

She knew that if he suspected any awkwardness he would want her to leave immediately. She could deal with awkwardness, and it would become nothing more than that.

"Of course I'm all right." But she added, "The earl is troubled. I think it's something from the war, which is not surprising. Perhaps de Vere suffers in the same way but handles it by creating mischief. It's not likely to affect me, however."

"If you're sure. But if you ask me, the mad blood runs in both sides of the family."

"That could be true. . . ." Yet she'd seen no sign of imbalance in Con all those years ago. He'd been the sanest, most even-tempered person she'd ever known.

They parted with a kiss in the great hall, and Susan went to the kitchen area to compliment the staff. She was still there when the bell rang. She told Diddy to go and see what the earl wanted. "Probably more brandy," Susan muttered, but she'd be happy enough if he drank himself into a stupor.

Diddy came back. "He wants to speak to you, Mrs. Kerslake. He's in the dining room."

Susan was strongly tempted not to go, but how would that look before the servants? The rest of the servants. And it wasn't as if this were a medieval castle and the earl had droit du seigneur or anything so absurd. Nor was she an unprotected waif. If she couldn't defend herself, she had a family of men ready to do so, or to avenge any wrong.

He must know that.

If he was sane.

If he wasn't dangerously drunk.

She hesitated, wondering if there was time to change into the defense of her housekeeper's clothes, but there wasn't.

She left the kitchen, but as she did so she said, "If I scream, come and rescue me."

She made it light, but she knew the women would do it. They'd lived with one mad Earl of Wyvern already.

She entered the garden a different way. With darkness almost complete the lamps created pools of light and shadowed corners. In the heart of the shadows the fountain still played.

The bride still drowned.

She detoured to the concealed wheel valve, and switched the water off.

Splash diminished into trickles, and then to peaceful silence. Susan walked through it toward the shining rectangle of the dining room doors, where Con stood waiting. Alone.

She hesitated out in the dark, but she would not be afraid. To be truly afraid of Con would be the final denial of all that had once existed between them.

She stepped into the room. "My lord? You needed something?"

He was blank, impossible to read. She wished the wide table stood between them, but he had waited for her near the doors. She wished she'd come in from the corridor.

She edged a little farther into the room to put more distance between them, trying not to make it look like a retreat. She was stopped by the table. To work her way around it would be ridiculous.

"In Spain, I almost raped a woman," he said.

She looked at him, seeking the meaning beneath the words and finding it. "That's why the fountain offends you?"

"That's probably why I am more sensitive to it than you. I regret implying that you are uncaring."

A flutter of something started within. Not hope, no. That would be foolish. But . . . pleasure. Pleasure that he could say that to her. That he wanted to and felt free to.

"Not uncaring, no. But I am callused," she said. "Crag Wyvern does that. The constant abrasion of the wicked and the bizarre makes us insensitive after a while."

"Like war. The constant abrasion of violence, suffering, and death. I tried once to peel away the calluses. It was a mistake."

She wasn't sure what had caused this moment of openness, but it was a treasure to savor. She leaned back slightly against the table between two chairs. "Why was it a mistake?"

As if mirroring her, he leaned back too, against the doorjamb. "Because I had to go back to war. Waterloo. Good calluses take time to build. Or restore."

Clearly he needed to talk and he'd chosen her to talk to. Privately, she gave thanks, but she simply said, "What happened?"

He shrugged. "We won. We lost. I mean, we lost too many good men. Ten thousand of them. I suppose it was worth it, but sometimes it's hard to see why. If they'd dealt with Napoleon properly the first time . . ."

He shrugged again.

"You must have lost many friends there." She hesitated, wondering whether mentioning his closest friends, something shared in the past, would be a mistake. But she did it. "The other two Georges? The Rogues?"

He did look startled—perhaps it was a flinch—but he answered. "One of the Rogues. Lord Darius Debenham."

She ached for him, but treasured the moment. "One of the Duke of Yeovil's sons. I heard of his loss. I'm sorry."

He said nothing more, and she sensed that this connection, whatever it had been, was fading. She'd recapture it if she could, but had no idea how. They stood in silence for a moment or two, and then he said, "What happened eleven years ago, Susan?"

The suddenness of it stole words. Eventually she said, "You know what happened, Con."

Did he think she would deny it? Try to claim it had been some huge mistake?

"I suppose I do. You made your ambitions clear enough. Did you try to marry Fred?"

She was poised on a razor edge. Did she admit that she'd never felt the same way toward any other man, that she'd bitterly regretted what she had done? Did she protect her pride with lies?

She could summon the courage to go only halfway. "Aunt Miriam had hopes. I suppose we all tried a bit, but my heart wasn't in it."

Do you hear what I'm saying Con? Do you care?

His eyes were steady, his face without any readable expression. "And your heart was in it with me?"

In the face of that daunting blankness, she could not make the ultimate surrender.

And of course he didn't care.

He had Lady Anne.

"Why do you ask, Con? It was a long time ago, and you are to marry soon."

His long lashes blinked over silvery eyes. "Ah, yes. Lady Anne. She has nothing to do with the past."

"She makes the past irrelevant."

He pushed off from the doorjamb and moved a step closer. "The past is never irrelevant, even if we wish it were. I wonder why you haven't married. If you are telling the truth and don't want the Crag anymore."

Through a tightening throat she said, "I am telling the truth."

The atmosphere had changed. He was still unreadable, but danger swirled with the candle smoke in the air. She'd told David she was in no danger here, and she'd thought it was true. Perhaps there were things men could sense that women couldn't.

"So," he asked, "why haven't you married?"

He was demanding surrender and offering her nothing in exchange. "The bastard child of a tavernkeeper does not receive many worthy offers."

"You said Mel Clyst provided you with a dowry."

"I have no intention of being married for my money."

"Just as I have no intention of being married for my earldom. But you do have money?"

She hesitated. Mel had bought property for her, but she'd poured all her recent income from it into supporting the Horde. She didn't want to tell Con that, however, and she would be repaid.

"Yes," she said. "I have money."

"Then why are you playing housekeeper?"

She realized too late that he'd come closer and closer until she was trapped against the table between two solid oak chairs with no way to escape short of pushing him out of the way.

Would he move if she pushed?

She didn't think so.

Heart pounding, she stood up straight. "I'm not playing. I work for my wages."

He put a hand on the back of each imprisoning chair, caging her. She gripped the table behind for strength. She didn't fear that he would hurt her. She feared that he would kiss her, and by kissing her, conquer her entirely. . . .

"What happened eleven years ago?" he asked again, his eyes dark now, the gray only a rim around his pupils. At least one of the candles behind her must be guttering, because it played erratic light over his somber face, creating saints and devils in turn.

"What do you mean? What do you want to know?"

He leaned a little closer. "When we kissed that day in Irish Cove, was it as much a miracle to you as it was to me? Or was it simply an opportunity?"

She couldn't deny him this. "It was a miracle," she whispered.

"Ah." He lowered his lips and she didn't try to escape, but it wasn't the fierce, experienced kiss she'd expected. It was the same tentative tasting she remembered. As hesitant. As wary.

As miraculous.

She sank her hips back against the table for support, clutching it for dear life as his lips pressed innocently against hers.

He licked her cheek and her eyes flew open.

She realized that tears were leaking. He straightened, and so did she. She brushed away the other betraying tears with her hands.

"Memories?" he asked. "Or regrets? Whichever, Susan, it's a damned shame you did what you did in Irish Cove."

He turned and walked out of the room, out into the silent garden. After a moment, Susan found the strength in her legs to leave by the corridor door and make it to the sanctuary of her rooms.

Tears welled up.

She never cried!

But the tears broke free and she collapsed into a chair to weep for what she had done to a fifteen-year-old boy in love, and for the living pain it had created. She wept for the man he had become and the loss of the man he could have been.

But she also wept for the loss of the man he was, a loss stated by those flat words. *It's a damned shame you did what you did.*

Because it said clearly: *Abandon hope. The damage done is irreparable.*

Con paused by the evil fountain, glad at least that the water was turned off, though it left the enclosed garden eerily quiet. The faint light of the two distant lamps still glimmered on the splayed legs and arms of the woman pinned by pitiless claws. Her dark mouth looked like a scream.

If he thought it possible, he'd tear it apart now with his bare hands. It would be gone tommorow. If Susan didn't see to it, he would. He couldn't believe that he'd tolerated it even for a day.

His mind had been fogged by Susan, but perhaps he was numb. Numbness was welcome sometimes, but mostly it was dangerous. He didn't feel numb right now.

He walked on, aching with the need to kiss Susan as he'd wanted to kiss her. That was the road to agonizing folly, however. That private discussion had been insane, but he'd wanted her to know. He'd not wanted her to think—

God, stop it. Put this place in order, then leave. Return once a year for an inspection. Next time bring armor. Bring Lady Anne, a wife.

He tried to summon a clear image of Anne, and could only assemble facts—slender, blond, a slight limp. That didn't do her justice, but it was all his struggling mind could come up with.

That was all right. They hadn't met that many times as yet, so it wasn't surprising that he couldn't summon a clear picture.

He knew she would make a perfect, tranquil wife.

✲ 14 ✲

SUSAN AROSE the next morning and set to work on her escape. She'd dreamed of being back in Irish Cove, of not saying those dreadful words, but a dragon had surged up out of the water. Con had tried to fight it, but been seared by flaming breath.

She'd lain awake after that, going over and over everything Con had said, seeking hope.

That was enough to tell her that she had to escape.

Over her breakfast, brought by Ellen, she drew up a list of three local women who could be housekeeper at Crag Wyvern. They weren't really of the caliber to run an earl's household, but this was not a normal earl's household, and Con did not intend to live here. If he managed to lease it, the new residents would hire their own principal staff.

She wrote letters to them, asking if they were interested in the position. At some point she'd have to ask Con if he wanted to interview them, or to leave it to her judgment. For the moment, however, she intended to avoid him.

Then, armored in her housekeeper's clothes, she emerged to send off her letters and to organize the day. She unlocked the store-cupboards to distribute necessary supplies, noting everything in the record books. She noted what supplies were running low and sent off orders to local merchants. She allocated tasks for the day as fairly as possible, then went to supervise the breakfast preparations.

Con's Spanish valet was in the kitchen, and he inquired about laundry facilities. She explained that washing was sent down to some women in Church Wyvern.

He seemed a quiet and proper man, but he was creating quite a flutter among the maids with his Spanish ways and his wicked smiles. Thank heavens the two other men Con had brought were living at the stables in the village.

Sarmiento had clearly been with Con for many years, and seemed both devoted to his master and proud of him. He was certainly ready to talk about him whenever one of the maids asked. Susan couldn't resist lingering in the kitchen to listen.

Then the valet turned to her again. "Mistress Kerslake, is the water for the big bath always available?"

"Yes, Señor Sarmiento. I have ordered the cistern to be kept full, and the fire fed with charcoal. Has the earl not used it yet?"

"Last night he was perhaps a little overtired. He asked only for the small tub. I will remind him tonight. He seems weighed down by his new responsibilities here, and would benefit from the luxury."

She couldn't resist. "What do you think of Crag Wyvern, señor?"

He rolled his eyes. "In my native land, dear lady, we often build with the forbidding outside and the sensual garden within, but we have the strong sun that must be hidden from and protected against. Here . . . here where the sun is like skim milk and scarcely warms the earth . . . ?" He shrugged and shook his head.

But then he said, "Now, Lord Wyvern's other home, Somerford Court, that is a suitable English home. There the gardens are outside and the rooms look out over distant vistas of the beautiful, green English countryside. People here say that this is not a good summer, that it rains too much. But I . . . I see the green the rain brings, and it is sweet to my eyes and heart."

Surely this was safe to talk of. "Somerford Court is on a hill?"

"On a hill overlooking the valley of a river called Eden. Paradise. In the valley is the village of Hawk in the Vale. An old place, and friendly in the way of old places." His dark eyes twinkled.

"That is to say, they look at a foreigner like me with suspicion, but do not actually throw stones. It is the same in my own village back home. The earl's close friend, Major Hawkinville, is son of the squire there. A great hero is Major Hawkinville, though he rarely raised a weapon. A warrior of the mind."

Susan wasn't quite sure what that meant, but she thirsted for more of this information.

"Major George Hawkinville, I assume," she said. "And the other George? George Vandeimen?"

His look was startled, and quickly hidden. "Ah. You know about the Georges, Mrs. Kerslake! He is Lord Vandeimen now. In that one, the family name and title is the same, which is not often the case, I understand. His family is all dead. It is a great tragedy. But now he is to marry a very rich woman. That is good, yes? He and my master have not met since Lord Vandeimen left the army, so I know only what I hear in the village."

"They haven't met?" She knew immediately that she'd stepped over the line she'd drawn for herself, but she had to know. "Lord Vandeimen has been out of the country?"

"No, señora. He returned to England in February, but has spent his time in London."

"What of Major Hawkinville?"

"He is with the army still. Even after battle and victory there remains a great deal for the Quartermaster-General's Department to do."

"It would be better if he were in England, though, would it not?"

Susan knew she was showing more personal interest than was wise, but she fretted about Con. If there was some problem with Lord Vandeimen, then this other friend would help. The Rogues did not seem to have penetrated the shell, and the Georges—the triumvirate—were lifelong friends.

"Lord Vandeimen visited his estate just before we left, señora," Sarmiento said. "He was in the company of the rich woman who is to be his wife. He will now be able to restore Steynings to its former state. But alas, we had to come here before there was chance of a meeting."

Susan realized that she was being told these things deliberately. Lord Vandeimen returned to his home and Con moved to Devon? There'd been no particular reason for him to come here now. And he'd sent no word.

It had been an impulse? A sudden need to escape?

She didn't need more concerns, more twists in the tangle, but she couldn't not care.

"And the Rogues?" she asked.

The valet's eyes lit. "Ah, the Rogues! *¡Qué hombres más admirables!* We spent much time with some of them in the winter." He shivered dramatically, but still smiled. "The hunting. In what they called the Shires. They chase around all day after a fox. Why a fox, I ask? It cannot be eaten. But the English, they spend a fortune on horses to chase a fox. They spend another fortune protecting the fox so it can be chased. They are mad, the English, but the Rogues, they are magnificent. And after that we went to London, also with the Rogues. My master, he seemed happy then, but underneath is still the sadness."

"Lord Darius?"

She'd startled him again. "He has told you of Lord Dare?"

Did Con speak so little of something that obviously mattered so much to him?

Sarmiento said, "A happy soul, Lord Dare, and worth mourning, but the darkness is not really Lord Dare, señora. It is war. War, she is like a fire that men walk through. As long as they do not see how hot it is, it does not burn. But then," he added with an eloquent gesture, "if that changes . . ."

Susan swallowed. She didn't want to know this. She didn't want to know that Con was suffering when there was nothing she could do. "And Lady Anne?"

"Lady Anne?" He seemed confused for a moment, but then said, "Ah. So kind and pretty."

What she wanted to know was whether Lady Anne was helping

Con deal with his devils, but to ask would be to go too far. She excused herself and went to deal with a question about peas, knowing she should force all she'd learned out of her mind.

It was impossible.

Con was at outs with the Georges? Because they were both connected to the war?

He was still close to the Rogues, but they didn't seem to be helping him.

It particularly worried her that he appeared to have come here expressly to avoid Lord Vandeimen.

She went into the pantry to check that the silver had been polished properly. "Stop it!" she muttered, pushing a drawer closed. She was powerless, and going around and around these things was likely to drive her mad.

Diddy came in. "The curate's here, ma'am."

Susan turned to go, but Diddy added, "The earl's got him. Taken him up to the Wyvern rooms. Wish I could see Mr. Rufflestowe's face when he sees that lot!"

So did Susan, but it reminded her of the fountain. She sent for Con's men, Pearce and White, and asked them to look at it to see how it could be taken apart. White was a mere child, pale and nervy, but Pearce was a substantial man who might be able to do the job. She told him to hire more hands from the village if needed.

Then she set out to search Crag Wyvern for clever hiding places. Con, as far as she knew, was still upstairs with Mr. Rufflestowe, and de Vere was in the office, presumably engrossed. If the gold was hidden in there it would be difficult to find. The man seemed unlikely to leave the room!

That had been one of the places she'd searched thoroughly, however, and it was hard to imagine a large concealed compartment that she hadn't found.

Thought of de Vere made her be systematic in her search rather than using her usual method—depending on inspiration. She considered where to start.

The great hall was an unlikely spot, since it was frequently used as a passageway. The kitchens and servants' areas could never reliably be private, and she'd never known the earl to go there.

Very well, on the ground floor that left the dining room, breakfast room, drawing room, and library.

She went first to the dining room, pushing aside all memory of the previous night. She had searched this room—she had searched everywhere—but now she tried to find clever, concealed hiding places.

The plain painted walls made this easier. It was impossible that there was a secret compartment behind them that could be accessed at will. She checked the dark oak floor and the plain ceiling and reached the same conclusion. There was an ornate plaster cornice but no other decoration, and she couldn't see how the cornice could disguise any useful opening.

Determined to be meticulous, she made her eyes travel the room again, seeking out anything suspicious. She didn't find it, but when her eyes passed over the glass-paned doors into the garden she wondered if the gold was hidden out there.

But no. She'd rarely seen the earl go there either. He'd preferred to move around the house using the outer corridors. She'd never thought of it before, but it had been as if even the enclosed openness of the garden had been too much for his irrational fear.

Even if he'd been in the habit of sneaking out to dig and bury at night, the garden had been under Mrs. Lane's assiduous care. She would surely have noticed the ground being disturbed.

Through a bush she could see Pearce over by the fountain. She resisted the distraction of going to see what he thought.

She moved on to the breakfast room, which with its monastic simplicity was easy to cross off the list. When she went back into the corridor, she realized that she had to consider the corridors themselves. But the outer walls were not of medieval thickness, and the inner walls were even thinner unless there was some very skillful disguise work somewhere.

She'd leave them for last.

She followed the corridors to the great hall, however, scrutinizing the surfaces all around, and then went on to the drawing room. Having been carved out of one end of the hall, it alone did not have doors into the garden. There was only one window, and the room was poorly lit during the day.

With paneled walls set with silk wallpaper, and elaborate plasterwork in the ceiling, it was a promising site for a hiding place, but it was only five years old, and she had been involved in some of its design.

She was almost certain that no hiding place of any substance could have been built in. She made her eyes seek for any thickening, any unusual crack or line. . . .

"Looking for something?"

She spun around to see Con standing in the doorway watching her.

"Cobwebs," she said hastily. "It's one of my housekeeperly duties."

"Poor spiders. Mr. Rufflestowe is suitably shocked by the books and manuscripts, and thoroughly enjoying himself. I've left him to it. How are we doing with the fountain?"

We.

She put that aside. "I've set your men to the task. You could go and discuss it with them."

"Why don't we go together?"

Oh, no. She glanced at the fob watch dangling from her high belt, though there was no duty hovering. "I am needed in the kitchens, my lord."

She expected some further argument but he merely said, "Very well," and walked out.

She blew out a breath, accepting that there was regret in her as well as relief. She wanted to spend time with Con, but she was determined to be sensible, which meant she must avoid him whenever possible.

Since the drawing room had only the one door out into the great hall, she waited a few minutes before cautiously leaving.

Con wasn't lurking.

She was a little disappointed about that too.

Truly, she was in a perilous state of mind, and the sooner she was away from here the better.

Having said she was needed in the kitchens, she felt obliged to go there. As she crossed the hall, however, she glanced out of a window, and saw Con in the garden down to his shirtsleeves, helping his men raise the dragon off its unwilling bride.

It would appear that the parts of the fountain were separate, but it did look strangely as if they were forcing the monster off the woman. Rescuing her.

She changed direction and ran up the circular stairs and along the corridor to the nearest room. She sneaked up to the window to watch.

The dragon was lying on the ground now, on a path, thank heavens, not on a bed of plants, but the woman still sprawled there. Free of water and rapist, she looked embarrassingly rapturous.

Were fear and rapture so close? Was rapture from the same root as rape? She must look that up. It certainly would cast a strange light on things.

Con leaped agilely onto the stone rim of the fountain and extended a hand for some tool. He'd unfastened his cuffs and rolled up the sleeves of his shirt. He'd taken off his cravat too, so his shirt was open at the neck.

He looked stunningly loosened, vulnerable, powerful, approachable. . . .

She breathed deeply as she watched him begin to work on something, a bolt probably, to release the figure.

Susan realized her hand was tight on the silk curtains—black silk embroidered with dragons. She was in the Chinese bedroom— the room where Con had slept the first night. This was the same window from which Con had watched her that first morning.

Yesterday morning. A lifetime in a day.

She should go. She shouldn't expose herself to this, and she certainly shouldn't let him see her here, watching him as he had watched her.

But she only eased back slightly. He seemed unlikely to look up. He was intent on his task, as if freeing the bronze figure was crucial to him.

Of course. In Spain he had almost raped a woman. Now he was freeing one. She ached for his obvious anguish, but rejoiced over it too. It must be easy for soldiers to grow numb to violence, but he hadn't.

Of course he hadn't. He was Con.

She realized she was crushing the precious curtain and carefully unclenched her hand, then smoothed it out. These Chinese dragons were a symbol of spirit and joy, but Con didn't have a Chinese dragon on his chest. He'd chosen a Saint George dragon, the evil oppressor who demanded the innocent as tribute. The dragon like the one in the fountain that violated all that was pure and good.

Why?

Why, when he'd always wanted to be Saint George?

She watched him toss the tool back to young White, then begin to lever the figure up off the base, legs braced, forearms taut with muscle. He wasn't a heavy man, but he was all muscle.

She realized she was licking her dry lips.

The big man, Pearce, used a thick stick to help, and then grabbed the woman's spread ankles so that she could be lifted over the side and onto the ground beside her slain tormentor.

Con threw his jacket over her.

Susan stepped back, taking what seemed to be her first deep breath in minutes. Even if Con had a dragon on his chest, he was still the heroic George. He could never be anything else.

And she must wish him happy with his chosen bride.

She couldn't resist one last temptation, however.

She left the room and went back downstairs to the library, hoping that neither Rufflestowe nor de Vere was there. She had every right to enter, but guilty conscience makes an innocuous task suspect, and she planned to check on Con's beloved.

The place was somnolently empty. Almost dormant, in fact.

Though full of books the library had been little used. The earl had kept his favorite books in his room like a squirrel hoarding nuts. The library had been given a thorough cleaning recently, but it had a sad air of neglect.

It contained a reasonably recent *Peerage*, however, and she took it down and opened it on the table.

Lady Anne Peckworth . . .

She soon had the entry. Middle of three daughters of the Duke of Arran. She was twenty-one years old, and both her younger and older sisters were married when this book was compiled two years before.

She frowned slightly, wondering why Lady Anne was still on the shelf. Idiotic to fret whether she was worthy of Con—he'd made his choice—but Susan did. He must have the best, a sterling woman who adored him. The prosaic details on the page revealed nothing about Lady Anne's qualities, however, or about her feelings.

How could she not adore Con?

Was it a long-standing engagement, delayed by the war? But in that case they would surely have married as soon as possible, not still be unwed nearly a year after Waterloo.

No matter how long she looked at the closely printed page, it offered no more enlightenment. She closed the heavy book, creating a flurry of paper dust, and tried to close her pointless and intrusive curiosity. All the same, she was thinking that if she left Crag Wyvern and went a-traveling, she could go to Lea Park and investigate Lady Anne. If she wasn't worthy of Con, she could . . .

What? Murder her?

With a wry laugh, she placed the book back on the shelf. This was no more her business than was the good government of India.

She turned to leave the room, then realized that she might as well search for the gold.

She'd recently supervised the spring cleaning, and every book had been taken out and wiped over; every shelf had been dusted. She had surreptitiously checked at the time for false compartments behind the books.

She went over to the window seat and opened it to check it again. Of course, the space inside was still the right size for the external dimensions.

She straightened, hands on hips and frustrated. Where the devil would the demented earl have hidden his gold? Probably closer to the Wyvern rooms, but that meant the whole upper floor, including the corridors, and the hidey-hole could have been built before she was born, perhaps even into the very fabric of the Crag.

Searching for it was beginning to look like a labor of Hercules.

She glanced out into the garden again, wondering how the fountain project was going. And yes, she admitted, hoping for another glimpse of Con. From the ground level she didn't have a clear view, but it looked as if Con and the men had gone.

Curious, she opened the doors into the courtyard and went out.

Yes, they'd definitely gone. She walked to the center and found that the dragon and the maiden had been taken away, but the chain remained, still connected to the rock at one end, the other end trailing limply into the dry basin. She wondered idly what Con would do with the two bronze figures. She almost felt the bride should have a decent burial.

All that remained was the rock in the middle upon which the bride had lain, and a simple metal pipe sticking up at one side where it had fed into the dragon. She wondered if they could still have the music of the fountain without the figures. The water would just splash onto the rock.

She went to the valve and began to turn the wheel.

It took about three complete turns before the water passed through, and it had to be fully open for the fountain to operate properly. She turned it quickly.

A spout of water exploded up. It pulsed roof-high then rained down again to hit the rock and splash out in a crazy pattern all around. Thoroughly soaked, she danced back, but she couldn't help laughing with childish delight. She looked up at the tall spout, then down at the diamond-sparkling water shooting erratically around, spraying grateful flowers and bushes.

And then she saw Con watching from the other side of the courtyard.

He was still in shirtsleeves, and suddenly, he smiled.

At her, probably, at her being wet and laughing at the water, but she didn't mind. He was smiling a smile she remembered with joy.

It was silly, it was nothing, but she couldn't help the laughter bubbling up and bursting free like the fountain water. She put her hand over her mouth, but couldn't stop.

It could only have been a moment, but her stomach was beginning to ache when she heard him say, "Don't you think you should shut it off?"

Gasping, she saw that he'd come close, over to the other side of the basin, but carefully in a spot between two arms of spray.

"It seems a shame," she managed to say.

"Such untrammeled pleasure in Crag Wyvern?"

The mad hilarity was simmering down. She wanted to say something about untrammeled pleasure, but had sense enough not to. She turned toward the wheel, but paused.

The deflected jet that had first caught her was still spraying the wheel, as if to prevent anyone putting an end to its freedom. She looked back at Con but he merely raised his brows, still grinning at her. She took a deep breath, prepared, and ran for the wheel, turning it despite the drenching spray.

The water stopped hitting her, but she heard a yell.

She turned and saw that the pattern of spray had changed now that the pressure was lower, and Con had been completely drenched.

Laughter won again, but then turned into a smile of simple delight. His hair was flattened to his head, water ran all down him, but he was standing there as if welcoming it, arms spread.

Shirt plastered to him. Breeches plastered to him . . .

She grabbed the wheel, but her hands seemed slippery and somehow weaker. Perhaps the water was truly fighting to be free. Suddenly hands were there to help her—strong hands, brown hands, hands marked with scars. Together they turned the wheel, shutting off the water completely.

In the last splashes and into silence, she looked up at Con.

He was no longer smiling, though something of it lingered in his eyes.

"Revenge of the water?" he said.

"I think it hated being forced through that fountain."

"Perhaps it just hated being forced."

His shirt showed every contour of his chest, and was almost transparent. It showed a dark shadow on the right side.

It could not be ignored.

She wanted to touch it but did not dare. She had to speak of it, however. "A dragon, I understand."

He seemed puzzled, but then his faced cleared. "Ah, the lusty maid saw it. Diddy, yes? We all had tattoos done—Van, Hawk, and I. The idea was that if we were searching for one another's mangled bodies, we'd find the task easier. Not a bad notion, as it turned out."

The sudden bleakness was not because of Crag Wyvern or herself.

"Who could you not find? Lord Darius?"

"There were so many dead and dying," he said, looking away again, but not in a way that broke the magic, "and some had been stripped, or trampled, or blown apart." He shook his head. "You don't want to talk about such things." He turned to the fountain. "What do you think we should put in place of the dragon?"

She wouldn't let the connection break without a fight. There would be only brief moments like this, when once they might have been eternal. "He was a Rogue, you said. I remember you speaking of them."

He looked back at her, dark, but not because of her, not directed at her, thank heaven. "You remember a great deal."

She hesitated a moment, then said, "I remember everything, Con."

His lips twisted. "So do I." But then he inhaled. "Yes, he was a Rogue. He wasn't a soldier, though. He shouldn't have been there. I should have stopped him."

"Perhaps he didn't want to be stopped."

"I should have stopped him anyway. Or prepared him better. Or—" He suddenly looked her over, and she knew, with clarity, that he'd remembered everything, and firmly closed a door. "That gray stuff would hide a tattoo, but it isn't hiding much, you know."

She looked down and saw that of course her dress was molded to her body as much as his shirt was to him. Her corset shielded her upper body, but her belly, her thighs, the indentation between her thighs . . .

Face flaming, she pulled the cloth away, flapping it to try to make it not adhere. She glanced at him and couldn't help a shiver of excitement at the look in his eyes, even though it wasn't proper, or respectful, or even particularly kind.

"You're not hiding much either," she said, and let her eyes look at his breeches.

"I know."

Her heart started to pound.

"Are you as curious as I am, Susan? To know what it would be like? Now."

Curious and more than curious. A warm heaviness grew inside her, an ache. . . .

After a moment she managed to say, "What of Lady Anne?"

"She isn't here, is she?"

Ah. Her throat tightened. She made herself swallow.

Curiosity. That was all it was for him.

For her it was a longing that went much deeper, but she wouldn't do this. She wouldn't be a convenient release and she wouldn't offend against the woman he had chosen, even if she wasn't here. She wouldn't reduce herself to a whore, not even for Con. It would destroy them both.

"She is here in spirit," she said, and stepped back. "I must go and change, my lord." She looked at the fountain behind him, however.

"I think it should be a Saint George," she said. "Crag Wyvern needs a hero to vanquish the dark."

Then she walked briskly into the house.

🜲 15 🜲

CON TURNED and leaned his hands against the rough, cold rim of the basin, looking down at the inches of water glimmering there.

Saint George.

A hero.

Where had that youthful idealist gone?

Susan had hurt him deeply but she hadn't killed the hero. The war had done that. Oh, officially it had made him a kind of hero. He hadn't been the dashing sort to attract a lot of notice, but he knew he'd done his job well for the benefit of his men, his general, and his king. Hawk had told him that Wellington had referred to him once as a "damned fine officer," which was praise enough for any man.

But the endless years, though full of excitement, triumph, and even pleasure among the bleaker times, had killed the saint. He didn't fear what the future would do to him, but what he might do to others in his soulless state.

Some fortune-tellers claimed to be able to reveal the future from reflections in water. What would anyone make of his?

He'd summoned Lady Anne as his defense, and now she was a barrier. Susan wouldn't come to his bed because of Lady Anne.

That was what he wanted, wasn't it?

What he wanted, ferociously, was Susan.

The sight of her laughing uncontrollably at the unpredictable spray had cracked something and carried him straight back to the sun-shimmered past. Then the sight of her body, lusher, more womanly in its mysteries, but still Susan, had undone him.

He couldn't let himself be used again, and despite the soulless need throbbing in him, he wouldn't use her. But could he bear to leave here without experiencing Susan as she was now?

He could always tell her that Lady Anne was a possibility rather than a commitment. Tempt her with the chance of winning Crag Wyvern for herself. She'd claimed she didn't want it anymore, but it must be a lie. Why else was she here?

He suddenly had a wicked vision of Susan—womanly, experienced Susan—setting her mind to seducing him. . . .

But Lady Anne was more than a possibility. He'd sent that letter. And she was the perfect, ideal wife for him.

If Susan married him, it would be for Crag Wyvern. Since he had no intention of spending more than a duty week or so a year here she would be miserable.

No, Susan would never wallow in misery. She'd fight for what she wanted. He'd seen men married to women determined to change them and their circumstances to suit. Seen them nagged into joining the army, leaving the army, changing regiments, spending beyond their means, saving beyond sanity.

No peace in those homes. He'd told Susan the truth about his ambitions. What he longed for above all was peace. Peace and gentle pleasures in Somerford Court, where he thought he might eventually rediscover his soul, and perhaps even his youthful ideals.

He leaned down, scooped some of the water, and splashed it over his face. It was warm from the sun by now, however, and did no good.

He pushed away from the fountain and walked back into the house. He'd change and ride out again. It was the only safe thing to do.

Susan was shivering by the time she stripped off her wet dress, and it wasn't entirely from the cold. She'd never expected to feel such urgent, physical need for a man. She hadn't known it existed!

With Con all those years ago it had been an unknown, a mystery. With Rivenham it had been a plan. He'd brought her to desire, but it had been a deliberate path for both of them.

With Captain Lavalle it had been a plan again, but a huge mistake. Physically it had been nothing.

Worse than nothing.

It had been disgusting.

Now, without even touching Con, she ached, she burned for him. Out there in the garden, she'd longed to touch him, to press against the hard muscles his wet shirt had so tantalizingly revealed, to embrace him, to comfort him, to be comforted and healed. . . .

She thumped down on the edge of her bed, still in her damp corset and shift, trying to understand this unexpected force.

She knew she *loved*. That was a force of its own, but it was one she could rule with willpower. She loved, and because she loved it was possible not to show it, not to distress him with it, and to let him go to the woman he had chosen.

But this . . . this was more elemental. Part of the ache, she was sure, was from struggling not to act, as if battling a fierce wind, or the pull of a stormy sea. It seemed all too likely that the force could overwhelm her, sweeping her into disaster.

Disaster for them both.

She shuddered, then stood to strip off the rest of her clothes, to rub herself sternly with a towel until her skin burned and the ache subsided.

She had to leave. Immediately. She had no explanation she could give anyone, but Con would understand. She'd return to the manor, and then go elsewhere—

She stilled, seeing many problems.

She had no money until the Horde was prosperous again.

She had nowhere to go, and no easy chance of employment. . . .

It didn't matter. For both their sakes, she had to at least leave Crag Wyvern. Mrs. Gorland could manage the household until a new housekeeper was hired.

She'd claim she was ill.

At the moment she felt almost ill.

She pulled on a dry shift and added another working corset. She took out her second gray dress and put it on. If she was leaving she could dress in ordinary clothes—but this was armor.

Yet it hadn't protected her from Con. . . .

She thrust away memory and added a starched fichu. She redid her hair, pinning it up tightly, and put on a cap, tying the laces.

It wasn't enough.

There could never be enough.

There was no protection except distance.

She looked at her possessions—books, needlework, ornaments. What could she carry them in?

She couldn't delay to pack them. She had to go now.

She walked out into the kitchen.

"We're almost out of butter, ma'am," Mrs. Gorland said. "And I could do with a nice sirloin."

Susan longed to rush by but duty made her pause. "Send down to Ripford for the beef, and buy as much butter as you need from the village."

"Very well, ma'am." Then the cook looked at her. "Are you all right, dear?"

The switch from business to personal was almost too much for Susan, but she found a smile. "Yes, of course, but I need to go down to the manor again."

"That's all right. We can manage fine."

"I know. Thank you." Susan left, wishing she could take a proper farewell of them all.

She felt she should sneak out by one of the small doors, but the main entrance was closest, so she headed there via the great hall. When she walked into that space a man was waiting.

Con!

No, not Con, thank heavens. Just Lieutenant Gifford. But he was someone else to talk to before she was free.

"Lieutenant. May I help you?"

He looked at her and blushed. She'd swear it was a blush. She looked down at her hastily put on clothes, but she couldn't see anything embarrassingly amiss.

He reached up and tugged at his military stock. "I came to speak to the earl, Mistress Kerslake. A maid is looking for him. For me . . ."

Speak to Con? About smuggling? And Con probably knew David was Captain Drake and might say something. Surely he wouldn't . . .

She couldn't deal with this now.

Dear heaven. Con would be coming here at any moment!

"Then if you'll excuse me, sir, I have an errand to run."

She moved to one side to go around him, but he blocked her way.

"I . . . I would prefer you kept me company for a while."

She looked up at him, trying to focus her mind on this. "I beg your pardon?"

"I would prefer your company," he said more firmly, looking a little alarmed, but also a great deal determined.

Insane humor tried to bubble up.

Was he going to propose to her?

Here?

Now?

She stepped to the side again. "My errand is urgent, Lieutenant—"

He blocked her again. "So is mine. Please, you will want to hear what I have to say."

Devil spit. Con could be here at any moment, or the maid returning to take Gifford to him! She pushed him hard on the chest with both hands, prepared to run if necessary. But he only fell back a step before grasping her wrists.

"Release me!" she hissed, wishing she dared scream for help. "Lord Wyvern will be here directly. He will not like to see you holding me prisoner like this."

"Got to you already, has he? That'll have to stop."

"What?" Either she was mad or he was.

He looked around wildly, clearly checking to see if anyone could see them. He was flushed again, but this time with excitement. It glittered in his eyes.

"I couldn't quite believe it," he said rapidly, quietly, as if they shared a secret. "But I saw you and the earl out in the courtyard. Only lovers look at each other like that, Susan. And to think I was advancing on your defenses so politely."

"Lieutenant—"

"Giles, Susan. Giles."

"Lieutenant . . ."

The flash of fury in his eye stole words for a moment. She made herself relax in his grip and look at him calmly. "Lieutenant, I'm very sorry but I could not possibly marry you—"

His eyes widened, and then he laughed. "Dear lady, I'm not after marriage. I want what Captain Lavalle enjoyed."

Heavenly mercies. Her legs threatened to betray her. She'd always feared this, that the cad would talk of it to other officers. It had been so many years, though. . . .

Too late, she tried to bluff. "I don't know what you're talking about."

"Oh yes you do. Keen for it, Lavalle said, and now I see how right he was. The earl's only been here two nights and he's clearly had you. So now it's my turn. You're a fine looking woman, Susan. I find you a real cock-stirrer, especially in your starchy gray and white, your hair all tucked up under that cap. . . ."

He was pushing her backward and she went, unable to think what to do. Her hips hit the center table and he trapped her there, licking his lips as he did so, pressing himself against her, trying to part her thighs.

"Are you mad?" she said in a frantic whisper. "Release me immediately!"

"A mere lieutenant not good enough for you after an earl?" He pressed harder so the table dug into her.

"Stop or I'll scream," she hissed, meaning it, though then he'd tell Con about Lavalle. *Oh, God. Oh, God . . .*

"No, you won't. Or I'll arrest your brother as Captain Drake."

Her throat seized up.

He knew.

No, she realized, her wits sharpening—he guessed.

She made herself meet his eyes and look astonished. "David? A smuggler? You *are* mad."

"David, son of Mel Clyst, Susan, just as you're daughter of Mel Clyst."

He stepped back and let her free, clearly confident now that she wouldn't run. Should she run to prove David's innocence?

Before she could decide, he said, "I wondered why you weren't respectably married by now, but you're not Miss Kerslake of Kerslake Manor, are you? You're the bastard daughter of a smuggler and a whore, and truly your mother's daughter, by what I heard from Lavalle."

"Whatever he told you, he lied. I assume men often boast of these things if they think they can get away with it. He tried to seduce me, yes. Five years ago, I think. He did not take my rejection well."

She saw a flicker of uncertainty and pushed her advantage. "I'd thought better of you, Lieutenant, than to believe such doubtless boozy talk."

Uncertainty disappeared. "He wasn't drunk, Susan, he was dying. We shared a mat on the ground in the crowded surgeon's tent after Albuera. I survived, and he didn't. But we talked of home, and one of the things he talked about was you. A beautiful, well-bred lady who'd just about begged him to tumble her. But he'd found out later she wasn't really a well-bred lady, and her mother was a whore, so it hadn't been such a miracle after all."

Susan couldn't think what to say, but relief was washing over her in a dizzying wave. It was possible that Lavalle hadn't talked of her in every mess tent in the Peninsula.

But she still had Gifford to deal with.

"Be my whore, *Mistress* Kerslake, and your brother will be safe."

Lord, and she'd thought Gifford a good man! Surrender? Or fight.

Fight, of course.

"My brother is the earl's estate manager," she said flatly, "and you, sir, are a cad."

He paled, but his lips tightened. "But you won't be telling the earl what I've done, will you?"

"He'd probably think that I'm as mad as you are. I doubt you're brave enough to admit your words to him."

"So he is your lover, is he?"

She met his eyes. "No. If I try to continue on my way, Lieutenant, are you going to manhandle me again?"

She had him rattled. He even bit his lower lip.

But then he stood straighter. "A week from now," he said. "When the moon is too full for the plaguey smugglers. Come to my rooms at the Crown and Anchor." His grim smile showed that he had his nerve back.

"The local smugglers have been trying for months to find a way to pay me off," he added. "Well, now they have it. For as long as you please me, Susan, you can be the payment."

Footsteps saved her from having to find a response. Both she and Gifford turned as Con walked in.

He paused.

What did they look like, standing so close together?

Con's face was expressionless as he came forward. "Lieutenant Gifford."

Gifford bowed. "My lord."

He sounded half strangled by sudden nerves, and Susan felt a bubble of laughter threatening. She kept forgetting that Con was an earl, that he was supposed to be regarded with awe and trembling.

Ah, no. She could do the awe and trembling very well indeed.

She knew that if she told him what Gifford had threatened, showed him the marks that had to be on her wrists, he would destroy Gifford for her. Doubtless here and now.

But she couldn't, because she'd have to tell him why.

And she didn't want to bring about Gifford's destruction. He'd been led astray by Lavalle's story, which had been essentially true. As with her other sorrows, she had brought this on herself.

Now, however, flight to the manor seemed pointless. The enemies were outside as well as in.

Con and Gifford had been speaking together, and now Con indicated that Gifford should accompany him. "Mrs. Kerslake," he said to her with chilly formality, "please have refreshments sent to the library."

She pulled on the manner of the perfect housekeeper, and curtsied.

"Yes, my lord."

Con led Gifford across the garden to the library, wishing he had an excuse to plant the man a facer. Gifford and Susan? Damnation, why would a Preventive man take up with a smuggler's daughter?

Perhaps he didn't know.

Gifford made some inane remark about the garden, and Con replied. He could drop the information into conversation. He assumed they were about to talk about smuggling.

They were passing the fountain basin and he remembered what had been there. He could not betray Susan. He was a dragon, but not a dragon of the foulest sort. Gifford was bound to find out soon, and if Con was any judge, that would be the end of any chance of a marriage, but it wouldn't come at his hands.

But then he wondered, if Susan was encouraging Gifford, did she truly not want Crag Wyvern anymore?

Or was she encouraging Gifford in the Dragon's Horde's cause?

The momentary hope faded.

Of course she was.

Poor Gifford.

Victim of the dragon in another way.

Susan gave the order for the refreshments, then scurried off to hide in her room.

What in the name of heaven did she do now?

She circled her haven, clutching her useless cap. She needed to warn David, but she didn't want to tell him about Gifford's threat. David always seemed levelheaded, but no man was going to stay levelheaded if told about his sister being blackmailed into whoredom!

He might challenge Gifford to a duel.

As Captain Drake, he might order Gifford killed out of hand.

That would be so wrong, and it would be disastrous to have yet another riding officer die on this stretch of coast. They'd end up with troops every few feet, and once the local smuggling master was caught, they'd find a way to hang him. If not, he too would doubtless fall off a cliff.

Gifford's threat was hollow. He couldn't arrest David. He had no proof. But now he'd be watching David and this area like a hawk.

She dropped her hands and sighed. She couldn't tell David any more than she could tell Con, because she'd have to tell them about Lavalle. Of all the things she had done of which she was ashamed, Captain Lavalle was the worst.

She wanted *no one* to know, and now it appeared that Lavalle had talked of it.

While she'd been speaking with Gifford she'd felt sure that Lavalle had spoken about her only when he'd been dying, but what if he'd shared the story with dozens? Or what if Gifford had spread it about since? No, no, he wouldn't do that. It was his weapon. But what if . . . ?

She recognized the ache of weak tears and fought them. But they broke free and she collapsed in a chair, trying not to sob out loud, trying to keep the storm quiet with her hand. That seemed to force the misery back painfully into her chest, into her bruised and aching heart. . . .

She managed to control it in the end, but Lord, she hurt. Her chest ached, and her throat, and her eyes burned. She couldn't imagine where the term "a good cry" came from.

But slowly she did begin to feel better.

Not good. But better.

She'd learned in the past that some things couldn't be changed and that the world did not crash to its end because of one person's anguish. She'd learned that life must be dealt with as it was, not as she wished it to be. She'd learned that she could not take life in her hands like wet clay and mold it.

This was simply another bruising lesson.

She stood and blew her nose. Her mirror showed her red and swollen eyes. How could she face anyone like this?

She ripped off her scratchy fichu, however, and her confining cap. Clearly they were not armor at all. In fact, she remembered with a shudder, Gifford had said they excited him!

With a shock of laughter she wondered if she was going about this in the wrong way. Perhaps if she flitted around the place half-dressed Con would not be affected, and men like Gifford would shy away!

But no. Her low bodice last night had not been safe either.

Gifford had given her a week.

A week to decide what to do.

A week to find the gold.

Which meant a week here, with Con, and already in two days things were getting out of hand. That force, that power that had driven her to run was still swirling through Crag Wyvern.

But the gold was the answer.

With the gold, David could lie low for months. Gifford could watch him until his eyes dried to raisins and not find a thing.

And with the gold, David could pay back the loans she had made. She could move far away. In fact, she thought, excited by the idea, she'd ask David to come with her to help her settle.

Bath perhaps. No, too close.

London.

Scotland?

Could she get him to take her to Italy?

The farther the better.

Perhaps she could keep him away for weeks, a month, even more. He'd have to return, of course. He'd have to be in danger in the future, but the critical danger would be past.

Gifford would surely forget about her once she was far away. He'd still suspect David, but the Preventives had more than suspected Mel. They'd simply not been able to catch him at it or prove anything.

Until helped by the old earl, apparently, damn his black heart.

Yes, that was a plan. For now, however, this was an excellent time to search for the gold.

Con was with Gifford in the library, and de Vere was presumably in the office engaged in his love affair with accounts. The bedrooms upstairs should be deserted.

She slipped out of the kitchen area without attracting attention and headed for the circular stairs. As she passed a window into the garden, however, she saw movement.

It was de Vere, out of the office, for once. It was one of the rooms she knew best, and had searched most carefully. She was almost sure that the money could not be hidden there, but she had better check one last time.

✸ 16 ✸

As soon as Susan entered she saw the effects of a new hand. The standish and pens were arranged differently. Piles of papers stood around the desk, each with a note on top. She glanced at them and saw one note saying, *Further investigation.*

What had de Vere found?

She flicked through that short pile but found nothing about smuggling. It contained mostly bills, and she supposed there was no record of payment.

It took only moments to assure herself that there was no hiding place she'd overlooked. However, she saw a small wooden box on the desk that had been tucked in a drawer for years. She opened it and found it half-full of scraps of paper, even chunks torn out of printed books.

She recognized the old earl's scribbled notes. De Vere must be collecting them as he found them. She took them out and flicked through them.

Some were nonsense. Some were clear. *Look up nao cha.* Some were cryptic. *Bats or cats? That is the question.* Two pieces made her frown, though.

One said: *Mel and Belle. Belle and Mel. Who should tell? Toll the bell.*

Another said: *Mel and Belle, Belle and Mel. Go to hell. To demon's land, in fact! Ha! Ha!*

"Ha! Ha!"? What a childish form of madness that illustrated, but what had impelled him to write these notes?

Gifford had hinted that the earl had played some part in Mel's capture, and the notes certainly showed animosity.

Why? Why would the earl have planned trouble for Mel and Lady Belle? Smuggling had provided the money he'd used to indulge in his mad pursuit of an heir. Until the end he'd seemed an enthusiastic supporter.

Did a madman need reasons?

She shrugged and put the notes back in the box. Whatever had stirred in his deranged mind, it was history now. He was dead, and Mel and Belle were at the other side of the world. She went to the globe that stood on its stand beside the courtyard window, turning it to look at Australia, so very far away.

She still couldn't forgive Lady Belle for taking all the money without regard to her son's safety, but perhaps she understood a little better now. Con's return had taught her something of the power of love, and now she knew the power of desire.

Her experiences with Rivenham and Lavalle had made her shut off that part of herself, made her deny that it existed. Easy enough when she hadn't met a man who tempted her.

She suspected now that she was beyond temptation. Eleven years ago, in two weeks of sunshine and friendship and one day of sinful exploration, she had been captured for all time.

She spun the globe idly.

Con had not been as trapped as she, thank heavens. He had escaped the shadows of that day to find love elsewhere, and it was proof that sometimes life was just. He'd done nothing wrong.

Her eyes were looking at the globe without seeing it, but something alerted her brain.

South of Australia. An island.

Van Deimen's Land . . .

To demon's land.

Dragon spit! The mad earl *had* planned to send Mel to the penal colonies of Australia! It sounded as if he'd planned for Lady Belle to go there too, but that was impossible unless he'd guessed that she'd do something so outrageous.

Did he know her well enough to be able to predict what she'd do? Susan wasn't aware of the earl and Lady Belle knowing each other at all, except, she supposed, as members of local society growing up together.

But even if he had planned to send them both off to "demon's land," why?

His madness had been a cunning sort, not completely wild. He'd always had reason for the things he did.

Why?

She was staring out of the doors into the garden as she thought, and she suddenly drew back. De Vere had come out of the library doors, and was heading this way.

She turned and walked quickly out of the room. The mad earl was history and she had an urgent present to deal with.

For the rest of the afternoon, between dealing with routine matters, she checked all the bedrooms for secret spaces. Nothing. To take care of the corridors she set Ellen, Diddy, and Ada to sweeping and dusting them, telling them to check as they went for cracks in the walls.

After a visit to the kitchen to check that all was in order for dinner, she climbed to the top floor, which would be the attics in a normal house. Here most of the space was taken by two large water cisterns.

The big one on the west side held water for the house, including the fountain, and was original to the house. Because the house sat on the cliff, the water was pumped up from the village by a clever screw design worked by horses. The smaller one on the north, above the Saint George rooms, held and heated the water for the Roman bath. That drew water from the main cistern by a gravity feed. Beneath it a stone hearth held charcoal to heat the water.

She noted that her orders were being followed. The fire was steady, and four buckets of charcoal stood nearby. If Con took it into his head to use the big bath, it would be ready for him. She was aware of a stupid tenderness about arranging such comforts for him. She was his housekeeper, for heaven's sake. She was paid to arrange every detail of his comfort.

Even so, it pleased her.

For the first time she wondered if the gold could be hidden in one of the cisterns.

She carefully opened the hatch and peered through warm steam. It would have been quite a cunning hiding place for something indestructible like gold, but there was no sign of a box or bag, or a line to anything submerged.

She went to the other, bigger cistern, and checked that. Nothing, though running the fountain so much had left the water low. She'd send a message to the village to get it filled.

She stood there smiling sadly at the memory of that encounter by the wildly spraying fountain.

Precious, but painful. A clear demonstration of what she had thrown away.

She moved on briskly to check the rest of the floor. She'd never known the old earl to come up here, but he might have sneaked up in the night. She had previously checked every box and piece of discarded furniture here. Now she looked for more cunning places, but poke around as she might, she found nothing.

As she prepared to leave, dusting off her hands, she noted the ladder that led up to the roof. She was sure the old earl would not have gone up there—into the open, by gad!—but she might as well be thorough. She kirtled up her skirts and climbed up, unlatching and pushing open the heavy trapdoor. It stopped just past the vertical, thank heavens, or she would have had to let it fall with a shocking bang. When she climbed out, she saw that it rested against a chimney.

She'd never been up here and she found herself on a wide walkway between the slope of the roof and the chest-high battlements. She gave thanks they were chest high—it was a long way down.

Up so high, however, the breeze was a brisk wind, cool and fresh off the sea. Enjoying it, she began a circuit, noting that the roof was shallow enough not to show from outside, and that it sloped from the courtyard side to the battlements. A groove ran around the walkway, and she finally came to a hole and realized that the groove collected the rain and funneled it here, which surely led down to the water cistern.

An efficient design. It made the recently added gargoyles particularly ridiculous, however. She leaned carefully out between two merlons to look at the one on the nearest corner. On true medieval buildings they were usually waterspouts. This one snarled uselessly into nowhere.

An image of something, that. She preferred not to look at it too closely.

She was on the sea side now, and she leaned her elbows on the rough stone to look out across the Channel. On this overcast day, the distance was misty, but up close the waves rippled silver on the steel gray sea, and fishing boats bobbed industriously on it. Shrunk small by distance, a sailing ship swooped along, heading west toward the Atlantic, perhaps to Canada, or south to Spain, to Africa or India.

Or to Australia.

Gulls swirled and cried, and the sea air whipped past her skin, brisk and unbearably clean. To right or left she could see misty miles down the coast.

Other places, other people.

Places she would have to go to, people she would have to live among. The old fear of not belonging cramped in her, but she made it release. She would do what she had to do.

She continued on her way, looking out all the time, dazzled by this new view of her commonplace world. Patchwork fields spread green or brown, the new grass dotted with animals. She had an angel's view of coppices and stands of evergreens, and the occasional majestic solitary tree. Of hills and valleys and silvery hints of water.

She looked down on the cottages, farms, and church spires of her familiar life—and out at distances containing secrets, and even adventures.

When she arrived back at the trapdoor, she almost could not bear to go down.

Trap. Indeed.

She'd thought she'd evaded the trap of Crag Wyvern, but she had come here, first by day, and then to live. And she was still here when she wanted to be elsewhere. . . .

Just a little while longer.

She quickly climbed down the ladder, managing the tricky business of bringing the heavy trapdoor down behind her, then latching it, sealing out the light and air.

The upper floor felt stale and suffocating now, and she hurried away and down the circular stairs to the floor beneath. Even there she was in one of the narrow dark corridors, and she hastened on, down and down, around and around, and out at last into the fresh air of the courtyard.

She inhaled, but it wasn't the same as the air she'd breathed above.

Once again she hurried to escape Crag Wyvern, but this time she wanted only freedom and fresh air. She burst through the great entrance arch and took a deep breath.

She was in the shadow of the house, however, and she picked up her skirts and ran, ran out of shadow into light, down to the cliff edge where the wind blew off the sea, swirling her skirts and tugging her hair loose from confining pins.

The sailing ship still billowed on its way, the fishing boats still danced on closer waves, the men on board letting down nets or hauling them in. The calls of the gulls were louder here, and the vegetation was alive with insects and small birds. Delirious with delight at everything, she sat, arms around her knees, to soak it in.

How long was it since she'd done this? Simply enjoyed the air and the world around. Too long. She rolled to lie on her stomach like a child, to look down at Wyvern Cove tucked below, to watch the people coming and going, the old men working on boats, or sitting mending nets.

The salt tang of sea and seaweed mixed with the smell of fish here, but she loved it. It was part of her world. Not for much longer. But there must be other places as sweet, and she would learn to belong.

She rolled away from the view onto her back, looking up at the misty sky. She felt small, but whole, or more whole than she had for a while.

She lay there a long time, knowing she should move. She was not a child anymore, but an adult with employment and responsibilities. She should be in the house doing something. . . .

She couldn't think of anything in particular needing her attention and so she stayed where she was, feeling rested for the first time in days.

Since Con had arrived.

It was more than that, though. It was the pull of the earth.

She'd used to do this all the time, to connect to the earth with as much of her body as possible, but somewhere along the way she had forgotten.

Had it been as long ago as eleven years?

Surely she'd done this since then. But she couldn't remember when. After Con, the appeal of the open headlands and the beaches had faded. No, not faded, but become shadowed by memories and regrets.

To Aunt Miriam's delight, she'd then spent more time with her cousins doing the things young ladies were supposed to do. Young ladies were certainly not supposed to sprawl on cliff tops.

Housekeepers were not supposed to either.

She really must get up and return to Crag Wyvern. . . .

It was as if the earth held her down with gentle hooks, however, or as if her hungry need of the earth pressed her there. She closed her eyes and let her other senses drink deeply.

Clean breeze over her skin, tugging at her hair, playing with her skirt.

Cries of gulls and curlews, faint calls from people below in the village. Children laughing. A dog barking. The ever-present rumble of waves on shingle.

All the wonderful mixed smells from plants and sea that she'd breathed in all her life.

A shadow fell across her lids. She opened her eyes, but she knew before regaining her sight who it would be.

He towered over her and she supposed she should be afraid, but all she could think was how wonderful it would be if he fell on top of her, if he kissed her. . . .

"You still like the cliffs," he said.

The sun was behind him, hiding any expression.

"Of course."

She should get up, curtsy even, but she refused to scramble to her feet like a guilty child, and the earth still hugged.

Of course, she was a very guilty housekeeper. It made her want to smile.

He suddenly sat by her feet, legs crossed, and she could see his thoughtful face. "Gifford knows your brother is Captain Drake."

She thought for a moment of denying it, but this was Con. "I know. He told me too." She sat up. She could meet him halfway.

"Why?" he asked.

She froze, unready for the question. But then here, outside in the sunshine on the cliffs, she had someone she could tell.

"He wants to be my lover."

"What?" His gray eyes seemed suddenly to become paler, silver.

"He has an excuse," she said quickly, then realized that pushed her farther than she wanted to go.

"You have been encouraging him?" Though he hadn't moved, she felt as if he were putting space between them. Telling him everything would probably drive him from her entirely, but wise or foolish, she had to be honest.

She looked away, though, away to the side at the wandering cliffs and the ruffled edge of the sea. "Some years ago, I made a mistake with a man. I . . . I thought I wanted to make love with him. But it was a mistake." *Dear Lord. How did anyone put these things in words?*

Say it simply.

She looked him in the eye. "I encouraged a military officer to make love— No, it wasn't love. I barely knew him. Whatever you want to call it. It was my idea, though he didn't need much encouragement."

"I'm sure he didn't." She could tell nothing from his tone.

She sucked in a breath and went on. "Apparently he spoke of it to Gifford as he lay dying, so Gifford thinks I do that sort of thing all the time." She managed a shrug. "Thus, he wishes me to do it with him. In return, he'll turn a blind eye to Captain Drake and the Dragon's Horde."

She watched him, fearful of his response, but immensely lightened by depriving Gifford of the power the secret would have held. She was lightened, too, by having someone she could tell about that painful event.

But Con?

Had the wild air gone to her head that she thought she could confide her most perilous secrets to this new Con?

"I'll destroy him." It was said with cool certainty.

She grasped his arm. "No!"

Silver eyes. Dragon eyes. "I see. You are not unwilling, then?"

"Of course I am." She was still holding him, through heavy cloth, but holding him. Was this the first time she'd touched him? "Don't duel him, Con. I couldn't bear to see you hurt."

He laughed and pulled free. "You don't have much faith in me, do you?"

Oh, Lord! "In a duel anyone can be hurt! And I don't want him killed either. I detest him now, but he does not deserve death."

He closed his eyes briefly, then looked at her. "Susan, I'm an earl. I don't need to call Gifford out to deal with him. If I want him posted to the tip of Cornwall, I can do it. I can send him to India, or to the hell pits of the West Indies, or to guard Mel Clyst in Botany Bay. If I want him thrown out of the service, I can do that too."

"But that would be unjust."

Too late, she realized it sounded like a criticism rather than a protest.

"It's an unjust world. What do you want me to do?" After a moment, he added, "I think I can still act Saint George on occasion."

He said it without expression, but it carried her back.

This wasn't Irish Cove, and they were both fully dressed, but she knew he, like she, was instantly back in another lifetime, before. . . .

"I'm not a maiden." What an idiotic thing to say.

It stirred the hint of a smile. "I believe I'm aware of that."

"I mean . . ." Suddenly it seemed essential that they have truth on this. "There have been others."

"You just told me that, didn't you?"

Now she wanted to clarify that there'd been only two others, and only two other times.

"There have been others for me too," he said, quite gently. "Rather more, I assume."

"Of course. And I'm glad of it."

But this was all going wrong. Her words weren't forming into the right meanings. She struggled to her feet.

He rose beside her. "Why are you glad?"

She tried again. "I don't want you to have suffered because of what I did that day. I am sorry, Con."

Oh, how inadequate that sounded.

He looked away, turning to face the vista of sea. "It's all so long ago, Susan. And it's impossible to imagine that anything could have come of it, isn't it? Two fifteen-year-olds. Me a younger son with my way to make in the world. You a young lady not considered ready for the world at all."

He was speaking so lightly that she wanted to protest, to insist that it was more than that. But perhaps for him it had been a simpler matter. Horribly embarrassing and painful at the time, but now a thing of the distant past.

And there had been many other women.

"That's true," she said, brushing off her skirts. "Even if I had ended up in a compromised condition they would likely not have made us marry. A visit to a relative, a family paid to take care of the child . . ."

She would never have allowed that, so like her birth and up-bringing except that there had never been any attempt at secrecy. But he did not need to know that.

He turned back to her. "I'll warn Gifford off. If he has any sense, he'll heed it."

"He thinks we're lovers."

He raised his brow as a query, but a blanket of . . . comfort was growing around them. He wasn't assuming she'd told Gifford they were lovers.

"He saw us by the fountain," she explained.

"We never touched by the fountain."

"Even so."

He grimaced. "Perceptive of him."

She remembered then that Con had propositioned her by the fountain—out of curiosity's sake.

"Let him think what he wants," he said flatly.

"He may think you sympathize with the smugglers too."

He shook his head. "Susan, I'd expect you to be quicker-witted than this. I'm the *earl*, remember. He'd have to find me hauling tubs up the cliff to even think of touching me, and even then he'd be a damned fool. The whole power system of Britain would rise up in rage at the thought of one of their own being dragged into the courts over such a petty matter. I'm damn near untouchable."

She hesitated for a moment because she wasn't sure what was happening between them, what it meant, but she asked anyway. "Will you protect David, then?"

His mouth tightened, but he said, "For your sake, yes."

"For his sake too." She put her hand on Con's arm again, delib-erately this time. "He didn't choose this path. He's Mel's son. Rival gangs were threatening to invade and no one else had the author-ity."

"I see. Very well. But I won't be here much. You know that."

It seemed to encompass more than the issue of smuggling.

"I know." She faced it squarely. "You'll be marrying Lady Anne soon, and living in Sussex."

The wind caught a hank of her hair, blowing it wildly around her face. She realized it had lost most of its pins and she must look a mess. She moved her hand off his arm to control the hair, but he was there first.

He caught it and tucked it off her face, behind her ear. "A plait was more practical," he said with a smile.

"It escaped from that too." She couldn't help but smile back.

"I remember." His hand lingered, but then he lowered it. "We were friends once, I think."

Her heart was rapid and high. "Yes."

"And again, I hope."

She sucked in a deep breath. "So do I."

"A man can never have too many friends. On the other hand," he added lightly, "an earl seems to have only one housekeeper. Shouldn't you be keeping house?"

She laughed and stepped beside him to walk back to Crag Wyvern, feeling suddenly as if she had found the only gold that mattered. By implication he had forgiven her for the past. She'd told him the worst about herself. And they were friends.

Certainly a person could never have too many friends.

By the time they went through the door into the cool of the house, however, delight was sliding into melancholy.

They were only friends.

He'd made it clear that friendship was all that could exist between them. She could weep over that for she didn't think she could bear to be only friends with Con. It would have to spin off into more dangerous waters, and that she could not allow. Despite temptation, she would not be the cause of Con breaking his wedding vows.

Any meetings between them in the future must be few and far between, and she would see that they were well chaperoned.

Con parted from Susan without a backward look and went directly to the office. Race was at a shelf, some sort of ledger in his hands, and as usual he looked up impatiently.

"Put that away," Con said. "We're going riding."

"How do you expect me to get this straight if you keep dragging me away?"

"Is it not straight?"

"Mostly, but there are some wonderfully arcane and tantalizing aspects."

Con propped his hips against the desk. "What do you think of Lady Anne?"

Race rolled his eyes and put the ledger back on the shelf. "I think you're more interested in Susan Kerslake."

Con straightened. "Who gave you the right to use her first name?" A fight might be just what he needed.

"No one. I'm tired of trying to decide if she's Miss or Mrs. Kerslake."

The inclination to violence dissolved into laughter. "The thing I like about you, Race, is that you don't give a damn that I'm the blasted earl."

Race leaned back against the bookcase, arms folded. "As I understand it, you have plenty of friends who wouldn't give a damn either."

Con eyed him. "The other thing I like about you—liked about you—is that you don't think you're entitled to dig into my personal affairs."

"Unlike the Georges or the Rogues." Race raised a brow. "Going to run?"

"I'm more likely to throttle you."

Race smiled as if offered a treat.

"Damn it to Hades." Con pushed off from the desk and paced the room. "I thought employees were supposed to do as they're told."

"Friends aren't."

Con looked at Race, remembering that civilized little exchange with Susan.

Friends.

God!

"Nicholas Delaney lives a couple of hours' ride from here," he said, then realized that Race wouldn't know what he meant. He'd mentioned the Rogues, but not in any detail. "He founded the Rogues. Sometimes we call him King Rogue."

"You want to visit him? Sounds like a good idea, but not this late in the day with an overcast sickle-moon night to come."

"That's as well. Nick's an interfering bastard."

Race's eyes twinkled wickedly. "Sounds like just the potion."

"Don't say potion in a place like this."

"Think a demon will rise?"

"If it's one of the old earl's potions, it'll be something else that'll rise!"

Race laughed. "If I find that one, it'll make my fortune." He straightened from the bookshelves and picked up his jacket from the back of a chair. "Let's go riding, then."

Con was aware of the strength of the pull to visit Nick, to talk to him about Susan, and Anne, and smuggling, and the Georges.

And Dare.

Perhaps more than anything he wanted to talk to Nicholas Delaney about Dare. He had something of a magic touch with tricky matters.

Not today though. As Race had said, it would be a wildly impractical thing to do.

So was riding around the countryside with no purpose.

He was simply running. He'd run from Hawk in the Vale to here, and now he was running from Crag Wyvern and from Susan. But he'd have to come back here. Like a hound on a long leash, he was tethered to the thing he most feared and longed for.

He'd agreed to be friends with Susan.

He wanted to howl.

S USAN HEARD that Con and de Vere had left Crag Wyvern, and she breathed a sigh of relief. It was like a pressure off her chest, though absurdly, she hated the thought of Con being any distance away.

Friends.

At least she had his protection for David.

Because she and he were friends.

It was more than she'd dreamed possible this morning.

It wasn't enough.

She made sure the dinner Con returned to would be perfect, and once again selected and prepared suitable wines. Then she checked that the table was perfectly arranged. Again, she took pathetic pleasure in doing these little things for him.

For her friend.

She could not stay here, could not be near, but perhaps there could be letters. . . .

Ah, no. She could control her feelings in letters, write and re-write them until they said only what she wanted to say, but his letters back would kill her slowly. . . .

"Hello." David strolled in and pinched a grape from the bowl on the table. "What's the matter?"

She looked at him blankly for a moment, then said, "Oh! I asked you to come up."

"Right. *Is* something the matter? Is it Wyvern?"

"No," she said, probably too quickly. "But I do need to talk to you. Come." She led the way to the privacy of her rooms.

Once there, she said, "Gifford knows you're Captain Drake. Or at least, he has the strongest suspicions."

"The devil you say. What does he know?"

"That you and I are Mel's children."

"That's all?"

"That's enough."

He shrugged. "It was bound to come out, though I'd hoped for a little while longer."

"This means that you can't have another run anywhere near here for a long time. He'll be watching—"

"Susan, when is he going to *stop* watching me? Probably never. I'll think of something."

"David!" But then she stopped herself from lecturing him like an older sister. She wouldn't tell him about Con's protection, however. Not yet. He was overconfident as it was.

"Wait for a few months at least."

"A few months." He laughed. "You know that's not possible. Unless you've found the gold."

She shook her head. "I've spent most of the day looking for cunning hiding places, and I'm running out of places to search." She paced the room in frustration. "It has to be somewhere the earl went, at least now and then, and he spent nearly all his time in his rooms. He used the dining room occasionally when he had guests, and the drawing room once or twice. . . ."

"What about the storerooms and cellars below?"

She considered, but then said, "I can't imagine it. He thought it beneath an earl's dignity to go into such places. I don't think he even visited the kitchens." She looked at him. "I can't stay much longer, and I don't think I'm going to find that money. I do wish you were just the earl's estate manager."

"Well you know," he said with a smile, "if I was I'd be dashed bored. Probably into all sorts of other trouble."

"Alas, how true." She took his hands. "For my sake, love, try to be at least careful."

He gave a comforting squeeze. "I am careful—because I have the welfare of everyone around here in my hands."

He might not have intended it as a gentle rebuke, but it was. He was her younger brother, but he was past her control and a commander of men. All she could cling to was that Con had promised to try to keep him safe. Unlike the old earl, he would keep his word.

She pulled free with a light smile for him, and told him about the notes she'd found. "It was as if he hated Mel and Lady Belle."

"Mel said a couple of things that suggested that he and the earl were at odds. He kept him sweet with money, but also with things for his collection." He grinned. "Some of it is even more bogus than it's supposed to be."

"Perhaps the earl found out about that."

"Possible, I suppose."

Susan frowned. "But why include Lady Belle in his animosity?"

"Jealousy? I did hear that the earl courted her when she was young. Before Mel."

Susan remembered that. "They must both have been very young. She was eighteen, wasn't she, when she took up with Mel? She could have been countess and she chose to live in sin with a smuggler instead? A wise choice, but extraordinary."

And so different from her own choice. For the first time in her life Susan wished she'd been more like her mother.

"And he held a grudge for nearly thirty years? Truly insane." David shook his head. "But by God, I'll bet he did bring about Mel's capture. I wish he were still alive to pay for that betrayal, but he's beyond my reach."

He was all Captain Drake, and suddenly she shivered.

He turned suddenly watchful eyes on her. "How did you find out that Gifford knows?"

She had to do rapid assessments. She'd confessed her past to Con, but she couldn't bear to tell David. "He told the earl, and the earl told me."

"So the earl's on our side?"

"To a moderate degree. I think I persuaded him of how important smuggling is here."

He nodded. "Good. I'd better go. I'm engaged for the evening."

"Not—"

"Dammit, Susan, I do have interests other than smuggling, you know. It's a cricket match over at Paston Harby."

She laughed with relief. "To be followed by a drinking match at the Black Bull. Do try not to get into another fight, love."

He kissed her on the cheek. "You too. Try to keep on the right side of Wyvern."

With a carefree smile he was gone, and she tried to begin as she meant to go on by not fretting about what he might do next.

She ate her meal in her rooms, served by a maid, as was proper for a housekeeper. As she ate she read a novel—*Guy Mannering* by Sir Walter Scott. The high emotions had appealed to her a few days ago, but now the book seemed ridiculous in comparison to the real, feverish emotions swirling through her life.

She exchanged the novel for a book about beetles and made herself concentrate on it and not think about smuggling, friends . . . or lovers.

At a knock on the door, she said, "Enter."

Maisie popped her head around the door. "The earl wishes to speak to you, Mrs. Kerslake. They're still in the dining room."

Again? Instead of fear, silly hope leaped inside her.

Idiot. They were friends.

Only friends.

Yet there was that matter of curiosity. . . .

"They?" she asked.

"The earl and Mr. de Vere, ma'am," Maisie said, as if it were a nonsensical question. As indeed it was. But Susan had the information she needed. He wasn't alone.

She hardly thought de Vere a pattern card of respectability, but she trusted Con not to do anything embarrassing in front of a third party.

"Thank you, Maisie."

She checked herself in the mirror, tempted to reach for her cap and fichu again, but there was no need for that. They were friends.

She was tempted to change into a pretty dress, rearrange her hair. . . .

They were *only* friends.

She settled her mind about that, straightened her spine, and went briskly to the dining room by the corridor route.

Con was relaxed at the table, fingers cradling a mostly empty brandy glass. He smiled slightly at her, but it was a deep, thoughtful smile. The decanter was over half empty and there was no way to tell how much of it de Vere had drunk. De Vere was on his feet waiting for her, looking bright-eyed. She wondered what was going on in his mischievous mind.

They must have decided that there was no point to formality, for neither man was wearing a cravat, leaving their shirts wickedly loose at the neck.

Con raised his glass and sipped from it.

"Yes, my lord?" She tried to make it crisp. Crisp as the starched cravat he so obviously was not wearing.

Race de Vere spoke, however. "We would like to see this torture chamber, Mrs. Kerslake."

Con raised his brows, suggesting that he thought it folly, too, but he didn't contradict his secretary.

"Now?" She glanced between them. "It would be better left until the morning."

"Did the late earl visit it in daylight?" Con asked.

After a moment she said, "No. But—"

"Then we probably should see it in the appropriate manner." He pushed back from the table and rose, steadily, it seemed. "Don't worry. We expect it to be suitably horrid. In fact, de Vere is depending on it."

She gave Race de Vere an unfriendly look, but he showed no effect of it.

Con said, "If it frightens you, give us directions and we'll go by ourselves."

"Frightens me?" she said, turning to him. "No, it doesn't frighten me." Then she saw the glint of humor in his eyes and knew he'd tossed out a deliberate challenge. The trouble with friends was that they knew you all too well.

Even across a bridge of eleven years.

She swept up the candelabrum from the table. "It's more ridiculous than horrid. But if you want to see it, come along."

She led the way down the dark corridor, but paused by the arch above the stairs that spiraled downward. These particular stairs had been made with true medieval narrowness, and were tricky, especially with the candles in her right hand. She transferred them to the left, then held her skirts up with her right.

Someone touched her arm, and she started.

It was Con. She'd known it was Con. She'd known his touch, like ice, like fire.

He took the candles from her and stepped in front. "I'm sure it's the noble hero's part to lead the way down stairs like this, and after all, I am suitably left-handed. Race, I trust you to fight off any demons or dragons that attack us from behind."

She entered the downward spiral, therefore, between the two men, encased in their fragile bubble of light and protection. She was truly relieved to have one hand free to trace the wall as they went. She didn't like these tight stairs. She always felt trapped, as if the air would go.

When they stepped out into a small, plain chamber she sucked in a relieved breath. She especially hated the stairs in the dark. She should have remembered that.

Only one narrow corridor led off the room.

"Down there, I assume," Con said.

"Yes. It was made narrow to increase the spine-chilling effect. It is all done for effect. Shall I lead the way, or do you wish to?"

He passed her the candles. "'Lead on, Macduff,'" he quoted. "If there's a trap, I assume you know how to avoid it."

"No trap. It is completely harmless, I assure you, though designed to stir fear."

She spoke calmly, but the narrow corridor pressed in on her, even three candles seeming feeble in the dark. The iron-bound door with a small barred opening seemed to waver in the flickering light.

She pressed down the cold iron latch, and pushed the heavy door open. It gave a long, eerie squeal. Prosaically, she said, "It was apparently quite difficult to make the door produce just the right noise."

"The miracles of modern engineering."

A hint of laughter in his voice warmed her and swept away fear.

Friends. Coming here with a friend was so different from coming here with the earl, as in the past. He'd insisted in showing it off to her three times.

She placed the candelabrum on a table among assorted strange implements, and stood back to watch the men's reactions.

"The room is not entirely below ground," she said as if giving a guided tour, her voice resonating in the chamber. "You will note the high barred windows, gentlemen. By day they let in a little light. For expected night visits, the torches on the walls are lit, and the brazier, of course, for heating hot irons and such." She gestured to the implements on the table. She didn't know what most of them were, and she didn't want to.

"The torches produce a lot of smoke," she continued, "but if the wind is right, it escapes through the windows."

Con and Race were wandering through the unsteady chiaroscuro of the room, studying the tools of torture on walls, shelves, and tables, glancing at the wretched victims. Three hung in chains on the wall along with ancient weaponry. Another screamed silently as his foot was crushed by the iron boot. On the pièce de résistance, the rack, a woman stretched, arched in agony.

The waxwork figures were astonishingly realistic, and the first time she'd come here she had been shocked. She looked at the two men, but couldn't read their thoughts.

"No waxworks of the torturers?" Con asked, flipping a cat-o'-nine-tails on the wall without expression. Of course, they were used in the army and navy on real flesh. They were used in the streets on thieves and whores too.

"The earl or his guests liked to play those parts."

Susan looked at de Vere, expecting to see him reveling in his treat, but he was looking around with a slight frown. "Why?" he asked.

She found herself sharing a look with Con. It was an excellent question, but to those familiar with Crag Wyvern and the Demented Devonish earls, it hadn't occurred.

"Because he was stark, staring mad, of course," Con said. He looked at Susan. "Does any of this actually work?"

She knew what he was asking: Had it ever been used? "Of course not, but it's designed to be played with." She went to one of the haggard wretches hanging on the wall, scarred, bruised, and burned. "The burns aren't wax, but painted metal over wood, so a hot iron can be put against them. They can be covered with mutton fat to create smell and smoke. There are bladders of red fluid in various places that can be pierced to bleed."

Con shook his head. "He could have joined the army surgeons and had so much more fun."

Susan was hit by a sudden feeling of associated shame. This place had nothing to do with her, but she had thought it merely ridiculous when she should have been deeply horrified.

Like the dragon's bride fountain.

She glanced at the rack, struck by a similarity between the arched figure there and the arched "bride" bound to the rock. What a foul and twisted mind it had been to think up such things.

She should have seen them for what they were. She should have avoided contact with the mad earl entirely. Instead she had chosen to work here, and thus had let Crag Wyvern coarsen her.

She had almost been snared by the dragon.

Thank God for de Vere and Con, who'd seen real horror and suffering, the suffering of friends and heroes in battle and under the surgeon's knife, while the demented earl and his idiot guests played mad games here.

She longed to leave now, but Con had walked over to the rack. "And this?"

"It is operational to a degree. Do you want to see?"

"Oh, by all means."

"Dammit, Con, it's a woman," de Vere protested.

"It's wax and a wig, and should we feel less pity for the tortured man than for the tortured woman?"

Susan went over and grasped the handle on the large, ratcheted wheel. It took all her strength, but she turned the mechanism another notch. The taut figure stretched another impossible inch. Its back bowed, and a high-pitched shriek of agony bounced around the stone walls.

"Christ Almighty!" Con leaped forward and pulled the locking pin, letting the wheel spin backward and the ropes go loose. The figure sagged, its waxen arms flopping bonelessly. A long wheeze told of the bellows mechanism relaxing somewhere inside.

For a moment they all stood like waxworks themselves, then Con seized a hangman's ax off the wall and severed the ropes at the victim's hands. The next blows cut through the ones at her feet and into the wood beneath. Then he swung again, to dig deep into the wooden wheel, splitting it.

De Vere hauled the victim out of harm's way, but then he shed his jacket and grabbed a mace. He smashed the heavy iron ball into the bed of the machine, sending splinters flying. Con laughed, ripped off his jacket, and swung the ax.

Stunned, Susan retreated from swinging weapons and flying wood and two maniacs who had moments before seemed to be civilized gentlemen. But her hand over her mouth was holding back laughter as much as anything—at the wildness of it, and the rightness. It was past time parts of Crag Wyvern were smashed to bits.

Perhaps she was dazzled, too, at the sight of Con in destructive fever, swinging that mighty ax. It should frighten her, but he was so magnificently physical that she felt dizzy. His back was to her now, and through waistcoat and shirt she could see the muscle and power in ferocious action.

From the first blow, there'd been nothing tentative about him. Her gentle, fun-loving Con was used to wielding weapons to destroy, used to swinging them to cut through to the marrow, to kill before he was killed.

It appalled her.

It made her prickle with raw lust.

She tore her eyes away to look at de Vere, equally masculine, equally ferocious. More so. His face was toward her, and there was something terrifying about the fury and passion with which he destroyed, as if he'd reduce wood and metal to splinters, to dust, to nothing.

His violent certainty, however, stirred nothing in her, while she wanted to rip Con's clothes off.

She looked back at him, wondering what his face would show. He suddenly stopped to stand looking at the destruction, leaning on the ax and sucking in breaths. His shirt was plastered to his skin again, this time with sweat.

De Vere was still smashing the mace down on the shattered machine. Would Con try to stop him? She thought he might be killed and braced herself to run forward, to interfere.

Instead he turned to face her.

No madness in his face, but a deep and dangerous fire that made her instinctively retreat. He walked toward her, his eyes dark, and she would have retreated further, but her back was already against the great door, cold iron bolts digging into her flesh.

She didn't know what his face showed, but she was nothing but instinct now. Instinct to flee. Melting instinct to surrender to the dragon.

He collapsed over her, hands and strong arms catching him but caging her, and lowered his head to claim a ruthless kiss.

She could, perhaps, have escaped. She didn't know what he would have done if she'd ducked away. She could have turned her head. Instead, she surrendered.

With the clang and crash of continued destruction filling the stone chamber and violence in the very air she breathed, she surrendered to a kiss that had nothing to do with the sweet explorations of eleven years ago.

Did she remember a taste? She thought so, but that could be illusion. She remembered his smell, though, strong now with maturity and heat, spicy and deep, and branded in her senses.

Lady Anne. The thought came from somewhere far away in the distant sanity of her mind.

For Lady Anne's sake she would not reach, or touch, or curl her arms around his wide shoulders. But she let herself stay to be consumed by the dragon's hot mouth and potent smell so that her nipples ached and her legs shook.

They betrayed her in the end and she began to slide down, the bands and bumps of the unforgiving door scraping along her back. He came with her, mouth still on hers until he straddled her and captured her head to demolish her entirely.

Hands clenched, she still would not touch, but tears leaked, perhaps *because* she would not touch. . . .

Silence.

There was silence.

Still ravaged by his hungry mouth, she forced her eyes open to the flickering room. She couldn't see de Vere, but he must be watching them.

She touched then, pushing at Con's shoulders and arms, fighting free to gasp, "Stop it!"

Silly thing to say, and far too late. He'd stopped anyway, eyes closed. Too late for other reasons, as well.

That kiss had kindled deeper, stronger fires. . . .

She could see de Vere now over Con's lowered head, apparently sane, watching them with knowing interest. Con still had her pinned to the floor with his weight and his legs. Her back was bruised and stinging, her legs cramping.

What was he thinking? Was he thinking as she was of fire, of greater fires? Or was he bowed by regret?

She made herself speak with quiet firmness. "Con, let me up."

He shuddered, looked at her, then quickly pushed away and rose, grasping her hand to pull her to her feet as he had that first day on the headland. Her legs failed her for a moment and she leaned back against the door. He was still holding her hand, looking at her as if seeking something to say.

What was there to say, particularly with a witness?

What would have happened if there hadn't been a witness?

For a moment, unworthily, she thought of it, the pleasure of it. She thought how it might have broken his commitment to another.

Then he shuddered—like a horse, with every inch of his body—and let her go. He turned to his friend. "Destroyed enough for your liking?" It sounded a little hoarse, but it was probably more than she could manage just yet.

"Sorry about that," de Vere said, like someone who'd knocked a cheap vase off a table. Or was he apologizing for watching?

"Perhaps it's a useful release." Con walked over to pick his jacket up off the floor and shake it free of wood chips. "I'm sure Crag Wyvern can provide plenty of things to smash."

They were both ignoring her. Was it a type of courtesy? If they didn't look, it hadn't happened?

Or was it an insult? *Ignore the convenient drab.*

Had she just been assaulted, or had they exposed a deep, forbidden passion?

Curiosity or passion, she wanted him. With a shivering ache and a hollow need, she wanted Con. If it weren't for Lady Anne she'd shed all pride and restraint and beg him to take her to his bed, even if it was to be only once. Like him she wanted to do what they had done eleven years ago, and do it this time with adult bodies, with knowledge, strength, and will.

And heart. And heart. But that was her secret to keep.

"I was sobered by something indestructible, actually," de Vere said.

His tone shocked her back to sanity. She focused to see him step back and gesture at the heap of broken wood and twisted metal. She pushed off from the door to stagger to the wreckage to see what was there.

A body?

Some new bizarre device?

She saw the glint of gold at the same time de Vere said, "Your missing money, I assume, my lord earl."

She halted and looked down at twisted metal and splinters of wood and the gold coins spilling beneath them. Some of the splinters were parts of the shattered chests that had contained the gold.

Oh, God. No chance now of claiming it for David. She'd not be able to stop him risking another run, and Gifford would be watching and waiting. . . .

But Con had promised protection.

She remembered to breathe. Con had promised protection. But could even the Earl of Wyvern stop the law if David was caught red-handed?

✴ 18 ✴

"W<small>E WERE</small> lovers when we were fifteen." Con was lounging in the enormous, steaming Roman bath, Race nearby. They both had their heads resting on the curved edge, looking up at the domed ceiling that contained yet another picture of a dragon claiming a bound woman.

It looked like the same bound woman. Same model for everything, including the waxwork on the rack. A beautiful young woman with a lush body. Generous thighs. Big breasts. Long, tawny hair. He wouldn't mind lying here enjoying her charms, but not while she was screaming for help and being impaled by a dragon.

A shame to ruin a piece of art, but it was going to have to be painted over.

Susan wasn't that lush sort of woman. She had all the right curves now, but she wouldn't be as soft. He was sure of it. Too much time spent climbing cliffs and swimming.

Did she ride? He didn't know. . . .

He'd wanted a bath for the past hour, but they'd had to deal with the gold first. He'd thought it best not to spread the word, so he'd summoned only Diego to help carry it up and cram it into the safe in the office. It hadn't all fit, so he had a bundle wrapped in a towel, and stashed in one of his drawers here.

Susan had disappeared and it was doubtless just as well. What was there to say about that kiss?

There was a great deal to think about it, but he couldn't bear to. Not yet.

When they'd finally finished, he'd remembered the Roman bath and told Diego to see if it could be used. So here they were, soaking together like warriors of old after battle.

It was heaven marred only by the persistent image of Susan in the water with him instead of Race.

And, of course, by the complete insanity of that kiss.

That damnable, betraying, annihilating kiss.

Race hadn't said a word about it, so in the end Con had felt he had to say something.

"I guessed," Race said. "Pretty good going at that age, especially for her."

Con wanted to defend Susan's virtue, but it had happened. And happened again since with other men, apparently. He hadn't forgotten that. He was trying to pretend it didn't matter. He remembered Nicholas saying something a couple of years back about the unfairness of holding women to a tighter virtue than a man was willing to accept.

There seemed to be an instinct to it, though.

He wondered if she were quietly raging at the thought of him in the arms of other women. In other women. It had mostly been a utilitarian use of whores.

It doubtless didn't bother her.

They were just friends, after all.

He laughed and it bounced around the tiled room.

"Life is damned funny at times, isn't it?" Race said idly. His eyes were shut and he looked blissfully relaxed.

Race was a friend, but more in the manner of brothers-in-arms than friends who shared intimate matters. In better times he could imagine talking about Susan with Van or Hawk, and even with a Rogue, but he'd not expected to be doing it with Race.

The Roman leaders had shared baths like this. Had it loosened their tongues? He amused himself by contemplating the effect on British politics if the powerful in London met naked in hot, communal water.

"She always was an unusual female," he said. "She was raised by her aunt and uncle at the manor house, but she's actually the daughter of the squire's wayward sister and the local smuggling master, Melchisedeck Clyst."

"Wonderful name."

"It's not uncommon hereabouts. He was transported a few months ago and apparently his lady went after him."

"Wild blood on both sides," Race remarked. "With a tendency to abnormal constancy."

"Lady Belle? She's certainly constant. Constant to the exclusion of her children."

"Children? How many did she have?"

"Three, apparently. Susan, David, and one who died young. Lady Belle treated Susan as just another girl, not even as a niece. Mel Clyst took a sort of interest."

He found himself telling Race about the time Mel Clyst had warned him off his daughter.

"I suppose she never told him then," Race said.

Con lapsed into silence, studying the fact that he'd never imagined that Susan would tell anyone, never mind Mel Clyst. Despite her behavior and her motives, he'd taken for granted that the friendship between them had been real, and therefore she wouldn't spitefully get him into trouble.

Of course, if she had, it might have ended with them married, which would not have fit with her plans.

She'd apologized today.

And meant it, he thought.

As he'd already accepted, most people came close to doing regrettable things in their lives. And the difference between *did* and *almost did* was often accident, or even weakness and cowardice.

Something inside him was cracking painfully open. He wanted to hold it closed with his bare hands, as he'd seen dying men trying to hold their innards in.

"Lucky you didn't get her with child," Race said.

"Very, though I was too callow to give it thought then. Astonishing to think about, having a ten-year-old child."

Children.

He'd never thought of children, though he'd assumed they would follow marriage. Now, however, he could almost picture them. Sons at Somerford, playing in the woods and valley as he, Van, and Hawk had played. Daughters too, perhaps, enjoying the freedom Susan had enjoyed . . .

He realized the children in his mind were his and Susan's, the daughters slim, agile, and adventurous.

Friendship.

What mad fool had talked about friendship?

"A ten-year-old," he said again, grieving a little for that nonexistent child.

"And a half dozen others by now, no doubt," Race teased.

Con splashed him, too lazy to have even a playful fight over it.

How strange life was, though. Paths taken, often for little reason, and others left behind.

He'd joined the army at Hawk's suggestion. Hawk had wanted to escape his unhappy family. He'd suggested that Van and Con join with him. Still raw from Susan, Con had agreed. He had been a second son who needed a profession, and one that would keep him far away from Crag Wyvern and Susan Kerslake seemed ideal.

Van had been an only son like Hawk, but with a loving family. He'd had more of a struggle, but he'd always been wild, and eventually his parents had let him go.

So they'd made plans to buy commissions in the same cavalry regiment, but in the end, Con had chosen the infantry. If he was going to do this, he was going to do it properly, and the infantry were the meat of the British army, where steadiness and discipline were key.

He'd served his country, mostly in ways he could be proud of, but all the same, his reasons for joining the army had been rooted in cowardice. It had been a way to avoid future visits to Crag Wyvern.

Over the years he'd come to see that as stupid, to think that there had been nothing to fear.

Now he knew otherwise.

Three days, and they'd exploded into that kiss.

It was more a sizzling blur now than a memory. It had overtaken him like a fever or a storm, and if it hadn't been for Race he'd have claimed her there on the stone-flagged floor.

If she'd let him.

Would she have been able to stop him?

Yes, he had to believe that, or he had indeed become the dragon.

He looked up at the damn rapacious dragon, then down at the one on his chest. At least it was just coiled there breathing fire.

"Dammit," he said. "Tattooing should be illegal."

Race opened his eyes, rolling his head sideways to look.

"It's rather a fine specimen."

"But permanent."

"Quite a few men in the regiment got a tattoo after seeing yours."

"Damned fools."

"Thought of it myself, but could never decide what would be most suitable."

"An angel, according to Susan."

A deep bracket dug into Race's cheek as he smiled. "Then I should have a contrast."

"A devil?"

"Doesn't appeal." He looked like a beautiful, decadent angel, his blond hair curling around his face. "Are you jealous of me and the angelic Susan?"

"Not if you're both behaving like angels," Con said.

"Angels being pure spirits, without carnal inclinations?"

"Precisely."

"I don't think either of us is an angel, then."

"Precisely."

Race laughed softly. "What are you going to do?"

"I don't know."

Had he acted the dragon in the dungeon? Con wondered. Had he forced that kiss on her?

She hadn't struggled until the end, but she hadn't touched him either. Even in the fever he'd noticed that. He hadn't touched her at first except for his lips, as if that would keep him safe, though in the end he hadn't been able to resist.

But she had.

Burning inside him like a twisted blade was uncertainty—had she hated every minute? Had she submitted out of fear?

Or worse, had she submitted because his first suspicions had been right and she still wanted above all to be Countess of Wyvern?

Out on the cliffs he'd been sure that wasn't the case.

Back inside Crag Wyvern suspicion stirred.

Race waved his arms, creating sinuous snakes in the water. "Did you see Miss Kerslake's face when she saw the gold?" he asked.

Con looked at him. "No."

Race's slight smile was angelic—if one remembered that the devil was a fallen angel. "She was devastated. She wanted that money."

It hit Con as a new betrayal. He could think back and see Susan staggering forward from the door to look down at the gold. Race was right. She'd been sallow with shock.

"Have you seen any evidence of her searching this place?" Race asked.

"Yes," Con said flatly, refusing to show how much it hurt. "Of course, that's why she's here playing housekeeper. It's hardly her calling in life."

Friends.

Friends did not steal from each other.

Criminal on her father's side. Whore on her mother's.

He stood, and water streamed back into the bath. "Blood will out." He forced himself to speak lightly. "It should be interesting to see what she'll do now."

"Try to seduce you, perhaps," Race said with a beatific grin. "Yet more theatrical entertainment!"

In preference to bloody murder, Con climbed out of the bath and wrapped one of the huge linen towels around himself. Normally he emerged from a bath feeling relaxed and soothed, but not this one.

He stalked into the bedchamber, where Diego awaited, politely bland, a clean nightshirt in hand. Con kept the towel. Despite everything, the thought of Susan seducing him had him hard.

Lady Anne.

He pulled Lady Anne up in his mind like a shield. Her sweet smile, her gentle blue eyes, her easy conversation about light topics, or more earnest talk of serious causes—education and the plight of the elderly poor.

What charitable causes did Susan support? All her efforts were lavished on a bunch of thieves and murderers.

Even for her elderly poor, Lady Anne wouldn't steal. She wouldn't involve herself in smuggling, not even to fund a hundred schools. She certainly wouldn't invite a worthless officer to her bed on a whim.

Race emerged from the bathroom, also wrapped in a towel, looking very like an effete angel.

A dangerous misapprehension.

How extraordinarily difficult it was to know what people were really like.

"That bath disgorges through a gargoyle?" Race said.

"Apparently."

"Let's go out to watch."

"Watch water? The deadly tedium of Crag Wyvern has struck already, has it?"

"Perhaps I simply want to get outside."

Race's words hit home, but Con said, "It's dark."

"Not entirely. The sun's down, but there's still light."

Yes. In this case, Race's instincts were sound. "Clothes," he said to Diego, flinging off the towel. Race grinned and went off to dress. Con wondered what would happen if he met a maid on his way.

He suspected Race would be delayed.

Sensible Diego brought just drawers, breeches, and a shirt. Con dressed quickly, then pulled on his boots. "Watch from one of the arrow slits and I'll wave when we're in position. Then pull the plug. And ring the bell, I suppose."

"*Sí, señor.*"

Con smiled as he left. Diego lapsed into Spanish when Con did something boyish. It seemed to indicate that he was pleased.

Boyish. How long since he'd felt a touch of the boy?

Mere hours. In the garden, pelted by cool spray. Susan laughing . . .

Damn her.

He collected Race, obviously uninterrupted by rapacious females, and led the way outside.

The sun was down, but pink streaks still shot through a vast shell of pearly gray sky, and light danced on the water, turning it into a blushing opal. The fishing boats were in now, but a mass of screaming gulls circled Dragon's Cove. Doubtless some fishermen were gutting their catch and tossing the scraps to the birds.

It was deeply beautiful and wholesome. And Crag Wyvern deliberately shut this kind of vision off. The garden was lovely, but it was inside and, in a way, artificial. The outer world was blocked off and could begin to disappear even from memory. The old earl had had a fear of the outdoors. No wonder he'd gone mad.

Yet Susan had chosen the Crag for many years, first as secretary, then as housekeeper. No wonder she'd become a conscienceless thief.

A breeze danced up, chilly in his still-damp hair, but alive and free. Even the scrubby headland had its charms, scattered with wildflowers. When he looked away from the sea, the Devon countryside spread in shades of green and brown from woodlands, hedges, and fields, dotted with church spires, each marking a village, a community.

"A sweet place," Race said. "Shame about the house."

"You think I should have it torn down?"

"It's a tempting notion."

"Indeed. But then I'd have to build something else, and even with that gold, I can't afford it."

"You could invest in smuggling."

"No. Come on." He led the way around to the north of the house.

This was the bleakest face of Crag Wyvern. All four walls of the house were the same flat stone broken only by the arrow-slit windows, but the north always looked grimmest. Perhaps it was the almost perpetual lack of sun. Could dark gather in stones like damp and moss?

"It does look remarkably like a stark fortress from out here," Race said. "Has it ever withstood an attack?"

"Yes, as it happens. During the Civil War. The earls of Wyvern were staunch royalists, and a Parliamentary force marched here but failed to take the place. It was halfhearted, though, in part because my direct ancestor, the then Sir John Somerford, was high in the ranks of Parliament. We've tended to take opposite sides all along."

"Don't tell me. The Devon Somerfords for Stuart, the Sussex Somerfords for Hanover."

"And the Devon Somerfords for James the Second, while my branch welcomed William of Orange."

"They must all be rolling in their graves to see a Sussex Somerford here at last."

"Quite. Which is why the old earl was obsessed with trying to get an heir."

"Ah. But I thought he never married."

"One of the many mysteries of Crag Wyvern. Rumor says that he wanted to try the ladies out first."

"Don't we all?"

Con laughed. "This one apparently took the testing seriously." He told Race the system that Susan had described.

"You do have an interesting family. Did many women accept his invitation?"

"Some, I gather. Doubtless not from the upper classes."

Race suddenly laughed. "You know, it's rather like the mythic dragon demanding maidens in tribute!"

"Except that they didn't have to be maidens, and he paid. The girls were sent home with twenty guineas for their service. Quite a nice dowry in a farming family."

"Droit du seigneur as well. What a splendid place!"

Con buffeted him and waved to where Diego was presumably watching.

The bath gargoyle snarled out at them from the middle of the wall, a crested dragon with a long forked tongue. In a moment the bell chimed, and the dragon spouted water. It arced down, silver, but touched with pink by the blushing light, to form glimmering pools and rivulets on the rough ground.

Race applauded, and Con said, "You are easily amused."

"Probably as well in this place."

"What? Three days here and you've had smuggling, a torture chamber, an energetic piece of destruction, and a treasure trove. Not to mention all those lovely papers to play with. What do you expect for an encore?"

"Some concupiscent nuns at midnight would be nice."

Con laughed. "You could probably have Diddy if you tried." Then he winced at the callous words, and remembered Susan's warning. "Leave the maids alone."

"I could take offense at that," Race said quietly.

"I know. I'm sorry. Look, go in, will you? I'm going to stay out here for a while."

Race—perceptive Race—touched him lightly on the shoulder, and went away.

Con looked again over the land, his land, settling softly into the subtle comforts of evening. Inside Crag Wyvern, it was easy to forget, to become wrapped up in his own twisted problems. Outside, he knew that these farms and villages deserved better than an absentee landlord.

That was all he could offer, however. He truly believed Crag Wyvern could drive him mad, but above all, he couldn't live near Susan.

She might be a thief. No. She was.

Despite appearances and his instincts, she might be a whore.

She was still the woman who'd lurked in his heart for over a decade, and who could now ignite him with a glance.

And here he was, afraid to return to his own house.

His mind was full of Susan and that kiss, and he wasn't sure he'd ever be able to think straight again.

He could hardly stay out here, however, and dark was deepening around him, stealing color from sky and land. He retraced his steps and entered the Crag, but not without a shudder.

He went directly to the garden, thinking it would be a haven of sorts, but all he could think of was Susan laughing in the spray. Susan, her damp dress clinging to every delectable curve.

His Susan then.

His Susan on the cliff.

His Susan . . .

A maid bustled out of a door, then froze and turned to go back. "Stop."

She turned back, eyes wide.

No wonder. He was still in just breeches and an unbuttoned shirt and doubtless looked wild. He walked over to her. "What's your name?"

She dipped a curtsy. "Ellen, milord."

She was slight, young, and looked frightened. Perhaps she was a lowly maid who shouldn't be here. Or perhaps she'd been taught to be afraid of any Earl of Wyvern, especially one who was acting in a strange way.

"Ellen, take a message to Mrs. Kerslake. Tell her I wish to see her in my room." She wouldn't come. He knew she wouldn't. She had to. "Tell her it's urgent."

The maid's eyes widened even more, but without suspicion. "Yes, milord." She hurried away almost at a run.

What the hell did he think he was doing?

He knew, though. He was in the grip of that mad force again, but he couldn't resist it.

She wanted gold, did she?

He'd give her gold.

He went up to his room and dismissed Diego. Then he glared at the picture of Saint George, pushing his hands through his hair in search of sanity. He should pray that she wouldn't come.

He begged heaven that she would.

She had to. He had to know her. He had to *know*.

How could he possibly marry another woman with this madness burning within?

How could he marry Susan, thief and whore?

Perhaps if she came tonight this obsession would burn out, leave him free.

If she came . . .

There was a rap on the door and he whirled to face it.

Susan walked in.

❧ 19 ❧

SHE WAS still in her modest, long-sleeved gray gown, but her hair was loosely tied back. She must have been preparing for bed.

Bed.

"Take it off," he said.

She stared at him, lips parted, pink flushing her cheeks.

"The dress. It's ugly. Take it off."

His mouth was working apart from his brain, but parts of him were in control that had nothing to do with brain.

She flushed.

Quickly, before she could refuse, he said, "You wanted that gold. I'll give you half for a night."

All the pretty pink drained away, leaving her ivory-pale. "You would make me into your whore?"

He wanted to deny it, to fall on his knees before her, but need raged over conscience. He found a shrug. "You clearly want the gold. I thought to offer you a chance to deserve it."

Fury flashed in her eyes, but she didn't leave. "A remarkably well-paid whore," she remarked, simply looking at him—mysterious, unreadable—for what felt like an aeon. Then, as his knees weakened at the sight, she lifted her hands to unfasten the buttons on the front of her bodice.

He watched, a part of him disbelieving, as she reached behind to untie something. It all came loose, and she raised the gown up over her head, revealing by layers sturdy gray stockings, a simple shift, and a plain corset.

He stared at it. He'd never seen such a plain corset before. It was clearly something only workingwomen wore, or only decent women wore. But Susan, by her own admission, was not a decent woman. That's why they were here like this.

"What do you want the gold for?" he asked, hoping for some explanation that would make sense of it. Of her.

"That is none of your business, my lord."

"Con," he said firmly.

"Con," she submitted, chin still firm, eyes steady on him.

Ah Susan, magnificent Susan.

"But you don't deny you want it. That you've been searching for it."

"No, I don't deny that."

She dropped the dress to the ground and stood there. She was wide-eyed, but not wide-eyed like little Ellen. Susan was no innocent, and she wasn't pretending to be. Nor was she reluctant. He saw—surely he saw—the same passions burning in her that were consuming him.

Battles could rage, kingdoms could fall, and he did not care. He wanted only this.

He walked toward her, looking at the corset, seeing hooks at the front. He put both unsteady hands there, at the top edge, between her breasts—the breasts that rose and fell against his fingers as he clumsily unfastened those hooks.

Susan wondered if she was visibly shaking, or if it was an insubstantial thing, this tremor in her heart, her soul. She'd come here with irrational hope, then been hit with cruel shock. But now . . . now all she could think was that she and Con were going to make love, that she would have this one night to remember.

I'm sorry, Lady Anne. But it is only the one night.

She knew she should have reacted to his offer with anger, with outrage, even. That, however, would have ended this. She knew

Con. He would never allow himself to do this if he thought her honest and virtuous.

For that reason she would not tell him that the gold belonged to the Horde. If he believed her he might give her half the gold, or even all the gold, but he wouldn't give her what she ached and burned for.

Himself.

But now, with his hands upon her, she didn't know her part. What should she do? She'd been bolder eleven years ago, carried on the courage of ignorance and instinct. Now she stood passively as he parted the corset and let her tingling breasts free. He spread it, pushed the straps off her shoulders, and down her arms.

Let it drop to the floor.

She gazed at the open vee of his shirt as he untied the ribbon that gathered the neckline of her shift, loosening it. Such a strong neck he had now, such a square, firm jaw, darkened by the hint of a beard.

He pushed her shift off too, so that it slid down her unresisting arms. As it passed over her sensitive nipples, she shivered, shivering more as it rippled down over eager skin to pool around her feet.

Only her stockings remained.

She sucked in a deep breath, watching him, seeking the reassurance of passion, if not love.

His eyes lingered on her body, then rose to hers, darkened. "I'm not forcing you," he said.

She didn't know if it was a question or not, but she said, "No, you're not forcing me. Even for the gold I wouldn't do this if I didn't want you."

It was honest. Every part of her, inside and out, quivered for his touch. The heat gathered again, but not just between her thighs. Everywhere. If he touched her, she was sure he'd feel raw heat. *Please let him touch me!* Her legs felt quivery, as when he'd kissed her in the dungeon, and he wasn't kissing her. *Please let him kiss me!*

He seemed frozen there, inches away. Afraid of hesitation, she moved closer and put her hands on his chest.

He broke then, kissing her as he'd kissed her earlier, so they folded down irresistibly to the floor, mouths desperately melded. She'd have taken him there and then, but he picked her up and carried her to the bed, laid her there, and began to strip.

In seconds he was naked and she sat up. "Stop."

She saw his face and quickly said, "I want to look at you! That's all. I want to look at you, Con. You are so very beautiful."

He laughed and pushed her down again. "Look later. I am so very desperate."

Laughing with him—she hadn't expected laughter—she scrabbled the covers down beneath her so she could get to the sheets. With one mighty pull, he dragged them all off the bed, then flung himself beside her, one leg trapping her, there where she wanted to be.

"Better than a beach," he said, his chest rising and falling, his hunger swirling in the air.

"And no fear of being caught." She twisted onto her back and dragged him over her.

"Susan—"

"Hush," she said, adjusting her hips and guiding him into her with her hand. Shuddering with him as they slid together.

"Hush," she said softly again when he groaned, but she didn't mean it. She loved the sound of his need satisfied, of pleasure.

She loved its echo in herself.

He filled her, filled her beautifully, and it didn't matter that she had so little experience of this. A powerful surge of womanly knowledge swept her along.

He began to pump into her and she met him, trying not to surrender to the fever growing within, because she wanted to give him this and she wanted to watch, to watch Con, to drink in his pleasure to the last drop.

To remember it.

She was swirled away, however, into private heat and darkness and only dimly aware of his gasp, his force, then his full weight upon her. Silence fell, hot, deep-breathing, sweaty silence in which she lay, slightly sick and trembly.

She felt him slide out of her, leaving her throbbing, almost in pain. Was it going to be wrong with Con, too? She couldn't bear it.

She hadn't felt this way the first time, with him on the beach. She hadn't felt this way with Rivenham. She hadn't even felt so horribly unright with Captain Lavalle.

He stirred, moved off her slightly, hand sliding down her side, over her hip. His mouth brushed across her aching breasts, then found a nipple. He gently sucked.

Her whole body leaped. "Con!"

He raised his head to say, "Hush," a trace of laughter in it, then went to work again as his hand slid between her thighs. She flinched, she was so sensitive down there, and his touch immediately gentled. Became exactly what she wanted.

He used the flat of his fingers, gently circling, and a buzz started in her head, lifting her away from herself. With deep gratitude she recognized it, welcomed it, and surrendered.

She lay there afterward, flat on her back, his hand still cupped against her, amazed at how perfectly she felt. Perfectly what? She had no idea.

She rolled her head to study him. He looked thoughtful as much as anything, but with endearingly tranquil thoughts. His short hair was on end in places, and stuck to his forehead in others. His dark jaw made him very unlike her Con of the past, and yet she felt only moments had passed between now and the last time they had lain together in sweaty satisfaction.

She looked down and saw the dragon.

She pushed him onto his back and sat up to trace it. "It's beautifully done."

He was watching her from under lowered lids. "By sheer luck we came upon an expert. But it took a devil of a long time." After a moment he added, "I've grown, which has spoiled it a bit."

The dark dragon coiled, breathing flames toward the center of his chest. "Why the dragon, Con?" She had to ask. "Was it because of me?"

She looked up again. He was still watching her. She thought he wasn't going to answer, but then he said, "Yes."

She sucked in a breath, but it was mostly gratitude for his honesty. "I am so very sorry. I wish I could scratch it away."

He trapped her hand. "No, thank you."

She heard humor and looked up to his eyes.

He said, "It's done. It can't be undone. Like many things."

Heart breaking, she understood. She worked at keeping a slight smile on her face. "But we have a night?"

He raised her hand and kissed it. "We have a night. I wish I hadn't wasted the bath on Race."

She did smile then. "Your valet asked if it should be filled again and I said yes. It won't have had time to warm much. . . ."

He was already out of bed, candle in one hand, pulling her with him with the other. "How is it filled so quickly?"

"A gravity feed from the main tank."

"Wonderful design."

They were in the bathroom then, and he went to turn on the big taps. Water gushed out and he put a hand under it, then smiled at her. "Not as cold as the sea, at least."

Memories. Memories.

If she'd been a wiser woman then—if she'd been a woman at all—she could have claimed a treasure greater than gold.

But at least she had one night.

He put the candle on the edge, where it danced strange shadows around the pictures on the wall and left mysterious corners where wickedness doubtless lurked. Then he dropped down into the waist-high tub, the water already swirling around his ankles. He held his hands out to her, but she went to a shelf holding fine china pots.

"If those are some of the old earl's potions, I don't want anything to do with them."

She looked back, smiling. "No doubts about your virility, sir?"

He glanced down. "Not with you, Susan. Never with you."

She knew she was blushing as she turned back. "These are just perfumes."

"We don't need perfumes either."

She picked up a pot anyway, and returned to toss a handful of brown powder into the water. As she walked down the marble steps, the scent of sandalwood began to fill the room.

"If we let the cistern drain into here, will the bath overflow?" he asked, coming toward her.

"It's not supposed to. Why?"

"I might lose attention soon." He pulled her into his arms, then leaned her back against the smooth, cold side of the bath.

She rested there, nervousness stirring. That hot passion had been all very well, but she'd given him the impression she was vastly experienced, and now, like this, all faculties alert, she didn't know what to do.

She knew her supposedly vast experience was another reason he was doing this. He mustn't guess the truth.

He nuzzled at her neck and jaw. "What's the matter? Something in particular you want?"

What did that mean? "No," she said. Then, "Yes. Kiss me slowly, Con."

He moved one hand to cradle her neck, sliding behind to hold her for his lips, which settled firmly, hotly. She opened to him, feasting, her own hand going to his strong shoulder, his neck, his hair. . . .

The water thundered, creeping up her calves. Sandalwood created spicy mysteries.

He moved back. "Like that?" he asked, smiling.

She smiled back. "Just like that."

He kissed her again, and she kissed back, her body stirring with primal knowledge. Perhaps it was all instinct after all, which emerged only with the right partner.

He pressed against her, and the water swirled around her wobbly knees. Perhaps his wobbled too, for eventually he sank down, taking her with him into water that was now chest-high.

He smiled.

She looked down and saw that the water was lapping at her nipples.

She laughed up at him, knowing exactly what he was thinking.

"You can touch them if you want."

"Oh, I want." He put both hands under her breasts, raising them, flicking the nipples with his thumbs. "I remember thinking that I was a dead man if Mel Clyst ever found out I'd touched his daughter's breasts. And that it was worth it."

His touch and his words sparked sharp desire. Through clear water she could see his erection. With an unsteady hand, she dared to reach through the water to gently touch it.

He put his mouth to her raised breasts again, and because of the rising water she had to stand slightly, bracing herself on his shoulders.

He seemed completely intent on his play—licking, tugging, nipping. He suddenly nipped sharply, and she yelled and pushed backward. He let go and she went right under, emerging spitting water and pushing sodden hair off her face.

"You bit me!"

"Mmm." Laughing, he grabbed her by the waist and hoisted her out of the bath to sit on the edge, then spread her legs wide. He smiled at her as he'd smiled at her breasts, then put his mouth there.

"Con!" She tried to wriggle back, but he grabbed her hips, looking at her with surprise.

She knew then that this was something experienced lovers did. She stopped trying to escape, but didn't know what else to do, what to say.

"You don't like it?" he asked.

"Of course! You just surprised me." Did that sound convincing? "And you bit me," she added as a distraction. "I thought you were going to bite me there!"

"No teeth. I promise."

He put one hand on the rim and leaped with agility out of the bath. He went to the pile of linen towels on a shelf and came back to spread them lavishly on the tiles.

She sat there, drinking in the beauty of his strong body, trying to look as if she knew what he was doing. She'd just lied to him, and she hated that. She wouldn't tell the truth, however. She couldn't bear for this to stop now.

He picked her up and sat her on the towels, then dropped back into the water. It was certainly more comfortable than cold, hard tile.

"Now lie back."

She did so, but he kept his hands on her knees so she had to leave her feet dangling, up to the ankles in water. Then he began to draw her toward him, and hooked her legs over his shoulders.

She knew better than to cry a protest now, but she lay there on her back, quivering with ignorant uncertainty, staring at the lewd ceiling, but shockingly aware of being exposed to his very close eyes.

Then she felt his hands beneath her, thumbs brushing apart sensitive skin. She stared fixedly at the dragon about to impale the screaming maiden, water still thundering into the tub, echoing around the tiled chamber.

His thumbs entered her, opened her, shuddering her, making her want to squirm away—and to wriggle closer. Then it was only his mouth, stroking and sucking. She almost felt too sensitive to be touched there, and yet immediately her body responded, demanded.

His tongue swirled around her and she gasped for breath.

Her breasts ached, and she reached up to comfort them, squeezing and stroking. A mere touch at her nipples sent fire through her, and she pressed there, squeezed there. Hot pleasure swept down to meet his mouth, making her arch toward him, but the dragon had her lower body chained, completely in his power.

Her demanding dragon with the mouth of fire . . .

A moan escaped her to bounce around the room. She squeezed her breasts harder as he sucked harder and that blissful darkness circled in.

She was being ravished by her dragon, but raptured, not raped. This was the most perfect, the most blissful rapture she could ever imagine.

Then fiercely he was in her, wonderfully big, hard, and strong, driving the velvety darkness deep into her until it swallowed her whole.

She drifted back to hard tiles beneath damp towels, to sweat and sandalwood. To silence. The water had stopped.

Curious, she raised her head to look. It had stopped a hand's breadth from the rim.

"Have we created a flood?" he asked sleepily.

She let her head sink back. He was half over her, his head between her breasts, and she stroked him there. "No."

"Pity. I wouldn't mind the end of the world."

She knew what he meant.

She moved her hand down, exploring the firm strength of his muscled back beneath the smooth, wet skin, a worm of sadness stirring. Never to do this again. A bitter shame, but better than never to have known it.

The one candle gave little light, and the room, the house, was quiet. Even their breathing had calmed.

Then he stirred, pushing up off her to stand. He extended a hand, and she put hers into it to be pulled up. As she stood, she winced. She was tender, but her legs were protesting unusual exercise too.

He smiled and pushed her into the water. She yelled as she splashed in, and it echoed around the room. Would it echo through corridors and courtyard to tell the world what they were doing here?

She didn't care.

He jumped in after her, and waves splashed over the edge, rippling down the steps.

"You'll bring the house down!" she protested, laughing.

"Good idea." He circled his arms to create waves, and she lunged at him to hold him still, his body slippery beneath her hands. They wrestled through and beneath the water, to emerge spluttering and collapse against the side.

"We could go out on the beach in the dark," he said, nibbling her ear. "Go swimming."

She shared his need to re-create the past, to make it whole and good, but she had to say, "There's not enough moon."

"Another time then." He said it lazily, but she knew from the tension of his body that he'd remembered that there wouldn't be another time.

Because there wouldn't be another time, every moment of the night became precious, and one thing she wanted was to know more about him.

She struggled up straight and embraced him in the water. "Tell me about the army."

"That's not something you want to hear."

"It's most of the years that divide us, Con. And there must have been some good times."

He moved back against the side, and she let him. When he leaned his head against the rim and let his body float, she floated beside him despite the distraction of his lovely body and soft, promising genitals.

"It seems barbaric," he said, "but it's true—there were some good times. Wild incidents. Insane acts of bravery and generosity. And pure farce, like the time the company tried to smuggle a bunch of piglets on a march . . ."

He began to talk, telling her stories, but leaving out so much. She wanted to ask: *Were you frightened? What was it like to kill? How often have you been wounded? How much did it hurt?*

They were stupid, invasive questions, but they made up a part of his life that she would never know.

She could tell from his body that he'd not been seriously wounded, but scars told of pain. She supposed everyone except an idiot was frightened sometimes. And certainly a soldier must kill.

Her sweet, gentle Con.

She turned to put an arm around him, to float against him. "I'm glad I was apart from you when all this happened."

He stroked her back. "But I was just telling you about the time Major Tippet made assignations with three Spanish women on the same night. That's not so terrible."

"I know," she said, without explanation, and he didn't ask for one.

"I checked the casualty lists," she confessed. "I knew that we'd hear the news eventually, but I couldn't bear not to check."

It was growing cold in the water, but she didn't want to move, didn't want to risk any change. "So many deaths. With each one, I thought what it would be like if it were you. I became intense about it. Uncle Nathaniel tried to forbid me to read the papers, but I always found ways. They couldn't understand, but of course, they didn't know about you."

"They had to know something."

She traced the coils of the dragon. "They knew we'd met. We'd been seen together often enough. But most of our time was out of sight. No one realized how much time we spent together. And of course, no one knew the whole of it."

"You never told anyone?"

She shifted to look up at him. "Did you?"

"No, of course not."

"Then why think I would?" It hurt, and she added, "It's not as if I wanted to be forced to marry you, after all."

They slid apart. "It was force you had in mind, was it?"

Appalled, she tried to repair the damage. "No! I thought you willing. You *were* willing! I simply encouraged you."

"But you'd have encouraged Fred if you'd realized he was the heir, wouldn't you? You did, in fact. I could tell from his letters that Miss Susan Kerslake was doing her best to be of interest to him."

She bit back tears. "I told you. Marrying the future earl had to be a worthy goal. I'd already sacrificed you on that altar."

"Any passionate little sessions on the beach with him? I doubt it. If you didn't have sails and a rudder, Fred would hardly notice you."

She sucked in a deep breath. "Don't do this, Con. It's so long ago now." Desperate for harmony again, she offered him a cautious bit of her heart. "He wasn't you."

He took it wrong. "That always was the problem, wasn't it?"

He yanked the plug out and water began to run away, taking her magical night with it.

She turned and climbed out by the stairs, grabbing a damp towel to wrap herself in, and drying herself as she hurried into the bedroom.

He followed, stark naked, watching her, silently.

"Are we finished?" she asked, knowing that too had come out all wrong.

"Oh, yes, I think we are."

She turned away to pull on her shift, to fasten her corset, to struggle into her dress. Her hair was still sodden, and she shivered at the water running down her back.

No, that wasn't why she shivered.

She'd constructed a time of lies here. She'd wanted him, and to get what she wanted she'd lied. As she'd feared, as she'd known, now she had only dust in her hands.

There was nothing for them now, but earlier there had been friendship, and tonight, together, they had thrown it away. What use was friendship, however, if they never met?

Once he left here, and she left here, they would never meet again.

She looked back at him still watching her, still naked.

The room smelled of sandalwood, and passion, and Con. She thought she'd remember it all her life.

What to say at such a moment?

In the end, she simply turned and left in silence.

20

C ON COULD finally allow himself to collapse into a chair, to sink his head into his hands.

Susan. Susan.

A thief, and a whore, and a liar.

He stood and went to the table to pour himself a glassful of wine, knocking it back in one swallow. He finally really did understand those poor fools entangled with worthless women. He could feel the bonds winding around his limbs.

What did it matter? a voice was saying. As his wife she'd have no need to steal. He should be able to keep her satisfied and in line so she didn't whore around.

But could he ever trust a word she said?

She lied so well. So convincingly. She'd claimed lovers to overcome his resistance to surrendering to his needs.

But it had been his idea. He remembered that. His insane, overpowering idea. He'd bribed her with half the gold. . . .

Was he mistaken? Was she honest?

How could he twist the lens to see her as honest?

"Lady Anne. Lady Anne. Lady Anne." He spoke it aloud, an incantation against dark magic.

Thank God he'd sent that letter. It bound him. It protected him. But even so, he had to get away from here soon.

Swann was coming from Honiton tomorrow, and Race had sorted out the essentials of the earldom's affairs. Even after giving

Susan half the treasure trove, there'd be enough to keep this place going for a while.

By tomorrow night he might be able to leave with a clear conscience and ride east.

To claim Lady Anne.

Sweet, kind, gentle, good—

He hurled the glass to shatter against Saint George's smug face.

Susan felt she could hardly breathe for suffocating sadness. She took refuge in the garden, but this was all too horribly like the past, without the brash certainties of youth to hide behind.

Then, for a while, she'd been able to think: *I made a brave sacrifice so I could continue to pursue my great goal.*

Now she could think only of might-have-beens.

They might at least still have been friends.

Where had she gone wrong?

Everywhere.

She should have reacted with outrage, as she'd wanted to, to being bought, and explained clearly why the Horde had the right to that money. He might not have agreed, but he'd have known she wasn't a greedy thief.

But then they would not have made love.

She circled the shadowy fountain, thinking of the dragon's bride splayed on her rock, screaming. Had she screamed in true terror, or because she was horrified at wanting to be ravished?

The chain still hung there, trailing limply into the stone basin. What had really chained the bride to the rock? What if she'd gone willingly, though shaking, to give herself to the dragon?

She leaned on the rough stone rim, shivering with loss, and with the prosaic chill of damp clothes and wet hair. What else should she have done differently?

She should have pretended more skillfully to be experienced.

No, no, she should have told him the truth.

But then they would not have made love.

Clearly she shouldn't have let her anger show at the end. Why not, though? Why not? Why shouldn't she be outraged at being thought of with no honor? Was that how he'd thought of her all these years, as a person who would stir up trouble out of spite?

But if she'd held her tongue, perhaps they would even now be making love again.

She pushed herself straight and took a deep breath. Life goes on. Despite lost chances and broken hearts, life goes on and must be endured.

As she continued through the shadowy garden she tried to comfort herself with the fact that she'd earned half the gold. She didn't know how much half was, but it must surely enable David and the Horde to lie low for a month or two.

It didn't touch the pain eating deeply into her.

Susan was wakened the next morning as usual by Ellen with her breakfast tray. Tea, a fresh roll, butter, and jam.

Routine, blessed routine, except that she had no interest in food at all. She'd hardly slept, but she managed a smile for the girl, and thanks.

"Was it something terrible last night, ma'am?" the maid asked.

"What?" Susan froze, wondering what people knew, what they'd heard. . . .

"The earl, ma'am. He said it was urgent, and he looked ever so wild!"

Susan choked down a laugh. "No, no. It was a minor matter. Nothing to worry about."

"That's good, ma'am." Ellen smiled. "He's a lovely man, really, isn't he? It'll be all right here with him as earl."

Susan poured tea into her cup. *Life goes on.* "Yes, he's a lovely man, though he's not going to live here. But you're right, Ellen. Everything will be all right as long as he's earl."

The maid left, and Susan spread butter and jam on the roll, took a bite, chewed, and swallowed.

Life must go on.

A lovely man.

He was.

Beneath the dark and angry moments lived Con, the blessing of her youth. With Lady Anne he probably was that man. At Somerford Court he probably was that man.

That comforted her. She thought perhaps she could bear this loss if Con was living a good life somewhere in the world.

She rose and washed and dressed as usual, unable to escape memories of Con taking off the same clothes. So she faced the memories, embraced them. Most of them were to be treasured.

She almost felt the events of the night should have marked her, but the most careful scrutiny in the mirror showed not a sign. Last night her skin had been a little reddened, her lips a little swollen. Now no trace remained.

Just as it hadn't eleven years ago.

She'd returned to the manor sure that everyone would know what she'd done, that she was marked, changed. It appeared not to have been so. Con and his father and brother had left three days later, and after that Aunt Miriam had remarked once or twice that Susan was missing him. Perhaps there'd been a hint of sympathy for a young love that had come to naught. But no more than that.

Today, no one would notice anything either.

What secrets lay in the other hearts around her?

With a sigh, she went out to organize the day.

She was inspecting the laundry that had come up from the village when Amelia bounced in, bright-eyed and beaming. "Hello. Where's the dragon?"

"Not in these quarters," Susan said, waving the maids off to put the folded sheets and pillowcases away. "What on earth are you doing here?"

She was smiling, though. No one could help smiling at Amelia, and all the shadows suddenly seemed to shrink.

"I do have a reason," her cousin said, eyes twinkling with mischief, "but I won't tell you what it is unless you tell me something exciting about the earl."

"I'm a servant here," Susan said, deliberately being difficult. "It is not a servant's place to gossip about her employer."

"Susan! We've gossiped about the earl enough in the past. What I really want is to see him."

"I have to pick some flowers to refresh the arrangement in the dining room. You can come with me if you promise to behave."

"I'm not a servant here."

"Behave like a lady, I mean. And," she added, picking up a basket and some shears, "you're much more likely to see him there than here."

That made Amelia enthusiastic. Susan fought off a touch of guilt. If she was any judge, Amelia wouldn't catch a glimpse of Con while in her company.

When they entered the courtyard, Amelia looked around. "This isn't much of a garden. If I'd known you wanted flowers I could have brought some from the manor. We're awash with tulips."

"Two gentlemen don't require a lot of flowers." Susan snipped some wallflowers and stocks.

Amelia was looking up. "All those windows. It's like being in a box, watched."

Susan looked up, realizing that Amelia was right—and that Con could be watching.

As if picking up the thought, Amelia asked, "Where is he? I do long to see him."

"I don't know."

It was true. He'd eaten breakfast but she knew no more. Mr. Rufflestowe was here again going through the curiosities. De Vere was presumably in the office. Con could be with either of them, or anywhere else. She didn't think he'd left Crag Wyvern, though. Mr. Swann was expected.

"How long are you going to stay here?" Amelia asked. "It must be pretty boring." But then said, "What does it mean? 'The Dragon and His Bride'?"

Susan looked over to see her cousin studying the words carved into the rim of the fountain.

"It used to have figures. A dragon and a woman."

Amelia turned to her. "What happened to them?"

Susan was remembering one of the problems she had with life at the manor. Everyone expected to know everything. The concept of private matters did not occur to them.

"The earl didn't like it, so he ordered it removed."

Amelia's eyes lit up. "Was it very improper?"

"Highly."

"I wish I'd seen it before it was destroyed. It really isn't fair. I never get to experience anything exciting."

Susan added some delicate rue to her basket. "You don't want to either."

Amelia wandered back to her side. "Not if it was uncomfortable, no. But a naughty statue wouldn't be dangerous, would it?"

Susan suppressed a wry smile. "You'd be surprised."

Con was with Mr. Rufflestowe, unwillingly fascinated by the strange and occult items being entered into a meticulous catalogue.

"People really do use eye of newt?" he asked, looking into a glass vial of small, dry objects.

"So it would seem, my lord," said the round and polished young man. He rose to take down a heavy, leather-bound book from the section already recorded. He flicked through the pages carefully and then pointed to a recipe.

"I can hardly read that writing, never mind translate the Latin after all these years," Con said.

"It instructs the user to dissolve four eyes of newt in mercury and pig's urine."

"And what is that supposed to cure?"

Mr. Rufflestowe went pink. "Er . . . a female complaint, my lord."

"Should certainly stop all complaints dead, I'd think."

Con was mildly amused, and Rufflestowe was surprisingly entertaining company, but essentially he was in hiding, waiting for Swann to turn up so he could arrange his escape.

Susan was somewhere in the house, and he wasn't going to see her, or speak to her if he could help it.

He glanced out of the window, however, and one resolution crumbled. Susan was out there. A new aspect of Susan, smiling and chatting with a plump and pretty young lady in a sunshiny yellow dress that was all the brighter beside Susan's gray and white.

Dammit, as her employer could he order her to wear something different?

Unfair, and dangerous.

But he couldn't stop watching the two women. There was something so comfortable and familiar between them, and he realized that it reminded him of his sisters together.

That must be one of her Kerslake cousins.

He knew he should move back, turn away, as if from a spellbinder, but he continued to watch.

Then Race stepped into view.

"Good morning, ladies!"

Susan turned to see Race de Vere sauntering out of the office doors, smiling angelically. "Speaking of naughty and dangerous . . ." she murmured.

"Oh, lovely," Amelia murmured back, giving de Vere her best flirtatious look.

"Mrs. Kerslake, do we have a new maid?" he asked, eyes twinkling.

Susan heard a little squeak of outrage from her cousin and had to fight a smile. She'd thought she'd never smile again.

"Don't be mischievous, Mr. de Vere," she said. "This is my cousin, Miss Kerslake. Amelia, Mr. de Vere. Lord Wyvern's secretary."

"And friend," he said, stepping closer and bowing. "It must mean something to be an earl's friend."

Amelia dropped a curtsy, dimples showing that she'd overcome any outrage. "Have you been the earl's secretary long, Mr. de Vere?"

"Mere months, but it seems like an aeon, Miss Kerslake. . . ."

Susan rolled her eyes and left them to their lighthearted flirtation as she looked around for suitable greenery. Amelia at least had what she'd come for here—an encounter with an interesting new gentleman. The selection in this area was limited and very familiar.

She wondered if Amelia had looked up de Vere in any books, and what she'd found. She was sure he was not a typical secretary with his way to make in the world. He was far too sure of himself for that.

As she worked her way around the garden, their voices and occasional laughter as background, she recalled Amelia's interrupted question. How long was she going to stay?

There was nothing to keep her here now.

Nothing.

A flutter of pain and panic told her how much she didn't want to leave. Not while Con was still here. It might be crumbs from the table, but if that was all there was she would stay for them.

And perhaps, just perhaps, he would summon her to his room again.

Wicked to even think of it, but she couldn't help it. And she didn't think she would be strong enough not to go.

Con felt unreasonable irritation that Race could stroll out there and flirt while he was pinned up here, a mere observer. Susan was now almost out of his sight unless he peered down from the window, and he wasn't about to do that. That left only the laughing, flirting couple.

How strange it was, however, to see such normal interaction within Crag Wyvern. He was sure it had been years, decades even, since two normal young people had enjoyed each other's company here.

Was it something to do with expectations? Could he and Susan get along better together if they weren't so aware of the poisonous nature of this place?

But then, it was their past, not their location, that had twisted everything into disaster.

A new person came onstage.

Susan's brother.

Ah, yes. Con remembered summoning him. If he was going to protect Captain Drake it might as well be an open matter between them.

For the first time, he wondered if he should warn Kerslake about Gifford's threat to Susan. She'd told him in confidence as a friend, he knew, and yet it was a matter that needed to be dealt with.

"Susan."

She turned to find David beside her.

"Good heavens. This is becoming a market square!" But then she said, "Trouble?"

"I don't think so. Wyvern summoned me."

"What?" But her sudden alarm subsided. "More poring over records with de Vere, I suppose."

He shrugged. "I was to report to him, not de Vere. Any idea where he is?"

David was Con's estate manager. It wasn't peculiar that Con wanted to speak to him. But prickles of alarm were running up and down Susan's spine.

Con couldn't want to talk about her. Of course he couldn't.

But men were so strange about these things.

He might want to talk about Gifford. Would he feel he had to tell David about Gifford's threat?

Would he want to talk about the gold?

What might he say about the gold?

She hadn't thought about how to explain the fact that she now had money for the Horde. . . .

"What's the matter?" David asked.

She found a smile for him. "Nothing. I didn't sleep well last night, that's all." That, at least, was true. "De Vere might know where he is. Otherwise we'll have to organize a search."

"A dragon hunt," David said lightly as they strolled over to the other couple.

Susan winced, but then she saw Maisie limping out of the great hall. "Mr. Swann's here to see the earl, Mrs. Kerslake."

"Market square indeed," she said, feeling as if the weight of three outsiders here—four if she included de Vere—was shifting something elemental about Crag Wyvern.

Or perhaps the change was all in herself.

"I'd forgotten," Susan said, going over to the others. "David, that's doubtless why the earl wants you here. Mr. de Vere, do you know where the earl is?"

"With Rufflestowe in the Wyvern rooms, I believe, ma'am."

How nicely formal they were all being.

"I'll go and talk to Swann," David said. "Someone else can dig Wyvern out of Wyvern."

With a grin he walked briskly off toward the hall. De Vere pulled a humorous face and said, "I'll go. I'm sure one day I'll be grateful for this exposure to fertility charms and auras."

"What?" asked Amelia as soon as de Vere was out of earshot.

After a moment's hesitation, Susan told her cousin about the earl's rooms.

Amelia was wide-eyed and laughing by the end. "Susan, I *have* to see that place!"

"It would be most improper."

"Foo. It would be no more improper for me to go there than for you, even though you are playing housekeeper here."

"I *work* here, Amelia. I earn my pay." It was appallingly tempting to tell Amelia exactly why they were different.

Amelia picked the shears out of Susan's basket and began to gather more blooms. "I've heard the rumors," she said. "About women coming up here hoping to get with child and become the countess. Strange they'd think it worth it."

"Very strange. But I talked to a couple of them and it was more a matter of getting a handsome dowry for nothing. I gather in recent years at least the earl was . . . incapable."

"Impotent?" Amelia asked, but then she pulled a face. "He'd still have wanted to touch and such, wouldn't he? Tom Marshwood tried to handle me in a most offensive manner at a picnic last week."

"The swine! What did you do?"

"Told him exactly what I thought of him, of course. He won't be so foolish again."

Such simple solutions among essentially decent people. Susan wondered if living in Crag Wyvern drove away all sense of proportion.

She recaptured the shears from her cousin. "This small garden can't afford such extravagance with flowers. Come to the kitchen and we'll have tea."

As they strolled there she chatted, but underneath her mind was fretting about the meeting between Con, David, and Swann. It should all be business, but it could turn to other things. . . .

Whatever was happening, she reminded herself, there was nothing she could do about it, and she had resolved to stop trying to force life into the channels of her choosing.

She settled to the haven of a session of light chatter and gossip with Amelia, wondering if there'd ever been a chance for her to be as straightforward as her cousin, or whether she'd been cursed from her irregular birth.

Con was glancing through a book about witchcraft when there was a rap on the door and Race walked in.

"Mr. Kerslake awaits below at your command, my lord," Race said like a bad actor in a poor play. His manner had become stranger over the past day, and Con wondered what the hell he was up to.

"But yet another waits below!" Race declared. "To be precise, in your great hall."

"Swann, I assume."

"So I am told, my lord, but it could be a mere goose, and the maid mistaken."

"A gander, at least, or the poor maid would be very much mistaken."

Race grinned. "Touché."

"And don't you forget it. Back to your den of archival iniquity, and prepare for invasion." Con realized Race's nonsense was infectious. "Are we ready to get everything straight?"

"Can a twisted tree branch ever be straight? We're ready to discuss matters as they are."

"That will have to do."

Con lingered a moment after Race had left and realized that he didn't want to set the earldom's affairs in order. Because then he would have no excuse not to leave.

21

TEA AND simple talk with Amelia seemed to bring some normalcy back into Susan's life. Perhaps it was helped by the awareness of other people in the house, though the kitchens had always been an oasis of sanity.

She and Amelia were sitting at the big table along with the other servants. With all the "betters" engaged in business, there would be no need of them in the other side of the house.

An aromatic soup simmered on the back of the modern stove Mrs. Lane had insisted be installed five years back, and fresh spice cakes sat cooling on a rack—those that weren't already on the table to be consumed.

She'd come to feel a sisterhood with the servants here. They were all, like her, at Crag Wyvern because in some way they didn't fit in elsewhere.

Ada and Diddy had come to try their luck with the earl and then stayed on. Diddy, at least, had tried her luck a number of times at twenty guineas a go. She was the one who'd told Susan that the earl was impotent.

"A lot of groping and complaining," she'd said, "but I can put up with that for a year's pay in a month. Pity, though. It would have been grand to be my lady, wouldn't it?"

When the earl had died, she'd said, "That's it, then. Time to start looking for a husband. With my nice little dowry, though, I'll be the one doing the choosing!"

Ada had spent only one month as a trial bride. Apparently the earl had been certain that a thin woman couldn't conceive. However, when Susan had realized that Ada had only a cruel father back home who had sent her up to the Crag, she'd added her to the staff and to the books, and if the earl had noticed, he hadn't cared.

That was four years ago, when she'd been secretary.

She'd employed Maisie and Ellen too. Because of her twisted spine, Maisie couldn't find good employment, and Ellen had been scared out of her wits by her first position with the Monkcroft family over near Axminster. What she'd said about that violently argumentative family had been a revelation to Susan, and when Ellen had found Crag Wyvern a happy haven it had shown that everything depended on the point from which one viewed it.

Mrs. Gorland had been cook here for nearly twenty years, and with her skills could work anywhere. She was, however, of a somewhat republican disposition, and would find it hard to deal with a lady of the house who demanded deference.

Susan knew she would miss this assortment of women as much as she would miss her family at the manor.

Though Amelia hadn't been in Crag Wyvern's servants' dining room before, she was at ease with the servants, sharing tales of the local families, and absorbing stories of the old earl. Reasonably decent stories, Susan was pleased to note, though perhaps there was no need to protect Amelia. No country girl with all her wits was naive.

At fifteen, and never having kissed, she'd known enough to seduce Con.

She settled into a mellow contentment with the moment. Eventually, however, Amelia had to leave. Susan walked with her to the main entrance, feeling extraordinarily better. It was only at the door out of Crag Wyvern that she remembered Amelia's arrival. "Didn't you say you had an excuse for coming here?"

"Oh, yes!" Amelia dug in her pocket and produced a slightly

battered letter. "This came for you. We think it might be from Lady Belle. Do you think she's reached Australia yet?"

"I doubt it. It's been only three months." Susan took the letter, which had been addressed to her at the manor, but showed nothing about the sender. "Why on earth would she write to me?"

"You are her daughter."

"Which fact she's ignored all my life."

She realized that she didn't know what her mother's handwriting looked like. That was strange, but then, her mother had given nothing to her in any practical way. So why a letter?

It had been roughly handled before it had come into Amelia's careless hand, and it was impossible to make out the smudged scribble that might have indicated where it had started its journey. It had come from abroad, however, and who else would write to her from abroad?

Despite a creeping reluctance, Susan snapped the seal on the thick package.

Perhaps one of her parents was dead.

There were three sheets of writing and a sealed enclosure, and at the end, the scrawled signature, *Lady Belle.*

Not *Mother.* Of course not. Did she really, after all these years, still harbor a hope that Lady Belle would turn into someone like Aunt Miriam?

Lady Belle. Not dead. And doubtless wanting something.

She returned to the first sheet. Lady Belle's writing was not an elegant hand. It was bold, splotchy, and sloped heavily to the right with big loops. Typically she had not tried to write small to save paper and postage. Instead she'd written extravagantly, and then turned the sheet to write crosswise over the first lines.

"What does it say?" Amelia asked, leaning closer. "Ugh. What a mess!"

"That sums up Lady Belle," Susan said dryly. " 'My dear daughter,' " she read, and couldn't help rolling her eyes. But then she made out, " 'I know the word *dear* has no real meaning between us, but how else could I open this letter?' "

Susan laughed. It was so typical. Lady Belle had never made any bones about her feelings or lack of them, nor made excuses. In a way Susan admired her for that.

Even more, however, she had a sense of foreboding about the letter. "I think I need to read this alone."

Amelia drew back from her shoulder, for once looking conscious of a need for privacy.

"I understand. How very strange it all is," she remarked, as if the peculiarities of Susan's parentage had never occurred to her before. "I should be going home anyway. Mother made me promise not to stay here too long. I'm not sure if she was worried what I would get up to, or that the wicked dragon would snatch me in his claws. And here I've not so much as set eyes on him. Remember that ball!"

With a cheery wave, she sauntered away.

Susan thought of retreating to her rooms to read the letter, but then instead she walked slowly to the headland, into open air and light, to the spot where she'd talked with Con yesterday.

Where for a brief moment they had found accord.

She'd known, she thought bitterly. She'd known that anything carnal would ruin it. But she hadn't been strong enough to resist.

Like mother, like daughter?

She sat down on the ground, smoothed out the paper, and began to pick out the words.

My dear daughter,

I know the word dear *has no real meaning between us, but how else could I open this letter?*

A sea voyage, I am discovering, offers a great deal of time for thought, and I have thought that my dearest Mel might disapprove of my taking the means to make this journey, though I have no doubt that he will be delighted to see me.

I have found myself remembering that you said the Dragon's Horde could be in difficulty due to a lack of funds, and that my son might have to take over control and put himself at great risk. Of course, there is nothing to be done about that now, but . . .

Susan had to turn the first sheet then and concentrate on the different layer of writing. What? Was there another cache of money somewhere?

> *. . . there is something which might be of assistance. Though you doubtless think me heartless, I am not completely uncaring about the safety of my only son.*
>
> *You threw up at me the fact that I never married Melchisedeck. I would have you know that this was not my fault, or Mel's either. Unfortunately, I had a prior marriage. I was wed to the Earl of Wyvern.*

Susan tilted the paper to make sure she hadn't read that amiss. No, that was definitely what it said.

Good Lord! Had her mother, too, run mad?

> *Wyvern courted me, and I confess that I was drawn to the idea of being a countess. He was not so strange in those days, though strange enough. He already had his obsession with producing an heir, and he actually made to me the proposition which became so infamous later.*

That ended the first page, and Susan flipped it over, having to turn it ninety degrees to get the next lines straight. Lady Belle must have realized that her letter would be long, for the writing became cramped and even harder to read.

> *Of course I refused, but he was so mad for me that he came up with another plan. We would marry secretly, and once I proved to be with child, it would be announced. He even offered me a normal wedding then. I was only seventeen, and I admit I was swayed by that. I have much regretted not being able to marry my dearest Mel in the church with all our friends around.*
>
> *How was this arranged, you ask?*

Yes, thought Susan. *I ask!* How could her mother, Miss Kerslake of Kerslake Manor, run off to Gretna Green and back and it never be noticed? Lady Belle had assuredly gone mad, or thought Susan a complete idiot to believe this farrago.

But irresistibly, she read on.

The means was so simple I wonder if it is not often done so. James Somerford was mad, but he was by no means stupid. He found a young whore who resembled me and went with her not to Gretna, but to Guernsey, just off the coast, where apparently the same convenience of marriage exists. Wasn't that clever? There the impostor declared herself to be me, and thus I was married without any inconvenience or discomfort at all!

When he returned with the marriage lines, we commenced our secret marriage, but without sullying your maiden's ears, daughter, it was not at all to my taste. In fact, it was quite shocking, and when I fled him in the night, I encountered Melchisedeck Clyst. It was a smuggling run, of course, and he kept me by him as he took care of business.

I am afraid, from what I know of you, Susan, that you lack the more sensitive emotions or a passionate heart . . .

"From what you know of me?" Susan muttered, switching to the next sheet. But she was totally caught up in this impossible tale. It was so impossible that she knew it must be true. And it did explain the great mystery of why her parents had not married.

. . . but to one such as myself, there comes a bond that cannot be denied, and that is for life, and such it was for me and Mel. I assure you, nothing short of an overpowering, tumultuous force could have impelled me into the arms of a mere tavernkeeper without the blessings of matrimony!

Susan laughed aloud at that. It was so completely Lady Belle.

Discovering that he was Captain Drake, and that smuggling was profitable, was some solace. It was also to my advantage that he was powerful enough to protect me from James, who could have claimed a husband's rights.

In brief, Susan, we all three agreed not to mention the marriage. That meant that James would be able to marry another if he managed to get a woman with child. In return for my discretion, James agreed not to interfere between Mel and I, and to protect the Dragon's Horde, for an outrageous tithe of ten percent of the takings. However, he vowed that if I attempted to go through a ceremony of marriage with Mel he would produce the marriage lines and exert his marital authority over me.

You can imagine that I prayed for a child at Crag Wyvern as ardently as James—except that he did not believe in holy prayer— for then I would have been free and able to openly plight my troth to my dearest Mel. I am a widow now, however, and thus I will do that as soon as I find him.

You see, of course, what this means for you.

"No," muttered Susan, almost dizzy from this strange story. Or perhaps it was just the strain of reading the crossed writing. She started the third sheet.

By the law, a child born of a marriage is legitimate unless there is evidence to the contrary. James never claimed David, of course, but nor did he deny him or you, and his clear evidence of insanity can doubtless be brought into play there.

For my son's sake, and to spite James, I admit, I have drawn up the enclosed sworn testimony that my children were fathered by the earl, but that in his insanity he threatened them, leaving me no choice but to give them into the care of relatives. That he then, in his madness, repudiated them.

You may not know, being a mere child at the time, but in the first years of my relationship with Mel, all was in secret. I continued to live at home, going on long visits for my confinements. My par-

ents and older brother hoped I would come to my senses and make a good marriage, you see. Once I was twenty-one, not long after the birth of David, I left my home forever. You will see, however, how this too could support the idea that you and David are the children of my marriage to the mad earl.

If you are wondering about evidence of my whereabouts at the time of the marriage, I went with my old nurse to visit a friend near Lyme Regis. Nurse is long dead, and I doubt anyone can remember the name of the friend. I certainly cannot.

I have no idea if this can be done, but the marriage certificate is somewhere in Crag Wyvern. James would never have destroyed it when it gave him power over us. Perhaps you can use it to make David earl, which would take away the need for him to risk himself as Captain Drake. And you, of course, will be Lady Susan Somerford, and may at last find yourself a husband.

There, I have done my duty to make amends. Do with it as you will.

Lady Belle

Susan sat back half expecting the letter to crumble to dust in her fingers like some mysterious artifact in a gothic novel. But it sat there, presumably still carrying its bizarre message.

David. She shot to her feet. She must speak to David about this! But then she realized that he would be with Con.

Con.

If she used this information, Con could lose the earldom.

But David as earl would be virtually untouchable. Leaving aside the benefits of rank and fortune, he wouldn't hang or be transported for smuggling. In fact, this whole area would probably enjoy decades of peace and illegal prosperity.

It wasn't right to use it. David wasn't the earl's son. But it was as tempting as the serpent's apple.

But Con.

They would be stealing title and fortune from Con.

She should destroy this letter and take the contents to the

grave. She began to tear it, but after the tiniest beginning, she paused. Shredding it and burning it wouldn't scour the knowledge from her mind.

David or Con?

Lies or truth?

22

TRUTH, SHE decided. Once settled, it was so clearly right that Susan could have wept with relief. She could see now that last night with Con had been a web of lies and untruths. Her intentions had not been bad, but all the same, it had been dishonest, and thus had fallen to pieces in her hands.

If she ventured into untruths again, her intentions would not be bad, but she would be back to her old ways, trying to manipulate life to suit her needs. She was through with that.

But then she realized that she really should put this in David's hands. It wasn't entirely hers to decide. Whatever David decided, however, she was going to tell Con the truth.

She returned to the house. If David hadn't left, she should be able to intercept him and talk to him alone.

In fact, she saw him coming out of the arch.

"David!"

As he turned, smiling, she found it easy to smile back. This was right, and it was good to be doing it outside the oppressive house.

"Believe it or not," she said as she joined him, "I have a letter from Lady Belle."

"What does she want?" he asked, and it made Susan laugh.

"Oh, she's all benevolence. Read it!"

He took it, but pulled a squint-eyed face at the writing. "I presume you've deciphered this. How about giving me the precis."

"No, I think you need to read it as given."

He sighed but then settled to it, complaining, but then falling silent as he reached the revelations. When he'd finished, he stayed silent.

She resisted the urge to demand his answer.

"She really is a most immoral woman," he said at last. "There's no trace of hesitation about perpetrating a deception, or making out false testimony."

"I know. It would be pleasant to discover that she wasn't our mother, but I'm afraid there's no hope of that."

"I'm proud to be Mel's son, especially now I know why they never married." He looked at the letter again. "She only sent this because she knew he'd disapprove. A sign of her love, I suppose, but still . . ."

She had to ask. "What are you going to do?"

"Do? Nothing. For heaven's sake, you didn't think I'd go along with this, did you? It's outright fraud!"

Susan was suddenly carried back to last night when she'd taken such fierce offense to Con's simple query as to whether she had told anyone about their lovemaking. Wrong again. Every step of the way, wrong, wrong, wrong.

She gathered her wits. "No, I didn't think you would. I hoped not. But I put it in your hands. I do think we need to tell Con, though. The documents might turn up, and I wouldn't put it past Lady Belle to stir the matter herself later. Now her husband the earl is dead there's no risk to her in asserting her right to be the countess."

"Except that letter," David pointed out. "It admits that we are Mel's children, and exposes her willingness to lie under oath."

Their eyes met. "So we have to give it to Con."

He folded it and gave it to her. "You do it." He hesitated a moment, then asked, "Can you tell me what lies between you two, Susan? Whatever it is, it isn't making you happy. I don't want to be unkind, but you are not looking your best."

With a sigh, she moved closer. "Give me a hug, David. I need a hug."

Susan appreciated his strong arms around her, and the certain knowledge that he would stand by her through life even if she continued to fall into follies. She thought soon she would be able to tell him the truth about some of the things she had done. But not yet.

She told him one truth as they parted. "I love him, David. I've loved him since I was fifteen years old. But he's going to marry Lady Anne Peckworth, who I am sure is a lovely lady and will make him very happy."

"Is it your birth? Is that what stands between you?"

She smiled. "No, of course not. He doesn't return my love. It happens all the time, I'm sure, and the world doesn't end."

"Eleven years, though. I wondered why you hadn't married. It would seem you share one thing with our mother. Eternal constancy."

"Hopefully not quite as obsessively. Go along. I'll give him this letter and tell you his reaction."

She watched him set off down the hill, then turned to enter the house. She supposed she needed to go dragon hunting. She crossed the courtyard, glancing in the window of the library, and saw Con still there with de Vere and Swann.

There was no great urgency about giving the letter to Con, and yet she felt it. Perhaps she was afraid that she'd weaken and try to persuade David to pursue safety through fraud. She wasn't entirely sure of her new skin yet.

Perhaps she simply wanted an excuse to be with Con again.

She took up a watching post in the breakfast room, from which she could see the library. She was soon rewarded when he emerged through the doors to the garden, leaving de Vere alone.

She hesitated for a last moment of thought, then hurried out. "Con!"

He turned sharply. She could almost see shields rising. "Susan."

"I have something I must show you, tell you."

He took the time to think, and it hurt, but then he said, "Very well."

She glanced up at all the watching windows. There were few people here now to watch, but all the same she said, "In the breakfast room would be better."

His look was both wary and suspicious, but he gestured for her to lead the way. Once inside, she shut the doors.

"This isn't something anyone should overhear," she said. At his expression, she quickly added, "This isn't some attack, Con. Please don't look like that. This is . . . a kindly act. At the least an honest one." She pulled out the letter from her pocket. "Amelia brought this. It's a letter from my mother. You can read it all if you want, though she writes in a terrible hand."

She glanced at the densely covered page. "I'd never seen her handwriting before. Isn't that strange?"

When she looked up, he was as blankly distant as if they were strangers. Why was she saying such irrelevant things?

"What does it say?" he asked.

She couldn't think where to start. "That she was married to the earl. I know, I know! But I believe her. It was a mad business, but he was mad."

She quickly related the details, seeing his distant coolness melt at least into bemusement.

She put the letter into his hands. "There. It's all there. The letter that you can use to stop her if she tries this again. The sworn false statement. Doubtless somewhere here are those marriage lines. If you find them, you can destroy them too, then she'll have no case at all."

"I believe records will have been kept in Guernsey as well."

"It doesn't matter. It's not true. Surely it can't be proved if it's not true."

"I wonder . . ." He looked at her. "You might have made it stick, then you'd have had Crag Wyvern at least through your brother."

"Dragon spit!" she exclaimed. "I do not want Crag Wyvern! I can't wait to escape this place."

"And yet you have just made sure that I keep it. And last night you proved I am vulnerable to you still."

She closed her eyes. "Con, please!" She opened them to look at him, to try one last time. "I know you have reason to distrust me, but in this I am completely honest. I, like you, will never stay in Crag Wyvern, no matter who owns it. I don't care about the title, any title. I'm deeply sorry to have given you reason to be so distrustful, but now, here, I am being starkly honest."

He was turning the letter in his hands as if it could reveal something extra from the outside. "Be honest then. How many lovers have you had?"

"Three," she said softly.

He looked at her, demanding more.

With a sigh she added, "On four occasions. I'm sorry for misleading you, but I thought that if you knew the truth you would not make love to me, and I was greedy for it. But it was wrong to lie, even by implication."

"Why only two other occasions? I have no right to ask, but I need to know."

She hesitated but continued on the honest path. "I was trying to wipe away the memory of you."

After a moment he put the letter in his pocket. "I need to think about this."

"There's nothing to think about. I told David about it, and he thinks as I do. It would be horribly wrong."

He continued to look darkly thoughtful.

"Con!" she protested. "Please. I will never do anything to hurt you again."

"I believe you," he said with a touch of a smile. "Don't leave here, Susan. I want to talk to you about this more."

"I am staying for a few more days at least."

He nodded, and left by the corridor door.

Con closed the door and paused to try to deal with the thoughts swirling in his head. It was no good. At this point, before making some crucial decisions, he needed an obviously sane head to help him.

He changed into riding clothes, then walked down to the Crag's stables and set off for the two-hour ride to Redoaks in Somerset, home of Nicholas Delaney.

He prayed Nicholas was at home.

As he rode it occurred to him that it was the first time he'd sought out any of his friends since he'd come home from Waterloo. He'd spent time with the Rogues in the Shires and then in London, but with masks and guards thoroughly in place. He'd been hiding within them rather than meeting them.

He'd last seen Nicholas in London a few months back when Francis had married his beautiful, scandalous wife. All the available Rogues had gathered to launch her into society. Being in hiding, he'd avoided Nicholas, who tended to notice such things.

The devil finds work for idle minds, so he'd kept his mind busy. He'd even gone to Ireland for another Rogue's wedding.

But in the end, the dark had crept in, and he'd begun to avoid those who knew him well. He'd sent chatty replies to letters from Hawk, who was abroad. He'd sent brief ones to various Rogues, who were busy with their own affairs. But he'd ignored Van's letters, because Van was too likely to seek him out.

He'd known Van had to be struggling with his own darkness, but he'd been too deep in his own hole to reach out to a friend.

Did he deserve to reach out to Nicholas?

He made good time and was soon looking at the brick house that was Nicholas's country home.

Redoaks was a simple place, but something about the proportions, the gardens, and the oak trees that gave it its name, all spoke of the kind of rightness that Nicholas would choose.

Quite a contrast to Crag Wyvern.

He turned his horse into the short drive, wondering what exactly he was going to say, but knowing that it didn't matter.

The door opened before he reached it, and Nicholas came out in an open-necked shirt and loose pantaloons, his dark blond hair obviously not cut for fashion. "Con! A surprise, but a delightful one."

He looked relaxed and welcome as a clear spring—which made Con aware that he was remarkably thirsty. He swung off the horse. "I'm at Crag Wyvern. You know I inherited the earldom?"

"Yes, of course. An interesting encumbrance, I'd think."

"That just about sums it up, yes." Con was smiling without any clear reason to, except that he was glad he'd made this journey.

A groom came running around from the back of the house and took the horse, and Nicholas led the way into a square hall painted a clear green and containing two pots of hyacinth. The sweet perfume of wax polish and blossoms made Con think of Somerford Court.

"It's what? About fifteen miles?" Nicholas asked.

"A little less, I think. This was an impulse, though if you'd ever visited Crag Wyvern, you'd know the impulse to go somewhere else is persistent."

Nicholas laughed. "I've known many places like that. I did look up a picture of it in a book. It was depicted suitably surrounded with dark clouds and stormy sea and looked rather like something dreamed up by Monk Lewis."

"Oh, a mere novelist could not do it justice. To create Crag Wyvern, you'd have to be completely mad. It runs in the blood."

He saw Nicholas give him a quick look as they went into a room that was probably called the drawing room, but which had a coziness that rejected such a formal term.

Of course there were books: books in bookcases, in small piles on tables, and three waiting on chairs. Sewing lay on one chair arm, and a chess table invited. Con wandered over, attracted by the unusual pieces, and saw they were some Indian design with elephants instead of horses.

"Metal," Nicholas said. "Very practical with little fingers around."

Con saw then that there were toys around the room, including a collection of dolls and carved animals set in a circle around a small lace cap.

"Guarding it, of course. It is currently Arabel's most precious possession. She and Eleanor are out, so you'll have to put up with crude masculine hospitality. What would you like?"

"Cider?"

"Of course." Nicholas went to the door and gave instructions.

Con put his hat, gloves, and crop on a table, feeling heavily overdressed. After a moment he stripped off his jacket and cravat and opened his shirt. When Nicholas returned, Con asked, "Why the devil do we men dress in so many clothes in May?"

"In recompense for demanding that women wear corsets."

"Do we demand that?"

"But surely they wouldn't ask that of themselves?" But Nicholas's smile pointed to most follies being self-imposed, which pretty well fit Con's thinking at the moment.

Nicholas would probably not ask any direct questions. It wasn't his way. Con, however, wasn't quite sure what he had come to talk to Nicholas about.

The Crag. Susan. Lady Anne. Dare. Gifford. Smuggling. Inheritance . . .

Inheritance was the blast that had blown him here, but it was all tangled with the rest of it.

The cider came in a sweating earthenware jug, accompanied by glass tankards. Nicholas filled both and gave one to Con.

At first taste, Con let out a sigh of satisfaction. At second, he said, "This is strong stuff."

"Home brew," Nicholas said. "If you're not ready to tell me your secrets now, you will be in a while."

Con sat in a chair and took another deep draft. "I suppose I wouldn't just be dropping by."

Nicholas sat opposite with his distinctive lazy elegance. He never looked as if he thought about movement at all, and he doubtless didn't, but his body didn't seem able to arrange itself in awkward lines. "Dare?" he guessed.

Typical of Nicholas to hit the spot. Or one of them.

"It's like a nagging tooth," Con admitted. "Not quite bad enough to drive one to the dentist, but perpetually stealing comfort and rest. It makes no sense. It wasn't my fault. But I can't close the door on it. If only we'd found his body."

"His mother's the same way, poor woman. She has this obsession at the moment about having the whole British army tattooed to make identification of bodies easier. I gather you are to blame for that."

"God. I did mention our tattoos, that we'd had them done for that reason. Careless of me."

"You couldn't expect her to cling to it, and it gives her a purpose of sorts." Nicholas took another drink. "I don't suppose Crag Wyvern helps. I know you never wanted the earldom."

Con shrugged. "Once Fred died, it was bound to happen one day. I had reason to hope it would be a long time, though. The mad earl was only fifty. The damned man killed himself with a potion supposed to increase longevity."

Nicholas laughed and demanded details, so Con told him about the sanctum and bedroom—the dried phalluses were a big hit—and what he knew of the mad earl's eccentric ways.

"I wouldn't mind a look at those books and manuscripts, you know. I'm a collector."

"Of alchemical absurdities?"

"Of alchemical curiosities, among other things."

"You just want the dried phalluses. Slowing down in old age, are you?"

"Creaking and groaning. So, is that the worst of Crag Wyvern?"

Con thought of the fountain, and Susan, the gold, and Susan, and the bath, and Susan, but didn't know where to start, or even if he wanted Nicholas's clear eye on these matters at all. He'd come to talk about the inheritance.

"I'm presented with a dilemma," he said, and gave Nicholas the bare bones of Lady Belle's letter.

"What an interesting family you have, to be sure."

"She's hardly family."

"She's Countess of Wyvern, after a fashion. I suspect it would be quite hard to prove that she wasn't the woman in Guernsey if she stood firm about it."

Susan's children . . .

"Con? Can you stay the night?" Eleanor asked.

He walked over and returned her distracting daughter to her. "Tempting, but I'd better ride back. I made no arrangement to be away."

"We could send a groom with a message."

"If he can ride over, so can I." Con wasn't sure why he was so insistent on returning. In part, he knew, he wasn't quite ready for a full-blown exposure to normal people, but he was also anxious to return, and worried about what might happen in his absence.

Susan might disappear.

He had no right to chain her, but he could not bear to lose her yet.

He picked up his belongings, saying, "You'll come over tomorrow?"

"I won't be denied."

"Excellent. And stay as long as you want. It's just possible you will have an antidotal effect on the place. You can have the Chinese rooms. I'm sure rampaging, fire-breathing dragons have no effect on you."

"Chinese dragons? I don't fear them. The scales of the dragon, the Chinese say, are nine times nine in total, and thus the perfect lucky number. It brings storms, but also good spirits, health, and longevity."

"Does it, by gad? I wonder if my mad relative knew that? I'll go odds he didn't or he'd have used those rooms himself!"

Con groaned. "That's all I need—Lady Belle in residence in Crag Wyvern. Thank God she took it into her head to sail off in pursuit of Mel."

"You could probably pull some administrative strings to see that she and this Melchisedeck Clyst get good treatment in Australia. Wonderful name, by the way. I wonder if Eleanor would agree to naming our firstborn son that."

"Probably not."

Nicholas laughed. "True."

Con was thinking about what Nicholas had said, however. "If they were treated well, they might stay after Mel's seven years are up. I suspect there's scope for a man of his abilities in a raw land like that. But what do I do if she insists her son is the true earl?"

"You have that letter. It should blow her case sky-high. A foolish woman."

"Apart from the letter, however, it could stick."

"Ah," Nicholas said, and drained his tankard. Trust him to see the possibilities immediately. He rose to refill both tankards. "You dislike being Earl of Wyvern so much?"

"And more."

Nicholas sat down again. "What a very intriguing idea. Deliciously Roguish, in fact. It's a shame Stephen isn't here with his legal wisdom, but I can't see why it shouldn't prevail. It would create quite a storm in society, and a devil of a lot of talk."

"I believe I can handle that. It would be a falsehood, however. I may not feel strong allegiance to the Devonish Somerfords, but it goes against the code to put a complete cuckoo in the nest. The whole damn lot will probably come back to haunt me."

"Perhaps they can only haunt Crag Wyvern. Stay away, and you should be safe."

Con looked at his friend. "You really don't see anything wrong about it?"

"I like to look at consequences not conventions. Who suffers? The Demented Devonish Somerfords, perhaps, but they died out without force from you. Who gains? You. This David Kerslake. The local people who will have a resident lord. The smugglers who will have a great deal of security. Is he able to be a good Earl of Wyvern, do you think?"

Con considered it. "Yes. He's somewhat brash and overconfident, but then, he's only twenty-four and hasn't been knocked about enough to age quickly. I'd say he is sound. He's certainly bright and hardworking enough."

"Lord above, get on with it! How many peers of the realm could be described that way?"

Con shook his head. "You make it sound easy. It's possible he won't agree." He was going to have to mention Susan. "His sister is my housekeeper. That letter was sent to her. Before she gave it to me, she'd talked to him, and he wants no part of a fraud."

"To his credit, but he must be persuaded. We don't always get to do just as we like. How would it be if I return with you? I can't resist poking my fingers into such a delicious affair, and I truly would like first pick at the arcane collection."

"I'd like nothing more, but it's an oppressive place. I think it truly can turn people mad."

"If I was going to be driven mad by places, it would have happened long since. Ah," he added, and rose before Con had heard the footsteps and the childish babble.

A moment later, Eleanor Delaney entered wearing a sprigged gown and a wide, sun-shielding hat tied with emerald ribbons. As always, she looked ordinary, sensible, and very attractive. She was carrying her daughter in her arms, but she put her down as she said, "Con, how lovely. Nicholas said that you would probably ride over as soon as you visited Devon."

Con glanced at his friend, but Nicholas's attention was on his daughter.

Arabel, in a copy of her mother's outfit except trimmed with pink, had toddled rapidly to fling herself at her father, to be swept up and kissed. Then and only then did she look around and give Con a wide smile.

"Crag Wyvern," Nicholas said to Eleanor, "is apparently full of arcane books and manuscripts."

Eleanor groaned.

"You wouldn't want me to miss an opportunity like that, my love. You and Arabel can come too—"

"No!" It escaped Con, embarrassing him, but he went on, "Truly, Nick, it's an unhealthy place."

"The air?" Eleanor asked.

"The atmosphere."

Arabel wriggled to be put down, so Nicholas did, extracting her from her hat, which had fallen down her back and was threatening to strangle her with the ribbons. "Very well. I'll go over by myself."

"But not tonight," Eleanor said firmly. "We're promised to the Stottfords."

"So we are. Can you stay, Con? I'm sure they wouldn't mind an extra guest, especially a temporarily eligible earl."

"'Lo!"

Con looked down to see Arabel, now with the lace cap perched on her head, greeting him, he thought. "Hello."

She raised her arms, and somewhat hesitantly he picked her up. He wasn't sure he'd ever picked up a young child before. She seemed to be a professional, however, and settled herself, firm and wholesome, on his arm.

"Temporarily?" Eleanor asked. "Are you about to be married, Con? It's about time. It must be, oh, at least a month since we've had a Rogue wedding."

"Archness does not become you, my dear," Nicholas remarked. "It would be best to tie all the Rogues up before they wreak more havoc."

Con had suddenly remembered Lady Anne, however. He should tell Nicholas that he intended to marry there, to tidy up a bit of Roguish mess. But the words stuck. They stuck because he couldn't stop thinking of Susan.

But he'd sent that letter.

He looked at the pretty child with the chestnut curls who was exploring his shirt and skin with small, soft hands, and the idea of marriage, of children, became appealing in its own right.

23

CON ARRIVED home in the late afternoon, feeling better for time away from the Crag. Feeling better, too, for contact with Nicholas, Eleanor, and their child.

There was such an aura of sanity and good health around them, and yet both Nicholas and Eleanor had been through troubles. They'd not let the darkness drown them, however. They'd fought back, and fought for each other.

He rode into the Crag Wyvern stables at the bottom of the hill rather than riding up and letting a groom bring the horse back down. Delaying his return, he supposed.

He needed time to think.

He'd had hours of riding to think, but had let them wash his mind blank. Astonishingly, he felt better for it. A clean slate.

He chatted to the grooms, noting their watchful eyes. He was key to their lives, and what they really needed was a sane earl in more or less permanent residence. Guests would be especially nice, bringing their own servants for company, and paying generous vails for service.

He left the stables, but instead of heading straight up the hill he turned back to the village and walked to the church. It was not called Saint George's, but Saint Edmund's. Of course it had been here long before the first earl's supposed adventure with a dragon.

He walked up the short path and into the cool interior, which was blessedly deserted.

He'd remembered that there were monuments to the previous earls here. The first earl had a carved marble memorial in front of the altar. Typical grandiosity. And the man had started life as a simple country gentleman. Find favor with a king, then marry an heiress, and here he was in stone robes and lace, his adoring family depicted in miniature all around him.

"Remember, earl, that thou art dust," Con murmured, "and unto dust thou shalt return."

Perhaps it wasn't so outrageous that the earldom return into a bloodline of gentry and yeomen. He seemed to remember that back in Tudor times the Somerfords had been only farmers.

He found the various memorials to the next five earls, but had to go outside in search of the mad earl. The sixth earl had neglected to make provision for his burial, and when Con had been asked for instructions he'd simply told Swann to arrange a suitable grave.

The suitable grave was a box tomb with scriptures engraved on all sides. Reading them, Con thought that the vicar and various others might have gained considerable satisfaction from encasing the old madman inside them.

> *For we must needs die, and are as water spilt upon the ground.* *II Samuel 14:14*
>
> *And the great dragon was cast out. Revelation 12:9*
>
> *Be not deceived; God is not mocked: for whatsoever a man soweth, that shall he also reap. Galatians 6:7*
>
> *Thou hast shown thy people hard things: thou hast made us to drink the wine of astonishment. Psalms 60:3*
>
> *The fear of the Lord is the beginning of wisdom. Psalms 111:10*

On the top it recorded that James Burleigh Somerford, Earl of Wyvern, had lived from 1766 to 1816 and had passed into the next life dependent on the infinite mercy of the Lord.

Another clever turn of phrase.

Con looked around the pleasant graveyard, which was swept

with spring flowers, and overhung by generous trees. A sweet resting place, but not his. Strange. Even in the dusty heat of Spain he'd
not felt such homesickness for Hawk in the Vale and Somerford
Court as he felt here in this equally wholesome place.

Was he contemplating chicanery simply to rid himself of a burden?

Yes, in part.

He knew he could cut through the graveyard to join the path
up to the Crag, and so he took that route. As he went he found
himself among the Kerslake graves. He stopped by one tiny stone
recording the brief life of Samuel Kerslake, born in May 1799 and
dead in June of that year. Susan's youngest brother, with no record
of his parents given at all.

Was the infant to be re-created the Honorable Samuel Somer-
ford, son of Isabelle, Countess of Wyvern and the Earl of Wyvern?
Put like that, he could see that it would be just about irresistible to
Lady Belle, no matter what David Kerslake thought.

He wandered through the other Kerslake graves, and found
one very interesting.

The clock struck five as he let himself out through the small
gate and walked the narrow path between green hedges full of
noisy, nesting birds. Where the path joined the wider one he encountered a middle-aged countrywoman in broad hat and apron.
It was her direct, shrewd look that alerted him to her being more
than she seemed, and he wasn't surprised when a smile lit her face.

"Why, you must be the earl. I remember you now. I'm Lady
Kerslake, Lord Wyvern. You and your family dined with us a couple
of times many years ago. You've hardly changed at all."

Con felt as if no scrap of that innocent youth remained, but as
he bowed he thought that such a positive statement doubtless came
naturally to her. So this was the generous woman who had given a
good home and unstinting love to her sister-in-law's carelessly discarded children.

"Lady Kerslake, I do remember. You were very kind."

"Oh, nonsense. A family of interesting strangers is an entertainment in these quiet parts. Are you walking up to the Crag, my lord? I'm going along that way a bit to see Will Cupper's grandmother at the stables."

They turned to walk together. "Susan says you don't plan to live at the Crag," she said.

"I know it will inconvenience the area, but I do have a home in Sussex. And," he added, "Crag Wyvern is Crag Wyvern."

"It is, isn't it? You know at various places along the coast the earth has given way now and then. I have thought it would be nice. But only if no one was injured, of course."

They shared a laughing glance that reminded him of Susan. So much of her must be from the family that had raised her—a good, solid family, all in all.

He was wondering what effect it would have on the Kerslakes if David established a claim to the earldom. He suspected that they were not the sort of family to enjoy the attention and speculation that would have to come.

At least the story was to their credit.

"I gather the Crag is built on a piece of reasonably solid ground," he said. "My relatives here have been peculiar, but not entirely crazy."

They had come to the stables and paused. "The first earl chose the building site, Lord Wyvern. I fear it has been all downhill since then. The lack of progeny could be seen as a sign of divine wisdom."

"I noticed in the churchyard that a Somerford woman married a Kerslake. Did that happen often?"

"Not to my knowledge. They've been peculiar all along. That would have been my husband's great-grandmother, I believe. A beauty, they say, but wild. The story goes that she danced herself to death by going to an assembly too soon after the birth of her third child."

Con sighed, looking up again at the house. "Do you think it's impossible? That anyone who lived there would be bound to go mad?"

Of course, David Kerslake wouldn't have to live there if he didn't wish to. He could build himself a house in the village here. But Crag Wyvern was still a burden any Earl of Wyvern had to bear.

"It's not a wholesome house," she said, "but it's the blood that is least wholesome, and that, thank heavens, has died out. Probably the place could benefit from some modern improvements and a lot of activity. My daughter Amelia has a great desire for you to hold a ball there."

"A ball! Would anyone come?"

"My dear Wyvern! Come to see the new mad earl? Most of the county would walk there in their bare feet."

He laughed. "A fashionable crush should certainly exorcise some ghosts."

"And if you need relief, come to dinner. You and your mischievous secretary. Take potluck. You will always be welcome."

"And Susan?" he asked, deliberately using her first name and watching for a reaction.

"She's always welcome, of course." She cocked her head, her eyes holding an appealing, practical wisdom. "You were good friends, I think, all those years ago. When we're young we tend to take such friendships for granted, thinking the world full of them. In time we see that they come rarely in life and should be treasured."

He noted the message. "Thank you. I do hope we can take up your invitation, Lady Kerslake, before we leave."

He opened the gate for her, closed it, and went on his way.

A rare and precious friendship. It was true, and he hadn't considered it that way, being generously provided with friends.

Or was he?

He, Van, and Hawk, being so close in age, and bound together by geography, had been destined to be friends. They were bound by time and proximity, but were in fact quite different in their natures. If they'd met elsewhere—at school or in the army, for example—they might not have formed such a close bond.

The same could be said for the Rogues. Nicholas had deliber-

ately gathered a varied group. There were commoners and aristo-
crats, scholars and sportsmen, thinkers and men of action. They
even had their republican rebel in Miles Cavendish, the Irishman.

There was a strong bond, but within the group other friendships had formed. During school terms Con's closest friend had
been Roger Merryhew, who'd joined the navy and drowned within
sight of England in a storm.

And then there had been Susan.

He and Susan could never be only friends and yet they could
not be more. He'd sent that damned letter to Lady Anne. Though
he'd love to wriggle off the hook now, he could not in honor do so.

Susan couldn't imagine where Con was. It wasn't the housekeeper's
place to be fretting over her employer's whereabouts, and yet she
couldn't help it. Had the letter so disturbed him that he'd ridden
off a cliff?

Then she heard that he was back safely, and soon that he was
sitting down to dinner with de Vere. She tried to put him out of her
mind and, having made sure all was in order for the next day, retreated to her rooms.

Then Ada came to knock on the door and tell her that the earl
required her presence in the library.

Oh, no. Not again. Tonight she would be strong. "Give him my
regrets, Ada. Tell him I've retired with a headache."

"If you wish, ma'am, but your brother's there."

"David?" She stood and hastily pinned up her hair. "Very well."

She entered the library, wary of a trap. However, she found
David there with Con. They were flipping through a portfolio of
drawings they'd spread on the long table.

"Look at these," David said to her. "The original designs for the
Crag."

He seemed completely unaware of any tensions or problems!

She went over, even though it brought her close to Con. A
darkly thoughtful Con. Unease prickled through her. Why had he
summoned David here? What did he intend to reveal?

"They were stained glass," she said, looking at a meticulous design for a set of glazed doors. "And one of the crazy earls had smashed them playing a ball game."

She caught a look from David that suggested that he wasn't completely unaware of tensions. Of course, she'd spilled the fact that she was in love with Con. She could only pray her brother wouldn't embarrass her.

Con firmly shut the portfolio. "I've asked you here for a reason, Kerslake. Take a seat, if you please, and you too, Susan." He sat on one of the library chairs, looking somber, and every inch the earl.

Susan and David sat on the opposite side of the table.

"Kerslake," Con said, "Susan showed you that letter from your mother."

"Yes. I hope you're not worried that I'll try to act on it."

It was all Captain Drake, and bloody arrogance.

"Not worried at all," Con said. "In fact, I hope you will."

Susan looked between them. David glanced at her.

"You want me to attempt to claim the earldom?" David asked. "Why?"

"Because," Con said, "I don't want it."

"You look sober."

"I am, and damned serious to boot. Listen. Even if the earldom was the wealthiest in England, and Crag Wyvern a place of beauty and refinement, I would not want it. I am foolishly attached to the place of my birth, and my father's title is good enough for me. I've accepted my duty, as we're all trained to do, but now I've been presented with an escape, and with your help, I intend to take it."

"And without my help?"

Susan realized that Con could use the papers without David's consent.

But after a moment Con said, "No. I won't force it on you."

David looked at Susan again, but she had no wisdom to offer. This had taken her completely by surprise.

"But I don't have a drop of Somerford blood in me," David said at last.

"That's not entirely true," Con said. "You probably don't pay attention to your familiar graveyard. The Kerslakes and Somerfords have intermarried at least once. Your great-grandmother was a Somerford."

"Lord, the one who danced herself to death? Mad blood, and it's a mere drop, thank heavens."

"Yet probably more than I share with this branch of the family. It's six generations since the first earl's younger son left here and ended up in Sussex. Since then, there's been no mingling at all."

David leaned back in his chair. "Perhaps I don't want it."

"We could fight over it. Loser wins all." Only a hint of humor suggested Con was joking.

"Do I want that kind of attention? Notoriety?" David surged to his feet and paced the room. "Captain Drake should be a shadowy figure."

"Then be shadowy. But instead of seeking the protection of the earl, you can protect yourself." Con put a piece of paper on the table. "Here is Isabelle Kerslake's sworn, signed, and witnessed testimony that she married the Earl of Wyvern in Guernsey, and that her three children were all sired by him. I have already destroyed her letter."

David froze to stare at him. "You really do want to get rid of this, don't you?"

"With all my heart, but not casually. I wouldn't do this if I didn't think you would be a good ruler for this part of England."

David flushed slightly at that, with pride. The favorable judgment of a man like Con was an accolade.

"There'll be a horrendous amount of talk," Con added, "and it will touch all your family."

"My family," David said. "One reason I'm reluctant to do this is my family. Uncle Nathaniel and Aunt Miriam won't like the fuss, but . . . I don't like disowning Mel Clyst. I'm proud to be his son. And I certainly don't like claiming the mad earl's blood."

"Few things come without cost," Con said. "It's your choice. I won't force it on you."

Susan thought before speaking, but then said, "Mel would love to see his son the Earl of Wyvern, David. It would be the perfect revenge."

"Revenge?" Con queried.

She turned to him. "As you know from the letter, the earl and Mel had a pact. According to Gifford, the earl helped catch Mel. He betrayed him."

"But according to Swann, the old earl made him work very hard to make sure that Mel Clyst didn't hang."

"Really?" Susan thought about it. "But of course. Death would be too easy, and would free Lady Belle to do her unpredictable worst. She probably would have marched up and installed herself in Crag Wyvern as countess. I wouldn't be surprised if he egged her on to follow Mel. For some reason, he finally wanted to be rid of them. She did come up here after Mel's sentencing. Perhaps to ask for help. If so, she didn't get it, because then she took the Horde's hoard."

Thinking aloud, she didn't realize what she'd said until it was out. Perhaps it was time to tell Con why she'd wanted the earl's money, but he didn't seem to have noticed, and she had to remember that he was pledged to marry Lady Anne Peckworth. It would be embarrassing to be trying to gain his good opinion.

David suddenly said, "I need time to think about this." To Con, he said, "Even though you claim not to want any of this, I thank you for your generosity. And for your high regard."

He left, and Susan and Con looked at each other. Awareness of each other, of being alone together, shivered through the room. Yet neither of them moved closer, or farther apart.

"Would it work?" she asked.

"I don't see why not. In addition to Lady Belle's statement, there must be records on Guernsey. Note, however, that the foolish woman didn't give a date. You were born when?"

"August 1789."

"So sometime before November 1788—"

"You're not suggesting I really could be the mad earl's daughter?"

"Unlikely, but if the marriage was about then, you'll probably never know." A teasing light in his eyes made her want to throw something, but warmed her. It gave hope again of friendship.

"I pray it was in summer. Wouldn't it be more sensible to take a sea voyage to Guernsey in a gentle month?"

"Definitely, but we're talking about the mad earl and Lady Belle."

Susan groaned. "Let's send immediately to Guernsey to hunt those registers."

"It might be easier to find the marriage certificate here."

"You clearly haven't tried a treasure hunt here."

He looked at her, gray eyes warm. "You regard that gold as belonging to the Dragon's Horde, don't you?"

"Yes. I'm sorry, Con, but the earl broke his covenant with the Horde, so he didn't deserve that money. It wasn't the whole of Mel's payments. He used to bring in all kinds of expensive curiosities to keep the earl happy."

"And without the money?"

"David will have to run contraband dangerously often. There are debts, and on top of that people depend on their smuggling income. If there's no work here, they'll hire out to other gangs. Once allegiance slips . . ."

"I see. Have you told him yet that half that stash of coin is his?"

"I assumed you had."

She felt herself color at the memory of what she'd done to earn her half, and then she also remembered the way it had ended.

"I'm sorry for taking offense at a reasonable question, Con."

"Don't take all the blame. I wasn't rational either. I'm not . . ." He spread his hands. "I'm not myself, which is a strange concept when you think of it, since we are what we are. I have no idea what myself is anymore, but I was beginning to find out before Crag Wyvern came crashing down on me."

"And I have made your situation more difficult. Perhaps it would be better if I left immediately. . . ."

"No." But then he looked out into nothing, a shadowy nothing. In the end he simply said, "Don't go, Susan. Not yet."

He rose, and she could almost see him pulling on a calm shell with practiced ease. "Tomorrow we'll have a hunt for those papers. By the way, a friend of mine, Nicholas Delaney, will be visiting, and will stay at least one night. I promised him the Chinese rooms."

"King Rogue. Was that where you went today?"

It was intrusive, even between friends, but his retreat inside that shell seemed all wrong to her.

He looked at her, deeply thoughtful, "You do remember, don't you? He has a lovely home. I'd like to take you there—" After a halted breath he continued. "You'll like him, I think. Perhaps your brother and cousin would like to join in the paper hunt. Do you have any other cousins at home?"

"Only Henry, the oldest, and he's not one for games."

He'd thought of taking her to visit his friend, then remembered Lady Anne. She longed to go closer, to help him, but that way lay disaster.

He suddenly fixed her with his silvery eyes. "Come to my room again, Susan. For nothing this time. We'd be careful."

Her mouth dried. "No need to be careful if it's nothing."

He smiled. "For everything, then." But the smile didn't warm the shadow in his eyes.

"It wouldn't be right, Con."

"Oh, yes, it would."

She wavered, almost a physical wavering toward him, which she fought to resist. She wouldn't even mention Lady Anne, for that might make it seem like a contest between them. "You'd regret it later."

He began to come around the table to her. "Regrets are hard to judge ahead of time. Have you noticed that? I have deeply regretted not forcing you to see sense eleven years ago." He was on her side now, and coming close, and she couldn't make herself run.

"Do you regret last night?" he asked.

"Only the ending of it," she whispered. "But—"

He pulled her into his arms and kissed her. The first joining of open lips conquered her resolve and melded her to him. When their lips finally parted it took all her strength not to say the fatal words, *I love you.* She gazed at him, tempted almost beyond will. Who could resist a tempest . . . ?

Then she realized that someone was tapping on the door.

Eyes met in guilt, and then they stepped apart. He went to open the door. Jane stood there, eyeing them suspiciously. "You've a visitor, milord."

"Who?"

"Says his name's Hawkinville. Major Hawkinville."

Susan's first, alarmed thought was that it was a new, higher-ranking Preventive man, but then Con said, "Hawk," and she remembered that this was one of the other Georges.

Here?

Now?

A blessed interruption, but she wasn't sure she could cope with any more shocks and surprises, not with her body still seething with forbidden passion for Con.

24

CON LOOKED back at Susan briefly, regretting yet not regretting the interruption. It would have been madness to have surrendered, and deeply wrong.

"Bring him here, please," he said to the maid. When she'd left, he said, "He's a good enough friend I could show him his room and ignore him, but . . ."

"But he'd guess, and we can't do this, Con. You know that."

Before he could unwisely protest that, she added, "You must remember Lady Anne."

His self-imposed prison. But she was right. Strong, honorable, and right. "I must, mustn't I? Very well, what rooms do we have available for Hawk?"

"The Jason rooms, and the Ouroboros."

"Oh, yes, the circular one with the dragon eating its own tail. But the Jason rooms have mazes on the walls, don't they? Arrange for Hawk to sleep in there. He enjoys a puzzle."

She was looking at him with a slight frown. "You don't seem happy to see your friend."

He shrugged. "I wonder why he's here. It's either trouble or curiosity, or both."

She began to say something else, but then they heard footsteps, and in a moment Hawk walked in looking the same as always. An elegant devil, even in ordinary riding clothes and after a long journey.

He was suddenly damned glad that Hawk was here, and grinned. After a swift, assessing moment, Hawk grinned back, executed an elaborate, archaic bow, and declared, "My Lord Earl!"

Con dragged him into his arms for a back-thumping hug. He'd have been glad to see Hawk again in any circumstances after a year, but he felt as if sanity had just swooped into his chaotic life. For a start, Hawk had always had a gift for puzzles, and Crag Wyvern was full of them.

Hawk glanced to one side and Con saw Susan standing there, the perfect image of a housekeeper except for her good looks and the lack of a cap. He was faced with a sudden decision.

"Hawk, this is Miss Susan Kerslake of Kerslake Manor, who's been kind enough to fill in here as housekeeper. She's also an old friend. Susan, Major Hawkinville. You've heard me speak of him."

She gave him a quizzical look, but then offered her hand to Hawk rather than bobbing a servant's curtsy.

Hawk took it and bowed. "Charmed, Miss Kerslake."

Con had no doubt that he was making a hundred rapid assessments and calculations and coming to conclusions, many of them correct. But he didn't regret introducing Susan as she was.

She said, "The Jason rooms then?" and when he agreed, she left with a pleasant smile.

Hawk looked at Con, but all he said was, "An interesting house."

"Wait till you see the whole of it. Trouble?"

"I don't think so," Hawk said. "Van's probably getting married."

"Probably? I saw the notice in the paper."

"That was a pretense. Long story. But now it's become real if only he can persuade her. I provided him with some ammunition that should carry the day."

"That's good, isn't it?"

Hawk had always been hard to read, and his years in army administration, some of it secretive, had perfected his inscrutability. But Con knew he was concerned about something.

However, Hawk merely said, "Excellent," and wandered over to consider the books on the shelves. "A conventional selection. I thought you said your predecessor was mad."

Con certainly understood an inclination to keep secrets, so he let it go. "The interesting stuff's upstairs. Come along and I'll show you."

But Hawk stayed where he was. "Perhaps I am jealous of Maria. A lowering thought. One George married. You here in Devon."

"I've no intention of living here, but our lives can never be as they were when we were sixteen. We will doubtless all marry."

Con thought of three new families—Van's, his, and Hawk's—linked as closely as the old ones, their children growing up as friends.

But it was Susan's children he saw, not Anne's.

Perhaps it would become more real if he put it into words.

"I have more or less offered for Lady Anne Peckworth."

Despite having been out of the country for most of the past eleven years, and being a schoolboy when they joined the army, it took Hawk's encyclopedic mind only a moment. "Daughter of the Duke of Arran? A good match."

"Yes."

"More or less?" Hawk wouldn't miss a phrase like that.

"I've arranged to speak to her father when I return east."

"Ah."

Con could see questions in Hawk's eyes, but at least he didn't ask them. "What of you?" Con asked, "A lady in mind?"

God, such a stilted conversation. Was there no real friendship to recapture?

"Give me time. I've been in England for only a week. Besides, unlike my fellow Georges, I have neither title nor large estate to offer. Since I have no intention of living at Hawkinville Manor with my father, I don't even have a home."

Trouble there too. Despite Susan, despite a tentative healing, Con flinched back from probing it.

"How is your father? I heard he suffered a seizure of some kind."

"Recovering. I haven't been there yet."

Conversation dragged to a halt again. "Perhaps we should be taking a bath," Con said.

Hawk's brows rose in a question, and Con laughed. "Come and see."

At sight of the Roman bath, Hawk whistled. "Crazily extravagant, but I can't say I like the decor. He really didn't like women, did he?"

"I presume because they kept failing him. A man like that always blames the woman. But sharing hot water seems to encourage confidences."

"I must remember that next time I have a deceitful supplier to question. Though," he added, "considering the personal habits of most deceitful suppliers, perhaps not."

They strolled back into the bedroom, and Con looked at the fresco of Saint George and the dragon. "Apparently this was modeled after my ancestor, the first earl."

"Not a warrior, I assume. I wouldn't bet on this one against that dragon."

"Nor I. Notice there's no cross bar on that lance? The beast would keep running up it and eat him as it perished."

They fell into a humorous, professional analysis, then progressed to the Wyvern rooms, joking about various aspects of the corridors. Con felt the old ease unfurling between them tentatively, but with all the sure power of an unfurling leaf, and gave silent thanks.

When he saw the bed, Hawk burst out laughing. "After all this, he never showed signs of fathering a child?"

"Ah," Con said. "Now that is a most interesting question." He sketched in the details of Lady Belle's letter.

Hawk smiled. "What a splendid notion. You think you can persuade young Kerslake to go through with it?"

"I hope so. Can you see any problem?"

Hawk contemplated the blank wall facing the bed. "No serious ones. It's suspicious that he fathered no more children, but these things happen. And his habit of drinking strange brews might have had a negative effect. I wonder what happened to the young woman who played the part in Guernsey."

"She might come forward when it becomes common talk?"

"More likely demand money for her silence. That can be the new earl's problem. And you know, from my very brief exposure to your predecessor's nature, I wonder if she survived."

"He pushed her off the boat on the way home?"

"And kept that marriage certificate in these rooms. He'd want it close. Sewn into a book's binding. Or in a cavity cut into the walls . . ."

He walked forward and ran his fingers around a blank piece of wall opposite the bed. "Has anything been moved from here?"

"I don't think so. Why? You've found something?"

"I've found a blank piece of wall in a room otherwise completely cluttered, and a mark. . . . Ah." He dug his nails in and pulled, and part of the faux stone slid sideways.

Behind was not a secret compartment, however, but a drawing of a young woman. It was a highly worked professional piece clearly showing the delicate lace trimming of her dress, and the pearls around her neck. Her hair was simply gathered up in the manner of a girl just out in society. Nothing could be told from her face, however, because the paper had been slashed like a pie, and the triangular pieces hung away from the gaping hole.

"Isabelle Kerslake, I assume," Con said. He'd thought he was past being shocked by his predecessor, but this was vile. "He lay in his bizarre bed looking at her, and hating her and Mel Clyst. I wonder why he suddenly decided to act on it."

"Men break. The last straw, and all that." Hawk looked around at the cluttered room. "I admit, it will be interesting to take this place apart piece by piece and find his other secrets along with that paper."

"We seek only to amuse," Con said. "Perhaps I should open this to the masses and charge a penny a gawk. Nicholas Delaney will be turning up tomorrow too. He doesn't have your eye for solving mysteries, but he can be perceptive in his own way."

"The founder of the Rogues? I look forward to meeting him."

Con shook his head. "Lord, but it feels strange to have people coming here. Ordinary people. Perhaps we should invite up the Kerslakes. I only worry that Crag Wyvern will split open and crumble away."

"Sorry if you're attached to it, but good riddance as long as no one's killed in the collapse."

"Someone else said that. And neither she nor you have seen the torture chamber yet."

"Thank the Lord. It wouldn't be surprising, you know, if this place had loosened some of your screws."

"As obvious as that, is it?" Con asked, navigating a way out of the room and back into the corridor.

"Is Diego still with you?" Hawk asked.

"Yes, why?"

"He'd only have come to England if he felt needed."

This was the astute assessment of someone who knew him well, the assessment he'd feared. Now it didn't seem intolerable.

"It's war sickness," he said as he locked the room. "I was getting over it."

"Dare?" Hawk asked, persistent as a surgeon after shrapnel.

In Brussels, before Waterloo, they'd all shared a billet—Van, Hawk, Dare, and himself. Van and Hawk, professional soldiers like himself, had been somewhat impatient with Dare's unshadowed enthusiasm, but they'd come to like him. Cheerful, generous Dare was impossible to dislike.

"Dare's death didn't help," Con said, leading the way down the corridor. "But it isn't insane to find the experience of death and agony unsettling."

"Of course not. But I gather you've been avoiding your friends."

"Not any longer," Con said, grateful to arrive at the Jason rooms. "Bring 'em all on. The more the merrier."

He left Hawk there, knowing it wasn't particularly friendly, but needing to be by himself. Friendship was unfurling, but he wasn't quite ready for the full power of it yet.

Where? In this fortress of rooms, where could he be sure to be undisturbed? In the Wyvern rooms, probably, but he wasn't going there.

The roof. He and Fred had found the way up to the roof and he thought he could remember it. He went up a circular staircase into the floor that contained the water cisterns. Then he found the trapdoor and climbed out.

Chill evening air hit him, blessedly welcome, and he leaned on a merlon to look at land and sea, at "outside."

Kerslake was reluctant to take this on for a number of reasons. Con wondered if it was pure selfishness to try to persuade him. But in holy truth he'd think himself blessed never to have to come here again.

Except that owning Crag Wyvern would offer the painful hope of at least seeing Susan again. If Kerslake did become earl, there would be no reason. No excuse . . .

He began to stroll around the parapet, but as he turned onto the south wall he stopped. Susan was there facing him, a knitted shawl wrapped around her for defense against the brisk sea air.

She looked like the simplest country woman.

She looked, as always to him, magnificent.

"I'm sorry," she said. "I was hoping you wouldn't notice I was here."

He didn't take it wrongly. He knew exactly what she meant.

He walked nearer. "Come to Irish Cove with me?"

She stared at him, but not with surprise. "It's a chilly evening."

"I wasn't thinking of going swimming."

She cocked her head, considering him, but then she said, "All right."

He led the way back to the trapdoor, but as he stood aside to let her go down first he said, "Would you change for me? Out of that gray gown."

She considered it again. "If you wish."

When they arrived at the garden level she said, "I won't be long," and walked off toward the kitchen area.

He'd like to go with her in case she changed her mind, but he made himself wait, hoping no one was going to interrupt this. Race was back in the office, but might pop out for some reason. Hawk . . .

He'd abandoned Hawk, and Hawk was doubtless drawing all kinds of conclusions. If he was drawing the right ones, he wouldn't interfere.

Though perhaps he should.

A gentleman engaged to marry one lady did not go for evening walks with another.

So why was he going with Susan to Irish Cove? To deal with shadows from the past. No more. It was certainly too chilly for a reenactment.

She appeared in a simple, high-necked blue cotton dress, her hair uncovered and in a plait, but with her shawl still wrapped around her for warmth. He'd rather she left off the shawl, but that would be asking her to suffer even more for him.

They walked out together and followed the path along the grassy headland for a while, contentedly in silence. He realized that this was a friendship he could accept in all its power, without reservation. If he hadn't built a wall between them.

Eventually they came to a slippage where they had to scramble over rough rocks. She laughed as she tried to hold up her skirts and cling to his hand. "This was much easier in a girl's shorter skirts!"

"Or in breeches."

She smiled at him. "Or in breeches. This is a mad enterprise, you know."

"Do you want to go back?"

"Not at all. Perhaps we'll be lunatic lovers, lost over the cliffs." Then she sobered with awareness of her words.

"We are lovers," he said, pulling her up to solid ground again. "Past, and almost present."

And future? almost escaped. But he didn't want to be Susan's lover. The carnal part would be wonderful, but it wasn't the essence of what he wanted. He wanted the golden friendship, the companion for life.

The wife.

He would not dishonor her by taking and giving less.

"Lovers are so often tragic, aren't they?" she said, wrapping her shawl more tightly around her and knotting it at the back. He helped, drinking in even this slight touch, his hands against her supple back.

"Because lovers are generally engaged in something illicit," he said.

"This isn't precisely licit, is it?"

Typical of Susan to insist on honesty. Could he live with anything less?

They walked on briskly, and gradually, out here where they'd roamed eleven years ago, they fell into the easy talk of the past, about plants and animals, and the sea and the sky. Then about the adventures of the years between.

First the light ones that carried no weight, but wove a fragile net between them. Then some of the more sober ones.

She told him more about working with the mad earl. He told her about army life.

He shared more about Waterloo and Dare, and she related with brief honesty her two times with other men.

The net they were building contained future pain as well as pleasure, but he was sure she was as willing as he to bear it.

Near an abandoned chapel, glassless windows showing a stark stone interior, they struck off across rough ground toward the cove. The route they followed was a faint smuggler's trail, mostly overgrown with weeds, and they had to watch the ground for unpredictable dips and bumps.

When they arrived at the steep path to the beach, Con hesitated. "Did we really go down there without a thought?"

"Too old to make it anymore?" With a teasing smile, she pulled the hem of her skirt up to her waist and produced pins to fasten it there, leaving her stockinged legs bare to the knees. Then she was off, finding handholds on roots, and on some rods conveniently driven in for the purpose.

With a laugh, he followed, not hesitating even when his boots slipped on the soft clay rock.

She jumped the last few feet to the pebbly beach and turned to watch him. He jumped too, and swept her into his arms. Just a hug, a friendly hug, but they clung in the salt air, and he knew she was absorbing him as he was absorbing her. Was she, too, feeling as if she was becoming a whole person here?

They drew apart in synchrony, perhaps both recognizing a point of no return, and looked around at the small cove.

"I think of it as bigger," he said.

"It hasn't shrunk, but there was more sand here. The sea changes. Like everything else."

She walked down toward the rippling waves, and he followed, admiring the elegant lines of her body, so different from those of a girl, but familiar, and not just from last night. A man knowing a young tree still recognizes it full-grown.

Last night. Had he been trying to prove something? To demonstrate his many lovers since her?

A smile fought through, and he said, "Susan?"

She turned, smiling, holding a strand of inevitably escaping hair off her face, her skirt still kirtled up to her knees at the front.

"Last night. I was trying to impress you."

A hint of a blush touched her cheeks. "You succeeded."

"I was fighting the memory of your many partners, all hugely endowed by nature, all possessed of the skills and experience of the world's greatest lovers."

She laughed. "Truly?"

"Truly."

"It wouldn't have mattered."

"I know." He had to speak the painful truth. "I'd welcome a chance to do better, but I have committed myself to Lady Anne, alas."

Her smile faded. "Alas?"

"Alas. Perhaps it would be better if I pretended otherwise, but I can only give you honesty. On my first day at Crag Wyvern I wrote to her and as good as offered marriage. I didn't come here with it settled in my mind, but I was drifting that way. It didn't seem to matter whom I married. She is a sweet young lady who deserves a husband. When I wrote the letter, however, I was using her—as a shield against you. Which she now is. Alas."

"And otherwise?" she asked.

Honesty, honesty. It could break his heart and hers. "Otherwise, I would have hope, at least, of winning you for my wife, my friend, my helpmeet all my days."

She turned suddenly away, hand still holding back her hair. From her stance he guessed she was fighting tears.

He walked up to her and put his arms around her from behind. "Once, you threw away what we had. Here, in Irish Cove. Three days ago I repeated the folly. It would seem we are tragic lovers after all."

He leaned down to kiss her wind-chilled neck. She lowered her arm slowly, letting her hair blow as it willed.

"All my life," she said, "I've been a fighter against fate. I've fought to make things be as I willed them to be, and what do I have?" She extended her open hands. "Wind between my fingers. But even so," she said, clenching those hands, "I am tempted again. Tempted to fight this."

He shook his head against hers. "I cannot draw back. A few months ago another Rogue, Lord Middlethorpe, courted Lady Anne. He didn't go so far as to offer marriage, but it was understood. She expected an offer, and he planned to make one. But then he met another. Soon the other woman was with child, and so one honorable necessity overrode the other."

She turned roughly in his hands. "I could be with child." But then she squeezed her eyes shut. "No, no! I don't want you that way, Con, with dishonor and regret around us."

He kissed her closed lids. "If you are with child, I must marry you, but I cannot in honor wish for it. And Lady Anne and her family will expect more from me before you can know. I told her I'd return in a week. I confess, I don't see how to handle any of this with decency, never mind elegance."

She leaned her head against his shoulder. "I'm praying not to be with child." He heard a soft laugh. "All my life, above anything, I have wanted to be normal. I wanted to be like my cousins, like David, who fits comfortably into the ordinary world. But a wildness beats in me. It drives me to disregard rules and conventions, to seek the open spaces and adventures, even as I long to be like others, to belong. I wanted a normal courtship and wedding, but my wild side threw me into your arms. Then made me tear us apart."

He held her tighter. "I don't want you to be anything other than as you are, Susan."

"But I seem to carry the seeds of destruction within me."

He deliberately chuckled. "I think you've been living too long in Crag Wyvern, love. Real life isn't so melodramatic."

"It feels it to me." She raised her head to look at him, and he saw tears glittering on the rims of her eyes. He didn't mention them. "Is there no chance that Lady Anne will refuse your suit?"

He felt her pain because it mirrored his own. "I don't know. It did occur to me that she might be less willing to marry Viscount Amleigh than to marry the Earl of Wyvern, but I don't think she is so petty. We got along together very comfortably, and I believe that is what she wants. It was what I wanted a week ago. Or thought I wanted."

Gulls gave their sobbing cries, swirling past on the winds.

He might as well tell her the rest of it. She'd find out one day. "Anne lives quietly because she was born with a twisted foot. It prevents her dancing, or walking long distances, so she doesn't have many opportunities for flirtation and courtship, but she wants marriage, I think."

He saw it register with her as it must. This was not an opponent she could with honor fight.

"It makes me think of breaking a leg and becoming crippled too."

He laughed because it was a joke, and because it was so very much a part of her to express what many would keep shamefully secret.

Despite the chill he could stay here forever, but the sun was beyond the horizon, and the pink and pearly remnants of light were beginning to fade to gray.

"We must head back," he said. "We don't want to be out in the dark."

She moved apart from him and openly wiped her eyes with the back of her hand. He pulled out his handkerchief and she took it to dry her eyes and blow her nose. "I don't want to go back," she said.

"But we have no choice."

"I do. I'm going home to the manor."

After a moment, he nodded. "It is time. I won't ask you to persuade your brother. It isn't an easy burden to take up, and I understand all his scruples. Will you come up to Crag Wyvern tomorrow to join in the paper hunt? Whatever your brother decides, we need to find those papers and deal with them."

"Yes, of course." She took his hand and they walked back up the beach, soft pebbles shifting beneath their feet. "I don't know what I want him to do either. I see all the advantages, but I wonder if there's a curse to being Earl of Wyvern."

"Curses can be broken. Perhaps one of those books says how." He looked up the narrow path. "Talking of curses, I think going up is worse than going down."

"The alternative is to drown, sir." With a saucy grin, she set off, agile as a cat. What could a man do but follow?

"Most battles are fought on fairly flat ground, you know," he called after her.

She only laughed.

There was still laughter, and that was a miracle.

At the top, however, looking down at the place that had been so crucial in their lives, she said, "Yours is the hardest part."

"Why?"

She looked at him. "Because you will do your best to be a good, loving, contented husband to Lady Anne, whereas I will be free to be a sour, eccentric spinster." She grabbed his hand and pulled him on, back toward the rest of their lives. "You can't imagine how relieved I am at the thought of not sleeping another night in Crag Wyvern."

"Oh, can't I?"

Though I'd sleep in hell itself, he thought, *to spend my nights with you.*

❧ 25 ❧

HE WOKE the next morning to a subtle awareness that Susan was not in the house, and that they had decided their future.

In harmony, but apart.

She'd spoken of the urge to fight, and it raged in him too. Fight to seize the treasure from the jaws of fate. Duty and discipline ruled, however. He had taken this course of his own free will, and since it involved another, he must follow it.

He got out of bed and managed to summon some enthusiasm for the day's paper hunt. On a simple level it could be amusing, and if David Kerslake accepted his part, it would pave the way to a kind of freedom, at least from Crag Wyvern.

Hawk was here, he remembered, and Nicholas had promised to come. Susan too. It could, for a miracle, even be a day of light-hearted fun. In the presence of outsiders, so much about the mad earl now seemed ridiculous rather than horrific.

He pushed to the back of his mind all thoughts about the future, as he'd so often pushed away thoughts of death and maiming before battle.

He found Race in the breakfast room, consuming his usual enormous meal, and then Hawk walked in. Con performed the introductions.

Hawk sat, saying, "We met, I think, at Fuentes de Oñoro."

"Lord, yes," Race said, for once looking a little awed. "I was a cornet then. I'm surprised you remember."

Con smiled. "Don't flatter yourself. Hawk rarely forgets anything."

"It's a curse," Hawk agreed. "But in fact, de Vere was left in charge when his senior officers were wounded, and I had to leave the orderly retrieval of his troop in his hands. Did what he was told precisely and efficiently. That is truly rare."

"Obedient to a fault," Race said, seeming to have recovered his normal manner. "Which brings me to ask, my lord, if you have any particular duties for me today."

Con realized that Race didn't know what was going on. Once the maids had replenished the dishes, he explained.

"Beautiful," Race said, with all the glow of the cherubim looking on the face of the Lord. "I wish I had known this Lady Belle."

"She'd have eaten you for dinner," Con said.

"Oh, no, I don't think so."

And on consideration, Con didn't either.

After another mouthful of thick ham, Race asked, "Did Lady Wyvern come up to Crag Wyvern shortly before she left?"

"I think Susan mentioned that, yes," Con said. "Why?"

Race smiled again. "She killed him, of course. Wonderful woman. He'd broken their pact and harmed the man she loved, so she came up here for vengeance. I assume he would let her into the sanctum, and while there, she slipped something deadly into one of his favorite ingredients."

"Because, of course," Hawk said with the same delight at the puzzle, "she could not have heard of his death on her travels, and yet according to your account, she assumed it in her letter to her daughter, yes?"

"Yes." Con absorbed it. "Of course she killed him. She is nothing if not consistent in her allegiances. She probably also calculated the advantages of having the influence of the Earl of Wyvern working for her—especially if it was her son. One wonders what will become of Australia—"

"Still at breakfast?"

Con turned to see Susan in the garden doorway in a becoming

peach-colored dress and modish bonnet. Another Susan, and one he could become very used to seeing in the morning. Beside her was a shorter, pretty young woman with big, sparkling eyes.

"I'm Amelia Kerslake," she said, without waiting for an introduction, though she did drop a curtsy. "I'm sure you can use extra hands, Lord Wyvern."

As he rose with the other men, Con said, "We can use extra hands, if you're not easily shocked, Miss Kerslake." He looked a question at Susan, wondering if she'd told her cousin the details. She only smiled, which was somewhat hard to interpret, so he said, "But we poor paltry males have only just begun our breakfast and need our sustenance. Will you sit with us?"

Once everyone was seated, Con introduced Hawk, noting that young Amelia was eager to test her flirtatious teeth on anything male. He was sure Hawk and Race could cope.

To Susan, he said, "Is your brother coming?"

There were other things he'd rather say, but during a night short on sleep, he'd arrived at a point of calm and acceptance. It would seem that she had too.

"He had some business to do, but will come up later. He still hasn't decided."

"There's no hurry."

"No, but we ladies are impatient to begin the hunt," she said to everyone, "so do eat up."

All the men laughed and cleaned their plates with speed.

"Army training," said Race, standing first. "The call to battle means don't waste what's on the table."

"Only to someone who needs a deep trencher to support a reed-thin frame," Con said, finishing more slowly.

Susan was amazed at how possible it was to be with Con like this, to be friends. Almost sisterly, though very unsisterly hungers swirled beneath. It was as if life had layers.

Like living water under ice, though that wasn't a good analogy, since the top surface of her life was surprisingly warm and almost joyous.

Like a delicious crust on a pie?

Like cream on a cake?

Like manure spread on a fallow field?

"What are you smiling about?"

She looked sideways at Con and told him.

He laughed aloud. "Don't take up poetry."

"Perhaps there's a place in the world for earthy poetry."

He winced at her pun. "Like the stone around the hearth," he offered. "Warmed from what it contains."

Smiling, they followed the others into the courtyard. De Vere was protesting that he was a great deal more substantial than a reed. Amelia had plucked a tall ornamental grass and was considering him against it, pretending the matter was in doubt.

Susan laughed along with everyone else, feeling a powerful rightness in the world, which was strange when her heart was breaking. Stones around fires did sometimes crack from the heat.

There was something so steady and strong between her and Con, however, that it was precious. Once this was over, they might not meet again. She was sure they wouldn't seek meetings. But the knowledge that the bond still lasted would be sustaining.

She still wished for other things, even prayed for other things, but not at the expense of another woman's heart.

She did wonder if Lady Anne would want a husband who would rather marry another. In the night, she'd fought and won the temptation to write and tell her. She knew Con would do his best not to let his divided heart show, and his best would be very good. Perhaps, in time, his regard for his wife and the mother of his children would deepen into a true love.

She had to pray for that too.

She had brought this upon herself. Con might try to take the blame for writing to Lady Anne, but he would never have reacted that way if she hadn't behaved so foolishly all those years ago.

She caught Major Hawkinville looking at her with far too keen an eye, and chose the bold approach. "The atmosphere of Crag Wyvern does incline to melancholy, doesn't it, Major?"

"Perhaps one has to be particularly susceptible, Miss Kerslake."

"And you are not of a melancholic disposition?"

"I'm far too practical. Why is this empty basin labeled 'The Dragon and His Bride'?"

She moved closer to it. "It had statues. The dragon and his bride."

"Ah. Having seen the Roman bath, I can imagine."

"Are you talking about the fountain?" asked Amelia, who had always been able to follow many conversations at once. "I'd like to see the figures."

"It's not suitable," Susan said.

"You've seen it, and you're as much of a maiden as I am."

Susan flashed Con a look, then knew it was a terrible mistake. She could feel her color rising and of course could do absolutely nothing to stop it. "I know it's shameful at twenty-six," she said in an attempt to cover it, "but there's no need to make such a point of it, Amelia."

"Susan!" Amelia exclaimed, going pale. "You know I never meant—"

"Yes, I know," Susan said, going over to hug her. "I was funning. But the statues are not at all pleasant."

She saw de Vere looking at her with raised, speculative brows and knew she might as well have shouted her sin from the rooftop.

"I think I should see it," Major Hawkinville said. "I need to see everything to do with the old earl if I'm to help solve this puzzle. But then," he added, with a slight smile, "I'm no maiden."

Susan thought he'd picked that up to cover the moment and said a prayer of thanks. As she expected, however, Amelia insisted that she should come too.

"Very well, but don't tell Aunt Miriam!"

She distinctly heard the major murmur, "I doubt she's a maiden either."

Con led the way, since he knew where the figures had been placed—in a windowless alcove off the great hall.

"We couldn't face trying to get them up or down stairs," he said, "and they'd be leaving through the hall anyway. They're only about half size," he added, drawing back a heavy curtain, "but dashed difficult to manhandle."

Susan stood back to let Major Hawkinville go in, but when Amelia followed, she felt obliged to look.

Apart, the figures lost some of their unpleasantness. The dragon lay on its back, its legs in the air like a puppy, making its large organ ridiculous and its snarl rather like a silly grin. She bit her lip, and Amelia laughed outright. The woman, however, was still somewhat embarrassing, if only because she looked as if she was in a private ecstasy.

Con stayed outside, though when Amelia laughed, de Vere went in. Susan heard him say something, and Amelia laughed again.

"Doubtless highly improper," she said to Con, joining him outside.

"Almost certainly."

"What are you going to do with those figures?"

"If your brother takes up my offer, it can be his problem."

The others emerged then, Major Hawkinville steering Amelia and de Vere like a teacher with young pupils. He gave Con and Susan a wry smile, but even so, she thought he assessed them.

He was one of those men, she decided, who couldn't help puzzle out everything they came across. She gathered, from things Con had said on the way to Irish Cove, that puzzling out things had been part of "the Hawk's" work for the Quartermaster-General's Department. Mostly he'd been engaged in the usual QM work—moving the army around efficiently and making sure it had the necessary supplies to live and fight with. He'd also, however, shown a gift for sorting out problems and investigating crimes.

A man like that would be bound to detect the feelings between them, she supposed. All the more reason for these to be their last days.

Lady Anne could be perceptive and intelligent too, and even if she did not see them together, others would. Stories would weave from place to place and reach her eventually. They always did.

"Did inspiration strike?" Con asked his friend.

"No, but I didn't expect it to. My method is the tedious accumulation of details. Eventually a pattern emerges that points to the solution."

"You are assuming some sanity at work."

"True chaos is rare. Madmen have their logic and purposes too."

"If you insist. I give you command of this, Hawk."

They all went up to the Wyvern rooms, Amelia exclaiming with delight at the gothic decor along the way. Yorrick the skeleton was a particular thrill.

At the sanctum door, Con took out his key, but it wasn't locked. They entered to find Mr. Rufflestowe busily cataloguing. He looked considerably startled at the invasion, and Susan at least was startled to find him there. She'd forgotten all about him.

"We're on a hunt, Rufflestowe," Con said. "A legal document that the earl misplaced, probably in these rooms."

"I have placed any papers I've found in the books on the desk, my lord, but none are legal documents. Most are scribbled notes, some are recipes."

Con went over and looked quickly through them. "As you say." He looked at the major. "What method do we use?"

"A systematic one," Hawkinville said, eyes already stripping the room of secrets. "We have six people and four walls, a desk, and the rest of the space. You take the desk, Con—"

But Mr. Rufflestowe interrupted. "If you will permit, my lord, I will begin work on the books in the other room."

Con's brows rose, but he said, "By all means, but keep an eye open for a legal document, or a place where one might be concealed."

The curate left, and Con laughed. "I wonder what devilment he thinks we're up to?"

"Here," Susan pointed out, "devilment is not a word to be laughed at."

"But laughter chases away the devil," de Vere said.

"Five," Hawkinville firmly interrupted. "Con, you should still take the desk, since there'll be papers there to do with the earldom. The rest of us will take a wall each."

Susan found herself with the door wall. That meant significantly fewer shelves to search, but even so, she was soon very weary of the painstaking business. She also wished she were back in her gray gown. Her hands and dress were covered with dust.

She glanced at Amelia and found her murmuring the odd comment to de Vere as she went through racks of scrolls, and laughing at his quiet replies. De Vere had the ingredients to explore, which he was thoroughly enjoying.

Con was sitting at the desk sorting papers into piles much as de Vere had done in the office, but when he looked up and caught her eye she knew it was not a task he enjoyed.

They shared a wry smile and returned to work.

Then the door beside her opened and Jane came in, her face disapproving as always. "A Mr. Delaney, milord," she said, looking around the room as if they were a bunch of children up to no good.

Con rose. "Nicholas. Good, you haven't missed the fun."

"As bad as that, is it?" said the man who must be Nicholas Delaney, leader of the Rogues.

As introductions were made, Susan studied him with interest. He was handsome in a casual style. Even his blond hair had a softer tone than de Vere's, and looked as if it was barbered only when he thought about it.

She remembered being intrigued by Con's stories of him. He had almost hero-worshiped him, though it hadn't been expressed as such. His name had simply come up a great deal, with many sprinklings of "Nicholas says."

Yesterday Con had mentioned visiting him. Though that had been about all he'd said on the subject, she felt the visit had helped him settle his mind about many things.

"Hawk's in charge," Con said. "I feel blessed to have the paperwork. Most of the rest of the stuff is foul in both physical and metaphysical ways."

"But remember," Delaney said, "I have an interest in these matters. Is that claiming to be mandragora?" he asked, going over to a jar on the shelves.

"Can you tell if it is or not?" Hawkinville asked.

"I was given an illustrated lecture on the subject once." Delaney opened the jar and extracted a withered, bifurcated root. "By all the sorcerers, I think it is." He popped it back in the jar. "You can sell that for a fair amount, Con."

"Excellent, but need I remind you that we're looking for a document?"

Nicholas laughed. "Aye-aye, sir!"

Hawkinville said, "If you have knowledge, Delaney, perhaps you could check for treasures while de Vere takes over my wall of books. I will search the spaces in between."

Susan saw Delaney nod as if this made perfect sense.

He caught her looking at him and smiled. She turned hastily back to her shelves of books, resenting another perceptive observer.

More than perceptive.

Knowing.

What had Con told him?

Nicholas Delaney worked quickly through the rest of the ingredients, then came over to study the books Susan had already opened and checked. "Did you see anything by the Count de Saint Germain here?"

"I haven't been looking at titles," she said. "But Mr. Rufflestowe has catalogued all these, I believe."

"He being interested in titles, but not in clever hiding places. I'll check his lists. Con has offered me first pick."

"You are a student of alchemy, sir?" She couldn't help but show her disapproval.

"I'm a student of everything," he replied with a smile, taking out a book, opening it, then returning it to the shelf. "You have lived in this area all your life, Miss Kerslake?"

"Yes."

"Probably you knew Con when he visited here years ago, then."

She grew belatedly wary, but wouldn't lie. "Yes. We are of an age."

"He clearly had interesting memories of his time here. Ah, excuse me." He reached in front of her to take a tall, leather-bound book off the shelf. "A *Physica et Mystica*. Con," he called across the room. "Your fortune is made. The last copy I heard about went for three hundred."

"The Earl of Wyvern's fortune is made," Con corrected. He looked at the desk and table. "I think I'm finished here. I suppose it was unlikely that the marriage certificate would be in such an open spot, and I can't see any secret compartments."

"No offense, Con," Hawkinville said, "but I'd like to check that." He pulled out all the drawers, checking for hidden compartments. Then he slid under the furniture on his back and they heard tapping and rattling, but when he worked his way out, he said, "You're right. Nothing."

He dusted himself off. "Nothing in the floor or ceiling. The shelves here are fixed very solidly to the walls, and there are no spaces between them. Windows, curtains, doors. All clear. The proportions of the room seem right."

So that was what he'd meant by the spaces in between. Susan thought of her haphazard search for the gold and knew they were in the hands of a professional.

She honestly wished she could leave it entirely in his hands.

"I think we should have a luncheon," she said, then realized that it was no longer her place to even think of such things. Even as housekeeper it had not been her place.

But Con said, "An excellent idea. We might as well invite Rufflestowe." He opened the door to the bedroom and Susan saw the curate bent over something on the cleared top of a bookcase.

"Found something?" Con asked.

The curate straightened, looking a little pink. "No, not really, my lord. I suppose this is not part of my ascribed duties, but the poor lady looked so . . ."

Con went in, and Susan followed. Rufflestowe had been bent over the slashed picture that had hung on the wall.

"I begged some egg white from the cook, my lord," the poor man said, looking as if he expected to be rebuked, "and used a sheet of thick paper on the back. It is not sticking down very well as yet."

All the same, the slashed scraps had been pulled together enough that a face existed.

Delaney demanded the story of the picture, and Con told it.

Amelia leaned closer. "She looks familiar. . . ."

"We think it's Lady Belle," Susan told her gently. "When she was younger than you."

"Oh, yes, there's a family portrait of her and Aunt Sarah hanging at the manor. This is probably a drawing for it. How horrid of him to cut it up like that and then keep it. If he disliked her so much, why not throw the picture away?"

"The ways of hatred," Con said thoughtfully. "I wonder if this can be picked up. . . ."

He did so, carefully, and it more or less stayed together. "Follow me."

He went out into the corridor and along to the Saint George rooms. Susan, realizing what he was thinking, hurried ahead to open the doors. They all ended up around the Roman bath with Amelia commenting wide-eyed on the pictures.

"It's the same," Susan said, whispering for some illogical reason, as if the woman on the ceiling, and on the floor of the bath, and in the portrait, might hear.

They were all the same person. All Lady Belle.

Her mother.

"And the fountain figure," Hawkinville said.

"By heaven, you're right." Con looked again at the slashed picture. "He had them all done in the image of Isabelle Kerslake, and doubtless saw himself as the dragon. God damn his black soul."

"Already done, I have no doubt, my lord," said Mr. Rufflestowe.

Con gave him the picture. "Take this back to the Wyvern rooms, Rufflestowe, then join us for luncheon."

The curate took the picture, but said, "I thank you most kindly, my lord, but I must return home. I am to preach tomorrow and must work on my sermon."

Con smiled wryly. "I think we must have provided much material for it."

The curate headed back to the old earl's rooms. The rest of them made their way thoughtfully down to the lower floor, coming to rest in the garden. Susan had no doubt they were all feeling in need of the relief provided by green and growing things.

They chatted about the strange items they'd encountered, and Susan wondered aloud where David was. Then she noticed Major Hawkinville still and silent. She glanced at Con, who was by her side as if it were the only place to be.

He said, "Thinking. He can become an island of calm in the middle of riotous disorder."

As if he'd heard, Hawkinville looked over at them. "Can I see those fountain figures again, Con?"

"Of course. You think there's a clue there?"

"Perhaps." There was something in the major's eyes that could almost be unease. When they paused outside the curtained alcove he said, "I'm not sure if decency requires that the ladies be excluded, or that only the ladies be permitted to search."

"Ladies should never be excluded," Delaney said. "Rogues' law."

"Really?" It was clear to Susan, at least, that Hawk Hawkinville thought this peculiar, but he said, "Come along then. Con, can we have a light?"

It was de Vere who went off to the kitchen to get a lighted candle. They all waited. Susan wanted to ask why Hawkinville thought they'd find the marriage certificate here.

"Because the fountain is labeled 'The Dragon and His Bride'?" she asked.

"It does seem somewhat pointed."

"And those figures are hollow," Con said. "But there are no openings to the inside. The pipe that fed water out of the dragon's, er . . . shaft? Is that it?"

"It would be nice," Hawkinville said, but Susan didn't think he was optimistic.

De Vere returned with a candle guarded by a glass funnel, borne very obviously like an angel bearing a fiery torch. Con pulled back the curtain, de Vere marched in, and they all squeezed in after.

In the flickering candlelight, the dragon did not look so funny, and its mouth did seem to snarl. It was an opening of sorts, however, where not filled with the long forked tongue. There was also the water pipe.

Major Hawkinville said, "Con?" offering him the job.

"Please," Con said, gesturing for his friend to have the honor.

Hawkinville poked a finger into the mouth, but shook his head. He rolled the beast to peer down the pipe. "Anything hidden in here would have to be waterproof, securely attached, and quite flat. And fairly close to the opening." He produced a long, thin knife from somewhere and probed, then straightened. "I don't think so."

"You never did think so," Con said. "Where?"

Hawkinville turned to the figure of the woman. The raped or rapturous Lady Belle.

"Where," he asked, "do you think the demented earl would have hidden it?"

The bride's mouth was open, but it was obviously a shallow space.

Then Susan realized and looked down between the spread legs. It hadn't been obvious in the fountain with the dragon pressed against her, but the figure was anatomically correct. There still didn't seem to be a hiding place, but she went forward. "I'll do it."

Her tentative fingers found something that wasn't metal. Wax. "A knife, or something," she said, hearing her voice waver slightly in the silent room.

Con knelt beside her, offering his penknife. "Do you want me to do it?"

"No, it should be me."

Wincing slightly, she dug the knife into the wax and carved it away. It became easier. It became only wax. And when the final bit came free, she saw a slender roll. She pulled it out and gave it to Con, then picked up some wax and pushed it back into the space as best she could.

Nonsensical, but she had to do it.

She stood. "I want this statue melted down and made into something else. Something good."

"Saint George?" Con said. He took off his jacket and spread it over the statue, then led the way out of the alcove.

"No. Something free. A bird, perhaps. Perhaps it has never been easy being Isabelle Kerslake, fighting to be free."

Con gave her a smile that said he understood, then unwrapped the package and unrolled the document. "The record of the marriage of James Burleigh Somerford of Devon, and Isabelle Anne Kerslake of the same county, on July 24th, 1789. Nearly a year before you were born, Susan."

He'd understood the depth of her fear that she might be the daughter of the mad earl.

"He probably never could father a child," he added. "Now, however, it's all up to your brother. You can take these to him."

She met his eyes, but he had himself under control as well. "Keep them, please. If he declines the honor, they are for you to deal with."

"As you will."

It was farewell, and they both knew it. They were under the eyes of others, but it was, in its way, a blessing.

"Come along, Amelia."

Susan did not look back as they headed for the exit to Crag Wyvern, but they were stopped by a young lad hurtling breathlessly in.

"Miss Kerslake!" But then he broke off, looking wild-eyed at the people nearby.

Sudden fear gripping her, she took Kit Beetham's arm and pulled him aside. "What?"

"It's Captain Drake, ma'am! He's holed up in old Saint Patrick's Chapel with the Preventives around him. Maybe wounded, too!"

❧ 26 ❧

"W OUNDED? How badly?"

"Don't know, ma'am. They flashed a signal down and my dad saw it. Trouble. Three of them there, and one or more wounded. Dad reckons Gifford will have sent for reinforcements and is pinning them there until they come."

Susan's heart was thundering, making it hard to think. *Stupid, stupid!* was running through her head. How had David been so stupid as to try smuggling in broad daylight?

"What is it?" Con appeared beside her. "What's happened?"

She shared the boy's message. "I'll have to try to organize a rescue. There's probably no one else. . . ."

"Of course there is. There's me for a start, and Hawk Hawkinville, and King Rogue."

She looked up at him. "You don't want to be involved in this."

His gray eyes were rock steady. "If you're involved, I am. And where I'm involved, so are my friends." To the boy he said, "Wait here for instructions."

"Yes, sir!" the lad declared. Susan could see an instinctive response to command, and the comfort of it. Someone was in charge and all would be right with the world.

She felt it too, but beneath it lay terror. David was in dire danger, and Con could be too, earl or not.

He led her back into the great hall and said to the men, "Council of war. The office, I think." To Susan, he said quietly, "What of your cousin?"

But Amelia said, "It's David, isn't it? I knew he'd do something stupid!"

"It appears she's part of our merry band," Susan said, startled that Amelia clearly knew more than she'd thought.

In the office Con related the basic situation. He included Gifford's threat to Susan without giving the history behind it. "He'll lose leverage by this. A strange maneuver."

"Perhaps not," Susan said. "Catching David red-handed would put even more pressure on me."

"But then why send for more troops? He'll want a quiet settlement with you."

"That's speculation. He might not have sent for anyone. He'll have the local boatmen. . . ." Then Susan sucked in a breath. "Con, Saint Patrick's Chapel is that ruin near Irish Cove."

Their eyes met. If Gifford had seen them embrace, he might be acting out of rage and envy.

Unpredictably.

And David might be wounded.

"I don't know what to do," she said.

Con took her hand. "It will be all right. How many men could Gifford have with him?"

"There are six boatmen here, but they usually go in pairs on land."

"We'll assume just Gifford and two for now, then." Con described the chapel to the others. "Easy to hold out in there against a couple of local men who don't want to get killed, and probably don't much want to kill either. The ground around is mostly open. I don't want this to be a pitched battle, but I want Kerslake and his men safely away. Suggestions?"

Delaney said, "Hawkinville and I are strangers here. That's a good card to play. If we happen upon the scene, we can't be blamed for getting in the way."

"Of a musket ball?"

"We take our chances. Meanwhile, you and de Vere can attempt your rescue."

"And me," Susan said. "I'll not be left behind."

"I want to help, too," Amelia said.

Before Susan could protest, Delaney said, "Of course. But like any inexperienced trooper, you'll follow orders. Yes?"

Amelia frowned, but then said, "Yes, sir!"

"I'm not military. I'm just a Rogue. Con, is there a map of the place here?"

De Vere produced one from a drawer, spreading it on the desk. He traced the coastline, then said, "I thought so. Here it is. Irish Cove, and the cross must mean the chapel. It seems to be not far from the road to Lewiscomb, but there's a break."

"There was a landslip there fifty years or so ago," Susan said, "cutting the road off. No one uses it anymore."

"Except smugglers," Con added.

"And people out for a stroll."

Their eyes met for a strangely peaceful moment.

"A road still suitable for riding?" Hawkinville asked.

"Up to the break," Susan said. "But if you ride out from here, you'll be cut off before you get to the chapel. Walkers can make their way over the rough patch, but not horses."

"We'll come around from the other way," Delaney said, tracing a path. "Even less connection to Crag Wyvern. As ignorant strangers, we don't know the road is a dead end. We ride along, see something to catch our interest, and approach the chapel."

"Gifford shouts to you to get out of the area . . ." Con supplied.

"And we hang around asking what's the matter. That gives you some room to act. With such open ground, however, it's going to be hard for the trapped men to escape without being shot."

"I'll deal with Gifford," Con said, "but we may need another distraction."

"Children," offered Amelia. "I take the schoolchildren for nature walks up there sometimes. He wouldn't be able to shoot with children around, would he?"

"It puts them at risk," Hawkinville protested, and clearly the other men shared his objection.

"They're used to taking part in smuggling," Susan said, "and we'll keep them out of danger. Go, Amelia, and take Kit Beetham with you."

Amelia turned to leave, but Con said, "Wait. We might be able to get the men away in disguise. Have two other women go with you—the tallest women available—and have them wear an extra layer of clothes that they can slip out of easily."

Amelia grinned. "Clever idea! But what of David? He's too tall."

"I know. He's my estate manager, however, and I'm going to be haughtily furious with whoever threatened him on my land. Get word to him if you can, Amelia, that that's his role."

"Amelia," Susan said as her cousin turned to leave. "The message said he's wounded. Bring bandages and such as well."

"Right." Amelia had paled at the mention of wounds, but she hurried off.

Susan swallowed. She'd supported using the children, but even with the utmost care, there could be a disaster. She saw Major Hawkinville looking at her.

"The commander's burden," he said. "It's never easy."

"I'm not the commander here."

"You're doing very well. Forgive me, but your charming dress does not seem suitable unless you're going to ply your wiles as a card with the riding officer."

"Oh, no." Susan's protest was instinctive. She added, "I have a better idea."

She hurried off, glad that she hadn't had a chance to move her possessions out of the house. The more strangers involved, the better. Gifford might not recognize her dressed as a man.

In short order she was in her breeches, shirt, and jacket, a neckerchief making a rough cravat. She looked in the mirror, unable to dodge the thought that she'd last dressed like this on the night that Con had returned.

She screwed up her eyes to force back tears and concentrated on completing her disguise.

She didn't usually bother with a hat, but she had one, a wide-brimmed countryman's hat. She pinned up her hair and crammed the hat on top. As a subtle touch, she wiped some soot from the chimney with her finger and made a bit of a beard shadow on her jaw and over her lips.

She studied herself in the mirror and decided it would do. Shame she wasn't tall enough to pass for her brother.

She made sure to stride boldly back into the office. "Well?"

Only Con and de Vere were there, but both looked impressed.

"It's pretty convincing," de Vere said, "and I have another idea. Back to your rooms, quickly."

Con came with them, and when they arrived, de Vere began to strip. "I can probably fit in your gown."

They were of a height, Susan realized, though she wasn't sure the shoulders of her peach gown would hold. She helped him into it and didn't quite manage to fasten the buttons all the way up the back. She dug in a drawer and found a pretty shawl to drape around his wide shoulders.

"Shoes," he muttered, looking down at his boots. "Con, my dear fellow, I have evening shoes in my room."

Con went off to get them.

"Hat," Susan said and found her straw villager one. She fixed ribbons so it could be pulled down at either side to hide his short hair.

"Too strongly featured to be a beautiful woman," she said, "but too beautiful to be a man."

De Vere fluttered a smile. "Ambiguous creatures, aren't we?"

"Not if anyone looks too closely." She dug out her rouge and reddened his lips and cheeks. "You're not quite proper, dear, wearing so much paint, and keep your hands inside the shawl. You'll have to distract them." She pulled stockings out of a drawer. "Here. Stuff these to make a bosom."

While he did so, she found her watercolor paints and mixed a little dark brown. "I don't think this will hurt your eyes."

"Thank you," he said with some alarm, but stood still as she painted dark lines around his eyes.

"Definitely not proper, but it makes you look more feminine."

"You can't imagine how reassuring it is to know it's such a challenge."

They were chuckling when Con returned with the black kid slippers. De Vere put them on and Susan said, "It will do, I think. So we are to be a courting couple, are we? And you, Con?"

"I'm going to be the bloody arrogant Earl of Wyvern. Your job will mostly be to distract his men so they can't hear what I'm saying to Gifford. Much as I'd love to throttle the man, we have to leave him a way out of this with his honor, such as it is, intact. Let's go."

Susan strode at Con's side in a blend of excitement and fear she'd never experienced before. A good part of the excitement was Con by her side. If nothing else, they were partners in this adventure.

This was the end of their time together, but it was a glorious end. As long as David came away safe.

Con had ordered horses brought up by Pearce and White, so they rode part of the way, dismounting only when they'd be in sight. The two servants were left with the horses while they approached on foot.

When they neared the landslip, Con went forward cautiously. "I can see the chapel with someone in the window, and at least one person in a dip, watching. Why isn't he shooting? Whoever is in the window is a clear target."

Susan was close behind. "Gifford's waiting for reinforcements. Or for me."

"Then why hasn't your brother broken out?"

"Because then they'd shoot. David will be hoping his signal is bringing help. He'll want to get away without bloodshed. Dead Preventive men mean endless trouble, and anyway, it's not the Dragon's Horde way."

"I wish we could get a message inside the chapel."

"We can." She pulled out the small mirror she'd brought. "I know the signals. I'll go over behind those rocks so Gifford won't see."

Con gripped her arm to stop her. "Do it from here."

"Why?"

"I want Gifford to see, wherever he is. I don't think he's down there. I wouldn't be. There's Hawk and Nicholas approaching, and I think I hear the children."

"I don't have to hide," de Vere said, and stood to stroll a little way up the slope, holding his skirts against the breeze. "It is. About ten children and three women."

"Excellent. Start signaling, Susan."

She angled her mirror to the sunlight and began sending the code that meant *help coming*.

De Vere said, "Did I get dressed up like this for nothing?"

"That would be a shame," Con said. "Go and distract the boat-men."

"That's more like it." De Vere flashed them both a wicked smile, and scrambled over the rocks to the smooth ground leading to the chapel.

As the three distractions converged, Susan had the panicked feeling that everything was sliding out of control.

Con gripped her shoulder. "Keep signaling."

She did so, blowing out a breath. "This goes against everything I've been taught, you know. I feel like a rabbit saying, 'Come and eat me.'"

"Just follow orders," Con said, a smile in his voice.

"Yes, sir."

He kept his hand firmly on her shoulder, and she welcomed the beloved warmth. For a moment, just a moment, she let her free hand rise to cover his.

She heard the children singing, then saw them marching in pairs, Amelia at the head, two other women at the rear, carrying baskets.

The two riders swung toward the chapel.

A voice shouted from the bushes, warning the riders off. She didn't think it was Gifford.

Hawkinville and Delaney halted their horses neatly between the bushes and the chapel, circling as if confused.

A man in the blue and white Excise uniform rose up, waving a musket at them.

More shouting.

The children broke ranks to run down the slope to peer into the chapel. The women rushed after, calling for order. Susan almost rose to scream for them to go back. They were in danger!

The trooper yelled louder.

"Someone's going to be killed," she said to Con. "We have to do something."

"Nick and Hawk will take care of them. Gifford's coming. In fact, it's time for you to be away from here, love."

"Then I'm going down to be closer to the children."

"Very well. Pursue your wanton maid."

She rose, but hesitated. "Will you be safe?"

"Just obey orders, lad."

She rolled her eyes at him, but then she heard hoofbeats approaching. Unable to resist, she pulled him to her for a rapid kiss, then hurried over the rocks.

Once clear of Con, she yelled in as deep a voice as she could. "Betsy, you damn whore. Get back here!"

De Vere looked behind, screeched, and hurtled toward the trooper. "Save me, sir! Save me!"

Con laughed and turned to look out at the sea as if he were merely admiring the view. When Gifford drew his horse to a rough halt beside him he turned. "Lieutenant! A pleasant day after the recent cool weather, is it not?"

"Damn your eyes, I'll see you in court for this, earl or no earl!"

"For what?"

"For signaling to smugglers, sir!"

"In broad daylight?"

Gifford looked down on the scene below, rose in his stirrups and screamed, "Shoot them, damn you. Shoot!"

Con launched himself and dragged him off his horse, knocking him half unconscious in the process. "Shoot women and children, sir?"

Gifford lay there, deep red with fury. "I'll see you hang."

"And I'll see you posted to Jamaica unless you do exactly as I instruct." He had the man pinned with a knee in the belly and a hand in his stock.

"I had smugglers trapped in that ruin, damn you!"

Con tightened his grip in the neckband. "If so, they're likely gone by now. Nothing to be done about that. But I take strong objection to your attempt to harm innocent bystanders. I also, of course, take violent objection"—he increased the pressure of his knee—"to your attempting to blackmail a lady into your bed. Don't say it," he interrupted, tightening the stock to the choking point when Gifford opened his mouth.

Gifford's red face began to purple.

"Miss Kerslake is a lady for whom I have the highest regard, Gifford, and if I hear of anyone suggesting anything to her discredit, anything at all, I will be forced to take action. Both as an earl and as a man. Are we reaching a point of understanding?"

Con took a gutteral noise as agreement and let him have more breath.

Gifford used it to curse at him. "You're hand in glove with the smugglers, are you? Just like the old earl."

"No." Con felt some sympathy for Gifford's attempt to do his job, if not for other things. "Gifford, there's little point in catching another Captain Drake, man. There'll be another, and another."

"It is my duty to catch smugglers, my lord, and you are a damned traitor for opposing me."

Con sighed. "Opposing you? I'm merely preventing a madman from firing on a group of children."

"You admitted—"

"What? I'm the Earl of Wyvern, man. I cannot possibly be a smuggler." Con rose, pulling Gifford to his feet. "Have sense."

Once free, Gifford grabbed for the pistol in a holster on his saddle.

"Ah," Con said to Hawk, who had climbed the rocks to this side. He'd seen him coming. "A witness."

He turned to face Gifford's pistol. "Shooting a peer of the realm in cold blood is looked upon very poorly, you know."

"What's going on here, Lieutenant?" Despite civilian clothes, Hawk's tone rang with military authority. "A trooper down there threatened my friend and I, then some children, then a young lady seeking his help. Are you his commanding officer, sir?"

Gifford's pistol drooped. "We are engaged in capturing some dangerous smugglers, sir."

"I'm Wyvern," Con said amiably to his friend, "and this is the local riding officer, Lieutenant Gifford."

Hawk bowed. "Major Hawkinville, my lord." To Gifford, he snapped a command. "Go and take charge of your men, Lieutenant."

Gifford stood to attention. "Am I to assume you are taking command here, Major?"

"Not at all, Lieutenant. I assume now your head is cool you see the way to go on."

Gifford glared at him in frustration, then thrust his pistol back in its holster. He stalked to the high point to look across the rocky slip at the chapel.

Con followed. Children were playing in and out of the church, watched over by Nicholas, while four women, Race, and Susan surrounded the bewildered boatmen. An earthenware bottle was passing around. Doubtless scrumpy cider, adding considerably to the men's bewilderment.

David Kerslake was sitting on the ground in a red-stained shirt, Amelia attending to him with bandages.

"By gad," Con said, "your demented trooper has shot my estate manager!"

"He's a damn smuggler."

"Kerslake?"

"Son of Melchisedeck Clyst, as you well know."

"I'm a relative of the late mad Earl of Wyvern, Gifford. Are you saying that makes me inevitably insane?" While Gifford attempted to come up with a retort, Con added, "Do you have any evidence against him?"

"I interrupted men bringing tea up from that cove, my lord, and Kerslake and some others held us up while it was carried away."

"Are you sure?" Con asked. "I told Kerslake to check this area to see if it would be practical to rebuild the road here."

"Then why did he hide in that ruin?"

"Zeus, if someone was shooting at me, I'd hide in whatever cover was available. I'm sure you've done the same many a time."

"But . . ." Gifford looked at Con, tears of fury in his eyes.

"You are not entirely wrong, Gifford," Con said softly, "though you lost my sympathy by your dishonorable behavior toward a woman who had shown you nothing but kindness. But be assured that you will have the complete enmity of the Earl of Wyvern if you disturb his people here."

"It is my job to disturb smugglers, my lord, and in these parts everyone is a damn smuggler! And Kerslake is that blackguard, Captain Drake!"

"Choose your targets, Gifford. Choose your targets. Captain Drake—whoever he may be—and the Dragon's Horde have the support and cooperation of everyone in these parts. It's been that way for generations. The Blackstock Gang to the west and Tom Merriwether's Boys to the east, however, are universally feared. They've both been known to flog men to death for crossing them, and rape women who get in their way. They flog and rape for amusement as well. One or the other murdered your predecessor, not the Dragon's Horde."

Gifford's lip curled. "Know that for a fact, do you?"

"I know their ways. Go after the other gangs and you'll get support. We learned in the Peninsula that a war can be won or lost on the goodwill of the local people."

Gifford whirled and marched over to his grazing horse. "I'll do you an ill turn if I can!" he declared as he mounted.

"Unwise to say something like that before witnesses," Hawk pointed out. "You'd better hope that Lord Wyvern doesn't suffer any kind of accident, hadn't you?"

Almost steaming, Gifford wrenched his horse's head around cruelly and spurred off.

Con pulled a face. "I feel somewhat sorry for him, but there's no place for personal vendettas in this."

They watched as Gifford raced inland until he could cross the slip, then hurtled down to berate his men and drag them away from temptation. He stopped his horse to look into the chapel, obviously hoping to find some contraband there, then glared around the area.

"Doesn't give up easily, does he?" Hawk said. "Shame, really. In wartime he'd probably be a hero."

Con noted that the two extra "women" had now slipped away, leaving the innocent intruders and David Kerslake. There also seemed to be a great deal of cider-fueled merriment.

"Let's go down and sort out our company."

When they arrived where Race and Susan were laughing together, he said, "Have you two made up?"

With a wicked smile, Race pulled her into his arms and kissed her. "My love! Forgive me."

In return, Susan bent Race backward for what seemed to be a ravishing kiss. When she straightened him, she said, "Only if you promise to behave."

"Sweetheart," Race fluttered, "I'm yours in all things."

Con felt a spurt of irrational jealousy. He knew neither of them was serious, but what if Susan did find another man to love? He had no right to mind, but it cut like a knife.

The thought of Lady Anne and him had to hurt her as grievously.

"How's David?" he asked deliberately, to turn her mind to other things.

She sobered and came over to him. "Not too bad. A ball in the shoulder, but not deep. What's Gifford going to do now?"

"Absolutely nothing, if he has any sense." He told her what had happened.

Her smile was brilliant. "Wickedly clever! As you say, now he'll have to be careful about any moves he makes around here. I do wish David would accept the idea of being the earl, though."

"Let's go and put it to him. This might have made it more attractive."

Nicholas and Hawk had gathered the children. Nicholas seemed to have confiscated the cider from the women as well. Con went over to where Amelia was finishing bandaging David Kerslake.

"Damn fool. Broad daylight?"

The younger man looked up, unabashed. "Creative thinking. Gifford's been all over this area with extra troops at night. I tried to bring the tea in here last night, but a navy ship came close. So I had it dropped as floaters. You know what that means?"

"Weighted so it rides just under the water with a marker on top. Seaweed or something like that."

"Right. We waited until Gifford was away from here, then brought round a couple of boats to haul them in and bring them to shore. Gifford and his men have been up all night the last few nights. They should have been fast asleep!"

"How did you get shot?"

"A boatman called for me to halt. I hoped he was bluffing."

"David!" Susan exclaimed. "You're lucky you're not dead."

"Lucky he was trying to kill me, you mean," Kerslake said with a grin. "The chance of Saul Cogley actually hitting his target is remote."

Con shook his head. "Have you had time to think about the earldom? It would make this sort of thing a great deal easier, I assure you."

Kerslake winced as Amelia tightened the bandage. She looked cross too.

"It's not a burden a man of twenty-four wants," he said, pulling a face. "Since I would be living here, I'd have to host a plaguey number of events and take part in county affairs. Then there's London and Parliament, for heaven's sake."

"The price of leadership," Con said without sympathy.

"Damn you."

"And you didn't even mention the fact that you'll instantly become a prize trophy in the marriage hunt."

"Didn't you say you *wanted* me to accept it?" But Kerslake sighed. "I don't really have any choice, do I, if I'm going to do the best for my people here."

Con noted that "my people" with a slight smile. Yes, willing or not, David Kerslake would be good for this area.

"Help me up, will you?" Kerslake asked, and Con supported him. "I wrenched my knee as well, which was another reason I couldn't make a break for it. Very well, damn you," he added as soon as he was standing. "I'll try to prize the earldom from your clutching fingers. As you said, Susan, Mel will be cock-a-hoop over it if it works."

Susan came to hug him and for a moment Con could steal a hug too.

Then he pulled apart.

This truly was the end. He could leave Crag Wyvern immediately. Perhaps even ride over to stay at Nicholas's place today.

Never have reason to return.

So be it.

After one last shared look with Susan, he turned his mind to the logistics of getting Kerslake back to Church Wyvern. Carry him over the rocks, or use one of Nicholas's and Hawk's horses and go the long way around?

He chose the latter course, and helped Kerslake into the saddle. Hawk prepared to mount to go with him, but then Race spoke up, in the arch, feminine manner that went with his disguise.

"My dear sirs, I do hope I can depend upon you for protection."

"What?" Con asked, sharing a look with Nicholas and Hawk.

"I have a little sin to confess," Race said, digging flirtatiously in his plump bosom.

CON SUPPRESSED an urge toward minor violence. "Race, this is no time for idiocy."

"Well really, my lord! That is rather a case of the pot calling the kettle dirty. Here." He pulled out a rolled-up paper and offered it, limp-wristed.

It was a letter of some sort. Con took it impatiently, but then his heart stopped. It beat again, it thundered, as he broke the seal and scanned it. It was! It was the letter he'd written to Lady Anne a lifetime ago.

Three days ago.

"Devil take you!" He glared at Race, not sure whether to throttle him or kiss him. "What right have you to hold back my letters?"

"The right of a friend," Race said in a normal manner. "I didn't read it, but Diego and I decided it couldn't be urgent and might be unwise. Send it now if you want."

Con looked again at his fateful words, thinking for a moment of Lady Anne. He was certain there was no grand passion there, but he must have raised hopes. He was truly fond of her. Not fond enough, however, to sacrifice everything now he had a second chance.

He looked at Susan who was staring at him as if afraid to believe. "I mentioned writing to a lady. . . ."

The last trace of color left her cheeks. "Con?"

Eyes on her, he ripped the letter into tiny shreds and let the breeze tumble them across the headland and into the endless sea.

"By a miracle," he said, "I have hope of winning you for my wife, Susan, for my friend, my helpmeet all my days."

Susan had so firmly sealed off hope that now she could not quite believe. "Con . . . ?" she asked again, reaching tentatively toward him.

He met her and took her hand, strong, firm, real. She wasn't dreaming.

"I'm not committed, Susan. I'm free. . . ." Then his eyes twinkled. "Oh dear, you've changed your mind. Race's luscious figure has—"

She threw herself into his arms to be swept up, to be swung around and around in the clean air and sunshine.

Then they kissed.

With scarcely a thought to their audience, they kissed as never before, because this time, after so long, it promised true eternity.

It was hard to stop kissing, to unseal their bodies for even a moment, but they slowly parted, smiling, blushing under the interested eyes of friends, family, and neighbors.

"Don't tell me you were sacrificing yourself for the honor of the Rogues, Con," Delaney said.

"It wouldn't have been a dire sacrifice." He turned to look at Susan, a look that made her breath catch and her toes curl. "Then."

She sensed his honorable concern and drew him close. "If Lady Anne is as good a person as you say, love, she'll find her true mate. Someone who loves her as we love."

Numbness, then delirium were turning into urgent purpose. "When can we marry?" she demanded.

His expression showed the same needs. "It is for you to name the day."

"Today?"

He laughed unsteadily. "I don't think even an earl can quite manage that." He brushed his lips close to her ear. "And though I desire you here and now, beloved, I want to celebrate our love with May blossoms, and ribbons, and grain thrown in promise of a bountiful future. . . ."

She turned her head to meet his lips in a kiss. "A *normal* wedding?" How had he known before she knew how much she wanted that? "How long will it take?"

"I have no idea. If we set Hawk to organizing it, it can doubtless be done in brisk military efficiency."

She laughed and turned to look at the major, but found that their audience was courteously moving away, leaving them blessedly alone.

Miraculously they had forever, but these first moments were a jewellike treasure.

Hands linked, they wandered to look down on Irish Cove, then sat together there in each other's arms in silent wonder.

"I still can't quite believe it," she said at last, turning to him, unable to resist raising a hand to touch his face, to trace the beloved lines of his face. "I longed for a miniature of you once, you know." She told him about the one his brother had brought to Kerslake Manor.

He trapped her hand and kissed the palm, slowly, lids lowered. "I had no picture of you. I tried to tell myself that I didn't want one, but it was a lie."

"Con, I'm sorry. I'm so sorry."

"Hush," he whispered against her skin. "Hush, love. Right or wrong it's all in the past, and who can say if it will not be better now, from this beginning? What did those children know of life, of temptation, of faltering steps and brave recoveries?"

He looked at her, smiling. No, more than smiling, adoring. Her tears began to flow.

"I know women have this damnable habit of crying when they're happy," he said, "but please don't, love. Listen to my words. You, as you are, with all your past, both good and bad, are perfect to me now. That is the Susan I love beyond words to express it."

She did her best to swallow the tears. "I can't imagine better words." She took his hand and kissed it. "I have always loved you, but I adore the man you are now, tested and true. I feel drunk with it, as if I could leap off this cliff and fly!"

He pinned her to the ground. "No, you don't!"

So like that first night, but now everything was different. It turned into a kiss. It turned into more, sprawled there on the rough greenery above Irish Cove, but they did not make love. They drew apart in the end, though seething with hunger.

"Cold water," she said, glancing at the sea. "I hear it's a good cure for this."

He leaped to his feet and took her hand to pull her up. "There's no cure for this save death, love. Let's go to your home and see how quickly a decorous wedding can be arranged."

With a license and many willing hands, it took only days, and could likely have been quicker except for the time needed for Con's family to travel from Sussex.

Van escorted them, and brought along his bride-to-be, Mrs. Celestine, as well. Susan understood that the matter had been uncertain, but no one could doubt the love and veiled passion between them now.

"I confess," said Mrs. Celestine, on greeting her, "you make me regret my setting a date some weeks from now."

She was an elegant, composed woman—except when Lord Vandeimen made her blush. Susan sensed genuine warmth in her, however. It was pleasant to think of them as neighbors and friends.

"I wanted a grand celebration in Van's home," Mrs. Celestine said. "A homecoming. A new start. A way for me to begin to belong, I hope. Please say you will take part, even though your wedding is to be here."

Susan took her hands with true gratitude. "That is so generous of you, Mrs. Celestine. Are you sure you won't mind? I confess, the idea of going to live among strangers daunts me."

The older woman smiled. "Van and I are not strangers. Nor is Major Hawkinville. Nor is Lord Wyvern's family."

Susan had already been warmly accepted by Con's mother and sister, and knew the words were true. She would not be going to live among strangers. Venturing forth into the world did still make her a little nervous, but it was becoming a more anticipated adventure day by day.

On the eve of their wedding, however, as they strolled in the orchard, Con said, "Somerford Court is not by the sea."

Susan kissed him. "I'm not a fish, love. I can live away from the sea."

"It's five miles away."

She looked into his eyes seriously. "I can live anywhere with you, Con. You are my world. I should have realized that long ago."

"No dwelling on the past." He pulled her close and they rested in each other's arms, a lark filling the soft air with song. "If I am your world, then I will work to make your world as perfect as humanly possible. That is, and always will be, my main intent."

"And I yours," she replied. "We have a second chance at heaven, and will treasure it."

Susan felt as if they said their vows then, but the next day, in a gaily decorated church full of family, friends, and neighbors, they said the traditional vows, then ran out together to be showered with grain.

When the first person greeted her as Lady Wyvern, she shared a look with Con, one that smiled at the folly of the past. It was only for a little while, anyway, and then she would become Lady Amleigh, a title that held no dark shadows or memories.

They shared their joy with everyone, but then at last they were alone together, man and wife.

Susan looked at the big bed, its sage-green coverlet strewn with petals. "Con, I have to say that I feel very strange about doing this in my aunt and uncle's bed."

He embraced her from behind, laughing. "I, on the other hand, am exceedingly grateful to them. I certainly had no intention of sleeping again in Crag Wyvern."

Henry and David had moved up there to make room in the manor, and they were playing host to a number of the guests. The Delaneys were sleeping there, along with Lord Vandeimen and Mrs. Celestine, and Major Hawkinville. There were some other

Rogues there, too—the Earl and Countess of Charrington, Mr. and Mrs. Miles Cavanagh, Major Beaumont, and Mr. Stephen Ball.

There had been warm messages and generous gifts from the Marquess and Marchioness of Arden and Lord and Lady Middlethorpe. Apparently both couples were awaiting a happy event.

Susan felt as if she were swimming in new and welcoming friends. It was terrifying in a way, but glorious, like swimming in the high waves.

Con nuzzled her neck. "However, if you truly don't think it right, we can wait. . . ."

She turned in his arms. "I could call your bluff."

"I'd win."

With a smile, she eased free the silk fichu that filled the low bodice of her gown. "Are you sure?" The bodice, by her design, was extremely low.

She saw his eyes darken and his lips part. Stepping back, she raised one foot on a chair and slid up her skirts to reveal a flesh-colored silk stocking embroidered with red roses. A red, rose-trimmed garter, held it up. Slowly, she undid it—

He fell to his knees beside her and took over the task. "You win."

"I thought so."

He looked up, laughing with her. "I am undoubtedly the happiest loser the world has ever known."

Later, lying limply in each other's arms, Con said, "Shame about that bath, though. There's no room for such a thing at home. When David's earl, we'll have to pay him a visit."

Susan rolled to face him. "Only when he's done considerable renovations." She traced the coiled dragon on his chest. "Shame about this too, but you are not the dragon, Con Somerford. You are Saint George. My Saint George." She had to refer to the past, though it was a past no longer able to hurt them. "I said it once, and I mean it now. My George, forever and ever."

"Amen." He rubbed his head gently against hers. "And I'm pleased to see that I was right," he murmured.

"Right?"

His tongue traced slowly around the rim of her ear, making her shiver. "I always suspected that when Saint George rescued the dragon's bride, his true reward came later, more or less like this. . . ."

AUTHOR'S NOTE

Dear Reader,

I hope you've enjoyed *The Dragon's Bride*, and had fun with a more adventurous side of Regency England. Some years ago, in preparation for writing this book, my husband and I visited the coast of Dorset and Devon, looking for likely locations. It was then that we first thought of moving to the area, and now here we are, having just bought a house on the Devon coast with a lovely view of the sea.

We've not settling in Dragon's Cove, however, which I invented, or even in the village of Beer, on which I based it.

I usually set my books in a real geographical location, with only the homes of the principle characters invented, but I had to do more invention here. Let me tell you why.

On that trip, we came across a village called Beer—an old and scenic place with a steep road running down between cliffs to a small bay that is still used by fishing boats. It was ideal for my smugglers.

I wasn't surprised to find that there had been smugglers there in the early nineteenth century, but I was very surprised to find that right at the time of my book, a very famous smuggler was hiding contraband in the caves of Beer. Jack Rattenbury is famous mostly because he wrote an account of his adventures, but I couldn't put Captain Drake and all the rest in Beer without involving the real smuggler, and that wouldn't do.

That's why I renamed all the locations, but it's still mostly Beer, and if you find yourself on holiday in east Devon, I recommend a visit. The cliffs are still there, but you'll have to use your imagination to see Crag Wyvern towering over the quaint old houses.

This story came to me in an odd way. I intended Con Somerford and Lady Anne to make a match of it, for, as portrayed in the book, she had been as good as jilted by one of Con's friends. When I tried to write it, though, it didn't go well. Lady Anne complained that Con was cold, and Con thought of her only as a good deed. Even throwing them into an adventure didn't make them get on any better. I'd always wondered what would happen if my hero and heroine didn't fall in love, and now I knew.

I fought them for a while, and then opened my mind to other possibilities. All of a sudden I was off with Con to this strange house in Devon, where he came face-to-face with a secret from his youth, pointing a pistol at him. And the rest is *The Dragon's Bride.*

The smuggling parts of *The Dragon's Bride* are based on truth, and Jack Rattenbury's memoirs were very useful.

Smuggling was the major industry all around the coast of England during this period, but especially on the south coast, so temptingly close to the Continent. During the Napoleonic War, smugglers conveyed spies, messages, and gold in both directions. With peace, matters became much more difficult, as shown in the book, but it will be another generation or so before the government brings about change by lowering taxes instead of throwing more and more money at trying to stop the smugglers.

It is also true that there were good gangs and bad ones. Some were thorough thugs, feared and despised by all. Others were led by clever businessmen who built cooperation and trust in an area.

The situation of the riding officers was often very difficult. In the past, Preventive men had often been local, but that led to obvious problems, so it became the rule that a riding officer be sent to a place far from his home. Friendless and unpopular, theirs was not an easy life because few people anywhere in England thought there was anything wrong with dodging a bit of tax. Even a parson reported in his diary paying his smuggler twenty-one shillings for a gallon of brandy.

The Dragon's Bride is part of a trilogy that I tagged "three guys called George." With four King Georges in a row, a lot of baby boys were christened George, so it's not far-fetched that three of them would grow up together and take nicknames.

The first story in the trilogy is called "The Demon's Mistress," and is about Van. That originally was published in a collection called *In Praise of Younger Men*, and then later in the omnibus edition of all the George stories, called *Three Heroes*. Its latest incarnation is as an e-book, released in July, but still easily available for the Kindle, Nook, Kobo, etc. If you don't have an e-reader, the story can be read on your computer.

The third book is *The Devil's Heiress*, with Hawk as the hero.

My recent new books are set in the eighteenth century, when men wore satin and lace, and also a lethal sword. I love this glittering, dangerous world, and I've set thirteen books in this time. The most recent is *An Unlikely Countess*, about an impoverished lady whose efforts to claim her rights from her family end up with her trying to make a life in the aristocracy, and come to terms with an exciting, challenging husband.

That was published in March 2011, and is available in print and as an e-book. You can find a list of all my Georgian books, in fact all my works, on my Web site at www.jobev.com/recent.html.

There you'll also find out how to sign up for my occasional electronic newsletters, where you'll hear about all the new and reissued books. I'm on Facebook, and I sometimes tweet.

All best wishes from Devon,

Jo

Jo Beverley is widely regarded as one of the most talented romance writers today. She is a *New York Times* bestseller, five-time winner of Romance Writers of America's cherished RITA Award, and one of only a handful of members of the RWA Hall of Fame. She has also twice received the Romantic Times Career Achievement Award. She has two grown sons and lives with her husband in England. You can visit her Web site at www.jobev.com.